D0840588

PUNKS

Punks 4 Life!

Richard Cucarese

RICH CUCARESE

Wordsmiths, Ink LLC

Published by Wordsmiths, Ink, Gilbert, AZ

This is a work of fiction. Names, characters, places, and incidents are the product of the author's imagination and have been used to create this work of art. Any similarity to actual persons, living or dead, events, etc. is completely incidental.

All rights reserved. Copyright © 2019 Richard Cucarese

Cover image copyright © Richard Cucarese

No part of this book may be reproduced or transmitted in any form or by any means, electronic or mechanical, including photocopying, recording, or by any information storage and retrieval system, permitted by law.

For information contact: Wordsmiths, Ink, Gilbert, AZ

ISBN: 978-1-64184-224-2 (paperback)

ISBN: 978-1-64184-225-9 (ebook)

Table of Contents

Prologue

THROUGHOUT ITS WILD, crass, storied, and controversial epoch, punk rock, its fans, and performers have dealt with their share of misunderstanding and animosity from parents, police, religious organizations, politicians, and the mainstream media over the past few decades.

Although some of its bad reputation can be attributed to the youthful exuberance and anarchy emanating from its volatile lyrics, guitars screeching feedback at maximum volume, accompanied by thundering, ominous, heart pounding bass lines and gut punching drumbeats, it would be a mistake to write the movement off as just a passing fancy of teen angst.

Born from the volatility brewing Stateside and across the Atlantic during the early 1970's and through the Reagan and Thatcher regimes, punk rock certainly gave a funny, if not campy glimpse into the boring, teenage life of suburban America and England, but it happily went out of its way to flip a big middle finger to the anti-war, campus protesting Baby Boomer hippies of the 1960's, who'd transformed into the greedy, self-important, yuppie pariahs of Wall Street by the 1980's. The Peace and Love generations, "never trust anyone over thirty" was replaced by the punks more caustic, "never trust a hippie."

Punk rock also addressed the despair and decay of Britain and the States inner-cities due to racial unrest, rampant unemployment in the heavily industrialized centers and poorly crafted socioeconomic policies; the impending annihilation of the planet through nuclear Armageddon by two, trigger happy Superpowers and in many cases, punk music demanded nothing less than the anarchistic overthrow of the so-called democratic, capitalistic forms of governance and economics the Western, X-Generation were indoctrinated and brainwashed to believe was in their best interests to preserve at all costs.

Bands with acerbic monikers such as the Sex Pistols, Dead Kennedys, Circle Jerks, The Slits and performers with stage names of Sid Vicious, Johnny Rotten, and Jello Biafra left grownups infuriated and deciphering lyrics, usually culminating with threatening calls to radio stations and all levels of government to completely ban this form of music.

There have been a few very well-made books, films and documentaries dealing with the punk movement and its music as a whole, but as far as what took place in the everyday lives of punk kids, there was not too much offered for public consumption.

'PUNKS' fictionally delves into as many of these aspects as possible, including how punk music and culture transcended certain racial and socioeconomic barriers, joining high school and college aged, rural and suburban kids with the more working class, city kids who also believed the world was failing them miserably.

'PUNKS' also doesn't hold back on the kid's strong, opinionated viewpoints and how vastly outnumbered they were in fighting against the societal wrongs of an American cultural, religious, economic and political landscape spinning madly out of control during the 1980's. It also takes no prisoners in the crude or vile language describing the very hardcore conditions and lifestyles of the street kids, especially.

'PUNKS' attempts to deliver a foretaste of three elements seldom discussed and shamefully overlooked; the artistic, vibrant club and underground music scenes taking place in Trenton, New Jersey, the Bohemian, starving artist enclaves of River towns such as New Hope, Pennsylvania and Lambertville, New Jersey and especially, in the city of Philadelphia; secondly, the street kids who found a home and a family in the throngs of punks engaged in the energetic, violent dance of 'the pit', or by forming the bands playing tirelessly and for not much money at the raw, disheveled clubs and underground events usually located in impoverished urban locations; and last, but certainly not least, the female punks who were an integral part of punk culture through their style of dress, political stances and their exceptional musical prowess in some very prominent acts (Joan Jett, Lita Ford, Debbie Harry, Wendy O. Williams and Siouxsie Sioux, just to name a few, all got their start in punk rock).

Gemma 'Swan' Stinson and Robert 'Robbs' Cavelli are the perfect microcosm of these aspects, thrown into the public eye for everyone to see; a middle class teen, writing the lyrical story of his and America's life, languishing in suburban hell with an overly religious, authoritarian, abusive and conservative mother, who meets the street girl with the smarts, looks, and a take no prisoner attitude from the wrong side of the city, who's over-come adversity and an addictive, hellishly dangerous childhood through her academic abilities and unbelievable musical talent. Theirs is the quintessential, punk story; fighting for what's right and just, fighting tooth and nail for your punk family, and fight-ing to be with the one you truly love, society be damned.

'PUNKS' allows for an unrestrained look into Rob and Gem's dreams, to be a part something special, to hopefully attain what they refer to as 'THE CHANCE' but never strays too far away from Philadelphia's dark alleys, ramshackle tenements, poverty, sadness and heinous characters looking to swallow whole these two young lovers and their patchwork family of tight knit friends known as the 'Misfits'.

Their bonds of friendship and family reveal the ties which still bind large numbers of real punks to the music and the move-ment decades later and have opened up this integral landscape of music and anarchistic activism for new generations to explore because truly, "Punk's Not Dead!!!".

Although 'PUNKS' contains songs from actual, musical acts, the names of real performers and events taking place at certain venues, it is still just a work of fiction and any resemblance otherwise to the 'real world of 1980's Philadelphia' is purely coincidental; so, please enjoy the emotional, roller coaster ride of events, the activist stances, the friendships, the music, the hope and the love not only in 'PUNKS', but also in the subsequent pages of the trilogy because in the end, we were not just golden, not just glorious, but we were and still are punks.

—Richard Cucarese

••• | •••

Like a Phoenix

"MEMORIES TO ASHES...ASHES to memories," it's a statement from her that I've replayed numerous times in my mind as we hold hands tightly, aiding in her quest not to fall upon the charred remains of this once hallowed ground of musical magic known as 'The Underground'.

Sunlight darts wickedly through the only warped, melted pane of glass remaining on the blackened, brick structure and the cooling winds of an otherwise, oddly warm, late October day whip around the police and fire department tape like flags on a river bound vessel, before we effortlessly maneuver past them to reach our destination.

"Hey babe, you know the Brody's will be back shortly to clear us out of here. Sarge McGuigan said the building can topple down at any moment." A slight nod of her head and the tossing of her long, velvety, deep auburn hair from side to side across the large, Social Distortion logo sprayed on the back of her roughened, black leather jacket is Gemma Stinson's hapless, solemn acknowledgment to the enormity of the destruction.

Breaking gently from my grip, she finds a piece of her past… our past, poking through the rubble. Deftly picking through the filth and debris with the long, razor sharp red talons she's utilized to play her wondrous music, she finds the neck, bubbled and burnt, with a few strings miraculously hanging on as if to say, 'there's still life left in us.'

Turning to me, Gem bravely smiles, but the eyes, those glistening emerald pools tell everything needed to be known as tears fall on the only recognizable piece of the body, where she'd penned her nickname so gracefully. Another piece of her young life is gone forever. "Oh, poor 'Robins Egg', you rose like a Phoenix from the ashes once before, but this time, you weren't so lucky. Life is like that sometimes, old friend," she laments, cradling its lifeless remains in her hands.

"You made music come to life with that old, blue Gretsch, girl. I'll never forget the looks when everyone watched you hand it over to Dil, so it could grace his wall of fame, along with so many notable relics from other artists.

"It held quite a place of honor," I reply somewhat cheerfully before blazing a Red to ease the pain of witnessing this completely unexpected loss of a place that was like a family to all who entered its large, ornate metal doors from a bygone era.

Through the billowing smoke, a hissing cacophony of soaked fur and snarling, long snouted hell, decides to show itself at this odd hour of the day. Not in the mood to ascertain if it's a displaced resident of the smoldering catastrophe, or a rabid sack of garbage out for a free taste, a ferociously hurled brick to its midsection sends the vermin sprawling painfully onto its side and squealing away in anger.

"Well done, Robbs, Vanquisher of Philadelphia Sewer Rats. Lena hath taught you well."

"Jesus, that thing was bigger than an alley cat."

Snickering, the verse flows from her black glossed lips as if it were yesterday. "Filthy city of rats…"

"Filthy city of rats, filthy city of rats…if they got any bigger, they'd fuckin' eat the cats…"

"Ha, ha, ha ha…damn…a jolt of laughter through the tears, Robbs. You always knew what would make the crowds…or me, for that matter, go wild, thinking…hell, loving…or hating your poignant, political lyrics and laughing our asses off at your sarcasm."

Aiding in Gem's escape from the smoldering pile, I wipe traces of smudged, black mascara from her pleasing, angular face but she pulls away, reassuring me that she'll soldier on with a flash of that disarming smile. "Wow, the memories we made in this club, Robbs…the first time we played here, when it was still just an abandoned factory in the Libs that Dil had broken into and rigged up the power…all so that the punks had a place to call their own…a place to play or listen to the bands and not catch any shit from the norms or the Brody's who never wanted to understand us or our causes.

"Poor Dil, I can't even imagine what went through his mind seeing his cathedral of music engulfed in flames and now like this, knowing that it was torched by some lunatic on a drunken, arson spree."

"You know Dil, Gem. If anyone can see this through and resurrect it for the next generation of musicians and fans, it will be him. That's why he made it a legit club, even though, I must admit, playing in it as a truly illegal, underground venue was an experience never to forget."

"Yeah, like when we saw Henry Rollins storming through the crowds at our one gig, only to have him approach us while we broke the equipment down, say that we kicked ass and then comment on what a hellacious stage dive you and Otto unleashed at the Black Flag show the week before in City Gardens.

"Or when Yuka and Otto came running up after one show to let us know Patti Smith was here to watch us jam…US…like we were something special, instead of just being street kids."

"Yep, or the time Lena did her best Wendy O. Williams imitation and tomahawked Otis' hood with a full bottle of Guinness just because it started on the first ignition strike instead of just rolling over and dying…as it always did on this street…and every other," I add with a chuckle.

3

"Oh my God, Otis, what a car that old, black Cordoba was," Gem replies cheerfully as the brisk winds push the warmth of the sun behind some puffy, white clouds invading an otherwise, bright blue fall sky.

"I told you anything that burps, farts and lurches ten feet, only to rumble, roll and die as much as that shitbox car of yours does, needs, to be named Otis, the stumble-fuck, town drunk of Mayberry's, Andy Griffith Show." Allowing us another well needed laugh, we eventually wade through massive mud pools left behind by the endless barrage from the cannons atop the Fire Department's pumpers which fruitlessly struggled to halt the carnage. The torched club was another in a long line of arsons sweeping mercilessly through this once proud, industrial swath of Philadelphia in 1995.

Where once stood progress and certain measures of working class prosperity before the draconian, Reagan 1980's and the sinister, recent years of Wall Street orgies foisted upon us by an Administration we thought would finally help revive the blue collar, lunch pail set, this part of the city was an unpleasant, unrepentant reminder of neglect bestowed upon the proletariat which built this country. Now, only despondency and hopelessness remained in its wake.

"Good Lord, Robbs, what the hell is happening to our city... our country anymore? They keep burning down the city's outskirts and turn their centers into fortresses of unbridled wealth and power hidden behind steel and glass monoliths...replacing good paying factory jobs with minimum wage inferiority and free trade. What does that even mean? Free for whom? Free for the countries whose workers and environments we abuse? More like free for the pillaging, raping corporations and their asshole buddies in Congress.

"We aggravate the Middle East enough that they try and level the World Trade Center a few years back and our own citizens hate the country enough to incinerate innocent children and their parents in Oklahoma City. What's next, kids wiping out their classmates with machine guns...fucking sick..."

Lighting a Newport, she angrily flips the match into an ashen, muddied puddle. "And we Socialists and punks are the pariahs because, heaven fucking forbid, we want all Americans to get a fair share as a reward for their efforts and hard work to live a better, happier life…such bullshit," Gem decries before the putrid, sulfur smoke wafting from the rubble brings on a round of hard, violent coughing.

Tossing her partially spent Newp to the ground, Gem's coughing worsens. "You know that you shouldn't smoke too much or anymore, for that matter, girl."

"Ha, okay 'Doctor' Cavelli…I'll try not to do it for a while… and anyway, that's a laugh from one who still smokes way too much," comes the acidic reply, with a slight, friendly push from the statuesque beauty who towels the dirt from her knee high, stiletto boots.

"Did you take your medicine yet, Gem?" I timidly ask.

"Three hundred milligrams this morning, love, but I don't think it's working so well, Robbs," she responds with a hint of sadness. "No probs, though. Tomorrow's another day and besides, I think I've seen enough hardship, so how about we return to New Hope and Lambertville this afternoon?

"I long for the kaleidoscope of colors swaying in the river breezes along the shoreline and the fresh air on this glorious day would do me some good…besides, I want so much to smell my beautiful strands of lavender by the canal falls before the cold of winter takes their spirited, calming scents from me again."

"As I told you before, Gem, the whole day is ours to enjoy and yes, the lavender is exceptionally strong now…just the way you like it." Upon carefully placing the remains of 'Robins Egg' in the trunk for what may become its funeral procession, I offer my assistance to get Gem into the Camaro, but her wry smile says it all…'I'm not a fucking charity case, Robbs. You know better,' therefore I acquiesce.

With its throaty V-8 thundering us through Center City and onto Interstate 95, Gem slides in a disc, bringing Fugazi's, 'Waiting Room' to life loudly until the wicked bass, guitar riffs and drums cease, leaving us to time the silence on our fingers and howling like wolves when the chaos kicks back in.

"I'm glad that you left the Epiphone in the car, if I'm feeling up to it, maybe we could do some busking on Main or Bridge Street. The town needs some of our music again, Robbs. At least nowadays, we can give the money to a charity besides us and our destitute tribe.

Remember when this was money to purely survive on, go see a gig, or buy a guitar string or a mic cord," she laughs heartily while running her fingers up my tanned, black inked arms and through my closely cropped, sun streaked hair.

"Mmmm...I'm still getting used to this shorter hair, with no curls, but it does make you look even more handsome...maybe even slightly grown up," she squeaks derisively.

"Ayyyy...Yo, piss off, Gemma Stinson! We said that we'd never grow up, like Peter Pan and the Lost Boys. Remember what you said years ago, we were like lightning in a bottle. Nobody could catch us...we were invincible!"

"Or so we thought," she tersely reflects, coughing slightly before twisting nervously at the simple, silver band on her right, ring finger, staring longingly at her other ring finger and constantly pinging her switchblade sharp skull and dagger earrings.

"Fuck it all, Gem...we're gonna' live forever," but the anxiousness towards changing the subject is evident, so I allow for the cynical backdrop of Rudimentary Peni's, 'Rotten to the Core' to achieve a proper segue.

"Robbs, let me relive 1985 and beyond as only you can retell our story...like how batshit crazy we were outrunning the yard Brody's and train hopped that freighter in Morrisville just so we could see a show at City Gardens in Trenton, or the gobsmacked day of roof running and surfing the El's subway cars in Philly to get away from Kellin's street gang...razzing the hell out of them after we beat them senseless, flipping them the bird when we pulled away from the station, but hanging on for dear life not to get pitched onto Kensington Avenue below us."

"Six of them against two of us and I still think the deck was stacked in our favor, Gem!"

"I tend to agree with you there, Robbs…so, tell me again about that day…about our magical times in New York, the protests, the shows, our tribe of Misfits, our college times…just let me hear everything for these next few days, especially our shows…those booze fueled, sexually driven, anarchistic nights and the insane happenings like skins being tossed through doorways by Dust and O because the Nazi's hated our political bent.

"But more importantly, remind me of those nights just wailing away up on this stage…on any stage, stripped naked to the world, so to speak" she says softly, pulling me closer to the warmth of her body.

"Some nights it was damn near a reality to be stripped naked, but you could listen to those stories from me nonstop, couldn't you? The good and bad times…the sad, the hysterical and the happy, all rolled into the story of us, just for Swan."

Staring at me deeply, she sighs. "I hope one day that you'll write the story of us, but yes, I will listen to them until my eyes close for the very last time, Robbs."

The ride continues through the city's outskirts, eventually reaching the remaining fields and forests surrounding the suburban, limo-liberal yuppie, cookie cutter mansions having laid waste to so many farmlands throughout Bucks County.

Proceeding to the New Hope onramp and the bucolic, River Road, Gem nuzzles into me when the Replacements, 'Unsatisfied' blares on dramatically. "Please, take me back there…in its entire wild, magical glory and don't stop even when you get to the parts you want me to forget like the epic magic of New York and what was…what could have…"

"Gem…we really don't…" Shuffling apprehensively in the driver's seat, I shoot her a pained expression, but she's having none of it. "Oh, but I do Robbs, even my broken, harrowing childhood and teens…because for better or worse, it became the story of us as well…

"Although you'll despise the correlation, I need that junkie's instant infusion…the flash of a poison laced rig mainlining that hideous evil into my being…stirring my demons…my thoughts…and not letting any of it escape me.

"I need that slap across the face hurtling me back towards reality and what really fucking mattered...the fight for what was right, the temptations of the opulent Eighties, the disparity of rat infested tenements, the back alley fights...like a photo album of memories running through my mind, so when we get to the old squat, sit with me on the deck while the sun warms my heart and the lavender, the falls and your voice warm my soul. Tell me everything, as only you can."

Winding past the glistening beauty of the Delaware's choppy waters, pointing us in the direction of the artists Valhalla and away from the hustle and bustle of the big city, I smile, responding simply, "okay," before taking a long, deep breath, lighting another Marlboro and gazing for what seems like an eternity into those mesmerizing eyes of green.

"Punks for life, Gemma...it's October, 1985...so, let our story begin."

••• 2 •••

1985

"GOOD GOD, HENRY, this train wreaks today!" We share a smoke in the aisle of the cloudy passenger car before the grizzled, bear of a conductor winces.

"I'm not going to argue with you on that one, Rob. Even these rotten Camels aren't hiding the stench of those burning brakes!"

The only salvation is that my stop, Rydal Station, will be next but poor Henry has to endure this putrid, shit burning in a paper bag smell for at least another forty minutes. "Christ, mate, SEPTA should give you hazard pay for sucking up this noxious shite! It looks like Pittsburgh in the forties down this hallway!"

"Okay, okay, I agree with you, kiddo. Now, onto to bigger and better things such as, why in the blazes do you look like someone ran you over? Burnin' the midnight oil again were we?"

"Yep, Gem and I had a small gig in the city last night and by the time she got me home and we said our goodbye's in the car..."

"Aye, so we were out with the pointy haired, redheaded beauty again, eh? Well, saints and angels, now I understand why

Mother Cavelli looked so miffed unloading yer' hide at the station earlier," he chuckles.

"Henry, Mother Cavelli ALWAYS looks miffed because her son's a Socialist, which in her estimation equates to me being a Commie..into punk, which she hates, so therefore, in her dead, dank world, it's the equivalent of saying that I'm a glue sniffing crackhead. She's ruthless, mate."

"We parents tend to be that way at times, sonny boy...so anyway, how went the show?"

"We played in Queen Village, at a coffeehouse on Third, although I must admit it smelled more like mold and stale piss than coffee and to top off the evening, a rat the size of poodle left a trophy sized pile of shit by my boot on stage."

"Ha, ha, ha, now that sounds like a night to remember!"

"Glad I can be the butt of your entertainment, Henry. Ah, piss off, it was all in a night's work, besides, the redhead and this drummer 'Stacks' who we borrowed from an ass kicking band in town just about blew the windows out of the place. We're getting closer to the chance, Henry.

"Anyway, ol' Gem just about lost it when the rat unloaded its contents and it gave her a great segue into our sped up punk ode to dirty, old Philly called, 'Filthy City of Rats'."

"Good Lord, I can only imagine the lyrics..."

Building up some air into the lungs and ample tension in the gut, I prepare to entertain Henry with the machine gun paced chorus. "Filthy city of rats, filthy city of rats, if they got any bigger they'd fuckin' eat the cats...Filthy city of rats, filthy city of rats, if they got any bigger they'd fuckin' eat the cats," and although Henry explodes into riotous fits of laughter through the burning brake and cigarette haze, I've apparently drawn the ire of a smartly dressed, refined businesswoman standing near us. "Sorry, it's not everyone's cup of tea, love," I snort.

"Apparently not," Henry chortles before the highbrow contemptuously turns back to her bible of the rape and pillager set, the Wall Street Journal.

"Ugh...man, I pity you putting up with the snoots on this train, Henry. I can only imagine this one's reaction when she heard the verses about our filthy, rat bastard politicians and I hate to keep beating a dead horse, but this crate really stinks, mate," I bellow acidulously, eliciting another glare from the prim yuppie princess who goes on reading about what CEO gleefully doled out thousands of pink slips in the name of austerity and profitability yesterday.

"Hang in there, Rob, hopefully next week, we'll have the newer cars and engine back. This one hails from the Depression Era." I smirk but Henry cuts off any chance of a snarky reply by delivering his middle finger salute.

"You do realize that's poor customer service, Henry. I could get you fired for such mistreatment." Henry scowls from under his salt-and-pepper, bushy mustache, taking the last drag of his Camel before pinching it between his fingers and sailing it to the tracks below. "You know, it's wise ass punks like you that make this Mick from Belfast think retirement looks better every day, Rob." He winks, opens the door, unleashing his best yawp to alert the groggy, working stiff masses of the next stop on their ominous ride towards perdition. "RYDAL STATION, RYDAL," and the bucking shitbox eventually sparks, screeches, and groans to a calamitous halt. Flicking my spent cig onto the platform, I give Henry a smile. "Thanks for the smoke, comrade. Be well."

"You do the same, Rob, and listen, don't be a stranger around here. I know you've got a car now but you're good company for this old man."

"No worries about losing this customer, besides I'm lucky if I can get Otis rolling forward twice a week and who can afford the gas anymore?"

"Tell me about it, kid. A dollar a gallon for gas and a buck-twenty for cigarettes, with no end in sight! I feel bad for you.

"By the way, what's with the spray cans?" he wryly questions, poking at the bulging backpacks side pouch.

"Got some walls to fuck up in the Student Union today, my friend."

"More than I need to know," he bellows with arms thrown wide. "Say hi to your pretty lass fer' me and BEHAVE!"

The train lurches forward, shooting sparks from its rusted underbelly and groaning out its death knell. "I'll tell her and don't worry about me, mate!" Raising a triumphant fist, I shout, "TO THE BOHEMIAN LIFE," when the train rolls away in a cacophony of fits and smoke, engulfing poor Henry in billowing, smokestack-like clouds of filth.

Bounding precipitously from the steep, grassy knolls of the meticulously kept, red brick and slate roofed Rydal Station, towards the winding, downhill roads ahead, I soon pass a picturesque mix of old and new wealth. Well-manicured lawns range in every direction, leading up to Tudor homes and stone castles of the self-important, reminding me of Yardley, the capitalist hell from where I reside. There's a nauseating amassing of wealth there as well, but I only get to view its excesses through the lives of thankfully, distant acquaintances.

The walks typically advance at a brisk pace, although lately my friend, Samantha Baird, eventually retrieves me, which I love, since she always has a warm greeting for me and a fresh pack of smokes to boot. The all too familiar sound of a Gran Torino horn makes me smile and Sammi gives me a big hug before we take off.

I usually put some punk, like Public Image into her cassette player and she'll actually give a listen now. "What's this shit?" was typically asked when the first attempts of punk selections were made, since she was more of a 70's arena rock girl, but there's a wicked evolution taking place in one, Samantha Baird, an evolution even more radical than she willingly admits to and I'm not just talking about politics or music. "So, what're we listening to today, Robbs?"

"I'm going mellow on you today, Sammi, with a little more of a new wave, dance vibe so here's The Smiths, 'Meat Is Murder'," leaving her chestnut eyes to actually sparkle at the prospect.

"Believe it or not, I like them. Play, 'How Soon Is Now'..I love that song." Shifting her peach colored, long, lovely legs while turning into the campus parking lot, Sammi's drop dead pretty and her legs are an equal distraction, especially on days like today when she's wearing ultra-short skirts and high heels.

So, as Morrissey keeps smooth crooning, "You shut your mouth, how can you say, I go about things the wrong way," Sammi dances in her seat and when it's obvious I'm enjoying her every move, she happily places her toned arms around my shoulders. "So, is there ever a chance that the punk guy will take notice of more than just my legs? Guys are all the same, you just want one thing. That's why I've given up," she replies with a dramatic sigh and wicked giggle.

"Are you kidding? Look, don't get me wrong. Your legs are exceptional…especially exceptional today, but you're an incredibly intelligent and pretty girl. I love hanging out with you." I run my fingers up and down her thigh as we move closer on the bench seat. The Smiths play on, Morrissey sings 'Nowhere Fast' and teenaged, Johnny Marr cranks out a western style warble on guitar. "So, let's talk about this giving up thing. You're done with guys, so, we're into girls?"

"Robert Cavelli, we're not talking about this and besides, goofball, if I said yes, your typical guy brain would be envisioning which girl you'd have in bed with me. I can only imagine the girl on girl grind and lick fest I'd have to hear about sometime down the road from your nasty piehole."

"Sammi, I take umbrage to that remark. I'm just a good friend, asking a question here."

Our eyes meet, and she smiles before mischievously pushing me away. "You're a good guy, Rob…a real cutie in most girls' estimations, including mine, but you can lock eyes with me all you want. When I look into yours, I already see her there." Sammi grabs my chin and her other hand traces the outline of my nose before running her long fingers through my hair. "I just love these loose, long curls…can't imagine these getting twirled and gelled into colored spikes. They must look sensational."

"Come out with us sometime, and you could see just how sensational they look." Her hands rest against my patchwork, leather jacket and smiling playfully, she unsnaps it before pushing me away again with a giggle. "Face it Rob, you are hers.

"Believe me, you can tell how much she adores you and thank God, she got you away from boring 'Miss High School'. What a bogus tart she was!" The interrogatory look soon overtakes the sweet demeanor. "You are still done with her, right? Fuckin' A, I couldn't stand Gargoyle, Jizzbisquit."

"You know her name's Giselle, wise ass."

"Giselle, Frizzelle…bitch can go to hell! Sorry…the blonde hair, blue eyed, fake ass, Barbie doll did nothing for you.

"I'm glad you found Gemma, and she found you. Dressed down, or tribal punk, she's exquisite, free spirited, smart as hell, thoughtful, spunky, gorgeous and madly in love with you.

"Keep ol' blondie in the rear-view mirror, Robbs, because Gem's the one."

"Thanks again, Sammi, as always, you're my voice of reason, even though you've given up on guys and apparently like sexing hot girls."

"For fuck's sake, shut up with the Sammi and hot girls thing already, you pre-teen dweeb twat and besides, I have to be your voice of reason, otherwise you'd still be with Gertie Bertie."

"Giselle…"

"Yeah, yeah, Giselle, what an ass…spying on you up here, while she's getting porked by every cock in sight! Oh well, piss off on her!" Sammi blurts out before retrieving my cassette. "Thanks for the music and for being such a big flirt, you made my day."

After successfully hood-surfing to open her car door, two cigs are procured and, as has become the norm when there's something to say, the glowing tipped smokes are hoisted skyward.

"So, who are we toasting today?"

"I'm toasting Giselle," is the devilish reply while I proceed to choke in mock horror. "Giselle..you, of all people are toasting.. Giselle?"

With a wry smile affixed to her eye-catching, round face, Sammi's eyes twinkle mischievously. "To Giselle, may the bitch rot in hell!"

"I agree, Samantha Baird…to Giselle, hope you're already there, ya' shitweasel."

"PISS OFF, SOD OFF," we bellow, while the befuddled masses view our rebellious chant, shake their heads derisively and trudge off to class.

Scaling the steep trails leading towards the Student Union building, the sun commences its usual game of hide-n-seek amongst the towering blanket of leaves overhead. Fall materialized rather early this October, leaving a palate of red, yellow and burnt orange swirling in the breeze like broken, colored glass in a kaleidoscope and as the wind howls, Sammi nuzzles onto my shoulder, buttoning up her petite jacket against the morning's chill. "So, where's my lovely, Bohemian girl today? Is she at the Student Union awaiting your arrival so you can piss off the University once more by painting album covers on the walls of the Socialist Party offices again? I see you've brought more spray cans."

"You know Gemma, she's more unpredictable than October weather. The Student Government President, Abby Rothschild, really got her bent with her recent proclamation about threatening a reversal on the college's approval for a Socialist office on campus, so let's go check the Union first, I have to get a dark tea and some more smokes anyway. Would you like a coffee, Samms? It's my treat since I got paid this week."

Besides going to school and enjoying new found freedoms like busking, I picked up a part time, office cleaning gig and was still waiting tables once in a blue moon at Kerrigan's Irish Pub near the campus. "Well thank you, my hard-working honey. Any chance you can get me some cheap smokes from the machine, babe?"

"As long as they are still a dollar-twenty, sixty cent smokes, coming right up." Sammi happily prances into the cafeteria to obtain some hot refreshments, allowing for my deliberate approach to the cigarette machine.

A friendly classmate toiling for a low wage, non-union vending company last summer gave a quick tutorial on 'purchasing' smokes at half price, so after scoping the scene, making sure no preppy snitches are surveilling, I grab change out of my shredded jeans...the ones with Sex Pistols lyrics scribed over every inch of fabric with a black Sharpie..slide the coins slowly into the slot and after some intricate, safe cracker artistry, a fresh pack of twenty Reds appears in the tray.

Upon performing the same sleight of hand for Sammi, the process is repeated for an exquisite lovely hopefully joining in our morning debauchery. Kneeling down, stuffing our prizes into the front pouch, a familiar clicking sound approaches me, accompanied by an entrancing song at an eerily moderate volume.

John Mc Geoch's guitar plays hauntingly, allowing Siouxsie Sioux's voice to roll out like a demonic purr..

> *"From the cradle bars*
> *Comes a beckoning voice*
> *It sends you spinning*
> *You have no choice..."*

The clicking and the music stop, superseded only by a spellbinding, sultry tone. "What's in the bag, handsome? You know, stealing cigarettes is a Federal offense, so stand up, turn around slowly, give up the contraband without a fight and no one gets busted. While you're at it, I'll take these off your hands too," she coos, slipping her deft, cat burglar fingers over the spray cans.

Turning to face the judge, jury and executioner, her early morning magnificence; the natural, light olive hue of her skin makes the green of her eyes even more arresting, the hair, which when left to flow freely, almost reaches the center of her back, is now pulled up, unlike the other night when it was gelled into what seemed to be hundreds of razor thin pink spikes. The Kool Aid neon has been washed out, revealing natural, deep auburn beauty, save for the dyed, shocked-white streak running through a few long strands.

With an acoustic slung across her back like a badass bandolero, the ensemble of thigh-high boots with precarious heels, sheer black stockings, short tartan skirt, black, homemade "ANARCHY U.K" t-shirt, covered by a short, well-worn, thrift store purchased, black studded leather jacket creates quite the dissonant effect in this predominantly, white bread, yuppie campus, where the Duran Duran or Culture Club, 'New Wave' demand of paying a high price to look trendy, exists in spades with this clique.

The balance of the Union inhabitants consists of Southern rock rednecks, who wear some degree of clothing comprising of an asshole Confederate flag, American flag or camouflage; the Quiet Riot, Twisted Sister types in their Spandex pants or ripped jeans, concert t-shirts and high hair or the motorheads in their black, Mopar, Ford and Chevy t-shirts. Never to be forgotten were the sweater boy jocks, and their annoying, fake ass cheerleader girlfriends carrying the high school, glory day cockiness pathetically with them into college life.

And then there were the Reagan Kids. Typically, from 'New Money', these were the future success stories of the boardroom, the courtroom or any other room they felt could be overtaken, raped and pillaged by their parents' money or vapid arrogance. Holding most of their fellow students at a tolerable arms' length, they held an aggregate amount of contempt for the banished kids in the smaller lunchroom of the Union.

This room, which we nicknamed 'The Gulag', contained black, Hispanic, Oriental, Indian and whites' of 'suspect' class or religious origin. The hideously beige, concrete block atrocity separating them from the 'norms' was nicknamed the Berlin Wall and was a source of supreme contentiousness with a certain, activist redhead leading the campaign to have it removed.

I'd developed enough diverse interests in the past year to move freely between all of these groups, even tolerating and actually becoming friends with a few Reagan Kids who were emerging and evolving from the President's and their parents bullshit conviction that the 1950's were some kind of white man's Valhalla to be repeated in the 1980's.

Sammi was from this moneyed group but was shunning many of these beliefs. Our bond as friends was initially because her parents and my mother were Reagan and Thatcher disciples, who believed in the Conservative, survival of the fittest narrative and were authoritarian in their belief system. It was a suffocating existence to say the least and we railed against it vehemently at times, especially after Gemma Stinson came into my life and turned everything even more upside down and for the better.

Initially, Gem viewed me with heinous contempt, surmising that I was a Reagan Kid, but her mood amended slightly when she happened past 'The Gulag', saw me reading her latest flier against the 'Berlin Wall' and hanging out with her gang, The Misfits while we listened to the Anti-Nowhere League and healthily debated over whether Public Image Limited was John Lydon being a sellout or a psychoneurotic genius.

Strutting with a purpose in worn, black combat boots, swinging her curvy hips in torn jeans and donning an equally tattered leather jacket, which had Black Flag painted on the back in red, she grabbed me by the wrist, searing through me with those penetrating, cat-like green eyes. "What's your game, Money? Are you slumming it today?"

Otto Lewandowski, the first punk I'd befriended on campus, quickly rose to my defense. "Bloody hell, Gemma, it's not like that, Rob's different than those Reagan Kid jagoffs. Yuka and I chatted him up at Rydal, waiting for the Philly train and he started saying what his favorite songs and groups were on the punk scene, oi, he just blew us the fuck away."

"Robbie, the Reagan Kid punk rocker," she snorted. "Yeah, we'll fuckin' see about that."

Hiking up my ball cap to give her a better look, she was a natural beauty, there was no doubt, catching my attention from minute one in our Humanities class. "Gemma, if you have some time, I'd love to take a walk with you. We could talk music, politics, whatever you'd like. I've got a full pack of Reds and I'll gladly grab some lunch for us too. C'mon, what do you say?"

I could see Otto from the corner of my eye trying in vain to make her be agreeable. "All right, Robbie Reagan, I'll give you a few minutes, only because Otto seems to think you're cool but don't get any ideas that we'll be fast friends here or that you can 'buy' me with your trinkets of lunch and smokes, though." Coffee in hand, a fresh pack of Newport's for her, we began our walk through the long and winding campus. The October winds blew a cool breeze, sending an array of crisp colored leaves swirling about the cobblestone paths.

It was supposed to be a short walk but turned into an all-day affair, skipping all of our classes, grabbing lunch at the Union, playing Frisbee football with the arena rock kids, sitting by the duck pond and talking into the night about everything and anything.

Needless to say, catching the late train home provided me with an ample wrath of shit from my mother. It was the one thing I detested about going to a satellite campus of a major college, it kept me home, nothing more than Thirteenth fucking grade but when I got off at Rydal the next day and saw Gemma waiting there to walk with me, everything became clearer. My world was peaceful, if only for those few hours. Our paths began to cross all the time; she, having an infinite trust in me, and I in her. Fast friends or maybe we were more than that?

I was still seeing Giselle but was increasingly tiring of her high school existence invading my life, whereas with Gemma, there were no boundaries, no secrets, the world was a canvas, and no one could stop us from painting our masterpiece together.

Now, in the midst of this new October and with Giselle out of the picture but interestingly enough enrolled at a campus less than two miles away, I had a pure vision of beauty standing there, badgering me like a street urchin for her smokes. "Well, Robbs, are you going to gawk at me like a fucking gargoyle, or are you going to hand over our spoils?"

"Well, Gem, I succinctly recall from the vast literature I've perused in my short but ubiquitous lifetime, that it's the victor who amasses the spoils." The impatience simmers to a boil, still, she can't help but smile. "You're really going to debate me on this, Robbs? May I remind you who was pleading for mercy in Forensics last year? Do I need to recap who walked away victorious from our tumultuous debate over the United States' stance on foreign policy in the Middle East?"

"I have a clear recollection that the majority of people viewed my thesis as being the righteous path to a more autonomous and coherent policy, Gem."

The cat eyes begin their demonic, darkening sizzle. "Do you know what I think?"

"No, but I am sure you will tell me," I groan sarcastically.

"I think you need to stop fighting me and make peace, Robert Cavelli." Pushing my backpack towards the floor, the lithe arms eventually reign me in...no gaps between us. "I have just the prescription needed to quell your hostility, young man, especially now that you've realized that the supposed dark side isn't too bad after all."

Moving closer together, the warm, sweet breath encompasses me. Much like Sammi, Gem's a statuesque girl, with the heels providing another layer to her entrancing aura. "So, how do you propose to repress this angry young man's hostile tendencies?"

"I think this will get you started on a more peaceful path," and her soft lips press against mine. I'm lost in her grip, our tongues dance, the embrace enjoyably lingers. "Don't ever break my heart, Robbs."

"No worries there, Gem. I would say that you've won my heart."

An angelic voice seizes the moment, crashing us back to reality. "Aww! Aren't you two just the hottest thing going on in this droll ass campus?" Sammi has returned with our coffee, tea and her daily dose of pleasantness, nudging me aside roughly to hug Gem. "Hello, my beautiful Bohemian girl, I absolutely love your look, and the white strip in the hair is sexy, sexy."

"Thanks, Samms and of course, you're looking Hollywood glamorous, and super sexy. So, did you take good care of my honey today?" Gem asks coyly.

"Actually, your honey took good care of me. He was the total gentleman and the consummate flirt as well. He played some good music and made me laugh."

Gem's green eyes sparkle, the fearsome, inquisitive gaze landing upon me. "Flirting with you, ay' Samms? Well, I can't say that I'm surprised, especially since you two are quite sexy together."

"Thanks, gorgeous, but I told him to enjoy the flirting cuz' it's the most he'll ever get from me, besides everyone knows you two are destined to be together," Sammi crows when the tortur-ous ribbing at my expense continues.

"You know, you may have something there, Samms because I think old Robbs may be a keeper."

I can only stare at the ceiling in mock agony. "Okay, enough you two 'cause this shit is almost getting sickening, syrupy. Please, let's try to focus ladies and get to the heart of the matter."

Sammi breathes deep and bellows "Friday!" as if life depended on it.

"True, true, Sammi, but more importantly, it is the Friday before The Cure's playing The Tower."

"You actually attempting to drive that bucket of bolts to The Tower, Robbs?"

"Very funny, Gem. Otis may take forever to get started, but he's a runner once he gets going. Besides, Otis is a battle wagon. Lena didn't even make a scratch on him this summer when she christened him with that full bottle of suds. So, who'll be meet-ing us?"

"Well, we have Otto, Lena and Yuka," Gem chirps before placing her wet, pursed lips seductively near my ear, "and of course, your date for the evening will be there." The neck becomes curi-ously warm when the enchantress moves her mouth about and it's quite an enrapturing aphrodisiac.

"As was stated previously, Robbs, you belong to her," Sammi happily intones.

Trying to regain some semblance of composure, I fail, shakily rattling off the itinerary while Gem continues nuzzling into the curve between my neck and shoulder, driving the senses wilder by the second. "So…mmm, Gem…you're killing me, babe…I'll meet you early at the apartment, right? The tribe will be over later and Yuka will perform her hair magic?"

The auburn-haired temptress ceases her wily ways only long enough to reply, "yes, on all counts, so pack your gear in the trunk tonight, so your mom doesn't spaz and give you any crap tomor-row like I know she must've after the hour you rolled in from the gig last night or about what you're wearing to school today."

Rolling her head back and forth lightly on my shoulder blade, the lament continues, "Parents…ugh…"

"Good God, Robbs! She's still not cutting you any slack over the whole punk thing or doing the gigs?" Sammi inquires before rolling her eyes in complete disgust.

"Yeah, she tolerates me a little better without Giselle around but she still can't break that total, authoritarian hold over me. She nearly lost my one brother with that stupidity, and she's about ready to lose me. Except for today, I rarely take the punk gear out of my car trunk 'cept to wash them at the Laundromat, and right into my spare backpack they go. It sucks, but it's better than listening to her shit all day."

"So anyway, you guys played last night and…"

"Samms, Rob brought down the house with his performance!" Gem gushes.

"Gem, your awesome axe, Stacks' drums and the stank of that shithole brought the house down."

"Very funny, butthead but you tore that place up with 'Filthy City of Rats'…slayed 'em."

"Hmmm…the 'Filthy City of Rats'…I don't think that I even want to know."

"Ya' probably don't, Sammi," I laugh before Gem gives me the once over.

"Cigarette break in the field, Robbs? We can discuss which wall is receiving Rudimentary Peni's 'Death Church' cover this time. Ugh, I get the okay on the requisition to paint the wall from those yuppie ass hairs' in Student Government and the University fascists and then they all flip out, saying the art's sacrilegious. What assholes."

"Alright, my activist hellion, let's take a breath and hammer this out, because you know they'll put you and Yuka on probation or worse if you're busted again and Pops Yamaguchi won't be happy with that. Otto is a chef with two left hands when it comes to wall art, so I'll do it and take the heat this time.

"You know how much I love to make art come to life and if I get busted, what the fuck do I have to lose? C'mon," I laugh, "let's hit that field and conspire." It sounds like the perfect plan for a

Friday morning before class, so we gather our belongings, progressing slowly into the effervescence of this picturesque autumn day. Sammi follows out, stopping long enough to embrace us before departing. "Goodbye, for now, young lovers, graffiti artists and University over throwers. I'll try catching up with you guys for lunch, if you're not incarcerated by then. Remember, Gem...no decking Abby, even though she's Giselle's little FBI bitch."

Gem keenly observes Sammi walking breezily through the leaf clogged pathways before unleashing a wicked, devil-may-care laugh. "She's so cool, Robbs, I'll make her into a hot, punk goddess yet," and the thought of our summery, apple pie girl becoming a night vixen makes me smile. "Let's get going, young temptress. Leave the pure of the planet to live in innocence for just one more day."

Sitting comfortably with her long, lovely legs crossed, Gem lets loose a few chords about a story of her young life she's comprised, although she doesn't delve too deeply into all of the lyrics. 'There's still many things I have to let you know about, but all in due time, Robbs,' she's accustomed to saying and I am more than patient enough to wait.

> "Staring out from behind a sooty window
> Look how the city lights shine so bright
> Woke up on the floor again
> The fuckin' filthy floor again
> Veins are hoping for some bliss tonight..."

Strumming lightly, her eyes meet mine. "It's going to take me some time, Robbs, but I'll get the lyrics to fill in the gaps. And I think I know the perfect person to assist me with their verbal prowess, but I still have many more things to tell you before I allow a perusal of what I've constructed so far."

"Whenever that day comes, Swan, I'll be right here for you."

Kissing me tenderly, she smiles radiantly, even hinting at signs of blushing. "Thanks babe, I know you will." Continuing with her entrancing playing, she hums sweet and true. The courtyard and winding paths have become increasingly empty and students scurry frantically to attend morning classes but that's of no concern to Gem nor myself since we have an hour before Literature class begins, so we continue regaling in the magnificent, October sun. The first month of school has been such an enjoyment and I know it's because of Gem.

We'd stayed in touch sporadically over the early summer months. It was during that time, Giselle and I were moving further apart upon painfully hearing rumors of her carousing and soon discovering they were quite truthful.

Giselle also became extremely jittery about my having contact with any girls who she deemed as pretty or as a plausible threat to our relationship. Eventually, I dispatched her to greener pastures, where she'd hopefully find a fool tolerant of her devious nature and coveting ways.

It was during this time I'd met up with some surfer punk buds of mine, who mused that a road trip to the town of Harvey Cedars along New Jersey's shoreline, would generate the perfect kick-ass release to make Giselle a mere memory on this hot, beautiful, July morning.

After a purely bitchin' early day of sun, swimming and of course, some radical surfing, the boys decided to cap off the day by heading into Philly, hitting South Street and with a lightning quick Chevelle under us and tunes from The Clash, Husker Du, and The Anti-Nowhere League peppering the college radio airwaves, haste was made down the Expressway towards our meeting place by the popular punk store, Zipperhead.

You couldn't miss Philly's more working class version of McClaren and Westwood's, Kings Row mashup, 'SEX', even if you tried, due to the fact that Zips had about seven, giant black metal ants crawling around on the buildings brick skin plus a larger than life, silver zipper in the center of the damn place which opened out of some poor bastards' head over the awning while the 'teeth' flared out until they hit the rooftop.

An army of punks, with hair ranging from brightly colored Mohawks, Liberty Spikes and cones, to the long, untamed, colored dreads of the rasta punks sprouting from under puffy caps, to your basic looking kid who had an equal love for the music and the politics of the movement, had congregated in front of the store and it was about that time, with the music of Brian Ferry blasting across a TV set showing a Live Aid feed from Wembley Stadium in London while simultaneously showing Madonna bimboing her way around our own Philadelphia's, JFK Stadium, I noticed a tall girl in knee high, stiletto heeled, black boots, fish net stockings, tattered, tight jean shorts, an Exploited concert T-shirt, and what seemed to be hundreds of razor thin, auburn spikes. Handing out leaflets to the amassed rowdies and some intrigued passerby, my mind raced with delight that it possibly was her.

Curiosity soon became pure elation when she turned, revealing a delicious smile and melting me with those piercing eyes, before letting go a plume of cigarette smoke as she sauntered my way, swinging those sexy hips of hers before happily handing me a flier containing some upcoming Democratic Socialist events along with some punk shows. "Slumming it again, Comrade Money? I'd have figured a big shot, capitalist, Yardley boy like you to be down at Live Aid with your yuppie tart princess."

"Never got the chance to tell you, Gem…Giselle and I are fuckin' done."

Haughtily releasing another plume of smoke, she revealed her innermost sympathy over the turn of events. "Damn, Robbs…I'm just so fuckin' heartbroken for that skank." Laughing, embracing her for what seemed like a lifetime, my mind raced as we held each-others gaze. Was this coincidence, was this meant to be, did it really fucking matter?

The girl who drives you crazy, debates you incessantly, who can be tough one minute, tender the next, was now in your arms, so without a second more of hesitation, my lips met hers, soon feeling her mouth open, revealing her intoxicating warmth. It was a kiss to be repeated numerous times in that whirlwind, summer of punk which now flowed into a busy but enjoyable Fall Semester. It was Gem and I against the world, we were golden and glorious, and nobody better tell us otherwise.

Reminiscing eventually becomes reality when Gem somberly glances at her watch. "Aww...well Robbs, our hour is almost done. Are you ready to move this day along? The sooner today ends, the better. Knowing I'll be with you all day tomorrow just thrills me."

Rapidly, we hit the paths back to class, kicking at the painters' palette of leaves wrapped around our feet. Opening the doors to Rutherford Hall, Gem darts ahead of me, daring the chase to begin. Skipping steps, damn near falling over each other, bursting into fits of laughter during this maddening pursuit, the solid wood and glass entrance doors of the second floor are impacted with a resounding thud. Regaining her composure, Gem takes me by the arm. "Don't ever break my heart, Robbs."

"No worries there, Gem, you've won my heart. Hey babe... fuck class today, let's go pepper those walls with some of Nick Blinko's kick ass artwork and our fine touches of worker portraits from the battles for unions in the Thirties. I have some rad' ideas that I freehanded for that in my sketchbook. The Student government will shit themselves and wonder when the Anarchy symbol and Hammer and Sickle are to follow.

"C'mon, let me do this. I'm not even on their radar yet, but they could toss me from school, toss the scholarship from me and I honestly don't care...they'll never split us up."

Feeling free to spin and twirl with childlike glee down the ancient, knotted and scarred wooden steps of this storied school building and out into the clean, crisp autumn air, Gem sighs peacefully. "You're crazy enough to do this for me and the cause, aren't you?"

"Punks for life, Gemma Stinson...punks for life." Golden and glorious, the adventure continues.

... 3 ...

Glorious Saturday

IT'S SATURDAY AND I'm up with the daybreak, not that this is anything new. The advantages of being an early riser consists of the usual routine; rearranging the bedclothes, consuming a rather sizeable breakfast, coaxing my body into performing a Spartan style slew of exercises and replenishing my energy with a warm shower.

After the wall painting fiasco, the ensuing verbal battle with the preppie Student Government President, Abby Rothschild and curtailing Gem's advances from giving Abby the quick slash of switchblade sharp talons across her cheek, or a bare-knuckled crack to her pristine jawline yesterday, I'm lucky to not be doing these activities from inside a jail cell, especially considering that I was about ready to curb stomp Abby's obnoxious, jock-itch, frat boy turd boyfriend, Jake Whitley, when he apparently thought his two cents really fucking mattered in the confrontation.

If Jagoff Jake continues running his mouth about Gem's politics, or especially about her personality, he'll be shitting teeth out of his tight, yuppie asscrack when we compete during the Intramural Hockey season.

With those issues put aside for now, eliciting a quick goodbye from my mother before things become increasingly contentious is the big hoop to jump through at the moment.

The acrimony of recent times has quieted down, especially since I sent Giselle packing. Giselle and my mom detested each other, making existence with an already dictatorial mother ever the more stressful experience.

Apparently, my mother, the oldest daughter of Giuseppe Antonini, a Pittsburgh born, leather craftsman and staunch union leader, was cut from the same taskmaster, disciplinarian mold of her father early on, remained that way even after Giuseppe moved the family from the hardscrabble, filthy steel town to the glitter of New York City, but became even more hardcore after my father was killed in a store holdup when I was only eleven months old. My oldest brother, Perry, took on a lot of the paternal responsibilities, while still attending high school and then college.

My other brother, James, seemingly unable to cope with the tragedy of losing a father who more often than not, was a gentle and nurturing soul, pulled further away from the normalcy already vanishing in late, 1960's America and by the 1970's inauspicious arrival, James was in full rebellion with society, Perry, and especially mom.

James was an exemplary, intellectual sort, receiving a full scholarship to Fordham prior to graduating high school but inexplicably, a year and a half later, James bid farewell to the Ivy League, grew a long, Jesus-style beard, adorned his dome with an overly large afro, incessantly smoked cigarettes, ingratiated himself into the drug counterculture, and began sporting unkempt jean jackets and bell bottoms as an everyday attire. He was often spotted walking the streets of our Brooklyn neighborhood in hippie sandals or even barefoot. To Anna Cavelli, this abhorrent rebelliousness was the ultimate slap in the face and an affront to her neighborhood status.

28

Frequently distressing about her upper-middle class way of life or what the hell neighbors would think, the fights between her and James became increasingly volatile.

Even though he towered above her, Mama Cavelli would think nothing of hitting James with anything she could wrap her lightening quick hands around and when Perry came to mom's defense, things became even more fitful. It was definitely not the 'Leave It to Beaver' reality my mom was bullshitting around the block, or to our extended family and once James had performed the act of basically proclaiming squatters' rights to the basement and painted beautifully scripted rock verses from Bowie and Pink Floyd on every inch of wall space, the battle turned into a war of sheer acrimony.

Eventually spending an inordinate amount of time at friends' residences to smoke weed, snort cocaine, work odd jobs, bounce in and out of college, or disappear for weeks at a time, James had become a lost cause in my mothers' eyes.

The laser focus for the perfection quotient was thrust into my very young hemisphere, commencing with private schooling and the supposedly innocuous attempts to clothe me as an upper crust young gentleman. When it seemed as if understanding that going the wanton ways of James would not be tolerated, the wooden spoon, the belt or her whip-like hands would soon remind her forgetful son that conformity to expectations would be met, or a heavy price would be paid.

Perry tried his best to be a nurturing big brother, but his calendar of events remained full upon graduating college, initiating his foray into the working world, plus trying to keep tabs on James' whereabouts. It was a daunting task for any young man to endure, even if he accepted the role without any sign of outward complaint or resentment.

Although exemplary, academic achievements were expected and accomplished, my free-spirited attitude didn't seem to fit into the private school realm and I was soon dispatched to our local Catholic school, Saint Valentine's, where the nuns seemed to have an equivalent affinity for Anna Cavelli's brand of harsh discipline.

Although I was still attaining good grades, my mischievous behavior earned me a familial reputation rivaled only by James. "If only you and James were more like your brother Perry, your time at Saint Valentine's would be a much more tranquil experience, Mister Cavelli," was reiterated by the uptight faculty more than once, so by Fifth grade, Anna Cavelli apparently had grown tired of Mother Superior's fruitless diatribes and unfortunately, a cataclysmic change was about to take place in my life.

The summer of 1977 was a tumultuous one in New York City, with the Metropolis still reeling from near bankruptcy; there were numerous strikes by the Sanitation Department which left the city buried in wretched piles of overflowing garbage cans, bags, loose mountains of refuse and an onslaught of rats.

The Son of Sam remained on the loose, gripping the city in fear and the death blow to our neighborhood came in the form of the biggest blackout on the Eastern Coast of the United States. With racial and economic tensions coming to a head, the bustling shopping district located on Flatbush Avenue was put ablaze, windows were smashed and stores looted. Witnessing her 'perfect world' coming apart, Anna Cavelli began dating a man from her past, Sal Pascala.

Sal was a diminutive man, who loved opera, wine and a good Italian meal. He'd earned an engineering degree in New York, and was immediately employed by a major oil company, shortly thereafter being relocated with his wife and four children to Yardley, Pennsylvania. Sadly, for Sal and his children, his wife was diagnosed with cancer and passed suddenly.

Within a year of her passing, Sal began courting my mother. We visited Yardley and although mom was quickly entranced by the beauty of the river, the farms and the manors of the small town, I viewed it as a death sentence, especially when I'd correctly surmised marriage would be in her future, thus tearing me away from my city, my friends and my entire family.

For the five years they were married, it was a constant battle over money, and the fuck if I know what else. Although there were rare, good moments with my step-family, I spent most of the time withdrawing into a world of my choice through a vivid imagination or by escaping to friends' houses. It was a trend I'd continue into the years after mom separated from Sal.

Even though notable achievements occurred in sports, academics and I'd significantly tamed my undisciplined school behavior, it was never good enough for Anna Cavelli. Her heavy-handed ways had not changed, so I would gladly disappear and test her will. My brother James, who very rarely visited because of his ongoing skirmishes with mom, even stopped in from New York recently, long enough to bellow, "Congratulations, mom. You're going to lose Rob even faster than you lost me!"

Buying Otis and paying for the insurance with my own work money safeguarded a certain amount of freedom from the contentiousness. As crappy a car as Otis could be, it made for many great escapes after it took forever to get started, puff, rumble and then finally roll. Sometimes it took a whack with a rubber mallet on the starter box to get him in the proper mood for mobility and today was no exception. Walking upstairs to finish my breakfast, I hear the tea kettle whistling, approach the entrance to the kitchen and pause…

"Well, I see the car is up and running. Are we out for the whole day? Keeping me up for ungodly hours while you and that girl did whatever it is you do in that city wasn't enough torture for your mother to endure?" The inquisition begins…

"Good morning, mom, it's great to see you too. You did happen to notice that all the dishes were done, the house was straightened out, my clothes were put away and there's seventy bucks on the table to use for whatever your heart desires."

Tersely smiling, mom's brain races for the next question to grill me with, like the bad cop in a smarmy 70's drama interrogation room ready to give you an ass whipping with a thick phone book, I decide to beat her to the punch before the routine is given a chance to flourish. "Oh, and even though our small-time gig went well…thanks for asking…all my homework, studying and my paper for Greek History is also completed." I can't believe I still have to say this crap to appease her; fucking Thirteenth grade.

"That's a good thing, Robert, but don't you feel any obligation to tell me what else is going on in your life?"

"I figured I'd achieved enough elation for you with Giselle's departure," I chuckle but my sarcasm is rapidly punctuated by another acerbic volley from the matriarch. "Best thing you could have done," she quips, sipping her tea, daintily placing the cup back on the saucer. "Giselle was a tramp anyway, but I guess you can't expect too much from a Levittown upbringing."

"Ah, the true crux of the problem, isn't that correct mother? The class divide of Route 1, or Route 13 trumps all, however, you do realize that the only thing keeping you from being over there is the money Sal gives you every month and the sale of our Brooklyn house."

With pure ferocity, the darkened, hawkish eyes hone in on their prey. "I'm keeping you from that existence as well! If it wasn't for me, you'd still be living in a Brooklyn that has gone to hell in a hand basket with all THOSE people that moved in. I saved YOU from that!"

Hopefully Otis is ready to get me the hell away from the proclivity of martyrdom and racism on display but not before I return some parting shots of my own. The quiet, passive son, who took his physical and verbal lashings in silence, is hushed no more. High school had made me find my voice, college has awakened my militancy. "You didn't save me from anything, you saved yourself and found YOUR paradise.

"Mom, admit to the fact that you have an affinity for wealth and strive to emulate people who've amassed it. You gravitate towards it and good for you, since you enjoy the pampered goings-on at your Garden Club luncheons with your wealthy church ladies and the like.

"I don't need that because money doesn't impress me and never will. It's why you like politicians like Reagan, his money men, and the sharks on Wall Street that you're ardently hoping I'll become someday.

"You've turned away from the good, working class life which Labor afforded you through Gramps' hard work but I abhor Reagan's policies, especially his treatment of people like the

32

thousands of steelworkers in Levittown who've lost their jobs because of his horrendous, trickle-down economics."

The tea cup misses the saucer altogether this time. "Damn you and your brother with that hippie, Democratic liberal agenda and now YOU have that vile, pointy haired punk garbage playing all the time! Its brainwashing you, just like it seems your college friends are achieving with great success!"

Just breathe deep and exhale, Rob.

"Well, thanks for another enlightening conversation, illuminating the reason as to why you receive limited or no contact with most of my new friends, mom. By the way, just so you are correctly informed...not a liberal, mother...I'm a Socialist."

"EVEN WORSE...A COMMUNIST!"

"Ugh...mom...they're not the same thing. Look it up in an encyclopedia or dictionary but until then, I can't deal with your 'Red Scare' McCarthyism, so I'm going into Philadelphia and seeing The Cure with my tribe and Gemma, who's such a good soul."

After kissing her forehead, I sigh harshly. "You know what I adore about Gem as well? She loves me for being me. You ought to try that with me sometime. By the way, the plan is to be out all night, staying in Philly and will see you sometime tomorrow night. Later, mom..."

"Yes, that's terrific, Robert. Spend more time in a city where the Mayor has to eradicate those MOVE thugs by dropping bombs on them. I just don't understand you."

Here we go again...

"Mom, we can't even talk about this because the 'burbs have tainted your view that there aren't some real, horrendous socio-economic perils going on in places like Philly now. You just choose to dismiss the fact that a white Police commissioner of a massively white police force just agreed to incinerate blocks full of houses, owned by innocent black families to remove a singular threat.

"If they'd done that in an Italian part of the city, you'd be screaming bias and bigotry from the rooftops. Listen, we'll never agree on this so, I'll see you soon. Much as you tend not to believe it, I do love you," I reply tartly.

Making haste through the museum quality appointments of the living room statuary, past the cherry tables with glass inlays, the polished brass lamps and the classically appointed sofas, finally heading down the plush, taupe colored carpeted stairs of her condominium, I hope one day she'll try to understand and accept me for who I am, but at the moment, that's all for naught. "Goddamn him," is mumbled from upstairs instead.

Jumping into Otis and hurriedly fast-forwarding Gem's mix cassette to Public Image Limited's 'Annalisa', the sputtering, lurching and fumbling begins, interior lights and the stereo start to fade in and out, before Otis lets out an enormous pop, springing painfully to life. "Come the fuck on, Otis, you doddering drunk! Let's go!"

I think he knows that I want to be out of Yardley faster than a space shuttle takeoff and with John Lydon screaming at full volume again, the black sedan gets hustled through the wooded back roads of Yardley onto Route 1 and in a few miles, pushed furiously onto Interstate 95, destination...Philly.

Lowering the window slightly before lighting a well-deserved Red, the morning chill mixed with the suns' blazing warmth is a welcoming feeling on my face. The temperature is supposed to hit about 63 today, 44 for tonight, which makes it a perfect day for hanging in Philly and heading to the Tower Theater later for a concert.

Yuka's not expected at the flat until two; that's when she'll reveal her art and hairstyling prowess once more, constructing me into a wild, gangland, Philly punk Misfit and Gem and I will finally receive some much-needed time alone beforehand, a thought which has me pushing Otis even harder than before. The Red's extinguished and Joy Division's, 'Transmission' pounds the windows mercilessly with its wicked bass lines.

Pretty much having the Interstate to myself this early in the morning and no cops in sight, mashing Otis' accelerator to conquer 100 on the speedometer is a given since the old boy still does have some highway chops.

I can't help but think again about Gemma, how our summer progressed, following that terrific, July night on South Street. She was renting a flat from Misty, a friend of Yuka's parents, the Yamaguchi's, on Fourth Street, an area which has an eclectic mix of artists, musicians, storeowners, a vibrant gay population a number of blocks away and its fair share of decadence and poverty distributed between some of the more tranquil, tidy, historic residences like the one in which Gem resides. I made the trip into Philly repeatedly that summer, and there were a few times when Gem rolled up my way in her prized possession, her dearly departed uncle's 1969 Camaro SS.

I always enjoyed the pleasure of rolling the silver colored bullet through the curves of River Road, streaking past the rippling currents of the Delaware River on one side, and the beautiful old manor homes, foliage and farms on the other, until we reached New Hope Borough; a great place for free spirits and oddities to hang out, so we fit right in, taking many walks across the New Hope-Lambertville Bridge, stopping mid-span to enjoy the ducks paddling and many types of fish coursing through the silt laden river below, share smokes and talk forever of our hopes and dreams.

We also spent our time by the riverbed, sitting along its rocky banks, staring into each-others' eyes; 'talking' for hours but never really making a sound as Gem happily wrapped her arms around my waist and nuzzled her head into the nape of my neck.

The thoughts of summer have to cease quickly, since approaching the city entails getting this black streak tamed because the cops (or as we refer to them, per 'JAWS' reference, Brody's) are very unforgiving, so I slowly weave my way through the accumulating traffic, bouncing at the last, possible moment to conquer the left lane exit onto Delaware Avenue.

The corner of South Front and South Street resembles the aftermath of a Mardi Gras celebration where trash bags, loose paper, bottles and cans roll aimlessly around the street after a heavy night of punk revelry and after grinning at the remnants of last night's orgy, I barrel up to Walnut Street and haul ass to Gem's flat on Fourth Street. Siouxsie and the Banshees remake of the Beatles, 'Dear Prudence' is blaring away on the stereo and I love this even more than their version because this is OUR song right now.

The front door of the well-kept, Colonial era, brick row home opens rapidly and Gem races down the cement steps to greet me with the sunniest smile. Donning another black leather jacket she discovered at a local thrift store, I helped put my artistic flair to this one as well with the Sex Pistols, "No Future" slogan painted across the back. I also added an Exploited, skull and mohawk on the one arm recently, which she shows off proudly on this bright, blue sky morning.

The signature, spray painted, ripped jean look is completed by a pair of 'bullet holed'…yes, I really did pump some real lead into them…enough said…Converse Chucks, adorned with red, black and blue splatters flicked across them. Her hair is pulled back again today, revealing the white stripe, but instead of a long ponytail, it's rolled in a bun with stiff spikes wildly sticking out and with no make-up on, she reveals the glamorous, light olive splendor of her skin tone.

"Good morning, love," she purrs and I immediately melt, making me want to hold her even more. We lean in for a kiss, so morning onlookers be damned because I've waited for this too long to let her out of my grasp.

"Do you want to take a walk around before we head upstairs?" I inquire, offering her a Red until she reminds me that she still has plenty of those sixty cent Newps to burn through. The Zippo's stainless body gleams in the morning sun as does the flame between our cigarettes. "So…you ready to venture, girl?"

"More than you'll ever know, baby boy." Taking hold of her hand, we're South Street bound to survey the glamorous carnage on a more up close and personal level. "The punks were out in force last night. It looked like Halloween came a few days early but I have to admit, it's becoming too filled with nodded out, junkie tourists and poser punks anymore and it pisses me off because it adds fuel to the yuppies fire on Front Street when they snottily refer to this part of Society Hill as Society's Ills.

"They want us out so they can blow up the cost of living down here and it doesn't help our cause when these interloping assholes are blazing their crackpipes and lacing their rigs in the alley by J.C Dobbs after the Brody's walked through. Are you fucking kidding me? We used to keep that shit past Seventh street where Brody's don't even dare to venture, especially once sundown arrives.

"Hell, last year they tried to drug raid Love Hall by Broad and South before it was condemned and got pelted with beer bottles full of piss and rasta punks were chanting for the release of Delbert Africa. It was pretty intense and they hate dealing with the tenements, squats and gangs for just that reason. The tribes like ours self-police those neighborhoods and keep the lawlessness contained and basically controlled.

"All the 'burb junkies are doing is quenching the yuppie scum manifesto of gentrifying our Bohemian enclave and making it lose the flair of originality we punks fought so hard to achieve. It's going to be a fuckin' police state soon...just like what the U.K. Subs sang about.

"Zipperhead and SKULLZ were way too crowded with the gawker set, so I bounced to Philly Record Exchange on Fifth to get a Flipper album and Social D and X-Ray Spex cassette. Then I busked on Fourth, took my loot across to Jim's for a cheesesteak and a Frank's, Black Cherry Wishniak."

"I'm almost jealous that you busked without me but bitchin' that you made some coin! Besides, I love Wishniak! Now, Whiz wid' or Whiz widdout?"

"Damn straight, Whiz wid'. A true Philly girl NEVER orders a cheesesteak without Cheez Whiz or onions. You former New Yorkers just don't get Philly etiquette. You don't even know what to call an Italian sub. It's a hoagie, not a friggin' hero. What the hell is that all about? A hero..."

This is how it usually goes between Gem and I, playful jousting and debating, which makes us laugh nonstop. At first glance, our friends assumed we disliked each other immensely but soon learned what we understood about ourselves straightaway. We fed off each-others playful sarcasm, relishing in its splendor especially when we could turn it on some yuppie prick or an asshole Nazi skinhead in the clubs we frequented or busked outside of.

Happily moving along, we playfully kick through the cans and bottles on the sidewalks around Second and South. "I'm thinking about a Penn's Landing stop…whaddya' think, Swan?"

"Why of course, Robbs. I can't think of a better place to chill right now."

Taking in the sights of this part of Philly is readily enjoyable with the mixture of apartments atop the storefronts and the murals depicting the shops or South Street life in general wrapped colorfully around their facades. Many of the buildings still retain their city charm with ornate cornices dressing the peaks, while cobblestoned roadways remain intact through most of this part of town. The steady breezes along South Front make the abundantly yellow tinged treetops sway to and fro like an uncontrollable mosh pit as we take the pedestrian bridge over the growing traffic on the Interstate and we howl spasmodically, wildly sprinting down the steps past some baffled, morning joggers readying to cross Delaware Avenue. "I bet they weren't expecting the likes of us to pull that one off, ay' Robbs?"

"It's not every day that a bunch of joggers get outrun by some fucknut, howling punk kids with smokes hanging from their mouths," I blurt out, grabbing the railing to steady myself before admiring the new tagging on the concrete walls separating us from the largesse of the river below.

CRACK WHORES TAKE PIPE IN THE ASS, is scrawled with artistic, colorful flair on one section, while further down, the massive, MISFITS RULE SOUTH STREET remains unscathed, as does SWAN IS THE PUNK GODDESS OF SOUTH STREET, which makes Gem blush. "Oh, the Wild Girls were so ridiculous doing that but I still love 'em!"

WHERE'S STREET CORNER SANDI? receives a loving rub, pat and nod of loving acknowledgement from Gem, but one which does raise her ire and receives a heavy heaping of spit from us both is the fading, x-ed out, TITUS AND THE SKINS RULE THIS TOWN, OI! "That drug dealing, abusive, pimp motherfucker will never rule this town as long as I'm alive," she snarls, kicking the wall with her Chucks for good measure before regaining her composure, latching onto my arm and smiling beautifully while we survey the river which has its fair share of bottles and oily slicks swirling around.

The government and the DER have broached the subject of cleaning up the pollution but it's a hard sell to ram through when people are losing the factory jobs surrounding the waterway in both Philly and Camden, New Jersey and want to put the blame solely on the environmentalists for the jobs moving away. The batshit loony brand of Conservative, radio talk show hosts have done their fair share of successful brainwashing on that front.

The Delaware has massive width and depth here, compared to its cleaner, narrower, rocky appearance between Yardley and Trenton. Barges and cargo ships of all sizes dominate the waterway this morning so we start guessing what each ship may be carrying.

I suggested that anything coming from the direction of my home base was probably carrying steel from the docks of the enormous U.S. Steel, Fairless Works complex at the mouth of Falls Township and the Borough of Morrisville. Gem points towards a northbound steamer, figuring that it was sending iron ore to the steel mill.

She leans slightly over the railing and I wrap my arms around her, enjoying our every movement below the waistline. "Mmmm…I totally like the way you feel, Robbs," she purrs but upon viewing the ship dematerialize into the distance, turning to me again; her green eyes becoming a darker, more serious shade. "Promise me something."

"Promise you what, Gem?"

"Promise me that if college does not work out the way you want it to, you will not get a job at that steel plant."

"Gem…"

"Let me explain myself, love, because I truly admire what those men and women do, but you can be and do so much more, Robbs. Even your friends' dads that toil at that mill have told you as much.

"You need to sing, you need to write, you need to follow your dream. Be an activist writer for the causes of working people at a newspaper or a magazine, or you could be their champion through song, just please, give it a thought. It's a dangerous place and too many good folks are getting hurt or killed there."

"Where's all this coming from, Swan?"

"Look, I know this is not where you wanted to really go to school. I know you had thoughts of Cal or Michigan; I know you were even thinking West Point but I have to honestly admit I'm glad that fell through. I understand the honor involved but, in the end, it's still war and annihilation when it's all said and done.

"You've also had people in your family trying to push you into the Wharton School of Business because they thought you to be a Wall Street darling and that being with Giselle put the brakes on your going away and now you regret that.

"I also realize that you need a break from your mom's authoritarian ways, so just think about what you really want to do before pulling out of school. You're extremely talented and I'll certainly not be the last person who tells you this in life."

Taking a long drag from my smoke, our eyes meet again; sighing, she begins running her fingers through my hair. "I love when you look at me that way, Robbs. Your eyes look almost golden, like they're smiling all on their own."

Gently caressing her soft cheeks, I eventually burrow into the warmth of her body. "You know how I feel about that place. It's like high school, Gem, but I'm trying to cope. Yeah, I let Giselle, my mom, too many people get in my way, but my bearing's getting a little clearer now.

"Listen, I have a lot of ideas that don't involve where I'm living or even the mill, but at least I know it could be a good stopgap measure if I need to pile away some money and move on. It will at least get me on my own and pay my bills until I do what I really want.

"Don't worry, Gem. I have no intentions of going there right now. I also have no intentions of being a Wall Street shark either, although I would probably be pretty good at it. That greed goes against everything I believe in anyway."

We take a long, parting glance at the rippling tides of the Delaware, and begin walking to the flat. The sunlight catches the beauty of her deep, auburn hair, making it look even more luxurious. "Money isn't everything, love," she quips.

"I know, Swan but it does put food on the table."

"So does farming."

"You need money to buy the farm equipment."

"Ugh, Robbs. Sometimes, you can just really be a piss ant capitalist," she moans, poking at my stomach and giving me a playful push.

"Hey! I'm a very big believer in the working man and trade unions so please do not discount my numerous, Socialist leanings."

"Oh, yes, quite the Renaissance Man you are, Rob Cavelli but if you weren't with me, you'd be in a button-down shirt, Brooks Brother blazer, slacks and wing tips. You'd have that Reagan Republican short, feathered hairdo too."

Snatching a crumpled soda can from the sidewalk, I curve it with deadly accuracy in her direction. "Fuck it all, Gem! You just described Alex P. Fucking Keaton. No way in hell!"

Returning the Franks can with maddening velocity, it nearly nicks my shoulder blade, allowing her a squeaking laugh at my expense. "Yeah, you're right, no way in hell. You're a true Comrade for the cause now!" She hoists her Newp into the air and I'm inclined to do the same with my Red. "To my dear Robbs, may he never be a Wall Street barracuda."

"Never, Gem."

"PISS OFF, SOD OFF!" The few people out on South and Fourth just look at us quizzically.

"It is our motto, folks, you'll never understand it!"

I start humming a tune as Gem's perfectly angular, gorgeous face beams with delight in the sunlight of this beautiful Saturday. "Sing it our way, not Siouxsie's," she whispers in her sexy, sultry way.

"Dear Gemma
Won't you come out to play?
Dear Gemma

41

Greet the brand new day..."
She joins in with me to complete OUR verse so beautifully.

"The sun is up
The sky is blue
It's beautiful, and so are you..."

Lifting her onto the stoop of her flat, kissing for what seems like an eternity, her heart beats wildly against my chest, allowing my mind to race about how we'll spend the next few hours before Yuka and the Misfits arrive. Pulling out the key, she turns around, batting her eyes, whispering seductively...

"Dear Robbs..."

Any bad feelings of dealing with my mother, Giselle, or anyone or anything else for that matter, is rapidly diminishing from thoughts of a painful past. Darting up the flats darkened, cherry stained stairs, she leaves me to sing the last line but I whisper it in her ear instead.

"Dear Gemma
Won't you come out to play?"

... 4 ...

Transformation

THE EARLY AFTERNOON sun peeks through Gem's bedroom window, laying a beam of light across her stunning body. Her breasts press into my hard chest muscles, and I feel the warm exhale of breath on my neck as I begin to run my fingers down to the small of her back, eventually cupping my free hand around her soft, round buttocks. .

We've played our game of cat and mouse, so now we stare at each other, relaying messages back and forth without saying a word. Lou Reed's sweeping epic, 'Sweet Jane' plays softly from her stereo boombox and I mischievously smile. "What are you thinking about, Robbs?"

"Already fast forwarding to when we come back here tonight, Gem. Damn, I just love being with you."

She flicks her long, sharp, black polished nails against my chest and giggles. "I figured I wore you out already but if not, you'll be begging for mercy tonight, love." Nibbling on her ear makes Gem giggle and squeak even more as I feel her long, shapely legs sliding back and forth under the weight of me. "Are you sure about that, Gemma Anastasia Stinson? You care to make a wager on that, Swan?"

"I'm not afraid of you, Rob Cavelli," she shrieks playfully, getting tangled up in the bedsheets and blankets, before finally escaping my clutches, only to lose her balance and slide off the mattress, landing with a thud onto the flats' hardwood floors. "Robbs, stop it, you goofball. Fred and Beth are going to think we're tearing the apartment up."

"That's not what you're worried about. You're worried they'll know what we're doing, so you'll blush with embarrassment next time you see them. The tough as nails, punk rock street girl named Swan is really just a timid dove after all," I chidingly reply. Standing in front of me with her hands on her hips, bare-skinned and beautiful, Gem flips me the bird. "Piss off, Robbs. I like Fred and Beth. They're sweet and don't judge me, so yes, I go out of my way to be respectful when they're home."

"I like Fred and Beth too, Gem. You know why they're a happy, older couple, because they were a happy, sexually driven younger couple at one time."

That remark earns me the dubious honor of a pair of painted Chucks sailed past my head and crashing into the knick-knacks and frames on her weathered, oak dresser. "You are a dipshitted dog right now, so I'm taking a shower before Yuka and Otto come over with Lena." She grabs a towel draped over an old, scuffed up, oak desk chair and prances away. "Don't you dare come in with me, we'll never be ready…and stop checking out my chassis." The temptress glances over her shoulder, batting her long lashes while her elegant cheekbones glow prominently in the rooms' streaking sunlight.

"Stop shaking it like that when you walk away from me, besides, you love the attention anyway, Swan."

"No coming in here, Robbs. I'm serious." The door latch clacks loudly, the water whistles through the showerhead but little does she know, Misty recently gave me spare keys for every door, so with a swift turn of the lock, I've entered the haze enveloped bathroom. Slinking quietly across the damp, yellow and black checkered, porcelain tiled floor, I reach for the sunny, yellow curtain and quietly pull on the chrome colored rings holding it.

Rinsing the soap from her face, Gem opens her eyes long enough to see me there with nothing on but my Cheshire Cat grin. "ROBBS!" Her shrieks of laughter bounce off the bright yellow and jet black tiles surrounding the tub. "We're never going to get done..." I wrap my arms around her while she melts into my frame. "Rob...We're..." The heat of our bodies rivals that of the water and we rapidly disappear into the mist.

● ● ●

Bounding up the stairs with my gear from Otis' trunk, Gem's already dressed, sitting on the couch in her splattered, ripped jeans and Chucks, as well as a snug fitting, black, Misfits t-shirt, which masterfully accentuates her fit as hell frame. The hair is back the way it was this morning, just completing her incredibly, bitchin' look.

I spill out the contents of my pack, get the nod of approval and a sexy wink prior to stripping down to nothing more than skivvies and a black t-shirt with Sid Vicious', snarling, 'fuck off' face across the front.

I compliment it with a pair of worn, torn Levi's. "So What?" is scrawled in black across the one knee, ANL is scrawled across the other, paying homage to one of my favorite bands, the Brit hardcore punks, the Anti-Nowhere League.

A pair of worn combat boots get thrown on and laced up tight and I've been in the habit lately of wrapping a bandana, bandit style, over the top of each one; one side black, the other red.

The wet, sandy brown curls are very wet, elongated to the point of touching my shoulders. It is almost 2 o'clock, and I'm ready for my transformation. "Damn, baby boy, you're going to look so outrageously good," Gem coos, already envisioning my appearance for the evening while she twirls a few curls between her talons.

Out on the street, the sounds of rowdy, hooligan laughter approaches, allowing Gem to leap excitedly from the couch and bolt to the window. "It's them! Hey guys, come right up, the door is unlocked!" Our crew of Misfits is here! Clomping up the steps in their combat boots and heels, I hear them laughing again. "Ummm...is it really all right to come in? I mean, we all know how the two of you get when you're alone for a while," Otto replies in his gruff voice and the two girls begin to giggle. "Gemma's in looovve...you better let that youngin' up for some air, Swan," Elena Lisowski (or as we lovingly refer to her, Lena) says coyly, as she, Otto and Yuka come rumbling in, past the heavy, creaky, wooden front door.

"Ayyyy, rat shit boot! Whaasssup' buddy!" Otto emits boisterously when we roughhouse for a minute.

"Hey, baby boy," shouts Lena, who still gets a kick out of saying Gem's pet name for me, since I'm a full year younger than my girl, making me the butt of 'little kid' jokes from the tribe. "Let's sing it, tribe! Filthy city of rats, filthy city of rats, if they get any bigger THEY'D FUCKIN' EAT THE CATS! What a hoot that was, Robbs. You, Gem and 'Stacks' tore it up and I loved the dedication to me! Ugh...fuckin' rats...I hate 'em. Little shits used to bite us in the squats when we were sleeping."

Yuka makes it a point to give me a big kiss, flirt incessantly and park her very toned bottom on my lap. "Mmmmm... Gemma, if I didn't care for you or Otto so much, this boy singer of yours would be mine," she purrs before nibbling my earlobe. "Anyway, let's focus on our task here." She glides her fingers through my hair. "Mmmm...baby boy, I know exactly what we are going to do to you, so there's no time to waste. Lena, get out the Kool-Aid packets that I brought and the hair conditioner from my bag, Gem, get me a bowl and a spoon to stir the mixture and Otto, my sweet?"

"Yes, my darlin'?"

"I am going to give Robbs a do' to rival your mowhawk, tonight. Yuka Yamaguchi's Liberty Spikes will be on display for all in the Tower to see."

Otto smirks, giving me the horns, in acceptance. "Brother, you're gonna' look fucking sick tonight. You want me to get your liquid cement mixture out of your backpack too, babe?"

"Absolutely, Otto, there is no time to waste," Yuka beckons, pulling a pair of latex gloves from her leather jacket. The girls are already furiously mixing the colors in bowls, with Gem stopping only long enough to blow me a kiss. "Gemma, you have to save that kissy, kissy shit for your boy until later; keep mixing and stirring, sexy Swan." When it comes to art and hair, Yuka is no joke, a veritable force to be reckoned with.

Otto brings her famous "cement" mixture over, which resembles a murky pool with the consistency of lumpy oatmeal and smells rather sweet as she now mixes the bowls contents between her fingers.

Her pretty, chestnut colored eyes meet with mine and she grins sinisterly. "Are you ready to be glorious tonight, Robbs?"

"I put all my faith and trust in you, Yuka, let's work your wonders." She quickly twirls the mixture through big sections of my damp hair, moving with amazing, catlike precision the whole time. While she darts about, I get a chance to take in her "look." The hair is in a shoulder length bob, with the bangs almost covering her eyes, and dyed a jet-black hue a la Siouxsie Sioux.

Looking absolutely Betty in a super short, hip hugging leather miniskirt almost covered by a long-sleeved black shirt, adorned with a large, red pentagram, she's complimented her Gothic style with a pair of thigh-high stiletto heeled black boots and sheer, black stockings to finish off her ensemble. The boots give her some height, considering Yuka's maybe 5'2" at best and it's honestly amazing to see how quickly she moves around in her death defying footwear.

She grabs another thick clump of curls, twisting them some more and the twirling continues with assembly line precision, as the smile on Yuka's face growing bigger after each one.

"Holy shit, Yuka that looks fucking kick ass!"

"Thanks, Otto but wait 'til you see the finished process, hon'."

Lena and Gem also add their shrieks of approval. "Wait until you see what you look like, baby boy, you're gonna' love this." I try to touch the spikes, but Yuka grabs my hand. "Oh no, honey, hands off the artwork, we have much more to do."

"I'll not make that mistake again, my artiste. Carry on, please." Hands firmly placed on my lap, she kisses me on the cheek, getting right back to her masterpiece in the making.

Gem says Yuka has been driven like this since she was a little girl. Though Gem bounced from place to place in Philadelphia and eventually into the streets for quite some time; then back to her abusive mother and father, and apparently an equally abusive, big time, drug dealer boyfriend not that long ago, Yuka and her parents managed to stay involved in her life, one way or another.

When she ran away for the last, harrowing time, the Yamaguchi's eventually took Gem in and kept tabs on her. Although many of their Japanese neighbors couldn't understand his interest in this gaijin, Masamoto Yamaguchi, child of the World War II internment camps, understood what it was like to be the misfit and he saw the potential and strength Gem displayed, if it was aided along by the right people. It was at this tipping point, Mister Yamaguchi decided to be that person.

It wasn't too long after settling into the healthy and loving routine of the Yamaguchi's life, that Gem found out her mom, Gabriella, or Gaby as she was infamously known on Kensington and Allegheny's 'Mean Streets', had overdosed in the basement of her filthy and disheveled row home, and her dad was found gruesomely stabbed and beaten to death in an abandoned lot not far from K&A's 'El'; the apparent victim of a hit put out on him.

For all of his anger and hate, Allan Stinson, a mean, paid enforcer of the street mobs eventually ran into someone who cared less about life than he did. I remember Yuka saying that Gem didn't even shed a tear when she was told of their demise, but instead quietly thanked the Yamaguchi family for making her aware that they'd passed on and summarily retreated into the quiet comfort of her bedroom.

Yuka's dad found her a job at a friends' restaurant, the South Street Diner and Gem vowed to keep up with her studies while she gladly earned her keep. Gem's life involved some massive turmoil and pain, but through it all, she excelled in school. When Yuka decided on which college she'd like to attend, the Yamaguchi's made sure the university understood it was a two-for-one deal and Gem's stellar grades despite her dismal life experiences sealed the deal with her garnering a full scholarship. The bond between the two girls was so tight, they thought nothing of referring to each other as sisters.

Since she now worked at 'SKULLZ' besides waiting tables at the Diner, Gem recently decided to move out on her own, feeling that the Yamaguchi's had done more than their share to take care of her.

There was worry of her doing this, mainly because there was a history of some hard drug and alcohol usage for a few years before the Yamaguchi's became involved in her life. Gem had gotten mixed in with a wild group, a vicious street dealer boyfriend and her extended family had been abusive to her in various, apparently sickening ways. It was a subject Gem had only broached with me recently, but even then she was apprehensive to tell me everything. "I know your temper and how protective you are of me, Robbs. I'm only doing this so you do not get yourself into trouble with any family members that are still alive or the drug dealing scum who took me in. I can't afford any more losses in my life." Reluctantly, I capitulated to her wishes.

As far as the drug usage, she was only smoking pot occasionally, swearing off the hard drugs so she could live life to its fullest, nevertheless, we all kept an eye out for any signs that her bad habits may return.

With the smells of Yuka's concoction wafting through the flat, Otto lights me up another Red before taking the bowls of mix from the girls. Everyone's ogling me with the excitement of perusing a new balloon in the Macy's Thanksgiving Day Parade and Lena can't help herself from twirling around happily or pinching my cheeks. "Oh cutie, this is going to be insane. You look so fuckin' wild!"

Yuka hands Gem the first brush of color, a strawberry red. "Would you like to do the honors, sis?" Gem nods, while quickly running the brush through the hardened spike or cone as some refer to this hairstyle. "Keep moving, Gem, we have to wrap it soon. Hurry everybody, grab a bowl, follow my lead and pick a spike to color, we have to get bookin'."

The crew takes on the task of this human art project vigorously and within minutes, they're done, taking a few steps back to admire their brilliant handiwork. Otto could not contain himself. "Sod off, Robbs, this is fucking brilliant!"

Lena sways her very fit posterior to and fro before she decides to shimmy onto my lap. If there's anything the Misfit girls absolutely love to do is flirt and cavort until I blush. "My cutie looks unbelievable!"

Gem kneels next to me, leaning in for a kiss. "I was right, you look so fucking good."

"Thanks babe, you look drop dead beautiful tonight," I respond to my doe-eyed, flirting, punk vixen but Yuka breaks up the love fest hastily. "Hey, we are NOT done yet, lovebirds! Sis and Lena, get the saran wrap. Otto, please retrieve my backpack, love, and get my little cigarette case because my finishing touches reside within."

The girls begin to wrap my hair while Otto brings back the case, grinning as he opens it. "Ha, ha…the finishing touches… fuckin' bril', Yuka babe! Rob, this is going to be epic, brother…"

Yuka hands me my trophies, little laminated cocktail flags of different nations on toothpicks. She picks up more hair cement while I hand her each flag, twisting them tightly into the tips of each spike, which are now wrapped to hold in the cement and the color. I'll have to stay this way for three more hours until the colors take hold and by then, Yuka will rinse each spike gently. It will not remove the cement (that will take a massive drowning of my hair tomorrow), but it will get the excess coloring out of my hair, making it look much more uniform.

Gem lights up a Red for me, gives Lena a playful bump to the floor and now has my lap to herself. "Sorry, my sexy Lena, but this boy's body is all mine tonight," she purrs while slowly straddling my legs, ending with her own enthralling bump and grind onto me.

Yuka laughs haughtily and places a barber shop mirror in Gem's hands. "Okay, okay, now that we've established who

OWNS honey bear's junk tonight, why don't you show your adorable guy what he looks like, Swan."

With the glass side still facing her, Gem shoots off a sneering, whiplash grin. "Are you ready, hon?" I nod yes as she turns the mirror to reveal a Yuka Yamaguchi Liberty Spike masterpiece. Twelve spikes, of perfect length and color now adorn my skull with the accompanying flags of nations on the tips making for the incredible, 'finishing touch'.

Yuka, mock stomping her boot heel, eagerly waits for a reply. "Well, what do you think?" I laugh, give her a kiss on the cheek and take another drag of the Red. "I think that in a few hours when this is a totally finished product, I could walk right over top of my mom or Giselle and neither would even know that it was me. Fucking brilliant, Yuka, this is your best yet for me! You're an incredible artist of the canvas, hairstyling and your 'do' will be the talk of the Tower, thank you so much."

"You're welcome, Robbs. I loved doing it. You and my sweetie, Otto, always have so much trust in me."

Otto runs into the dollhouse sized, tidy kitchen and raids the fridge. "Beer and smoke break outside," he bellows in triumphant jubilation. He pockets the bottle opener, adeptly snatching five bottles of "Irish Gold" as we all spill down the steps and onto the stoop.

Gem's neighbors, Fred and Beth come outside as well to see what all the commotion is about and Fred can only shake his head. "Holy crap Beth, lookie what they did to poor Robert's head! He looks like a Technicolor porcupine in a plastic wrap trap."

Yuka smirks, putting on her best pout. "You really don't like my artwork, Fred?"

Beth pokes at Fred's arm. "Ignore him, sweetie, I like Robert's porcupine look."

"Yuka, of course I like it," Fred chuckles. "I just had to have some fun at poor Robert's expense. Listen kids, this is your time to shine, enjoy it while you can because before you know it, you will be growing up with tons of responsibilities to take care of.

"I was your age once, believe or not. When I was courting my beautiful Beth, I was a jazz loving, sharp dressed Zoot Suiter."

Otto nearly chokes on the smoke from his cig. "Mister Fred, a flippin' Zoot Suiter, who would've thought?"

"Whoa boy, did her dad dislike my look, Otto, but he respected all of the other qualities that I displayed. He knew I would settle down my appearance when I got older, and he knew I always had his daughters' best interests at heart."

Beth tosses the long, pale blonde hair away from her glowing, glamorous face and grabs Fred's arm. "And he still has those best interests to this day," she says lovingly.

"Mister Fred and Miss Beth, would you care for some liquid refreshment on this killer, sunny, October afternoon?"

Beth says no thanks, but Fred's eyes widen like a teenagers' at the proposition. Tall and slender with a full head of naturally colored brown hair, it's hard to believe Fred is an elder statesman and Beth is an absolute vision of timeless beauty. "Otto, this is a splendid idea." With Otto rumbling upstairs for another beer, Fred takes the time to breathe in deeply and smile since he always enjoys our company. "So, my young friends, what are the plans for today? We're not planning on parading Rob around in plastic wrap all afternoon, are we?" Laughing at the prospect of such a spectacle, I inform Fred we'll be catching a New Wave concert at the Tower tonight. "New Wave, I thought you were all into that punk rock. Hmmm…diversity in music is a good thing."

"Wow, this is so great that you know the difference between the two, Mister Fred."

"I've always been a lover of music, Robert. I know that you and our eclectic, young Gemma are as well. If I remember correctly, just this summer I heard you playing Mussorgsky's, 'Pictures at an Exhibition'…a wonderful masterpiece, if I do say so, myself."

"I apologize to you and Miss Beth if we were playing it too loudly."

Otto hands Fred the chilled brew, returning to the stoop to repose with Yuka. "Thank you, Otto," he replies happily before drawing his attention towards Gem and me. "Nonsense, young Robert, there is no such thing as playing a work of art such as that too loudly. You need volume to immerse yourself in it, just like you do with your modern music, now if you'll excuse me for just a second…"

Seemingly distracted by some other goings-on, Fred glances towards the street level, quietly spying some well-dressed, middle aged couples glaring at us disapprovingly. They especially seem transfixed to my plastic wrapped hair, but I pay them no mind, as I take another swig of Guinness. We're normally nonchalant to stares and indifferent attitudes but it certainly seems to have rankled Fred.

"Hey, what the hell's the matter with you people looking like that at my grandkids'? This is their time, and if you don't like it, don't come down this block," Fred shouts while shaking his fist.

"How dare you judge these fine, young people just because of their appearance? You should all be ashamed of yourselves!" I've never heard Beth raise her voice above a whisper before, but she unloads her vitriol towards these folks pretty loudly. Turning away, the couples shake their heads, muttering to each other and scuffing along the cobblestone sidewalks until disappearing around the corner.

The Misfits break into raucous laughter, delivering whistles and thunderous applause to our saviors of Fourth Street. Lena gives them a hug, only to be followed by Yuka and Gem. "Mister Fred, do you really think of us as your grandchildren?"

"Yes we do, Gem. Beth and I lost our William as a baby and were never able to have any more after him. When Misty informed us she'd be having a young lady living with her, and that she'd have friends here, we were elated. You kids have been a breath of fresh air on this otherwise vanilla block."

Otto pops the cap off another Guinness before doing the same for me. "Well, let's enjoy the time before the show, Otto, but first a toast. To Fred and Beth, the best damned grandparents we Misfits could ever have," and as Fred drapes an arm around Beth, he astutely smirks. "I'll drink to that, kids."

··· 5 ···

The Tower

OUR DRINKING AFTERNOON with Fred and Beth has come to a terrific culmination, so it's back into the apartment for the official unveiling, where the saran wrap is finally peeled from the new 'do, which is sprayed and cleaned for the whole world to see. More than likely, most of the older people will be repulsed by the looks of us walking down the streets. Their generation and even the sixties, hippie folks who are now turning into the yuppies we absolutely abhor, do not understand us at all. Oh well, screw them because I want to immerse myself in some well-needed time with my friends tonight.

Everybody is all geared up and looking great, starting with Otto, who is sporting a worn leather jacket with "Misfits" spray painted in white across the back, torn jeans and engineer boots.

Lena is her darling, street tough self, with her beloved, studded rings on every finger, pink lemonade spikes topping her head, with the sides shaved tightly to her scalp. A Dead Kennedy's t-shirt, which is cut fairly low, reveals her ample breasts and thigh high boots and an equally short red leather miniskirt slit up the side looks just killer, and to complete her ensemble, she puts on her leather, adorned with a splatter painted, red anarchy symbol, courtesy of yours truly.

The spray painting of jackets, and splatter painting of other clothing has turned into a lucrative, sideline biz for us Misfits. The alley by Misty's house has become a great, makeshift, open air workshop, especially for Gem and me.

Tossing on my latest beat up, airbrushed leather artwork, it slightly resembles Gem's with an Exploited skull and Mohawk on the arm, but I have ANL scrawled in yellow paint on the opposite one; on the back, I took countless hours to ornament it with the Black Flag, 'My War' album cover, complete with Ronnie Reagan hand puppet and dagger.

Yuka, Otto and Lena rumble aimlessly down the stairway, already engaged in their usual, animated conversation about how the night should go and as I wait for Gem to lock the door, she grabs my arm, nuzzling into me when we depart. "You know that I'm madly in love with you, right Robbs?"

"I sure do Gem, and I think you know that I adore everything about you," I happily reply as she holds me close to her. "Don't ever break my heart, Robbs."

"Don't ever break mine either, Gem." I draw her in for another long kiss. "Love you, babe." Smiling, she opens the door to raucous applause. "Shit, we thought you were heading back upstairs for more fun," Otto barks.

"Plenty of time for that later, buddy," I reply mischievously. "You're so fresh!" she exclaims, pinching my side with her talons for good measure.

Our three partners in crime point to Gem's, Motown perfection, 69' Camaro and then towards my Motown rejection, shitbox Otis. "Cordoba or Camaro, folks…c'mon, let's bring it to a vote," Otto commands.

Tapping Otis' hood, Gem cracks a mischievously, sly grin. "Well, as always, I was in shock and awe that Otis even made it to Philadelphia intact, so why don't we put him in the drunk tank for a nap?" I feign a look of painful dismay, Gem of course gets a good laugh at Otis' expense. "Fine, fine, we'll take the

Camaro but know this, I'm appalled at the mistreatment Otis gets from this tribe. You know, this car's gotten us out of quite a few close calls before."

"Oh, you mean like the time at City Garden's when all hell broke loose in the parking lot and we told the cops not to arrest us because we couldn't disperse immediately when it took YOUR car ten minutes to warm up?"

"Well, all right Otto, there was that time."

"What about the time I put on the air conditioner and the car's power cut off in the left lane while we're going fifty on Route 13 in rush hour traffic?"

"Well, ok Lena, so there were a dozen or so volatile commuters swerving not to hit us, but we came out of it unscathed, right?" I look at Otis and his gleaming, black hood. Soothingly patting his vinyl roof, I offer my final exhortation. "It's ok, Otis, because I will always know your true value. Well, pile into the Bullet, wise ass Misfits."

"Ok! Let's get a move on," Otto blurts out, as he Yuka and Lena book into the street, anxiously waiting to hop in. I walk around to open up the driver side door for Gem, but she hands me the spare keys instead. "I told you earlier, baby, I am your date tonight." The purr of her sultry voice is just driving me wild and after I walk her around to unlock the passenger side, our three, ruffian partners-in-crime collapse into the back as I give Gem a kiss, quickly holding up the evening traffic in the process. "Come on, love, I don't want to lose a door or my butt out here."

She slides in and motorists gawk at my do', giving equal stares to my passengers who all make funny faces at their captive audience. We've discovered this maneuver disarms tense situations rather well, but if people really push our buttons, we're ready to throw fists and fight 'til the death if need be because the punk code runs deep in our Misfit ranks, whether we're, as Yuka puts it, 'tribal' like tonight or more bare bones, as we normally look.

Gem understands how much I really appreciate the honor of driving this ride since it's basically one of few possessions she has to elicit pleasant family memories for her. It was her Uncle Ronnie's car, and it was bequeathed to her when the cancer from

Agent Orange being dropped on him in the dense jungles of Vietnam became a horrific death sentence for the poor man a few years ago.

Ronnie was the only person she had any attachment to and Gem valiantly tried to care for him until he passed away, prompting another tough blow in a long line of disappointments thrown her way by an extremely dysfunctional family, but it made running away from her home life easier after he'd passed on.

I turn the key, and Ronnie's 396 SS thunders to life. Gem's so meticulous in the upkeep of it, much like her Uncle was... always washed, vacuumed, a full tank of gas and besides that, Ronnie taught her how to do oil changes when she was little, so Gem does them religiously. It's another trait of hers I find endearing. We can talk shop about cars and cycles all day long.

A new model Datsun waits to jump into our grave, so I drop the floor shifter and slowly rumble away from the curb. Gem puts her hand over mine, giving it a gentle squeeze.

The traffic isn't really heavy yet, so we haul ass through more historical neighborhoods, followed by some not so hospitable ones, ultimately hanging a hard, tire smoking left onto Walnut Street, where before long we'll arrive at The Tower's famous doors. Gem's been playing Suicidal Tendencies and when 'Institutionalized' comes on with Mike Muir scorching the refrain with machine gun rapidity, the wild, singing Misfits join in.

"I'm not crazy–in an institution
You're the one that's crazy–in an institution
You're driving me crazy–in an institution
They stuck me in an institution
Said it was the only solution
To give me the needed professional help
To protect me from the enemy–myself..."

The rumble of the Chevy perfectly blends with Cyco Miko's psychotic vocals and we're having a bitchin', killer time reworking the lyrics...

Otto: "And I didn't even hear Gem
And then she's screaming, ROBBS, ROBBS!"
Me: "And I go: what's the matter with you?"
Lena: "I go: There's nothing wrong, Gem"
Yuka and Gem: "And she goes: Don't tell me that,
You're on drugs!"
All of us: "All I wanted was a Pepsi, just one Pepsi,
And she wouldn't give it to me
Just a Pepsi!"

"We're here!" Lena screams pointing towards The Tower's ornate, red illuminated marquee with the gigantic, lighted, art deco radio tower adorning the structures roof. Even though The Cure is not what one would consider punk, they are consummate musicians with a punk pedigree and we do enjoy a little segue.

I find a spot and the SS's growl and thump have attracted the attention of our other hellacious looking Misfits hanging by the wall. "It's Dusty and Steph," Lena blurts giddily from the back-seat. I jump out of the car, quickly opening the door for my punk princess. "A gentleman, no matter how you look, Robbs...I like that." She grabs my chin, pulling me in close for a long-awaited kiss. Our tongues intertwine and the intense heat of passion rises. "Mmmmm...I like that too, baby boy. C'mon love, let's catch up with Dust, Steph and the tribe."

"YO, MY MISFIT BROTHER!" Dustin Bollinger yells (or as we'll forever refer to him, 'Dusty') and bear hugs me... his trademark Camel hanging from his mouth. His Mohawk is cemented up high and colored blue tonight. "Look at this motherfucker with Yuka's Liberty spikes, and what in the bloody fuck, flags on the tips? That is motherfuckin' brill, and now you get to book around in the SS? Boy, I know Gem's got a thing for you, when you're driving her ride, kid. I've never seen anyone else in that seat but her!"

"That's what I hear, Dust, apparently the die has been cast." Gem slides over, resting her head on my shoulder. "Yep, there is no getting away from me now, Robbs. Yo, Dusty!" She hugs him and pecks his cheek. "Goddamn, Gem, you still know how to get to me, you truly are THE Punk Goddess of Philly," he laughs boisterously, wrests her into his thick, tattoo covered arms, elevates her feet from the cracked, cigarette-butt filled sidewalk and swings her around like a rag doll.

Gem squeaks and pulls away laughing, "Jesus, Dust, you're strong as an ox."

"Still dumb as one too, my beautiful, tribal queen, Gem," a chuckling voice exhorts from behind us. It's Dust's girl, Stephanie Magnuson, or Steph, who hugs Gem for a long time before giving me a playful push and a peck on the cheek. She has a powder blue Mohawk and large numbers of bad-ass tattoos that are rivaled only by Dusty's.

"Yo, Steph, it's always good to see you, girl. So, it looks like a full house tonight…what's the plans for after the show, Dust?"

"Well Rob, we're thinking about bookin' over to Fairmount Park. There's gonna' be a good amount of the tribes around tonight, so they're all going there for some brew and roll some fatty's afterwards. Swan knows the spot well."

"I know that I'm up for anything, so let's do this, Dusty," I reply, handing him a fresh twenty to cover anything we may consume tonight.

"Damn bro' a fresh Jackson is way more than enough to cover us, thanks Rob."

The Misfits stridently march into The Tower, moving hastily to the upper level. An eclectic, colorful show of street and tribal punks, plus the more glam, mall loving, money spending New Wavers make up the majority of the crowd around us, the complete diametric of the rough and tumble club atmosphere in places like Trenton's, City Gardens, where you can get your ass stomped at any moment and usually at the hands of your friends just having a good, hell-raising time. Outside of what looks like a small pit area by the stage, the venue reminds me of where I used to see symphonies at Brooklyn College or Philly's Academy of Music, so it seems like this will be a nice, chill evening for a change.

It's become much easier to enjoy times like this due to Gem's free spiritedness. With Giselle, everything had become a disturbance or an argument with her spazzing out like a pure asswipe over something trivial. I honestly felt relieved when we broke up, like the weight of the world had been lifted from my shoulders.

Upon taking my seat, a number of concertgoers stop by to discuss the merits of my "bitchin' spikes," as one New Wave kid so deftly puts it and I enthusiastically point towards Yuka, who's more than willing to converse about how she achieved my 'look' and I think she gets a few phone numbers from people seeking to have her work some magic on them.

Of course, they'll be paying and as well they should, since Yuka puts a lot of time, talent and effort into her work, whether it's on canvas, clothing or hair.

Settling into our comfortable seats, Gem nuzzles into the nape of my neck, making the night special in an instant. "Thanks for doing this, Robbs. I know The Cure isn't high on your list of bands to see right now, but the girls needed a chill night for once. We've been going full steam ahead in the pits at punk shows lately and you and I made a good take from busking and the small gigs recently, so we may as well enjoy the fruits of our labor."

"No, this works for tonight, Gem...a good change for all of us. The Cure's a very talented group, besides we'll be full steam ahead again next week," I smirk, laughing aloud.

Otto looks over and shrugs. "Whatcha' laughing about, bud?"

"I'm laughing about no dipshits trying to break our heads, spit beer at us or throw bottles everywhere for one night, Otto. No barfed-up shitters, no spent hypos to hop over in alleyways or rats crapping on our boots tonight, bro."

"Don't worry, Robbs. That'll take place at City Gardens, with Motorhead on Halloween night because it'll truly be sick as fuck!"

"Getting a head rush just thinking about it, Otto."

I light a Red, thrusting it into the air and the Misfits quickly follow suit, until the ushers bellow shrilly for us to extinguish them. "A toast...to tonight and the many adventures that'll follow."

"PISS OFF, SOD OFF," comes the boisterous reply, only to be followed by wails of "Oi, oi, oi," from a number of 'Roosterheads' sitting alongside Dust and Steph. Exhausting the remainder of our cigs, billowing smoke cascades lazily towards the high ceilings of the Tower precisely when the lights flicker and finally dim. Gem grabs me enduringly, preparing herself to be entertained and mesmerized by The Cure for the next few hours.

··· 6 ···

Fairmount

HANGING OUT UNDER the bright lights of the Tower's marquee, the tribe's engaged in quite a candid conversation about what an absolutely astounding, brilliant show we've witnessed. Everyone agrees that Robert Smith, lead singer and ex-Siouxsie and the Banshees guitarist was at his theatrical finest. Gem and I couldn't stop admiring the dynamism and passion he puts into a show, especially since the band banged out easily over twenty-five songs, including encores. 'Let's Go to Bed' had all of our dead-sexy girls up and moving their bodies in every direction, so neither Otto, Dust nor I could even attempt to conceal our shit eating grins, taking in such a pleasurable spectacle for the young, male senses.

Amped up to no end about the show and the ensuing festivities in Fairmount, we bolt to the SS, leaving a trail of smoke and burnt rubber down Market Street once we've escaped the concert traffic. Gem's hand finds its way over mine again, while the other starts moving playfully up and down my thigh. "I love feeling your strong leg muscles," she whispers loudly over the stereo as our favorite Philly college station, WXPN plays Killing Joke's, 'Love like Blood'. I glance into the rearview, catching Yuka in a full lip lock with Otto, while Lena gently nibbles on his neck. It's nothing for the three of them to share time with each other, even though Otto and Yuka are the mainstays of the relationship.

Lena enjoys playing around but is definitely more into pursuing girls than guys at the mo'; although she readily admits to Gem and Yuka that she'd easily crush with me or Otto, if given the chance.

Putting that aside, even with his wild appearance, Otto has no trouble getting females to look his way. His pleasant demeanor and boyish face have made many a girl, punk or not, want to be with him.

I regain my focus, mash the gas pedal, hastily racing the SS down towards North 52nd and Lancaster. This big 396, V-8 has a lot of play left and I'm more than willing to have some fun with it this evening, especially when The Specials, 'Ghost Town' floods the airwaves.

The apartments atop the red awning shops along 'The Strip' have started to see better days and you'd better have your wits about you because this is not the place to be if you lack streetwise presence. Most of the shitheel, douche bag burb' twats I live around would crap their pants if they drove through here late at night. Get stopped at any corner, it's best to give a nod to the locals, followed by a thousand-foot stare dead ahead.

Within another few blocks, the slow roll begins into Fairmount Park, which I'd heard in its heyday, could easily bear comparison with Central Park as a beautiful, safe experience for the denizens of Philadelphia to behold, but the budget cutting, austerity filled 1980's made it neither good, nor safe times for much of the city and with tensions still high from the MOVE bombing, Philly at times teetered on the brink of bankruptcy, with an all-out race riot occurring to boot.

Nevertheless, the avarice and stupidity created by the older generations will not deter us from a night of revelry with our punk tribes, since most everyone leaves us to our own devices anyway. The only people you really had to watch out for were the drug dealers or the occasional group of skinhead assholes who were looking to throw fists. Dusty, Otto and I had rolled a few of those fascist scumbags at a show in Philly this past summer, so we're constantly on the lookout for retaliation from their unfortunately growing ranks.

I peer into the rearview again and grin, given that Otto basically has both girls in some orgasmic state of passion. Gem turns to view what's caught my attention but instead gasps, mouthing 'holy shit', before shaking our heads and laughing lightly. "Where you see the fire burning, Robbs, that'll be the place." The Avengers remake of the Stones, 'Paint it Black', was now blaring through the speakers as I bring this awesome piece of machinery to a stop far away from where four metal trash cans full of leaves and branches were keeping everyone warm on this chilly, October evening.

"Should we leave the three of them alone, Gem?"

"Hell no...they're not doing that crap in my car, let them grab a blanket from the back and mess around in the park. Yo' lovebirds, we're here! Let's party!"

Our three horny compatriots regain a semblance of composure, eventually finding their way out of the car, wearing the sheepish look of teens caught by their parents jerking off or boinking in their bedroom. A grinning Gem opens the trunk, tossing them a couple of big blankets. "Just in case the three of you get the urge to do that again, I wouldn't want you dying from exposure to the elements."

Orangey yellow embers race towards the clear, evening sky and we soon locate Dusty, Steph and some other tribes stomping to the sounds of D.O.A's, 'Fucked Up Ronnie' coming from a battered, black, 1960's style, Cadillac Coupe De Ville, parked by the raging fires. "Yo' kids, glad you made it, booze up tribe, your case of Bud and bottle of Jack is over there by the trees and we are rolling you up some fine fatty's as we speak. It's time to get wasted, motherfuckers!"

I grab a beer for Gem, before Otto snarfs the Jack and some brews for our tribe who wind their way through the crowd of punks. It's a great group to be around since most of us know each other from shows on the weekends, and whoever we don't know, we're eventually introduced to.

Dusty hands me a joint which I quickly slip to Gem and the girls. "Not partaking tonight, Robbs?"

"Nah, not tonight Dust, I better make sure I stay clear headed so I get our tribe home in one piece." He takes a hit and exhales. "I have to tell you man, I'm glad Gem and all of them are with you, cuz' you're mature beyond your years, brother. You know how to cut loose and kick some ass, but you got an eye on all of them too. Anyone gets too freaked, you're always there to chill em' out."

I take a quick swig from my bottle and drag on my Red. "Losing your pop at eleven months old to some dickweed drunk packing heat will do that to you, Dust."

"Yeah, Gem told me and Steph about that…sucks man. Well, you got family here, kid. We have a few jerk offs from time to time, but yo', most everybody is chill."

The night moves along flawlessly, we break off, mingle and I run into one of Dusty's good friends, Oren Jones, introducing him to some of the other tribes. Oren's a black punk who lives in Montgomery County, another predominantly white suburb of Philadelphia. Sporting what he refers to as a "frohawk," standing over 6'2" and easily weighing in at 260 pounds of solid muscle, his massive arms and thick neck are covered with wild, black ink tattoos.

We see each other from time to time at our gigs and the shows in Trenton, so he's very popular with everyone in our tribe. The black punks in Philly have been welcomed into the ranks pretty well, especially with our city having a kick-ass, black group called Pure Hell.

Not surprisingly, the 'White Power' Nazi's or skins, seem to be the only dissenters to this welcoming of different races and many of us have no tolerance for their racist garbage, happily throwing fists with the scumbags on a regular basis. And with Oren's size and boxers speed, you'd have to be a pure dipshit to mess with him.

"Planning to be at City Gardens on the 31st, O?"

"Damn straight, Rob," he replies in his smooth, baritone voice. "I just have to see Motorhead because my boy Lemmy is the shit."

Dusty hands Oren a fatty and sparks it up for him. "He sure is, O'. Me and Steph are gonna' go too, so oi', you're more than welcome to tag along, brother."

"I'll ride down with you guys, Dust. That'd be great. Are Otto and the girls coming too, Rob?"

"Sure are, O and your girl Lena will be there, brother." Oren's pleasant demeanor perks up even more at the sound of Lena's name. "Damn, I like her, cuz' that Icy is one hot, brawlin', badass girl. Where is she?"

"I think she's by the fire with Gem and the girls." Trying to spot Gem, I notice her with Lena, Yuka, Steph, and some stocky looking punk with thinly spiked, blonde hair. The four girls look like they want nothing to do with the guy, especially Gemma. Steph and Lena keep pushing him from her side, but he's being obnoxiously persistent. "Hey Dust, who is the guy the girls are keeping away from Gem?"

Dusty turns around, his smile rapidly evaporating into a brawler scowl. "Goddammit."

"What's wrong, man?"

"That asshole is Gem's old supplier and boyfriend, Kellin. Fucker always thought he owned Gem like a piece of real estate. Guess he's trying to get her back on the train, if you know what I mean."

"I sure as fuck know what you mean, and that ain't happening," I reply as my blood boils and before I can make a beeline towards the girls, Otto, Dusty and Oren temporarily block my progress. "Chill out for a minute," Otto pleads. "Be careful with this asshole, he always carries a switch or short knife, ain't afraid to use it either, Robbs. Shitbag's been known to pack heat, so just be on your toes bro.

His scumbag legions must be lurking around the park, so we'll have your back if you rumble with this jerkoff, but be sensible, keep your wits about you."

Walking briskly towards the fires Gem catches my expression while I begin surveying the landscape for anyone who thinks they're going to impede my movement. Otto, Dusty and Oren trail behind at a fair distance but it's Gem sprinting towards me that catches my attention. "Robbs, it's ok, really it is. I told Kellin to bugger off. He's just being an asshole but he'll leave eventually."

"Gem, I know who he is…he's leaving now." Gem attempts obstructing any advancement but her efforts are in vain. "Robbs…please…he's not right in the head and neither are you right now. Please…please…just stop," but after throwing her a smile and a wink, my head's on a swivel already, spying to see if anyone's decided to join the party.

Gem runs off, her fading voice pleading with the boys to impede my progress but I approach the fire rapidly, keeping the cocky prick dead in my sights. The girls become increasingly agitated with his presence and when shadows approach through the dancing firelight, Lena's eyes grow wide, reaching hurriedly for Yuka's arm. "Robbs, oh no! It's ok hon, Kellin was just leaving, right Kellin?"

Turning to face me, with a smart-ass smirk across a pock-marked face, he's a stocky fucker, but his knuckles are meat grinder raw, the signs of a true scrapper. "Actually, I wanted to meet the savior of our Gemma, so…fuck na', I won't be leaving, Lena. And I think by the looks of him, he's somethin' to get off his chest." Ashen grey, sunken eyes deliver a twisted, demonic appearance but two can play that game.

Bringing my breath down a notch, my heart rate lowers by the second. It's a trick learned from a close confidante who was a nasty brawler back in my Brooklyn neighborhood, placing the focus on nothing but your surroundings, people, objects, things to grab, smash or if needed, pierce or gouge someone with, heightening the ability to listen for things your ears normally wouldn't pick up, like the sound of approaching footsteps, twigs and branches snapping, or leaves rustling…all sounds which were flooding the ear canals at this very moment.

My eyes narrow in on this prick and even in the mixture of glare and shadows being thrown off by the firelight, I surmise he's noticing the change as well, giving him the hardened stare of someone equally not giving a fuck about going a few brutal rounds or getting hurt badly. Lena, Yuka and Steph attempt setting a block, but a shake of the head lets them know the point of being reasoned with has evaporated quicker than drops of water on a blistering, summer day. Guys dealing grass was one thing, but these scumbag meth, crack and heroin pushers I have no tolerance for, especially one who surmises that Gem is his property to abuse, misuse or otherwise, so with no chance of brokering peace, they recede to the tree line.

"Well, so I finally meet Gem's protector…must say, not impressed all in all." Swallowing a little harder, he's trying to figure me out with each second.

"Didn't give a fuck if you were impressed or not, Kellin." The breathing's almost non-existent, my senses, trigger like. "This was supposed to be a night of good friends getting together, tribes having a good time….it doesn't seem like you're wanted here, man."

I watch for all the signs of this remark igniting the feelings of his territory being pissed on. "So, some newcomer fuck to the game from out in the sticks is coming into my backyard to tell me HE holds sway here? Fuck off!"

The mind game has been worked to perfection, drawn his ire and finally produced the three other bodies I heard rustling through the parks' darkness. They take their place behind Kellin, the king and his court in their perceived seat of power start to chuckle, spittle forms around his mouth. "Think you are going to dictate to me now? We hold the high ground here, asshole. I will get Gem back with or without you running interference on me. Your choice, but you're fucked either way!"

Laughing manically again, his piss-ant legion of skinheads follows suit, their shaved heads gleaming from the fire's glare but I laugh even harder which annoys him immensely. "Do you think this is a game, prison bitch, pretty boy? Your life is hanging by a thread, you cunt!" The heart rate slows dramatically while sizing up my four antagonists but I make sure to hold Kellin in my gaze.

Locking eyes, the words roll from my lips in a simmering boil. "You'll never get Gem in your grips again. Neither you, nor the three Nazi fucks behind you will stop me from making that happen. You'll get hurt tonight, one on one, four on one...your choice. Either way, you'll be out of her life, starting right here, right now. Peddle your shit and abuse elsewhere, or I'll end it for you tonight. Are you getting it now asshole, make a move to touch her and it'll be your last one."

Conversation around the party's come to a crashing halt, leaving only the De Ville's stereo ominously to blare the Misfits, 'Die, Die My Darling'. I've called him on his bullshit, await the response, verbal or non-verbal and when none comes, I take the game to the next level, chuckling before turning my back on them. "That's what I thought, nothing but a scared shit talker." Glancing over my shoulder, I never let them out of my sight because Kellin won't control his rage for long.

The leaves rustle spasmodically, twigs snap violently and ahead of me, I spot the tribe yelling, but don't hear any noise except for the approaching footsteps of just one person because Kellin's unhinged and bearing down on me. Swinging around, crouching into a defensive hockey position, it's like I'm waiting for a hard check at mid-ice because he's running too quickly to stop, so the advantage is now mine. I lift up, feeling the weight of his body rolling over my shoulders and he crashes hard to the ground. Wasting no time, I pounce on him, pinning his shoulders under my knees. He easily outweighs me by forty pounds, so I move rapidly to get the advantage, unleashing three quick cracks to the face, while the fourth one thrown lands squarely on his nose, splattering blood in all directions. He gurgles, gagging on thickened, brownish red fluid, gasping heavily under me, as I hurriedly look up to see his three goons approaching. Preparing for the onslaught, I lift my weight off of the fallen, immobilized Kellin. Leaves rustle, several very distinct voices yell and glass cracks violently.

Before I know it, Lena, Yuka and Steph stand in between me and the goons, broken beer bottles in their hands, ready to slice anyone who's daft enough to rescue Kellin. Dusty, Oren and Otto join them to form an impregnable wall. "Get the fuck outta' here now, you Nazi shits, or I'll turn this whole fuckin' place loose on you," Dusty explodes, which invites ten or twelve punks from other tribes to stand with the Misfits. Realizing they're vastly outnumbered, the skins tuck tail, sprinting into the darkness of the park.

Feeling the weight off his shoulders for an instant, Kellin rolls out from under me, throws a quick boot shot towards my chin, catching me slightly off guard, as he struggles in vain to regain his balance prior to reaching into his pocket at which point the distinct click ejecting from its housing is heard, the villains weapon produced, catching the silver gleam of steel in the moonlight. Being slightly dazed, seeing the blade slicing and slashing about manically knocks loose any of the cobwebs I haven't already shaken off.

The first lunge is a staggering one, only enough to nick the arm of my thick, leather jacket. Lena screams, but it's a very quick distraction and I manage delivering a kneecap into his chest cavity. Kellin loses oxygen, falling hard into the crumbling bark of an oak tree while flaying about and hitting nothing. The grip on his switchblade falters, so I crack him hard in the nose again. Tears stream down to blend with the snot and blood mixture already caking Kellin's face. The knife flies far enough away not to be a threat anymore, and I see Dusty pocket it. Feeling no pain from my arm or the heat of blood trickling, I pursue Kellin, giving him a quick crack behind the ear, obliterating his equilibrium.

Vividly aware the three skins may acquire some reinforcements, turning this battle into a war, the tribes rightly scatter for their cars or through the forbidding darkness of the sinister, surrounding neighborhoods, bolting the park before the skins return or the Brody's invade Fairmount. With Kellin in my sights, a thundering kick to his ribs sends him reeling to the grass, where I pounce again, this time pressing my fingers into his neck and my thumb pressuring his Adam's apple until wheezing and writhing underneath me, he fights for his pathetic existence.

Steph, Dusty and Oren yell for us to get going before hauling ass to parts unknown, leaving only our small tribe to view him gurgling on his own spew before I peer into his fading eyes. "This is only a taste of what you will get if I ever see you or your goons around Gem again," I snarl, spitting in his face for good measure.

Finally releasing the death grip, Kellin lays still, struggling for air. "I mean it, call off your dogs, or I won't be so generous next time." I lift him slightly from the ground by the blood-soaked collar of his leather jacket. "Are we understanding each other now, asshole?" He nods, heavily collapsing onto the turf, moaning and agonizing over his plight. I mull over kicking his skull in for good measure but my concentration is interrupted by chaotic bright lights, explosive sound and squealing tires when the silver SS slides, violently turfing every square inch of grass in sight. "Get the fuck in," Gem screams angrily. "Those animals will be back soon enough for him!"

The resonances of howls and yips approach from the distant woods, reverberating louder by the second. With Misfits diving wildly into the back and passenger seats, Kellin is left to remain beaten and bloodied, a gruesome eyesore hopefully reinforcing that Gem's not to be fucked with, or there will be dire consequences. "Remember what I said, Titus. It fuckin' ends tonight! YOU RULE NOTHING IN THIS CITY!" Gem spins more grass behind her, the silver stallion screams madly across the field, finally stampeding wildly onto 52nd Street.

The car is as quiet as a tomb, except for the radios' low hum. Gem's eyes remain focused from the windshield, to the rearview, to her sideview mirror, keeping her attention on 'The Strip' traffic while furiously smoking a Newp. I ask if she's ok, but after receiving no reply, glance back at Otto, Lena and Yuka to see if they're cool. Smiles and the nodding of heads are my reply before Otto decides to pipe up.

"Listen man, I always figured you could handle yourself...I mean, I've seen you moshing and throwing some people around who were way bigger than you. I saw you brawl those fake-ass mobsters in the alley alongside Gem when they stole her money, but what you did tonight was fuckin' outrageous! You fuckin' were ready to take on those skins by yourself, mate! Insane, fucking insane."

"Lena and I were scared shitless of what you were going to do to Kellin when we saw the look on your face. Kellin was getting a lump in his throat, Robbs. You had him and his goons jarred." Yuka grabbed Otto's cig, taking a long drag before handing it over to Lena.

"Personally, I am glad you cracked that dick," Lena chirped. "He's been hell-bent on getting our Gem back in his grips. Fuck him, his Nazi pricks and that bullshit they tagged down by the River. That's why we got out in front when we saw them rushing you. No way you were getting hurt, cutie!"

"But you could have gotten hurt, Icy," a voice growls dimly from the driver's seat where another Newp was already hanging from the Punk Princesses' mouth.

"Gem, we were fine..."

"Bullshit! You didn't know that for sure, Lena! That's why you, Yuka and Steph were holding those bottles like switchblades, right? None of you knew what to expect from those fucking goons, except you, right Robbs?"

With eyes wildly focused on only me, her neckline flashes blood red splotches. "You just jumped right into the fray, giving me that cocky wink and smile of yours, ignoring my pleading... begging you to just let him be."

"Gem, you were agitated and the girls were trying to get him away from you. He wasn't going to leave you there peacefully." The car picks up more speed, as does her temper. "You didn't know that, Robbs! You just found out who he was and you lost it! You were gonna' prove to an abusive pimp and dealer with a bad reputation and a murderous side to him that his tag on the wall was a farce...that he didn't rule Philly or especially Gemma

Stinson, right? You were going to be the knight, the savior of poor, defenseless Gem!

"Well guess what sweetheart, Gem can defend herself! Gem was punching, kicking and gouging eyes out long before you came along! Who the FUCK do you think was protecting me when I was living on the streets? Who protected me when I found out what an abusive, sadistic, piece of shit Kellin Titus was? Was it YOU, Robbs? FUCK NO!

"Were you there when the male 'protectors' in my family were passing me around like a rag doll, using me for whatever their pleasure of the moment was, Robbs? Were you there to save me from any of that?

Were you there to see my drunk, piece of shit dad fucking the hell out of me while my piece of shit mother was passed out on the floor from all the blow she put up her fucking nose? NO, YOU WEREN'T! Nobody fucking was! NOBODY! MOTHERFUCKING NOBODY!" She furiously pushes the SS past the Art Museum, cutting off a few cars in the process as horns blare wildly behind us.

The air escapes in furious exhalations, what she hadn't wanted to divulge was spewed with pure vitriol. Gasping at the thought of her ever being violated in such a way, I regain my composure if only for Gem's sake.

"Gem, if I was around then, I sure as hell would've done anything to stop what they were doing. Believe me, I would have." I was barely whispering at this point, and could hear Yuka and Lena lightly crying, peering rearwards long enough to see Otto shaking his head, muttering "damn it, he didn't know," every so often in between drags of his Lucky.

Tears roll down Gem's cheeks and she violently slides the car into a spot on the Ben Franklin Parkway, irately clawing at my jacket, the venom from years of hurt being readied to swallow me whole, unleashed in the form of a vicious, sarcastic laugh.

"You still don't get it, Robbs! They would have fucking KILLED YOU! They would've done it just to prove that they could keep me under their control! They could rape me at will, no matter how hard I fought them and my evil, old man would laugh his ass off...all fucked up on booze, drugs and hate.

"Now you know why I became a street kid. The one thing I wasn't ready to tell you...I had to because you didn't listen tonight. You didn't want to hear me pleading, you didn't see me crying when I ran to get the car, hoping that I wouldn't come back to see you lying on the ground, covered in blood!

"You just didn't care that you could have been gone from me, another person, taken the fuck away from me!" Shutting off the car, pulling the keys from the ignition, she violently lunges at me. "Damn you! DAMN YOU! You could have been taken from me!" Flailing viciously with fists and talons, I don't attempt to repel any shots.

Otto and the girls struggle valiantly to capture her arms, screaming for her to stop but I beg them to let her go, willing to have her unleash all the pain and anguish on me, before she pulls away, thumping hard into the seat with her eyes still afire, tears cascading from her cheeks. "Damn you, Robbs! You could have died tonight! The only one I have ever cared for like this in my life and you could've FUCKING DIED!" The door swings open, Gem stumbles towards the sidewalk with reckless abandon, eventually passing one befuddled onlooker after another.

"Just stay here, guys, give me a few minutes." They solemnly nod, still shell shocked from what's transpired in the past few minutes. Hurriedly jumping out, I sprint past more pedestrians who stare blankly at my appearance, eventually catching my heartbroken girl. Gently placing my fingers on her shoulder, Gem's sobbing rather heavily. Seeing her this way, knowing what I do now about her earlier life is just breaking my heart. I wipe the tears away from her cheeks and she grabs my hand strongly.

"Gem, I'm so sorry that I've hurt you. It wasn't my intention to do so. I was just infuriated that he wouldn't leave you alone. You've been doing so well and I didn't want him peddling his crap around you again or laying a hand on you, but I promise, I will follow your lead from now. I'll always try to protect you.. please understand that."

74

The sobbing becomes a whimper, then contemplative silence, reeling in my heart with those beautiful, soulful eyes. "I…I'm sorry too, I just went manic because I was so afraid of losing you tonight. I know we've only known each other since last year, but I adore you like no other person I've ever been with.

"Can you understand better now, why I ask you to never break my heart or leave me, Robbs because you are a piece of me. I breathe you in and I never want to let you go." She reaches out to hug me. "I am so sorry, Robbs…I shouldn't have blamed you for…"

"Shhh, it's over, Gem, you don't have to apologize to me. Don't ever hold back on me because I love you for being you. You never have to hide anything from me." Wiping away the black mascara that's cascaded down her cheeks, I hold her close. The sobs diminish, she nestles into my chest, breathing calmly before I swear that she giggles nonchalantly. "What was that little laugh about?"

"Otto was right about you tonight. I knew that you could hold your own, but holy crap, you certainly put a beating on that bastard." Halting the celebratory haughtiness for a moment, I receive a serious stare from the green-eyed beauty. "I adore that you want to save me but please, be sensible too. You were lucky Kellin sliced only your jacket and didn't cause worse damage than that."

Our lips meet…the Punk Princess and her Punk Prince pitted against the world once again. We look down the street, noticing our Misfits leaning up against the Silver Bullet, smoking, waving and whooping it up. Gem asks if I'll drive and I happily agree before we finally get a chance to take in the splendor of the Museum of Art, Philadelphia's own Parthenon, ablaze in lights.

Giving each other happy, playful glances, there's no doubt about what's happening next as the Misfits have their own Rocky moment, scurrying past Eakins Oval's overwhelming fountains and statuary leading towards the Museum steps. Otto and I sprint to the apex in leaps and bounds but break into hysterics observing Gem aid the girl's navigation of the terrain in their death-defying heels. Springing down to give them a hand, we all reach the precipice together, releasing our pent up, youthful, punk tribalism in the form of howls, war cries and the like while a few straggling tourists look on in utter amusement, with some even cheering on our efforts before heading on to their evenings of enjoyment.

The summit offers one of the best views of Philly's skyline and on this clear night, the city sparkles brilliantly in the distance. Lena spins like a ballerina, stopping only long enough to give us one of her radiant smiles. "It looks so beautiful out there...the city is glowing for us tonight, Misfits!"

"It sure is, Lena...our city is shining like a diamond tonight," Gem adds before Lena and Yuka begin hugging her tightly. "I love you, Swan," Lena chirps in her ear, kissing her cheek, while Yuka stands on her tiptoes, to kiss Gem's forehead. "I love you too, sis, you know that, right?"

"I do know...I really do...I was just so scared...I'm not used to being that way. You understand that, right?"

I walk slowly towards Gem, staring deeply into her eyes. "I know that I understand, now more than ever."

Agreeing that it's been a hell of an emotionally exhausting evening and we should run our three Misfits back to Otto's place, I plow through the late evening, party town traffic, reaching his apartment in record time. We promise to regroup at the flat for an early Sunday brunch, which has Otto psyched for the upcoming morning.

The return trip to Gem's is a lively discussion of everything and anything and it's delightful to see her spirits rejuvenated, a resilience she seems to have acquired from dealing with so much heartbreak, but I admit, a part of me is still stricken, acknowledging the pain she endured at the hands of her family and Kellin. For tonight though, unless she brings any of it up, I will let the subject pass.

Fumbling for the keys to her apartment, the giggling continues. "Are you getting nervous or are you overly excited to get on the other side of that door, baby?" Reeling me in with those eyes again, God, between them, her sunshine smile and stunning body, I do not stand a chance.

Finally advancing through the opened door, she presses us up against the wooden frame, leaving me only seconds to break away and smirk. "Mmmm...this is all well and good but let me lock up first."

Misty is gone until tomorrow night, so there's no worry about having to be discreet, the upstairs is totally ours again. Sweeping Gem off her feet, she amorously kisses my neck and the warm, darting movement of her tongue feels unbelievable. In no time at all, our bodies are entwined on her large bed, with clothing quickly tossed in all directions as another round of intense ardor ensues.

Rolling on top of her, I open my eyes long enough to see her incredible figure making perfect movement with mine. Gem digs her nails into the small of my back, losing herself in the moment, as beads of sweat trickle between us.

"Don't make this night ever end, Robbs," she coos repeatedly. In the darkened peacefulness of her bedroom, with the radio playing softly to the sound of The Replacements, 'Kiss Me on The Bus', I have no intention of making that happen.

··· 7 ···

What Remains of the Day...

STREAKS OF SUN MAKE it through the curtains to begin shedding playful, dancing rays of light across the flats' contents. Although it's an older place, it attains a certain elegance with its high ceilings, turn of the century windows, and ornamental plaster moldings. Gem's space is charming as well. It's a meticulously kept room; "a place for everything, and everything in its place," she has a habit of saying with a sense of glee. It's the spot she's always dreamed of having, a happy, reserved space to furnish and appoint with her meager but important belongings.

Bulletin boards found in an abandoned school were carefully covered with fabric and adorned with fliers from the many punk shows she's seen throughout her young life. Two of her most beloved possessions, a medium blue, 1950's model Gretsch electric that she calls 'Robins Egg', which was retrieved from the bowels of a music store set ablaze a few years back and lovingly restored by an older friend who owed her a debt, and a well weathered, acoustic Epiphone, given to her as payment for painting some custom designs on a street punks leather jacket, stand proudly against a vintage dresser that Misty helped her sand and stain, while an old, second-hand, durable, tube amp sits on the floor next to it.

In homage to our folk hero, Woody Guthrie, Gem's written 'This Machine Kills Fascists' in permanent black marker on the body of the gleaming Egg, and I think it's befitting of her personality, railing on against the Nazi's and Skinheads who attempt to unsuccessfully infiltrate our ranks and spread their hatred.

A small black and white TV is on the corner of a long dresser. The loop antenna is in good shape but the wand antenna has seen better days, resembling a dismembered, metallic twig after being harpooned by a combat boot when my Rangers beat her Flyers in an exhibition game we viewed recently. AN EXHIBITION GAME, FOR CHRIST'S SAKE! If there's one thing you're made aware of rather succinctly, Gem takes her love of Flyers hockey and hatred towards my Rangers very seriously, so thankfully, the antenna took the brunt of her acrimony and not me!

Numerous records and cassettes are stacked alphabetically in milk crates adorned with the same fabric as the bulletin boards. The clothes are always tucked away neatly in the dresser or hanging in her closet and the many tidbits of history, poetry and the greats of American, Russian and Western European literature purchased at the local, secondhand bookstore are placed carefully in a fairly large sized, wooden bookcase that she unearthed from the same school housing the bulletin boards. I still enjoy listening to the joyous recounting of how she and Lena lugged that piece through the streets of Philly and upstairs to her flat. Trying to envision two totally decked out punk girls transporting a bookcase through South and Fourth Streets alone must have been an amusing sight in its own right but that was Gem, no pretensions, no bullshit. She was a breath of fresh air, a girl of so many sorrows and triumphs in her life already, you just wanted to know everything about her.

The sunlight finds its way over her body, illuminating Gem's beauty. If an hour of sleep was attained, that was a lot, considering most of our time was spent entwined in a never-ending embrace, talking on and on about everything from her troubled past, to what transpired in the park.

She was struggling valiantly to kick all of her past demons and readily admitted to the many failings which had occurred. It was a hard road to travel, but she was doing her best, succeeding much more than she was willing to give herself credit for.

Apologizing profusely for allowing an erratic temperament to get the best of me last night, Gem's beginning to understand my protective nature more each day. "It was always a defense mechanism for me, Gem. When we lived in Brooklyn, my mom would think nothing of taking a piece out of me for making the simplest mistake. Shit, sometimes she'd do it just because she was pissed off at James and I was the replacement, whipping boy.

"She would smack me with those bony hands of hers until you'd feel the air come out of you. If it wasn't the hands, it was a wooden spoon, a metal sauce spoon, a belt, you name it. When she was really having one of those truly mental breakdown days, I would get tossed into the bedroom closet, sitting in the darkness, waiting for her to calm down or beat on me some more."

A tear rolls down Gem's face. "Jesus, why did they do things like that to us, Robbs? What did we do to deserve that treatment? Why did they hate us so much?"

"We did nothing, Gem, it was their madness, their uncontrollable anger. I will tell you something though, the darkness of the closet was solitude for me. If she thought it would play on all the fears that she knew existed in me, it accomplished the opposite effect because it left me emboldened never be afraid of her or anyone else.

"Until recently, when I was able to open my heart to you, it's why I never cried. I refused to show her that the pain she was inflicting on me even registered at all. Hell, some days, I would burst into fits of laughter and the harder she beat me, the more I grinned. It's a part of the reason I'm very protective of anyone whom I truly love and will never let them endure suffering at the hands of some animal unable to control themselves."

Regaining her composure, Gem recounts the painful narrative of her woeful, abuse laden history. "As a young girl, I'd close my eyes and think of fields of flowers with me running through them or recall any music that made me forget what my family... what my dad or Kellin was doing to me.

"The abusiveness dragged on excruciatingly, until I started to fight back in high school. It's partly why I started filing my nails into dagger points and if he tried to grab me, I would slash at his face or his eyes. If he kept coming, I would aim for his knees or his crotch with my boots. He tried stabbing me on one occasion but when he lunged and missed, I pulverized his skull with an almost empty bottle of vodka. I was surprised that I didn't kill him...some days, I wished he'd died at the fury of my hands instead of someone else's.

"Anyway, my dad's doped up friend tried grabbing me from behind to hold me down but I donkey kicked him in the sack. That was the night I told my mom I was done being a punching bag and sex doll for the family."

"Jesus, I'm so sorry you had to endure that, Gemma. Those sick bastards! What did your mom say to you? Did she even try and protect you?"

"Gabriella Stinson? Ha! She couldn't even stand up long enough to tell you what it looked like outside," Gem snorts through her sniffles. "She was a stone-cold junkie for years and used drugs to forget how shitty her life had become, the same path I was going down too. I still worry that it's a path I may try again, Robbs. I'm petrified of the thought and I know it's a horrible excuse but I still feel very fragile sometimes.

"I worry most that I may try and find my way back to the needle because although I did it infrequently, it was the best way to separate my body from my mind, even if it left me rattling, nauseous and shivering on the streets after the comedown."

Sniffling again, the toughened, streetwise exterior returns in spades to quell the anguish. "So, what did Gabriella Stinson do? Well baby boy, when I informed her that I was leaving before I killed one of these pricks, her response was, 'so now I have to put up with all the hell again? Thanks Gemma, take your clothes, your music shit, take your dead uncle's car and just go, bitch.' So much for the warmth and love of the mother-daughter bond, eh?"

"That's just fucking unbelievable."

"What about you, Robbs? Has your mother ever tried to hit you again?"

"She stopped beating on me after I was ten and we'd moved here. She fed me a line of utter bullshit that it was because she'd realized that brutalizing a child was not the proper way to handle conflict or anger. It was such contrived, patronizing garbage on her part.

"Her fucking epiphany occurred because Sal never disciplined his children and if he'd seen the way she beat on me, he would have called her an animal and probably never married her. The free ride out of New York and into the sappy ass suburbs of Bucks County would've been nixed."

"Oh my God, how hypocritical…how nice…so we don't beat our son anymore because the perceived gravy train of dollars will stop flowing from a new husband. Wow! Did you ever call her on this?"

"During the summer before I started college, we got into a big argument over Giselle and a million other things that were pissing her off about the life I was leading. I honestly never should have stopped cracking you, she said, so I began laughing, replying, do you really think that the verbal mind games you play are any better?

"You're relentless, no matter what you try, and the only reason you stopped hitting me is because Sal would have thought you to be psychotic, calling your whole escape to Yardley off."

Gasping loudly, Gem sits up, clutching her pillow tightly. "Wow…I couldn't even fathom what the response would have been to such an accusation like that?"

"Typical of my mother, her face turned blood red, the bony hands gripped the end of the kitchen table, slamming it hard onto the tile floor. Her verbal response was typical as well… goddamn you."

"Don't you just love parents? Well, here's hoping that we're never like them and if or when we have little ones in our lives, they'll know nothing but being cherished, supported and loved. Robbs, I am so sorry for what you went through."

Holding her close to me, I kiss her forehead softly. "Listen, I'm not trying to make light of my situation, Gem, but you can't even equate the abuse you received at the hands of more than one person to my situation. I had it relatively easy compared to the mental and physical pain inflicted upon you and I also had a much easier go of my conditions."

"Whether emanating from the elevated towers of the elite, the bucolic, suburban landscapes of the bourgeois, or the derelict domiciles of the downtrodden, a beating is equally brutal, a rape, equally ravaging," she replies in an eloquence and strength beyond her years as the fiery green of her eyes fall upon me.

"Wow, what a sobering tale of heartache and woe, Gem. It sounds like something written by a turn of the century, Russian poet. Who was it?"

"It was written a tad more recently than that but you do have the Russian background partially correct," she says mildly while wrapping her long arms around my waist. "It was from Gemma Anastasia Stinson, in the early 1980's."

● ● ●

Gem reluctantly rolls out of bed to grab some new gear, throwing it on quickly to warm up, since leaving the window open has left her bedroom chilly on this beautiful October morning. Upon making the decision to shower after everyone departs (when I'll regrettably have to wash out Yuka's Liberty Spikes), we stumble groggily towards the kitchen to share a glass of cold orange juice and one of Gem's delicious, homemade blueberry muffins. The big feast will take place in a few hours, so we refrain from spoiling our appetites.

Donning our leather jackets and snagging her Epiphone and notebook, we escape to the stoop for an early morning cigarette and some apparent brainstorming. Outside of a few joggers and some churchgoers slowly ambling towards Old Saint Mary's, Fourth Street is ours.

Strumming lightly, Gem speaks in a serious tone between puffs of her smoke. "When you fell asleep, I wrote more of that song from the other day at school. Now that you know what happened to me as a kid and young teen, I really want your honest opinion and help. Soooo...Take a look."

Scanning the page and a half of brutal honesty, I sing in a hushed tone, trying not to drown out her playing or let my voice crack due to the pure, raw emotion of the lyrics.

"Staring out from behind a sooty window
Look at how the city lights shine so bright
Woke up on the floor again
The fuckin' filthy floor again
Veins are hoping for some bliss tonight

Heat the spoon and tap down the needle
Why'd I let everything fall apart?
An innocent glance led to painful touches..."

It's killing me to sing this aloud, but there's no way in hell that I'll knuckle under here, especially when Gem needs my support and honesty.

"You stripped me of my innocence and crushed my heart..."

Slapping the strings, she smiles awkwardly. "Wow...that was really powerful. I love the way you're matching my chord structure."

"It was easy to do, Swan. I sang it like you would perform it on your own. You need to sing this song...on your own."

"Robbs...I'm going to need a lot of cheering on here...it's gonna' be hard..."

"I know it will be and I'm here for you, just like I was last night."

"Ahhh...my sweet, guardian angel," she happily sighs. "I love you so much...but I will love you even more if you can figure out some verses. I'm coming up empty with something to put here. It needs something before I progress."

Perusing further down the page, a flow of words and emotions flood my brain and I motion for her to resume strumming as I try hard not get aggravated with myself for being unable to write as fast as the verses are spinning through my skull.

Scribbling, cursing, throwing the pen from the stoop only to retrieve it and apologize profusely when it almost impales a lady jogging with her puppy, I'm finally confident that I have something, which makes me roll my hand in a cueing motion for her to continue playing.

> *"You were supposed to be the sun and moon for me*
> *What could I have ever done?*
> *You said that if I told, you would take my life*
> *So I prayed for strength to fuckin' run*

> *What you did to me*
> *The way you broke my heart, but now I'm finally safe and warm*
> *Had to escape your evil…get away for good*
> *Seeking shelter from your violent storm…"*

Ready to jump right into her incredibly strong words, she stops dead, with tears streaming down her face. "How did you know?"

"I just do, Swan…nothing more to say, nothing more…you know how that is."

"I sure do, baby boy…and the last line before the chorus…it's all you…always…you…" she replies defiantly strumming harder on the Epiphone's strings, letting all of her emotions be laid bare.

"Sing the rest, Gemma. This is all you, girl," and as if summoning spirits from above, sings it so strong and true…

> *"Standing on the ledge of this beat down ol' apartment*
> *The city lights don't look so bright*
> *I'm so lost right now, so fuckin' lost right now*
> *Wondering if it's all gonna' end tonight*

But then he comes to me
This beautiful new soul...says he wants to talk things through
I never felt this way...like someone really cares
And now I'm free again, free, flying like a bird
Is there a chance that life begins anew..."

And with her steel trap memory gathering the refrain precisely, she adds it before the final lyrics...

"What you did to me
The way you broke my heart, but now I'm finally safe and warm
Had to escape your evil..get away for good
Seeking shelter from your violent storm

I'm never lookin' back again
I'm never lookin' back again
No, I'll never look back again
Never fuckin' lookin' back again..."

Gazing deeply into one another's soulful eyes, she lays the guitar on the stoop and embracing as if it were our last day on earth together, sob audibly, no longer the prisoners of our abuses or abusers, until the slight breezes as if on cue to warm our hearts make the sun-bleached colors of fall dance around above us.

Gem, wiping the tears from her cheeks, breaks away, hops from the stoop and playfully pilfers them from the sky, pulling down two, beautiful orange leaves, wraps the stem of one around the flag in my spike and starts to giggle and squeak incessantly. It's times like these that I find her even more endearing than usual, when she finally allows her innocent, young girl side to come shining through.

I confiscate the other leaf, wrapping its stem through the hoop of her eyebrow piecing. "Now I look like a pirate princess with an eye patch." Racing madly onto the sidewalk, she picks up a small branch and starts swinging it like a sword. "Aargh!" she yells, before giggling even harder. Not allowing her to have all of the fun, I snag an even bigger branch by the curbside and begin stabbing her in the arm. "No Punk Pirate Princess will ever triumph over the Royal Navy," I laugh, allowing the wild rumpus to continue until we hear familiar voices approaching.

"Good Lord, can we ever leave these two alone for a minute, people?" Otto playfully inquires.

"Nope, not for even a minute, love, and what the hell is with leaf patch, sweetie?"

Gem twirls her twig sword in a parrying motion. "I am the Punk Pirate Princess of Fourth Street, Punk Lady Yuka!".

"Dare I even ask what you are supposed to be with that leaf attached to your flag?" Yuka questions, while trying not to crack up.

"I am Commodore Robert, savior of the Royal Navy and pursuer of the ruthless Punk Pirate Princess Gemma of Fourth Street."

Lena and Otto put down their grocery bags, pick up branches and join the fray. "Oi, I will fight for the colors of the Union Jack against the tyranny of the Punk Pirate Princess," Otto bellows.

Taking a defensive stance, Lena rolls her eyes mockingly. "Yo, I'm not getting all that dramatic…I just wanna' fight by the side of a sexy, Punk Pirate Princess."

Taking a long drag from her cig, looking like an exasperated mother outnumbered by her rambunctious children, Yuka flicks the spent butt to the ground, sighs…picks up a branch. "Well, if I must…c'mon Princesses!"

The girls attack us with vigor, although Otto and I stand our ground valiantly if only for a few minutes, eventually succumbing to their vicious onslaught. Otto unties the bandana from around my boot, painfully thrusting it in the air, admitting imminent surrender but it's of no benefit.

"Never," Gem cries, launching the branch like a javelin into the clear, blue sky while the girls pounce, eventually knocking us all to the sidewalk, quite the sight on an otherwise peaceful Sunday morning.

With the Misfits nearing exhaustion, we grab our bags of soon to be brunch and make haste to Gem's kitchen. This is becoming a weekend tradition since right before school commenced…a night of hard charging, followed by a brunch fit for a king or a Punk Pirate Princess. We may rub nickels together some weeks, but lately our paychecks have improved reasonably, freeing us up to enjoy more occasions like today.

Otto and I eagerly whip the eggs before dropping fresh bacon and sausages from his butchers' job at D'Angelo Brothers, in the Italian Market, onto the griddle as well as two scrumptious looking tenderloin steaks.

Otto is a workhorse for their shop, so the old man doesn't mind throwing him some freebies. Occasionally, Gem and I go to help clean up the store and sidewalk, earning us some cash and meats too. It's all about hard work and hustling to reap some well-deserved rewards and it gives me the chance to needle Gem about how some aspects of capitalism aren't necessarily bad, which usually earns me a wry smile, a lecture on how socialism is still the better path to a harmonious existence and a middle finger salute.

We begin pan frying the tenderloins, tossing spices and sliced mushrooms into the mix. Yuka and Gem methodically cut up fruit and stir batter for some pancakes, Lena gets the coffee, tea and music going with some Youth Brigade's, 'Sink With California'. The kitchen fills with every aroma imaginable and we break loudly into song…

"And we'll sink with California
When it falls into the sea…"

Otto slices the mouthwatering, juicy steak into thin portions, pouring the sautéed mushrooms over them as I toss the hot, juicy sausages and crisp, but not burnt bacon onto a platter, stacking the steaming, buttermilk pancakes next to them. Gem finishes cutting up the strawberries, oranges and apple slices, adroitly pouring them into one of Misty's large, blue, hand blown glass bowls, while Yuka and Lena tend to setting the table and readying the beverages, a picturesque, Norman Rockwell painting of a feast for the sight and senses.

The morning moves delightfully along with the Misfits pigging out in the living room, enjoying each other's company immensely. The conversation gets animated with the events of yesterday being replayed and Lena keeps the music going with Patti Smith's, 'So You Want to Be A Rock and Roll Star', followed in quick succession by the U.K. Subs, 'Warhead', the Ramones, 'Rock and Roll High School' and Iggy's, 'Seek and Destroy'.

The gastronomic contents of the delicious feast firmly lodge in our bulging waistlines and the Misfit ladies give Otto and I a break, meticulously cleaning Misty's kitchen and the rest of her flat until it sparkles. A pleasant breeze from the wide-open windows, plus plenty of light dart through the living room, it leads to a few moments of blissful relaxation until the decision's made that it's high time for the night creatures to invade the daytime crowds of South Street. Gem grabs her Epiphone and grins. "You never know when a song may come to us, baby boy."

"That's my Swan, always striking out into the wild streets with a plan in hand."

The smell of cigarettes and food envelop our senses soon after we hit the corner, so needless to say, Otto and I are already scoping out our next culinary conquest while the girls just groan. "You guys are such hogs," Lena blurts out, instigating a motherload of our loudest pig imitations, which soon drown out her admonishment. "Ugh, grow up you two piggy's'!" Doing our best to drive them batshit crazy, the snorts and squeals become deafening. "Real mature, you pudwhackers," Yuka chortles while walking away in a mock, snobby fashion.

Gem wants badly to be part of the 'Pig Parade' but the girls grab her to join the growing throng of roosterheads in front of SKULLZ wild, S&M window display of the week, which usually makes the norms cringe in disgust or go red faced in embarrassment. Two of the younger roosters, our Misfit apprentices, Skate and Tim already cozy up, trying to snag some free smokes. "Filthy city of rats...filthy city of rats! Yo', well if it isn't the singing stomper of Fairmount Park," Skate pipes up, rapidly grabbing the mobs attention.

"Jesus, news travels fast, Skate."

"Sure does, man. The beat down you put on that asshole Kellin has been the talk of the street, Robbs, an' everybody says 'at he deserved it. Yo, the punks respect the fuck outta' Gemma 'round here, so you earned some major cred' by crackin' his grill."

"He may be licking his wounds right now, Skate, but I know he'll be looking for payback. I'm ready for him, though, 'cause nobody's going to hurt Gem," and when the young roosters voice their approval, Gem blushes from all the attention. "You see that, Gem, you truly are the Punk Princess!"

"Gemma Stinson, The Punk Princess of South Street, now that's bitchin'," yells Tim. "Oi, oi, oi!" comes the deafening retort from about twenty roosters, to which Gem slings her guitar around to perform for the punk delegation. Finger picking and giving her best two-step, she unleashes into a wicked hillbilly twang and revamps the 'Beverly Hillbillies' theme.

"C'mon an' let me tell ya' a lil' story
'Bout a punk named Robbs
Don't like skinheads or dope dealers
Who act like fuckin' knobs

And one night in Fairmount
Titus went too far with his old lass
So Robbs came outta' nowhere
And stomped his ass

Kicked it that is...
All over the park...
Left him for dead...
With black eyes, busted lips and a boot to his ballsack..."

"Yeee haw...Gemma Stinson...the Storyteller of South Street," I explode while Skate and Tim go into hoedown mode and rebel yells fill the air. In appreciation for their boisterous cheers, Otto and I give the boys a few more smokes for the day before continuing our walk through the growing hordes of sightseers and gawkers. The euphoric feeling of owning the street after the news spread about last night gives us a spirited sense of holding sway here, but I dare not let it give me an over-zealous air of cockiness.

I'll have to keep my wits about me for at least the next few weeks, because Kellin and his crew will be looking for ample opportunities to stomp me in retaliation, so there's enough intel-lect within me to understand that 'what doesn't kill you makes you stronger' is definitely a statement of infinite truths.

The Misfits close in on Second and South, where the rau-cous sounds of punk have some new, exciting competition. The equally militant tunes of rap invaded this corner recently and a group of young black guys and girls in leather pants and stud-ded jackets commence break dancing besides performing some wicked pop and lock moves.

The punks have been pretty receptive to this incursion of equal rebellion, since punk and hip hop seem to share an equal amount of 'life on the street' stories mixed with a smattering of anti-establishment themes. Gem and I hang out with this group every now and then after we busk across the street by the rock club, J.C. Dobbs. We're not quite sure how the whole hip hop tribe feels about our music but a handful of them seem to be receptive to ours when we perform.

The Misfits have certainly embraced the music with open arms and ambitiously attempt the latest dance moves. When Lena and Yuka start rotating their hips furiously to Grandmaster Flash and the Furious Five's, 'The Message', a few of the hip hop girls dressed in brightly colored jackets, neon, skin tight Spandex and high heels join right in on the fun, latching onto our girls' waists from behind and matching their every move.

Otto slides onto the cardboard which has been laid out for breaking and before long, spins on one knee, immediately twist-ing his body into almost pretzel-like fashion, ending up on his back, twirling like a top, which draws a big cheer from the hip hop tribe.

Gem holds my hand as we start to pop and lock and pretty soon, we're surrounded by the rest of the breaking crew, doing our damned best to put on a show for the masses gathering on the corner. We happily give up the dance area to the professionals, but not before receiving a round of enjoyable applause from the crowd along with a few hugs and high fives from the hip hop kids.

After feeling rather heady and psyched-up about our break-dancing 'debut', we journey onto Delaware Avenue, viewing the glimmering beauty of the river nestled in between the decaying, vacant shells of some turn of the century warehouses, while we're smoking, laughing, absorbing the joyous afternoon for all it's worth.

The day seems to lazily roll by, so apprehensively, I ask a passerby for the time, before guiltily shrugging to the tribe. It's time for me to find my way back to the stifling 'burbs, even though, every day more, this ragtag city of abandoned cars, graffiti and working-class heroes feels like my true hometown. Gem gives me the sexiest pout but understands fully. "I had so much fun with you, Robbs, I can get very used to this."

"So can I, Gemma...so can I."

Running with reckless abandon through the heavily trafficked streets and making it to Gem's flat in record time, Otto goes out to give Otis a full warm-up and Lena retrieves my backpack. Yuka and Gem tackle the arduous task of detangling my now wet, knotty mess of curls in the bathtub. The colors have drained out for the most part, but I throw on a ball cap and hood for the ride home. Lord knows, after having such a fun weekend the last thing I want to deal with is my mom bitching about the tint of my hair. I toss off my punk attire and am back in my 'normal' gear. "Ugh!"

Gem gently pinches my neck, "Oh, stop it now, you're still adorable as hell..." Catching up with everyone downstairs, I give Yuka and Lena a big kiss on the cheek, Otto gives me a bear hug and I thank them again for an awesome time. "We're just getting started, bro! Motorhead on Halloween..that show is gonna' kick ass."

"I can't wait, Otto." We say our goodbyes' and our three compatriots roughhouse their way past the well-kept brick row homes and alleys of Fourth Street. Quickly disappearing from sight, Gem and I are alone, perched atop Otis' long, black hood.

"I'm going to miss you tonight, Robbs. Being with you all the time is something I can really get used to."

"Same here, girl. I could easily make this an everyday routine." Gem nuzzles into my chest and I reach under her jacket and shirt, caressing her back softly before losing ourselves in an amazing kiss. Staring into those eyes, I feel as if I've recognized that comforting gaze forever.

Reluctantly sliding behind the wheel, a Red is lit and the column shifters dropped into drive. Hopefully, Otis will not die in the middle of Fourth Street, even though part of me wishes for the occurrence of remaining stranded with my lovely, Punk Princess. The warm, sinking sun glistens over Gem's lovely auburn hair as she smiles and blows me a kiss. "I love you, Rob Cavelli. Thanks for your help with the song, it sounds fabulous. When you least expect it, I just may perform it," she radiantly replies.

"I love you too, Gemma Stinson and you're very welcome. I look forward to the day you decide to play it. I'm your number one fan, Swan. Punks for life!"

Otis lurches, chugging down the block, so to keep the old boy going, the gas pedal is punched and Siouxsie's version of 'Dear Prudence' remains cranked through the speakers when I look in the rear-view mirror to see Gem's solitary figure waving from atop Misty's stoop. "See you soon, girl…"

"Dear Prudence, let me see you smile
Dear Prudence, like a little child
The clouds will be a daisy chain
So let me see you smile again
Dear Prudence, won't you let me see you smile…"

··· 8 ···

Effin' Monday

THE RETURN HOME delivers its fair amount of contentiousness, with a mixture of well-rehearsed, theatrically dramatic angst from the matriarch. "So, we don't bother to say when we are coming home, anymore? Well, I just told your aunt again, that you and James have never cared about the strain you put on my health. I will be in the grave before you know it..."

It becomes very hard to take these proclamations seriously, especially when her doctor said for about the thousandth time that she's the healthiest dead person he's ever met, but years of well-honed Catholic, Italian-American mother guilt has earned her this vaunted reputation. Mom has been 'dying' for damn near fifteen years now, quite an amazing feat, but I've learned to endure the harrowing, painful narrative, taking it with a grain of salt.

Inquiring how her day went only amplifies the 'guilt game'. "Oh, now we want to know what I did for the almost two days you were gone. Well, I sat in the house, watching television, wondering what I've done to deserve such treatment from you and James. I went to church and asked God why Perry seems to be the only one who cares what will become of me? He is such a good soul."

I could argue my case about accomplishing a multitude of duties and tasks around here without even being asked or showing respect to a person who is insanely judgmental, massively racist and incredibly homophobic, but I've debated or sparred ad nauseam. Sometimes it's just worth saying good night, retreating to my room and slapping headphones on, becoming immersed in a variety of music. Tonight, how ironic is it to have Bad Religion's, 'How Could Hell Be Any Worse' on cue, but as much as I want to give it a listen, I have to make a special call.

The phone rings a couple of times before the sweet, sultry voice greets me. "Is it my honey, telling me that he's home?"

"Ha, ha, what if it hadn't been me on the other end?"

"I just know your ring, it has a certain tone."

"Well, that's good to know, funny girl. I just wanted to thank you again for an incredible weekend."

"It was a terrific one, Robbs, with another memory posted to my board via a ticket stub and our band flier from the other evening at The Daily Grind."

"Listen, I'm going to get a move on here, before the Inquisition starts up again."

"Oh boy, try and hang in there with her. I know she may not be the easiest person to live with, but at least you have a roof over your head, until you go away to school or get a job and move out. You don't want to live on the street, baby. I know you can hold your own, but you don't want that kind of life. No one really does."

"I get that hon, but it's enticing at times. Well, we'll save this conversation for when I meet you at school tomorrow. I love you, Gem."

"Love you so much, Robbs. Sweet dreams."

"You too, babe." Cranking my stereo, the sounds of Bad Religion envelop my ears before slowly fading into peaceful slumber.

• • •

The morning breaks with a superlative sunrise, only to be sadly overtaken by heavy cloud cover on what's developing into a chilly, gloomy October day. "Another effin' Monday," is how the Misfits deridingly refer to the first day of the week.

I pack a long bag with my hockey gear, since we have an important intramural match at the Leopards Ice Rink this afternoon. Tossing on my beat up, old Rangers cap, pulling up my hood to still conceal the ever-fading colors of my tremendous weekend, I slip into the kitchen, grab the backpack and say my goodbyes.

Mama Cavelli's still looking perturbed, continuing the martyr role to a tragically, operatic level, but I really don't have the time to psychoanalyze all of her mental maladies at the present because I have a pack full of books, a ten-ton hockey bag along with a handful of sticks in the garage waiting to be wrestled with.

Otis continues the pathetic chug and burp and with the trunk already open, the pack, bag, sticks, boombox and a truck-load of cassettes are dumped in there as well. Motivational music for the pre-game warm-ups should never be looked at askance.

Closing up shop, I spot the punk gear neatly folded in the rear corner of the Cordoba's cavernous compartment and it's got me psyched, jazzed and reflecting about the incredible girl I've enjoyed an unforgettable weekend with. Damn, I can't wait to see her today, pressing those full, wet, soft lips against mine, losing myself in her passionate kisses.

No time to waste, I've got to get Otis haulin' ass. I blaze a Red, crank up Specimen's, 'Kiss, Kiss, Bang Bang' on the stereo, slam the shifter into drive and cantankerous Otis has rolled all of ten feet, belching out a noxious plume of black, oily smoke. The painful process of being an Otis owner begins in earnest, opening the trunk to secure the rubber mallet which strikes the starter and a flat head screwdriver to jam in the butterfly valve so the carburetor obtains enough air.

Furiously emitting clouds of smoke from my nostrils, I hastily perform the ritual, cranking the ignition to the point where

Otis finally springs to life. Hustling the old bucket onto the Pennsylvania Turnpike, then through the burgeoning Route 611 morning rush insanity and within forty minutes, the campus grounds are in sight. The Dead Boys, 'Sonic Reducer' piss pounds my eardrums and I mischievously power slide Otis into an open spot by a familiar vehicle, laying on the horn until Sammi peers over, greeting me with her radiant smile.

Out of her car like a flash, she's exquisite today in tight black leggings, an oversized pink sweater, large hoop earrings and thigh high boots very similar to Gem's. Her pretty, sandy brown hair is pulled away from her face and into a bun with small spikes sticking out of it. "Wow! Check you out! Very sexy look, Sammi. I can't put a finger on it, but it's similar to another tall, gorgeous gal I know. If I didn't know better, Samantha Baird, I would say that you're trying to seduce me." She's eye to eye with me and looking so pretty, until I receive a roundhouse punch to the arm.

"Robbs, you're such a big dope. I think between getting beaned by baseballs and hockey pucks, you've totally lost brain cells. Gem showed me this look with the hair, so I bought some new gear and tried out the hairdo myself."

"Well, Gem did a good job wrapping up an already pretty package, but I do take umbrage to your earlier remark, Samms, since I have quite the stellar GPA."

Exhaling a plume of smoke from her Newp, she sighs. "Good looks, book smarts and dumb as a board when it comes to common sense."

"HEY!" And in the process of roughhousing with Sammi, she knocks my hat and hood off, revealing the rapidly fading tints.

"Oh, my God, look at all the colors Yuka put in your hair! Gem said you looked fucking incredible."

"You talked to her last night?"

"Yep, are you surprised by that? I am just a nosy gossip and your personal Cupid."

Feeling uneasy over the notion of Gem and Sammi discussing any events that transpired over the weekend, I painfully inquire, "did she tell you.... everything? I mean...well...you know."

Sammi giggles uncontrollably. "Why, Rob Cavelli, you're blushing worse than one of your hair colors and anyway, I'm not at liberty to tell you what we discussed, so you're going to have to let your vivid imagination run wild.

"She did mention what occurred in Fairmount Park though. What the hell were you thinking, babe? Those skins and her old, bastard boyfriend could have hurt you bad, Robbs. You better keep yourself safe. Do you think you can fight against all the evils that may try and hurt Gem?"

"I'll sure as hell do my best, Samms. Would you expect anything less of me?"

Sammi gets a twinkle in her eye and sighs. "No, and I told Gemma that you will fight to the death for her, as I know she would do for you."

"I know she would." Giving Sammi a playful push, I feel compelled to inquire about her earlier declaration. "So, what's with the dumb as a board comment, girlie?"

"Ooooooh…did I touch a nerve, tough guy? You know, I'm not afraid of you, Robbs." With the books, purse and keys dropped dramatically onto the blacktop, Sammi displays her best boxers' stance. "Let's rock, tough stuff."

Bobbing and weaving around her tall, nimble frame, I let her throw a few punches my way, adroitly eluding them all. A swift uppercut nearly catches me by surprise but Sammi becomes entangled in her stiletto heels, leaving open the golden opportunity to hoist her over my shoulder as she shrieks in laughter. Our unruly horseplay is only interrupted by the clicking of heels approaching, followed by a lighthearted voice. "Hey! Am I going to have to really start keeping an eye on you two?"

"We're good, Bohemian girl. Tough guy here thought he could take me on but I showed him a thing or two."

"Yep, she sure did. She showed me that she fights even shittier in heels than she does in sneakers."

"Oh piss off, Rob. I could've taken you down at any minute, you airhead!"

"All right, Rocky and Apollo, go to your neutral corners," Gem squeaks.

"It looked more like Rocky against Bullwinkle out there, Gem," I mutter after blowing smoke at Gem and Sammi's upturned noses. "Piss off, Robbs!" is their amplified refrain before flipping me the bird.

Gem's Monday wardrobe is usually kick ass and today, she's hit the knockout punch, accentuating her curves with skin tight red leggings, thigh high stilts, a tight black sweater, and her "No Future" leather jacket, adorned with concert pins and 'Reagan Sucks' buttons. Spiked bracelets and belts finish off the sexy display and the new 'do' is quite captivating, with the left eye almost completely covered by her soft, deep auburn hair, while the balance is slicked back into a bun with thin spikes sticking out, a very similar look to her Saturday masterpiece, except for streaks of black mixed in with her natural color.

The tall beauties stand next to each other and could almost be mistaken for twins which I do not hesitate to make known, much to my chagrin, for stating the obvious readily gives them the ammunition required to make me blush a second time. "Do we look hot together, Robbs? Does it make your mind just race at the thought of what could be?".

Gem sexily cuddles into Sammi, biting her earlobe, letting her tongue trace over Sammi's pursed lips, eventually giving me a devilish wink and all I can do is bury my head into cupped hands. "You two are really killing me right now. You do know I have a game to concentrate on today, correct?"

"Yes, we know, Robert," comes the giddy reply. "The big, one o'clock match against the 84' Champs, the Blazers. You're going to crush those Reagan Boy creeps today. Otto, Yuka and most of the Gulag will be there to watch the spectacle unfold."

"The Gulag...really? I figured most of the Gulag didn't give a piss about sporting events."

"They don't, but they love knowing that a punk kid likes to play hockey, and they know I'm a rabid Flyers fan, so..."

"The Flyers...UGH! It's the one unforgiveable fault you do have, Gem."

"Piss off, Robbs! What about the Rangers? Really? Your sorry ass team hasn't won a Stanley Cup in forty-five years, and honestly, you need to get rid of that scuzball, abortion of a hat."

"You just wait, babe. My Broadway Blueshirts are going to trounce your little pretty boys Peter Zezel and Derek Smith. You just wait, Gemma!"

Sammi can only grin, tapping her boot heel loudly on the pavement. "Ahem...well, if you two lovebirds are done hating each-others hockey teams for the moment, we really should be moving along to our classes."

"Oh shit, you're right, Samms, I gotta' jet over to Woodlawn. I'll see you two at one for the game."

"I wouldn't miss it for the world, Robbs. Thanks again for this weekend."

"I can't wait to do it again, Gem.."

The girls begin their onerous journey to Sunderland, hearing them laugh hysterically while miserably navigating the hilly, gravel trails in their perilous footwear. Chuckling to myself, I marvel at how Gem always manages to turn even the gloomiest day into a terrific one. It's a feeling I've never encountered before and hope it's never taken away.

··· 9 ···

The Uninvited Guest

"ROBBS, ROBBS, ROBBS, oi, oi, oi," echoes wildly through the stands, followed by the ear-splitting mayhem of Gem, Sammi and the Misfits flooding the still packed, Leopards Ice rink with a car crash mixture of air horns, bongos and cowbells. To a bunch of ragtag punk kids, the blissful dissonance is music to their ears as the boys of our blue collar, working class Blades hoist me in the air for scoring our winning goal with four seconds left in regulation and our brilliant, Canadian born goaltender is elevated soon after for keeping thirty-five shots away from the netting, preserving a 2-1 victory over the massively dejected, blue blood, yuppie Blazers.

A match between these bitter rivals amounts to a Rangers versus Flyers showdown and todays' game did not disappoint anyone in attendance, with great scoring chances by both squads, bone crushing checks and a few fisticuffs to boot, including one between myself and Jake Whitley. After our little squaring off today, I don't think Gem will hear a peep from his piehole anymore.

A good portion of our fans have overtaken the ice and with bodies crashing around her, Gem swiftly slides through the madness and the boys return me to terra firma to receive a very enjoyable celebratory kiss from my Punk Princess. "I think for today, I'll let you off the hook for being a Rangers fan, Robbs! Wow, what a game!"

I absorb the joyous occasion immensely, until witnessing a streak of long, white blonde hair racing through the crowd only pausing by the exit doors long enough to converse with a few snooty Reagan Girls she knows at the school. Continuing her vitriolic diatribe with Gatling gun precision, she stares coldly at Gem and me. I knew this day would eventually come, considering she's only a few miles down the road, but goddammit, not today, not right now! Fuck it all to hell, Giselle is here.

Gem feels my muscles tense up, the anger no longer able to be hidden. "Babe, what's the matter? Robbs, you should be so happy right now." Glancing over her shoulder, her cat-like green eyes sizzle with pure animosity. "What in the hell is that tramp doing here? Goddamn, Reagan Bitches, think they're going to start some shit with you today? It's not happening, Robbs. I'll tear that two-timer and those little prissy twats from head to toe, especially Abby Rothschild!"

"Gem, she's not worth your time. Giselle's a coward and if you get angry enough to wallop her, she'll have you arrested. Please, let me deal with this. Please…"

Stomping her heel hard into the Leopards center ice logo, Gem acquiesces. "Okay, Robbs, you're right. I'm telling you this much, though, I'll be keeping an eye on her. I don't trust her, I think she is out to hurt you and make your life miserable. If I see you get upset for even a second, I can't promise that I won't put one under her chin, or the chins' of the chickenshit, troublemaking bitches who brought her here today."

"Fair enough, Gem, I'll deal with this." Taking some time to chat with friends, the Blazers players and my teammates, while enjoying some more congratulatory handshakes and high fives along the way, I skate from the ice onto the concrete by the glass doors where she strikes an uppity stance with her trouble-making team of Stella, Carol and our nemesis, Abby Rothschild. Swallowing hard, trying in vain not to tell them all to fuck off, I feign a smile of warmth to Giselle's little clique of snot-nosed snobs. "Hello, girls, too bad about your boyfriends on the Blazers losing today, they played a damn good game though."

"Yeah, you had a nice game yourself, Rob," Stella replies while annoyingly snapping her gum like a stereotypical Jersey girl. "You know, the Blazers wanted you before you started hanging out with THAT other crowd. Oh, nice hair colors, by the way," she snorts derisively, which apparently breaks Giselle and her crew into fits of childish laughter.

"Thanks, Stel, but you should have seen how incredible it looked on the weekend. Hell, it was the talk of the Tower, Fairmount Park and South Street."

The obnoxious gum snapping goes into overdrive. "Mmmm... ya', I bet..."

"Listen girls, much as I'd like to exchange pleasantries today, I really could use a few minutes alone with Giselle, if that's possible, thank you."

Giselle gives them the nod and her minions disperse like rats off a sinking vessel to gossip with the yuppie elite. "Giselle, can we please head outside? I'd like to have a cigarette." She pushes on the door and we head out into small rays of sun trying to break through this otherwise gray day.

Even though she always fretted about, in her estimation, coming from the wrong side of the tracks, she was trying to 'valley up' her image a bit by wearing her hair in a high, Duran Duran style, and her short, frilly skirt was awash with fall colors. She wore black leggings underneath it and had on shorter black heels, making her not appear much taller than the 5'7" height she thought was quite regal, until she caught sight of Gemma's statuesque frame.

"So, to what do I owe the displeasure of this visit today," which gets her hands immediately affixed to the hips in a defensive stance. "There's no need to be so cynical, Rob. I was invited to the game by the girlfriends of the Blazers and had no idea they were playing you."

It's damn near impossible not to laugh at the infantile ridiculousness of her ways but I try my best. "So, you had no inclination that the Blades were scheduled to play them today?" Her bright blue eyes quickly lose connection with mine. "Well, at least I know that you're still a horrendously shitty liar. Remember, it's what got you into trouble this summer with me. You remember that whole scenario, the spying on me, while you're having sex with someone else? That was epic Giselle, so it looks like nothing has changed, and you are still here spying."

"Please Rob, don't flatter yourself, there are more fish in the sea than just you."

"Oh, I'm well aware of how many fish you know about, Giselle, considering that your lure was bobbing in the ocean quite a bit while it was supposedly just you and me."

"Fuck off, Rob."

"Ah, that classy attitude just comes shining through. Thought you were trying to yuppie up your act, 'Selle. A quick word to the unwise, it needs some refinement."

Ignoring the brusque comment, she gets right to the heart of the matter. "So, the taller girl in the tight punk clothes that was kissing you, that's who you've been running around with this summer? She's kind of pretty and the hair is interesting, if you're into that kind of look, I guess. What's her name?"

"Giselle, you already know her name and what she looked like way before this afternoon. The gossipy gaggle of girls who are friends at your school and mine let each other know everything."

"So, this little fling you have going on, you do realize you'll come back to me." She moves in closer, running her fingers through my hair. "All this craziness of pointy hair, colors and punk clothing, your singing down in Philly, all these people you hang out with, you realize it will come to an end sooner than later, Rob." Pushing her hand aside sternly, the steely stare I return Giselle reeks of pure contempt. "Nothing is going to end with Gem and I, unless we want it to. She understands something that you'll never grasp, Giselle, she understands love."

"Oh, give me a break, Rob, I understand love."

"No, 'Selle, you understand sex, not love. Getting laid is not love, girl. What you consider love is nothing more than animal instinct. Gemma is in love with me...mind, body and soul. That requires effort, something that you refused to give us. Now, if you could please keep your distance, Giselle. You have your life and I have mine."

"It'll never last, Rob. She's not me..."

"And I thank the goddamn heavens every day that she's not you, 'Selle. Gem's a free spirit, whereas you always overanalyze and demean everything, you yearn for wealth, whereas she understands money is the root of all evil. You don't value commitment, she embraces it. Gem cheers on my dreams and builds them up, while you consistently found ways to tear them down and be derisive. She loves me for me, 'Selle, no matter what I want to do or be. She's the only person ever to invest that kind of time into me, so please don't try and destroy what your heart cannot possibly understand."

With Giselle rendered utterly speechless, I take the advantage to reunite with a happily approaching Gem, who flips the bird to her startled, cowering nemesis, throws her arms around my neck and presses her lips to mine. Our mouths open and her warmth covers' me like a cloak. I succumb to every emotion filtering through me right now.

"I absolutely adore you, Robert Cavelli. You are my warrior! I've had enough of this petty, Barbie doll bitch trying to rain on your parade, so let's go celebrate this win.

"Oh, and Giselle, a word to the wise...keep your distance from Rob or next time you're dealing with me, tramp." Cuddling each other as we glide back into the still rowdy gym, I peer through the glass doors, no longer observing Giselle outside, but instead, the marvelous palate of fall colors swirling through the breezes allowing more sun to take over an otherwise melancholy day. Gem wraps her arms snuggly around my waist.

"Let's have some fun today, Robbs. You deserve it...we deserve it."

WE CERTAINLY DO...

••• 10 •••

The Ash Heaps

IT'S THURSDAY! ALL Hallows Eve has finally arrived, and not a moment too soon. Gem's placed calls to our tribe and everyone is psyched about seeing Motorhead at City Gardens tonight. I woke up at four this morning to get my backpack filled, grab breakfast, and say goodbye to my mother, who knows that I will not be back for the balance of the week, so needless to say, she's not enthused.

I hate having to argue that this is a part of growing up, but it's almost like I have to remind her of the fact, since it's an aspect of her life which seems to have died a long time ago. Hopefully, one day she'll understand this before it's too late.

Otis actually gives me a good morning with very few gasps or gags, so I'm able to make haste to Gem's apartment, where Yuka's crashed to work on my hair bright and early. This will be the first time anyone at school gets a full glimpse of my still rare, weekend transformations.

I'm going crazy at the thought of seeing Lemmy and Motorhead in one of my favorite places. Most people would argue, sometimes vehemently, that they are a metal band, but to me and many others, they're sound definitely has punk kick to it and we say Lemmy is a Godfather of Punk, much like Lou Reed or Iggy. Either way, it'll be one interval where all of the long-hairs and roosterheads can have a good time in the same venue.

Now, City Gardens is a place unto itself. It's the equivalent of a cement warehouse dropped in the heart of Calhoun Street, Trenton, New Jersey. The name, City Gardens, has to be a play on words because there wasn't a tree, shrub or flower within a motherfucking block of this tomb.

If Calhoun Street was ever a pleasant place to live or work, it would have only been depicted that way in old photographs but as of right now, it's very endemic of what's going on in every city along the Northeast corridor of the United States. Thanks to the horrendous policies of Reagan and his ilk, all of the good man-ufacturing jobs were either moving to the cheap wage South, or even further down the map into Mexico and the rest of Central America. All that was left behind was horrendous poverty, hor-rific crime, a drug epidemic second to none, and burnt out shells where factories or homes once proudly stood.

Enter City Gardens into this uncontrolled chaos. Roosterheads in the projects sounds fucking insane, but it's a perfect fit. The punk movement gained traction during the end of Carter's Presidency and has exploded during our current President's, jingoistic, "everything is ok white suburbia, America; just avert your eyes from the cities burning down around you," run in office.

By enlarge, the punks I know despise Reagan and his ilk, and the punk movement has given clubs like City Gardens a great place for us to catch some great acts, have some fun, but also vent out some frustration about the bullshit we see going on around America. As far as we're concerned, the Anti-War hippies were now the Wall Street pariahs they'd said to never trust when they were young. Fucking sellouts...

The inside of the Gardens was not anymore pleasing than its exterior. The walls are painted black, half of them were tagged with graffiti, and you'd rather drain your kidneys behind the place than actually do it in their bathrooms. In other words, it was an awesome place to be.

It's also the best place to stage dive, in my opinion, so you can really hurl yourself into the crowd and they'll send you for an unforgettable ride. Randy Now, the club's promoter, is always on the PA yelling "NO STAGE DIVING!" The last time Black Flag was here, he got pretty pissed at me and Otto for launching ourselves right past Henry Rollins. I have been tame about going into orbit from the stage since then, out of respect for Randy. He's a pretty cool guy, but Motorhead is coming tonight, so sorry Randy, but I'm taking to the stage, running past Lemmy, going airborne and happily landing in City Gardens mosh pit. You can pitch me out of the club for a week, but I AM doing this. Sometimes, as Gem says, you just have to be golden and glorious.

Avoiding the city's rush hour traffic is great, booking right down Fourth Street, parking directly behind Gem's SS. It's a gloomy morning, but a ray of sunshine is waiting for me on the stoop and she looks gorgeous for tonight's' event, wearing black leggings so tight, they appear painted on, combat boots with bandannas tied around both of them; one orange, the other black, a Motorhead t-shirt, with a long-sleeved purple tee underneath. The 'No Future' leather is draped across the steps and a Newp is rapidly procured from its pocket.

The hair is similar to the way she wore it on Monday at the hockey game, but a temporary dye makes it jet black with orange streaks through it and sporting black lip gloss makes her look vampiress sexy. "Hello, Punk Queen of the Damned. Girl, you look good enough to eat."

Her warm breath tickles my neck and the senses are in overdrive but they tragically must come to a crashing halt when the front door opens and a familiar, admonishing tone travels down the stairs. "Hey young man, we don't have any time for that frisky stuff! I have a job to do." Gem snags my keys and skips to the car for my gear after Yuka, who's decked out appropriately in combat boots, shredded jeans splattered with orange and black paint, donning her 'Nazi Punks..Fuck Off' leather jacket, in homage to her favorite group, The Dead Kennedy's, gives me a warm kiss on the lips, twirls my hair between her fingers and seductively nibbles my earlobes. This is way more sensual overload than any eighteen-year-old, hot blooded guy should have to endure this early in the morning and both of these demonic, night crawlers of the damned know it.

Hauling ass into the flat, Misty is up, greeting me with a hot cup of tea, along with an ashtray and a warm, motherly smile. She's a very dear lady to put up with all the Misfits hijinks but will readily admit that our chaos and subversive political talk keeps her young. "Thanks, Misty, you're a doll for letting me do this here."

"You're welcome, Rob. Oh, you'd better get a move on," she chuckles, pointing towards Yuka, who is already standing by the chair tapping her foot.

"I think I'd better, Misty. Never keep the artist who's doing your hair waiting."

"You've got that right, mister, now get hoppin' to Gem's room and get changed already."

"Yes, boss...I'll get a move on." I grab my gear, shuffle past her and playfully goose Yuka's bottom before she shrieks, picking up a roll of paper towels to hurl in my direction but I laugh manically, slamming the door shut before it harpoons me.

Setting out the gear, I hurriedly throw on a long black tee, a Motorhead short sleeve over top and a torn pair of jeans with different sized ace of spades, spray painted in black and placed in various spots on the garment, and throw my other tattered leather on Gem's chair, which has an Exploited skull painted in white on the back with the words 'Dead Cities' written below it, and I just recently added some silver, ace of spades on both sleeves.

Hustling back out, Yuka starts surveying her newest artwork-to-be. "I was thinking of a Halloween theme, but that'll be too commonplace tonight, so we're going with a Brit theme to celebrate Motorhead's coming to City Gardens. Sit tight... you're in for a helluva ride again, baby boy." She gives me a peck on the cheek before she and Gem are off to the races. A lot of smoking, giggling and bedlam ensue over the next few hours. 'Liquid Cement', red and blue mix for the colors and more little cocktail flags to twist into the tips of my Liberty Spikes…Union Jacks for Christ's sake. When the wraps are off and cleaned, Gem and Yuka take turns getting pictures with me while Misty gets one of me and the artists' extraordinaire.

Finally getting a chance to throw on my combat boots, Gem gives me red and blue bandannas to tie around the tops. Misty thanks us for being such animated company this morning and for organizing the flat back to its pristine condition. Otis, in all of its sputtering, farting cacophony awaits us, so we haul ass outta' Philly since there's still classes to get through today. Gem nuzzles up against me on the bench seat and happily leaves off from Yuka's earlier seduction, nibbling ferociously on my ear-lobes. Yuka, who looks thoroughly exhausted, takes up residence across the back seat, falling into peaceful somnolence on the ride to campus.

Gem goes through my mix of cassettes, beginning our venture with Bauhaus', 'Bela Lugosi is Dead'. We stop off at the Wawa to buy smokes and coffee as we get closer to campus since the vending company owning the machines at the Student Union figured out our half-priced smokes scheme when the change box was damn near empty but all the cigarettes were gone. Word of a good thing travels fast, so they unplugged the machine, leaving the Bohemian student population to fend for themselves. Capitalism in all of its greed and ingloriousness fucking wins again.

The enjoyable sojourn culminates with us swinging wildly into the campus lot, listening to our Philly punk act and friends, The Dead Milkmen, who always have us in stitches with their songs, so 'Bitchin' Camaro' is no exception, especially when Gem is in the crowd for a show and they dedicate it to her and the 69', silver SS, so she loves the song for obvious reasons…

"Bitchin' Camaro, bitchin' Camaro,
Donuts on your lawn,
Bitchin' Camaro, bitchin' Camaro

Tony Orlando and Dawn

When I drive past the kids,
They all spit and cuss,
Cause I've got a bitchin' Camaro
And they have to ride the bus..."

Stoked from the music, still laughing and singing our fool heads off, I'm amped to survey the reactions since this will be my punk debut at our college and already, I can see there are mixed reviews from some bewildered onlookers. Most of the kids I know come up are just wowed and readily accept the fliers we hand out about an upcoming anti-nuke rally the Socialist Union will be having at Philly's, Love Park, but the Reagan kids are keeping their distance. I guess their yuppie value system has truly been offended and the Student Government drones in their ranks are still pissed to no end at the spray painting of walls galore by our Socialist offices and the fact that I threw it in their face, pleading guilty for whatever 'crimes' they feel are deserving of punishment.

The 'prim and proper' girls of the group just stand with their mouths open and the guys walk away shaking their heads. Oh well, you're not going to make everyone happy all the time but my attitude towards them lately has been more of a 'go fuck yourself, sod off' one anyway, especially since the Giselle incident.

Gem and Yuka laugh joyously at the reaction their Punk Prince has received already, so they pull me into the Union for a minute. Pointing out that we still have a few classes at Sunderland to attend, Gem playfully raises her index finger.

"We have to wait for someone who'll be coming with us tonight. If you think the reaction you got was interesting, wait until they get a glimpse of our newest creation." Gem torches a Newport, smiling brightly when the glass doors of the Union open to reveal Yuka Yamaguchi's and Gemma Stinson's newest protégé. The sassy, sexy statuesque figure approaches in spray painted combat boots, tight orange leggings and a studded leather jacket looking suspiciously familiar to the one a certain, beaming girl standing next to me owns. Her hair is done exactly like Gem's, right down to the colors, except her right eye is covered.

Gasping at an equal volume, we can't remark on the others appearance quickly enough. "Holy shit, Robbs. You look bitchin'! My God, look at the colors and the flags. Yuka, you are an artist."

Yuka playfully bows in appreciation, nudging me to say something about our newest Misfit. "When in the hell did you do all of this? I can't believe you are dressed like this, right down to the black lip gloss. The Misfit girls transformed you into a night creature, Sammi Baird and I love it."

"Well, I wouldn't have been able to pull this off, except for Yuka and Gem inviting me over to the apartment last night, cuz' they got me all tribal punked out."

I glance over to see the two culprits sporting devious grins. "So, that's what you two were up to when I called and heard all that giggling. I figured it was Lena."

"Oh, she was there too. We were all having a good time, and then Misty started telling us about her hippie days. What a hoot she was as a college gal'! It was a real fun girl's night at the apartment."

"I bet it was Gem, but admittedly I'm curious as to how the new look was dealt with at the Baird household." Samms takes a drag from her cig and smirks. "They were more receptive than I thought they'd be but they did request not to make it an everyday thing, and I said that was fine."

It's shaping up to be a terrific day but our morning objective still must be dealt with and I tell the girls it would be my pleasure escorting them to their classes, so they happily accept. Yuka and Sammi depart to Anthropology, Princess Gem strolls casually with me to our Literature lecture.

We grab seats in the back, away from everyone as our Professor speaks of Fitzgerald's, 'Gatsby'. The great, epic failure of Jay and Daisy rolls out through clouded thoughts and a life full of secrets, tragedies, yearnings and passions, never to materialize, but painfully documented by Nick Carraway. Gem's radiant green eyes meet mine, instantaneously I succumb to their spell. Her smile has me trapped as well, those beautiful, wet lips just yearning to be kissed.

Unlike Gatsby, I have already won the heart of the girl…or have I? There are so many complexities about Gem and I'm only starting to peel away some of the understandable layers she's put between herself and the ones around her, even though she's confided on a few occasions that the trust level between us is something she's never experienced with anyone else.

With her head resting comfortably on my shoulder, I feel a warm, trickling fluid between our tightly wound fingers. Gemma Stinson, my Punk Princess, hard as nails, who learned early as I did, not to cry, not make anyone know how much pain was inflicted mentally or physically, has done something that no other has ever been able to experience. She's given me her true self, her emotions laid bare for only me to see. "Promise me, we will never be like Jay and Daisy…promise me there will be no secrets." The sweet whisper, like a warm summer breeze rushing around me continues. "Promise me that we'll not end tragically…promise that it will be you and me in the end…that I will wake up in your arms and you'll shower me with kisses every day. Tell me that day will come." I feel another tear trickle between our fingers, followed by another. She's managed to break down my barriers as well and I wipe my cheek.

For the first time in years, I have let myself truly feel…not afraid anymore to wear my heart on my sleeve. The young child with the smile on his face, but the aching, sorrowful eyes, was no longer a prisoner to his thoughts. The dam had burst open with furious scribblings of verses on papers, wrongs to be righted in newspaper articles or on political fliers, songs and stories to finally be told. The young boy, who was beaten and left in a dark closet to cower, now the young man who embraced the dark with no fear, relishing and embracing the shadows of night as much as the warm rays of sun to follow.

"Promise me, you'll never break my heart, Robbs. Love me forever." Wiping away another tear, I place my mouth next to her ear, breathing warmly…"You have my heart, Gem. You are mine…always…always…always…"

● ● ●

After emotionally expressing our innermost thoughts and feelings, the day progresses rapidly. Our classes are at an end for the day, so we scamper down the pathways with Yuka, Otto and Sammi in tow.

Otis putters to warm up, so the tribe share some laughs and smokes. The excitement is building up to have a bitchin' bit of anarchy at City Gardens tonight so it's high time to give Sammi a quick rundown of what to expect, since this will definitely be culture shock for her. Rowdy crowds are the norm at a City Gardens event but the majority of the people going to shows there on a regular basis get along just fine, with the only negative elements under a watchful eye being certain skins. If you get mostly Trenton skins, they are ok since we all mingle at the shows but if their locale boasts from Allentown and Reading, watch yourself…things could get volatile, especially if they are skins indoctrinated into the true Nazi belief system. They are pure pricks and can make the evening go to hell very rapidly.

We tell Sammi not to worry though, since Oren, Dusty, Lena and Steph will be meeting us there, providing her with a lot of protection and muscle if the shit hits the fan. The norms, the yuppie Reagan Kids, the Mods and the old timers may deride us, denigrating our appearance, ways and music in a multitude of unflattering terms, but there is one thing they can never take away from us, an unwavering loyalty to our tribe of Misfits. If anyone is senseless enough to mess with us, we have no problem giving it back as good as we get.

Giving Otis some gas, the old tin can rumbles and belches to a complete stop in the middle of the parking lot. Undeterred, I hop out, lifting up the Cordoba's hood, while Otto grabs the rubber mallet and begins pounding the starter box. Gem loosens the wingnut on the filter cover and immediately jams the flathead screwdriver into the butterfly valve. Sammi hops behind the wheel, readying herself to crank the starter and Yuka comes around from the trunk with a funnel and a can of motor oil. "It sounded like your valves were tapping a little, Robbs. Better safe than sorry, isn't that right baby boy?" Otto is the man, but the Misfit ladies are in a class unto themselves.

"Okay, Samms, prime the engine and let her rip," Gem commands. Otis coughs out a blackish, gray cloud from his tailpipe and hacks back to life and after Yuka finishes filling the oil reservoir, the valve tapping slowly dissipates. Gem pulls the screwdriver out of the butterfly valve, tightens the filter cover and slams down the heavy hood. Otto and Yuka tumble into the back seat, with Sammi sliding over to make room for Gem and me on the bench seat.

"Yo, Sammi honey, you can sit back here with us."

"Thanks, but you looked so tired Yuka. You guys stretch out...relax."

"We're fine up here with Sammi, sis. I'll be right next to Robbs, anyway, so siesta, young lovers." Gem grabs a cassette from her bag, happily loading it into the tape player. "And... a little mix of Gem's music to get us ready for tonight, Misfits." With shitbomb, rustbucket Otis moving, she cranks up the volume and we're on our way to Trenton with Lemmy performing his inimitable, sandpaper throated growl on the 'Ace of Spades'.

The tunes roll along through the knotted up, rush hour traffic and the plan is to start taking some back roads into Bucks County shortly. Checking the rear-view mirror, Yuka and Otto are already gassed and sprawled out...Gem's wrapped around my arm but keeping up a very animated conversation with Sammi, who you can tell is a bundle of nervous energy about tonight's show. This is totally foreign to Samms, so Gem just keeps telling her to follow our lead. The stereo speakers' strain under the blasts of Husker Du's remake of the Byrds classic, 'Eight Miles High' before Gem's mix shoots right into Animal's vociferous diatribe on Anti-Nowhere League's, 'So What?' and 'I Hate People'...

"People ride about all day
In metal boxes made away
I wish that they would drop the bomb
And kill the pigs that don't belong

I hate people
I hate the human race
I hate people
I hate your ugly face
I hate people
I hate your fucking mess
I hate people
They hate me...."

Traffic thins out slightly, but the town of Bensalem is still too built up for my liking since the bucolic, rolling farmlands have all been plowed under to be surreptitiously replaced by obnoxiously, endomorphic shopping malls or the mini-mansions of yuppie, white-flight Wall Street expatriates from New York and Philadelphia, causing the roads to become congested with an overflow of vehicles.

Barreling Otis further along Route 13, we pass the simple, two story, asbestos shingled or aluminum sided, working class homes of Croydon and Levittown, which was mainly built for the thousands of mill workers who came to toil in U.S. Steel's mammoth Fairless Works.

With a few thousand workers laid off in the past few years, the town's showing its age, with overgrown yards, paint peeling on structures and blue tarps spread out over leaky, unfixed roofs, the main shopping center was all but boarded up, and there's always news or rumors about shutdowns of certain operations, with more layoffs to come.

The well-to-do WASP's on the other side of Route's 1 and 13 have never accepted the influx of blue collar, union workers, or the large numbered, 'ethnic', European Catholic families into their backyard and never hide their feelings over wishing for the mill's demise.

I always viewed the WASP's as such short-sighted fools, because once these hard-working union toughs had nowhere to go and there were no jobs to be had, their plight would soon become everyone's nightmare with more social ills foisted onto the community as a whole.

Besides, as true capitalists in their thought process, you'd think the WASP set would totally understand the driving mechanism to a healthy economy is a well-paid working class consuming everything in its path, which is exactly what the mill workers had accomplished for the past few decades since they were vaunted into the ranks of the middle class, but I can only fathom that snobbery and avarice trumps common sense…'I got mine…fuck it if you don't have yours.' The rugged individualist Reagan has brainwashed people into believing they really are is tearing the country apart even more, but nobody seems to notice or care, as long as they have their central air conditioning, TV dinners and cable TV to rot their brains.

Iggy strains out 'The Passenger' as I shoot off 13, slowing to a crawl through Tullytown Borough's old, weathered clapboard mansions and smaller residences approaching the man-made, twin lakes on Bordentown Road. The lakes take on the creepy appearance of a Hollywood, B-movie horror set shrouded in a constant mist, and on this Halloween evening it is no different. Those not familiar with the area always ask why this strange phenomenon exists, but we locals know better. The 'fog' is created by the ongoing polluting from the mighty Fairless, which sprawls out in its maddening, deafening glory, dead ahead. Sammi, who seems to be drained by all the excitement has fallen asleep on Gem's shoulder, only slightly stirring when Gem occasionally caresses her head.

The eerie orange-red glow from the multitude of stacks illuminates the sky ahead of us as the rust orange façade of the open hearths and phallic shaped enclosures of the blast furnaces churn out massive pools of molten metal creating the arsenal of American democracy and capitalism. The ground rumbles underneath our feet and the hum from massive power lines snaps like a whip through the air when we near the plants rear entrance.

Everyone in the car is stirring from the clamor, so I eagerly await their reactions. "Jesus Christ, did you drive us to gates of hell," Otto blurts out while Sammi and Yuka absorb the calamitous hum and bustle of activity, as does Gem. This is only a fraction of the colossal plant but the noise level is incredibly impressive to people who've never witnessed such harnessed power and somewhat, controlled chaos.

Gem smirks wryly, exhaling her Newp. "No Otto, this is Robbs future, if college doesn't work out. Isn't that right, baby boy?"

I know she's trying to get everyone riled up to the fact that I've inexplicably deliberated ditching college, vaulting instead towards the ideal of making a good and steady paycheck, but I allow for the remarks deflection. "I just wanted you to see the mill in all of its glory, tribe, since its macabre appearance would be appropriate on the night of ghouls and goblins." I give Gem a kiss as I put my lips near her ear. "It really is the only reason I brought them this way. I thought it would be neat for every-one to witness the nighttime eeriness. It is awesome in its own right." The Misfits decide to deliriously cling onto the chain link fence, viewing the 'Mighty Steel', becoming engrossed in its overwhelming ability to transform the pitch black of night into day but Gem hops up on Otis' hood with me, her eyes widening to the incomprehensible spectacle of mass and mayhem from behind the gates. Hastily peering down, she takes another drag, keeping purely focused on the gravel underfoot, a modern-day Daisy averting the ash heaps. "You are thinking about leaving college, aren't you? It's not really what you want right now, is it?"

Smiling because of Gem's incredible thoughtfulness, I gen-tly lift her chin so our eyes can meet. "Gem, I'm doing well in school, but it's true. There are so many other things I want to do. I want to start making money, get out on my own, to keep writ-ing lyrics, maybe even have us start a full band…hell, maybe I'll even write a novel. There's so much going on in my head. Part of the reason I feel alive like this is because of you."

"Listen, I'm in a whirlwind period of my life now too. There's so much I think of doing, and I want so many of them to be with you, Rob."

"Just be patient with me, Gem. I really have to think things over. If I leave school, I'm only doing it long enough to get my life straightened out. I'll figure out what I want to do about furthering school only after that happens. For right now, I want to get through this semester and focus on you as well. Wherever you decide to go, whatever you decide to do, I will support your decision and I'll figure out a way to always be in your life, if that's what you want."

The reddish glow of the night sky highlights the fire in her eyes, as she touches my face. "Baby, you will be in my life, no matter what happens. I just need to get college figured out. It will be my only way never to go back to a life on the street." I kiss her lips softly, feeling her tremble in my arms. "I want this for us, baby boy. I want you to be a part of my soul forever..to complete how I feel, Robbs."

"I want this too, Gem."

"No regrets, love?"

"What, regret us meeting, getting to know each other, falling in love with you, no way, Swan, no regrets, whatsoever." We look to the fence line separating the average person from the harsh realities of what takes place in these foreboding cathedrals of industrial might. Our friends stare in awe at the fury of flames and molten metal being poured into torpedo carts, while a loco-motive waits to pull them from the bowels of Hades fortress, the blast furnace. Gem and I approach, witnessing firsthand their childlike expressions of amazement until the devil's playground unleashes a torrent of underground reverberations as explosions roar in the distance.

Everybody jumps or flinches and I laugh, remembering all these sounds touring the mill with my friends, whose dad's toiled mercilessly in the open hearth. "Jesus Christ, what in the fuck was that, Rob?"

"That Otto, is the tap hole being dynamited in the open hearth, which is the building belching the orange haze into the sky. Once that happens, they have a process called tapping the furnace and about 100 tons of steel or more gets poured through a trough, the excess slag or impurities are skimmed away and the steelmaking process is on its way when they cast the molten metal into ingots."

"Jesus mate, you really not scared about working in a place like that?"

"No, not at all. I'd actually find it peaceful, in its own weird way." I happily point out the other massive buildings and points of reference on the sprawling property like the now shuttered coke works, the docks, the rolling, sheet and tin divisions where the cooled off metal is actually rolled and formed into everything from automobiles, appliances, decking for bridges or skyscrapers, to a multitude of other products.

Sammi tosses her cig into the gravel and shakes her head. "Cutie, your and my idea of peaceful differs massively," a wry statement that has everyone laughing, until headlights followed by a blinding searchlight pierce through the mist, coming to rest on our figures. The thick, steel sound of truck doors echo into the eerie, orange night sky while smaller flashes of light now surround us. I look in between the beams of light to see a familiar uniform of plant security for the steel mill approaching and when the one guard lowers his torch, I break into a giant grin when the barrel-chested frame and bushy mustache give him away in an instant.

"Okay, smiley...you and your friends have to take your Halloween act somewhere else!" he bellows authoritatively. "This is steel mill property, you know. It's kinda' dangerous to be out here."

"Hello, Mister Madison..."

"Hey, how do you know me, kid?" Shining his torch in my face, he begins to chuckle. "Robert Cavelli, is that you? What in sweet Jesus do you look like that for or your friends for that matter? Aren't you kids a little old for trick or treat tonight," and the Misfits can't help but laugh at Mister Madison's quizzical expression or his comment.

"I dress like this sometimes, Mister Madison. We're going to see a punk concert at City Gardens in Trenton." He pulls a Camel from his pocket and I hastily furnish him my Zippo. "Thanks, son. So, that's what you're into these days, Robert? God bless you, 'cause that music is too loud for me, but then again, my Mom and Dad couldn't stand my music either. Are you still in college, boy?"

"Yes sir, I am."

"That's good to know. Not planning on coming here, are you, 'cuz things have been rough lately. I'm trying to tell Adam to enroll in college and get the hell out of here. They just laid him off last week, so maybe this'll be a wakeup call for him. Damn Jap steel and all these Reagan robber barons are killin' us!"

I inform the tribe that Mister Madison's son, Adam, was in my graduating class, and we were teammates in quite a few sports as well. "Wow, that sucks about the layoff. I should really give him a call soon."

"I'll let him know that I saw you and good Lord, wait until he hears about this get-up you're in and your hair! He'll never believe it!" He chuckles, taking another drag of his Camel.

I introduce him to the Misfits and they all exchange pleasantries. "Listen kids, you have a very good friend here, in Robert. He stuck with my boy through some tough times at school, when a lot of his other so-called friends left him blowing in the wind.

"So, a punk concert at City Gardens in Trenton? Calhoun Street? Whew, it's getting tougher over there every day! You boys better take care of these pretty young ladies tonight. Ahhh, what am I saying, if you're a friend of Robert's he'll fight tooth and nail for ya'. Still, all in all, be careful."

"We will, sir." I go to shake his hand but receive a strong hug from the bear of a man. "I'll never forget what you did for my boy, Robert. If you ever need anything...ANYTHING... you just let me know. Don't be a stranger, you hear me?"

"I hear you, Mister Madison and I promise to keep in touch." He retreats to the patrol vehicle along with the other security officer, vanishing like apparitions into the haze of Vulcan's workshop. We continue watching the outlines of steelworkers toiling in the blazing torrents of molten metal and Gem leans on the fence, gripping my hand tightly. "If you don't mind me asking, what was it that you did for his son, Robbs, that he's so grateful?"

"There were some jock asswipes harassing him in school, because there was talk going around that Adam was gay. It was getting pretty nasty and a lot of his other friends basically ditched him or joined in the nastiness. All I did was stick up for him and that I'd crack them if they kept their shit up. I would never care if Adam was gay or not, it had no bearing on our friendship. I came from a very bigoted family, my mom is ultra-religious, so she always had nasty things to say about gay people. I grew up with all those beliefs as well, not realizing how ludicrous they really were until Adam.

"I decided life's too short to miss out on all the people that I was avoiding with my ridiculous thought process, so there was never any hesitation about sticking up for him after I came to terms with not wanting to be so close minded, Gem.

"Hell, if I'd stayed in that frame of mind, I'd have never talked to any of you and what an incredible tribe I would have missed out on.

"Listen, I was definitely one of those jerk-off's early on in high school who turned a blind eye to a lot of bullshit taking place in and out of school and regretted immensely that I didn't speak up. I was worried at times that my so-called credibility would take a hit, but in my last few years there, I changed for the better, tried to raise my voice against injustices…credibility be damned."

Gem quickly kisses my cheek. "You never cease to amaze me, Robbs. You are my Renaissance Man." Holding Gem's hand, we leave the sparkling spectacle of mass and might, returning happily to Otis. Everybody else jumps in, taking turns thanking me for making an impromptu tour of a venue the Misfits may never see again.

Otto seems to have enjoyed it the most. "I think I understand why you love it so much, Robbs. The raging fires, the rumble, the hum, the violent, screeching sounds of molten metal being made into something…it sounds punk. I totally get it, man."

"That's so true, Otto. The primal energy of punk has so many similarities to the raw, brutal, primitive feel of industries like steelmaking. Think about this, guys, the punk and labor movements have similarities as well. They cut against the grain, stand against the norm, and have a certain sense of anarchy within their ranks. Hell, think of the Molly Maguires sending coffin notices to the robber baron mine owners or blowing up the Pinkerton's."

"Right you are, love," Gem adds. "The union workers in there have fought against the norm for years. They were willing to lose everything, including their lives to stand up against the status quo." Gemma Stinson's in her element, holding sway on this fanfare for the common man. "Think of the 'Grapes of Wrath' and Tom Joad's awakening to the injustices going on around him. Look at John L. Lewis, Chavez, Lech Walesa standing up to the Supreme Soviet and martial law in Poland. The Solidarity movement has embarrassed the Soviets. All these Movements are truly Bohemian…punk to me."

No longer afraid to avert the ash heaps, Gem holds up her cigarette as Otis lurches past the enormity of Fairless. "Here's to the Bohemian life, Solidarity…all those brave trade union-ists in that steel plant, confronting the dangers and rebelliously standing up to their corporate enslavers. They are the true punk rockers."

"I agree Gem, so here's to them. Solidarity, the Bohemian life, and the punks! PISS OFF, SOD OFF, TO ALL OF YOU CORPORATE FAT CATS!"

"You said it, Robbs!" Gem fast forwards her cassette to The Exploited singing 'Dead Cities' upon crossing the magnificent architecture of the turn of the century, Calhoun Street Bridge. The bridge has two precariously narrow lanes, but the danger of feeling like you are only inches away from being ominously pitched into the chilly, murky depths of the Delaware River below, strangely adds to its charm.

Otis continues his death wobble over the water and except for our newbie, Sammi, we all blurt out the lines of the song with The Exploited's front man, Wattie, if for no other reason than to release some pent-up energy.

"See the man in the electric chair
They beat him up and shave his hair
There is no future to behold

In the city of dead you'll be there

Dead cities, dead cities
Dead cities, dead cities..."

Otis shakes back and forth with ferocity and a mini mosh pit has erupted inside. Our howls of anarchy can be heard filtering through the many vacant, red brick homes and burnt out shells of the shuttered businesses lining Calhoun Street. New Jersey's capitol city has fallen on some excruciatingly hard times, but there's still a place to party, dance, slam, mosh and raise hell in its confines. It's called City Gardens and Otis screeches and smokes towards it with reckless abandon.

••• 11 •••

Into the Abyss

THE PUNK AND metal worlds' have converged onto this small plot of earth in the bowels of the capitol city, making City Gardens buzz with hyper activity. The glow of headlights, low rumblings of engines and static energy of the crowd bring a well needed liveliness to the grim, trash strewn lots and urban decay sadly swallowing up the balance of Calhoun Street. Otis' hood is a great vantage point to take in the human freak show that is all of us tonight. We've met roosters and bangers from New York City, Philly, different parts of Jersey, even Baltimore and D.C.

Oren, Lena, Dusty and Steph have found us easily enough in the throngs amassing and brought young Skate and Tim along to witness the insanity of tonight firsthand. Gem cranks up 'The Ace of Spades', initiating an uncontrolled mosh on the gravel lot. Some of the D.C. and Baltimore tribes join in, the local bangers' start tossing beer bottles through the night sky in a mock celebration of the impending anarchy and when the crowds' mass in volume, the mood stays lively and enjoyable for the moment, although the bouncers have come out to keep a wary eye on the growing numbers of chaos punks congregating on the perimeters.

Dusty, Oren and I lift the girls onto Otis' hood for some refuge, but they begin dancing and swaying to the hard charging beats before Gem and Lena jump off and into the fray, tossing some of the Philly tribes around for good measure. A few of the Trenton boys jump in to roll us all hard, amounting to some good, clean payback for a stomping they received from us at a recent Dead Kennedy's/Butthole Surfers show.

Trent, one of those boys, who happens to have a boxers' frame and a few breaks in his twisted nose to prove it, heaves me into Otis' chrome bumper, dropping my ass like a ton of bricks. Crowing like a rooster, he peels me from the gravel, pats my back and rubs his scarred knuckles. "Damn son, I know you didn't crumble like that with Kellin in Philly last week!"

"How the hell did YOU know about that?"

"Shit son, I got ears everywhere in Philly. My phone was ringing off the hook the next afternoon, with everybody talking about some kid hanging out with Gemma Stinson put a massive ass thumping on Titus in Fairmount Park. Fuckin' knew it was you, soon as I heard you left him a bloody mess, son. Gemma's a great girl, Rob, she's worth protecting."

"She sure is, Trent." The exuberance of our moshing seems to have invited some unwanted attention from inside the building. "Yo, we better calm these boys down, 'cause look who's coming outside."

"Oh shit! Here comes Randy!" Club promoter Randy Now approaches quickly, looking like he's about to have a massive, hemorrhaging shit fit. Trent grabs a couple of his tribesmen, and I grab Dusty, Oren and Otto to quell the wildness of the crowd down a notch or two. Randy doesn't look any happier once the dust has settled and the former postman sticks his finger towards both of us in a demonstrative, father scolding his kids' type of way.

"REALLY...YOU TWO? Look, I get that you're having a good time out here, but for Christ's sake, a hundred people moshing and brawling in the gravel is not what I need right now!" Trent tries to relax Randy's frayed nerves. "Randy, the boys are just letting off some steam, trying to have some fun. We've got it under control now, son."

I chime in, attempting to take the heat off of Trent since they've have had a strained relationship as of late. "Look Randy, I had the girls turn the music up to get everyone in the mood for the show tonight. If we got carried away, it was my fault, man. I fucked up." Randy accepts the apology, but still appears aggravated.

"It's ok, guys...it's just that we're having trouble with the band. I don't even know if we're having a show tonight," a response leaving Trent spitting his mouthful of Bud skyward. "Yo, what the fuck, Randy?! That's some bogus bullshit! You got people out here from NYC, Baltimore and even D.C.! What the fuck're they supposed to do if they cancel, son? They 'sposed to just go home?"

"You don't think I know that already, Trent? Listen, I need you to not say a thing. I'll know soon enough. Just keep every-body calm, ok?" We agree to say nothing but it still pisses us off that this event may not occur. We've been waiting to tear ass in the Gardens for weeks!

Hopping dejectedly onto Otis' hood with Gem, she shoots me a sarcastic, sly grin. "Getting into trouble with Randy again, babe?" I peck her cheek, snarfing a fresh Red from the pack to share. "Don't say anything, but we may have to ditch tonight. Randy said they're having trouble with Motorhead and they may not play."

"That sucks, Robbs. People have been waiting for this show to happen for a long time."

"Well, I guess we'll find out soon enough because here comes the staff and they don't look particularly happy." Randy jumps onto a motor home that was already in the lot, dolefully inform-ing people that Motorhead has cancelled their appearance. Word swirls through the crowd rapidly that the band was not happy with the accommodations. What the FUCK, Lemmy? This is hardscrabble Trenton, City Gardens for shit's sake, not Madison Square Garden! Projectiles become launched in every direction like a missile strike gone awry, a smattering of derisive catcalls resonates through the crisp, evening air, but it was out of Randy's hands.

He always tries his hardest to give us kids a good show, so I can't see this cancellation being anything that's his fault. The City Gardens staff refunds our tickets and that fast our Halloween night's shot in the ass. Dusty rolls his scarred, squeaking Ford Grenada across the lot, parking it next to Otis. "Piss off, what the fuck are we going to do, guys? Halloween's in the crapper now."

"Yo, you got that right, Dusty. This fuckin' sucks," Skate replies dejectedly as he and Tim kick beer bottles to and fro.

I flick the spent Red into the gravel and try to dissuade the Misfits from totally giving up. "Just chill for a minute, Skate, there's gotta' be something going on to salvage this night."

"There is something," replies a meek voice from behind our cars. Florian McDonnell, a thin, scrappy runt of a punk from Trenton typically appears out of nowhere at almost any City Gardens function we attend, so tonight's no exception. "Gather around guys, I think you might like this idea." We encircle him as he pulls out a band flier and immediately let out war whoops and tribal screams that shake the heavens above.

"Are you for real, Flor? This is just sick...pure fuckin' crust man," Dust blurts out.

The flier reads like a Who's–Who of hardcore acts...

Mammoth
Nevermore
Ultra-Violence
Psychos
Reagan Youth
Murphy's Law
Cause for Alarm
And headlining...The Cro Mags
AT CBGB'S!

The Zippo's orange-yellow flame lands under another Red before huddling up the boys for a brainstorming session. "Listen, this would be a fuckin' brill' night but we have to make sure a particular girl understands what kind of crowd this is gonna' be. Sammi's never been to a show before, so it will be like tossing Christians to the lions for her."

"Fair enough, bro', we'll talk to them right now."

"We have to do it soon, Dusty, cuz' Jersey Transit will be leaving in under an hour. We don't catch it, we miss the last acts," Florian adds.

Spilling our narrative about how hardcore the night may be, Sammi seems psyched about the change of events before Gem grins and hugs our newbie Punk Vixen. "Don't worry Samms, you will have a ton of bodyguards tonight. We'll be like a fortress around you. Hell, Oren is a fortress on his own."

Gem yanks on his massive forearm and her eyes widen to the size of silver dollars when he hoists her off the ground like a rag doll. "That's right, love, old Oren here will take care of em'!" The big man grins, snatching Sammi up for good measure, which immediately amps up the tribe in anticipation of the night possibly being salvaged. Florian tries not to be too much of a killjoy but points towards his wristwatch. He's absolutely right, we have to haul ass.

"All right, so we're all good on this? Flor, jump in with us. Dust, follow me over to the train station. We gotta' get booking, brother."

"Yo, Rob, I'll be right behind you, just keep that motherfuckin' Otis moving!"

With Otis miraculously starting up in a flash, everybody's in the car and psyched about the prospects of a wild night in the Bowery. Darting through the dark, mean streets of Trenton, sewer rats scatter when our headlights hit their bulging eyeballs and with Dusty giving hot pursuit, there's a few times I chance it, blowing through consecutive red lights to make up time.

Dusty wails on the Grenada's horn, flashing his high beams in approval. The ride plays out like a chase scene from a bad, B-Grade, 70's detective movie and the Misfits are laughing their asses off at how ridiculous these two oil burning, bucking bombs must look flying through the potholed, scarred, city streets. With a hard turn, our tires are squealing relentlessly until both cars come to a smoking, screeching stop in the stations parking lot.

Tumbling out of the cars like a Chinese fire drill gone awry, sprinting across the street with reckless abandon, everybody lets out their best war whoop, while Gem runs alongside of me hysterically as we invade the train station. What a beautifully ridiculous sight we must be to the commuters groggily going about their mundane travels tonight.

Our group of Bohemians is in blissful disarray, making sure funds are available for Manhattan, the club and the return trip home. Dusty, Steph and Otto say they'll pay for Tim and Skate, our true, street punk cat burglars, who very rarely have two nickels rubbing together at any given time. Their drug of choice right now was speed or crystal meth, and they're notorious for smoking it to get a full 'rush.' The hard charging days into night of no sleep or eating has them looking older than their true age of sixteen, making it a lot easier to pass them off as college age at clubs.

Eventually, we get into line. I've had several supreme months of income from work, a few shows and busking, so money's not a big issue today, which is a rarity in a punk kid's life. I take care of Gem's ticket, and alert Otto, Yuka, Lena and Sammi that I'll foot their door charge at CBGB's.

There are a growing number of people staring at us and the late night, Wall Street expatriates give us their fair share of contempt. Much as we'd like to give them a hearty "fuck off," we keep our tongues in check, since there's an overwhelming Brody presence in the station tonight and we know whose heads those tossers will crack.

Sadly, the homeless population simultaneously overtakes the remaining areas and there have been a few instances of assaults on them lately which infuriate Gem and I to no end. Like Gem has said before, "no one chooses to be homeless." Sleeping bags and clothing are strewn haphazardly on the station floor and their hollow eyed, unwashed faces stare out from behind ratty blankets. This epidemic of despair is tragically replayed throughout every major American city and industrial town unfortunate enough to be raped by the global economy and the awful scourge of Reaganomics.

A girl, possibly a few years younger than Gem, catches her attention. She sits alone in a tattered, light green jacket, with what look like her few worldly possessions scattered about. An empty canvas bag and a blanket are at her side and her eyes are swollen and red from what must have been endless bouts of sobbing, drugs or heaven knows what. Gem puts a tight grip on my hand, sighs and rests her head on me.

"That was me, four years ago, in despair, shivering in the cold, all spun out from a daily diet of booze, speed and sometimes heroin." The pain in Gem's eyes is hard to bear and she can't stop staring at the bedraggled girl who looks blankly in her direction. Lena and Steph notice the girl too, as both of them now hold Gem's hand tightly, giving her a sad nod of acknowledgment... these sisters of the street, so sympathetic to the despair and vulnerability of this young girl.

"Babe, give me a minute. It's not much but there's something I have to do."

"Steph and I'll come with you, Gem," Lena adds in an angelic, soulful tone. The girls depart to the vending machine, purchase some coffee and slowly approach this bedraggled waif of the streets.

Kneeling down alongside the young girl, she initially recoils in their presence, but Gem smiles, leaning in tenderly to reassure her that they mean no harm before handing the girl the coffee, creamers and sugar, and for the first time, this young, threadbare soul smiles lightly at their gesture.

Gem's a true angel of mercy, holding this girls' hand and speaking to her so peacefully. Lena offers her a reassuring smile and Steph pulls a small brush from her jacket, finding a water fountain near where this young child of the hardscrabble streets sits. She runs the brush under the water, quickly returning to kneel on the ground and carefully strokes it through the girls' straggly hair.

Yuka and Sammi, the ever-caring den mothers, gather the girls' possessions together, put them in the canvas bag, and take the pilled, worn blanket, gently placing it across her legs. Yuka softly rubs her back and smiles. "There you go, baby, you need to stay warm tonight." The rest of us surround her and Gem introduces us to Claire, who says she's been on the streets for the past three months.

Claire smiles sheepishly, thanking us profusely for the warm drinks. Otto, Dusty and Oren spot another vending machine, scrounge up some loose change for a few sodas, peanut butter crackers and place them in Claire's bag.

Oren pats her shoulder lightly. "Make sure YOU use them, little girl. They're not for anyone else," he says in a fatherly sounding baritone. She shyly inquires if we have any smokes to spare, so I offer a few Reds, and Tim hands her a pack of matches. We try to keep her company for as long as we can, until our trains arrival is announced for Track Four.

Steph gives Claire a light kiss and tells her to keep the brush, which she now cradles like a prized possession. The rest of the Misfits wish Claire well before making their way downstairs to the platform, leaving Gem and I alone with our young, new-found friend. Gem strokes Claire's cheek, softly expressing that she must find a way to escape the dangers of the street and Claire suddenly clutches onto Gem's arm as if begging her not to go.

Gem leans down again to give Claire a long, thoughtful embrace. "I know where you've been, little sister. Get some rest and please get some help because you owe yourself that much, Claire." I kneel down next to Gem, discreetly putting a ten spot in Claire's tiny, doll-like hands. "Keep this hidden, little one. It's not much, but if you use it well, you can feed yourself for quite some time. Take Gemma's advice, Claire, please get off the streets. You have your whole life ahead of you."

Claire hugs both of us tightly and kisses Gem on the cheek. "Thanks so much, for just caring, Gemma. You're my angel...I won't forget you." Tears stream down Claire's cheeks but Gem holds her closely, wiping her tears away. "Don't let anyone out here ever see you cry, do it in private and be strong...get help. We'll be back in town sometime tomorrow. I promise, I'll look for you, little Claire."

Their hands slowly separate as we say goodbye to Claire, who's already starting to drink her second coffee. Gem and I sprint quickly towards the entrance, turning long enough to observe Claire smoking a Red, smiling and waving to us. Gem blows her a kiss before we run downstairs, jumping onto the platform, where our tribe eagerly awaits to board, but not until our conductor partakes in some good-natured ribbing about our looks.

Luckily, the passenger car is half empty, so we're able to sit together and immediately converse about Claire and how we hope she'll be alright. Gem sits quietly, holding and caressing my arm as we pull away from the station, her eyes focused on the outside world until she loosens her grip, pressing both hands against the window. Lena has the same reaction, and soon all of us are against the glass, glancing up to the passenger waiting area, where little Claire stands with her tiny hands pressed firmly against the large window. I just about make out the warm smile on her face before we all wave goodbye to our little sister. The train picks up speed and Claire's outline grows smaller by the second.

Gem, the hardened, shivering girl from the street, wipes a tear away and forces a smile. She takes a breath, letting the words swathe through the passenger car as only her strong, soulful voice can do.

"Look me in the eye
Then, tell me that I'm satisfied
Were you satisfied
Look me in the eye
Then, tell me that I'm satisfied
Hey, are you satisfied

And it goes so slowly on
Everything I've ever wanted
Tell me what's wrong..."

I lend my voice to the refrain and the strength of our sound has caught the attention of the Misfits and some weary travelers.

"Look me in the eye
And tell me that I'm satisfied
Were you satisfied
Look me in the eye
Then, tell me I'm satisfied
And now are you satisfied

Everything goes
Well, anything goes all of the time
Everything you dream of
Is right in front of you
And everything is a lie…"

Any of the Misfits who know the rest, now add their emotional refrain…

"Look me in the eye
And tell me that I'm satisfied
Look me in the eye
Unsatisfied
I'm so, I'm so unsatisfied
I'm so dissatisfied
I'm so, I'm so unsatisfied
I'm so unsatisfied

Well, I'm a-
I'm so, I'm so unsatisfied…."

The singing ends with nods from the tribe because we understand what this song means to all of us, the words, the emotion, it fits us completely. The aching, strain of Westerberg's lyrics, it is our lives, our hopes, our fears, the painful reality of our abuses and abusers, the not so distant past of street life for some of us and the painful realization of Claire and those who face its hard-ships now.

The green eyes glisten and after latching on to me, as if ready-ing for an epic fight against all the worlds' evils, her warm breath reaches my ear and the words which follow make my heart melt. "No matter what you do, whatever you decide, I'm yours, Robbs. I will love you forever."

The train glides hastily over its steel skeleton, on past the cold, brick facades of factories with their ominously billow-ing smokestacks, past rolling hills leading into dark, menacing forests, past the harsh realities of the hollowed out, burnt and boarded up squalor of urban tenements, only to be followed by the bedazzling glitter emanating from the towers of wealth and power.

New York, its lure of dreams come true and hopes dashed into the abyss lies dead ahead.

••• 12 •••

All Hell's Breaking Loose

"OUR NEXT STOP WILL BE PENN STATION," the buzz-
ing speaker crackles for the last time. It's been quite a trip from
Trenton, so needless to say, we're psyched to hear some maddening, skull crushing, hardcore acts at CBGB's.

Snatching our meager belongings, hustling rapidly from
the stopped train, keeping our brisk pace through Penn Station,
you can't help notice the same story being played out in the Big
Apple as well, where the homeless seem to reside everywhere
and the smell of shit, piss and jizz permeate the senses.

"Jesus fuckin' Christ, this shithole smells worse than CBGB's
bathrooms," Dust blurts out to no one in particular. I toss a Red
in my mouth, lighting it quickly. "Smoke em' up, Misfits, at least
it'll kill some of the odor!"

Bathroom humor was definitely going to happen during
this trip, because anyone who's been to CBGB's knows what the
bathroom situation is like. The toilets have no enclosures, filth
and graffiti scar and scab the walls and if you have a smart-ass
friend at the urinal, or some fuck ass, drunken dick who wants to

make life miserable, you may just end up with your boots getting pissed on. In other words, it made for a great, memorable night at, as Gem puts it, the 'Cathedral of Punk.'

Gem and I take the lead, running the gauntlet of night crawlers, pimps, hustlers and pushers, only stopping long enough to absorb the grand view of the sparkling Empire State Building looming above us. Spotting the green globes' friendly glow above the entrance for the 34th Street Herald Square subway, we roar downstairs skipping over randomly accumulating newspapers, empty vodka bottles and the like; jump the turnstiles, catching the next train to Broadway-Lafayette Street Station and sprint into the subway car, laughing our asses off about how a crew of batshit crazy punks gipped the TA out of their blood money and left the TA Brody's grabbing for air.

We're only riding for a few minutes, but if you've never had the pleasure of experiencing the NYC subway system, it could be quite traumatic for the weak of spirit or stomach.

Whereas the Misfits may be looked upon in the confines of a suburban Philly SEPTA rail car as a menacing presence or a nuisance, in a New York City subway car, we're nothing more than odd sorts of kids inhabiting some space. Our Thursday night ride has accumulated its fair share of earlier rush hour litter, while graffiti covers its walls and windows from one end to the other. The chaos, despair and decadence witnessed underground, are vital elements which have spawned a rebirth of the punk movement in this country under the not so incredible Reagan Administration, evoking a sense of where we feel the future is heading for many Americans, a future of good jobs being lost, immeasurable poverty and a post-apocalyptic feel in many cities and industrial towns. Don't get too haughty, suburban America, because if this cycle continues, your demise will soon follow.

A growing number of punks have become savvy to the realpolitik being peddled in America and aren't buying into the "Morning in America" line of shit that a second-rate actor, a former CIA head, and a carnivorous Wall Street tyrant have sold to the seemingly gullible masses.

Gem and I are personally disgusted with the legions of 1960's, anti-establishment activists, who said never to trust anyone over thirty but reverted into Neo-Conservative, modern day pimps whose mergers and acquisitions are tearing the country apart. In their minds, American Jesus, wrapped in the American flag by Jerry Falwell and Lee Atwater, has showed them the righteous path through leveraged buyouts, layoffs, mergers, acquisitions and a military that is the biggest, best trained killing machine to hit the planet since the days of the Roman Empire.

And as far as the Democrats go, fuck them too, since the limousine liberals have moved so far away from being the perceived 'Party of the People', they should honestly be ashamed of themselves; reminiscing about the days of JFK and their college protests against Vietnam, while they sip overpriced wine at their lunchtime benefit galas, summon the drivers to get their brats from private school and finish the day in their study reading the New York Times where haughty Libs write puff pieces about how inferior the lunchpail and hardhat set is and how enlightened their Ivy League asses are.

There are those in the punk ranks who believe the system should be totally overturned in an anarchistic fashion to bring about true democracy. There is a frighteningly Orwellian feel about America lately and many in the punk movement need an avenue to display their vitriol against it. CBGB's has stood as a shining beacon for most of us, because it's given punk music a platform to demonstrate its disgust at the system, our schools, even our parents, through the music.

On a more generic level, it affords us some commonality at a place where we can let loose and not feel like we are freaks, misfits or rabble who constantly get harassed by the redneck elements or Brody's in our respective towns. The hippies had their Woodstock, punks have CBGB's.

A thumping, screeching halt ensues at Broadway-Lafayette Station, leaving the acrid smell of burning brakes pouring inside during our escape. Gem torches a Newp, sniffing the putrid, fetid air encircling us. "Rome is burning, Robbs," she says with a smirk. "Sure as hell is, Gem. Well, if we're going to witness the fall of the Empire, no better place to do it from than CBGB's."

Tattered jackets and filthy blankets adorn the restlessly sleeping homeless in our midst but the gang of twelve marches up the steps like a victorious army laying claim to what's viewed as a place of pure debauchery, disorder and desolation to most. Gem can't help but laugh as I blaze up a Red and grin from ear to ear, the Punk Prince and his Punk Princess, in their element and owning the night. After a few minutes on East Houston, we turn the corner and I raise my arms towards the night sky. "Misfits, welcome to our nirvana. Welcome to the Bowery... the place from where the forgotten ones will lead the next, true revolution!"

Dusty, Oren and Otto lift their smokes together as we roar our intense war cry, "PISS OFF, SOD OFF!" Skate and Tim, our young Philly street punks absorb the spectacle that is the Bowery, with its tragic yet mesmerizing visual of all that we see wrong with America today. "Fuck dude, I thought where we've squatted in Philly is fucked up, but this is bullshit poverty, man," Tim confides in Skate.

People sleep on skids, in doorways of ramshackle shops, fires glow in trashcans and the living dead, with vacant, bloodshot eyes, wander aimlessly about. It's almost maddening to look at this and hear my mothers' generation blathering on like complete assholes about how this is the greatest nation to live in. Come out of your bucolic, fake-ass, suburban life of finger sandwiches and tea parties to see what the fuck your cities, industrial towns and rural farm communities look like now, mom's generation, because your ignorance and apathy allowed this America to die.

Ambling timidly past the filth ridden alleys and tent cities, Sammi tenses up until Lena grabs hold of her arm tightly. "Take it from a street girl, cutie, don't let anyone sense fear in you out here, or in the club." She pulls close to Sammi, giving her a reassuring peck on the cheek. "Don't worry gorgeous, you've got some rough and tumble beauties with you tonight and I won't let anything happen to you." Sammi smiles shyly at Lena who is domineering tonight in her high heeled boots, leather and spikes. "Thanks, Lena. I feel safer already," Sammi replies, resting her head on Lena's shoulder, who purrs into Sammi's ear, "no problem, beautiful girl, Lena's got you tonight."

Scurrying to reach us, Yuka discretely gets Gem's attention. "Hey sis, I don't know if Samms is aware of this, but Lena appears to have a big girl crush happening."

"I was wondering about that when we were all at the apartment the other night," Gem whispers excitedly. "Lena was quite infatuated with her and got really bummed when Sammi was ready to jet. The two of them were outside for a quite some time. Who knows, maybe they were snogging..."

"Well girls, if nothing else, Sammi will literally be in good hands with Lena at her side although I do though feel quite bummed for my man, Oren here, since he was hoping to get some time with lovely Lena tonight."

Big Oren wraps his thick, black inked forearm around my neck, giving me a forceful, but good-natured shake. "Yo, don't sweat it, Robbs. If I play my cards right, maybe I will end the night with a beautiful girl on each arm."

Yuka, Gem and Steph both give Oren a push from behind. "Oren Johnson, you dirty dog...are you trying to get a threesome going for yourself?"

The big man hits the girls with his handsome, Cheshire Cat grin. "The night is young, Miss Steph, so I've got quite a few hours to work my charm." Finally alighting under the infamous awning at 315 Bowery, 'CBGB...OMFUG', I happily approach Florian. "Flor, since you are the savior of this night for all of the Misfits, I'm taking care of your door charge and drinks. We also think you should be our lead man into the club."

"Thanks Robbs, I'm really glad you let me hang with you all. I know not everyone wants to do that because of me being gay but the Misfits have never given a shit about what everyone else thinks."

"And never will," I pipe up. "Flor, you and your boyfriends are always welcome."

"Yo, Rob is right. We're all fuckin' Misfits here, kid, every bleedin' one of us, marching to the beat of our own drum and lovin' who we damn well please, so don't you ever forget it," Dust chimes in. "Now, let's get this ass kickin' night going, kid."

Approaching the club's door, we hear, Cause For Alarm's blistering, 'Time Will Tell' rolling in waves onto the street and we're immediately amped but Karen Kristal, owner Hilly Kristal's wife, gives us the stern, once over at the entrance. "Where are you kids coming from this late?"

"Just bounced in from Trenton," I pipe up.

"Like the flags in the hair," she replies in her dead, matter of fact tone. "Listen, the three up front and you look like you're thirteen and the girls look young as hell. I know you came a way to get here, but I don't want any crap. Are you all at least sixteen?"

"Everybody here's in college or working, except for these two," I reply while pointing to Tim and Skate, "but they're both sixteen."

"Let's show some ID's then, people," and she methodically examines them, like Checkpoint Charlie viewing your papers at the Berlin Wall, only then stamping our hands. "All of you that are nineteen enjoy it because on December first, drinking age will be twenty-one." She points to me and smirks wryly. "Flag hair, sucks being you at eighteen, so let me make it clear that if you or the 'sixteens' get caught drinking, you're all tossed out."

Florian opens the punk palace's doors only to be greeted by the crushing sounds of ear splitting bedlam before snaking through the packed club, trying to absorb the atmosphere in an instant. Punks and skins give the Misfits a good once over and we gladly return the favor since everyone seems to be in a receptive, festive mood tonight. Otto, Dust and I spot some familiar faces from shows that we saw this past summer and give them a wave, as do Gem and the girls, so any wariness that may have precluded our acceptance seems to be diminishing. Dust and Oren give me a pat on the shoulder. "Yo, I know Hilly's wife is bein' a hard ass right now, but when Cause For Alarm goes off, I'll sneak some brews out for us so you can drink in the alley!"

"Sounds bitchin', Dust!" The music is drowning us out...the masses of bodies begin storming wildly around the floor. I wrap my arms around Gem, her hips sway back and forth and I love the way we feel together even though I'm trying to keep a keen eye on everyone else's whereabouts.

The tribe's keeping close quarters, so Flor, Steph, Dust and Oren get some cold brews for everyone. Otto and Yuka squeeze in next to us, begin pogoing and Lena has a tight hold on Sammi who takes in the intense sounds and surroundings with a mouth agape as Skate and Tim try to work their way forward to engage the frenzied atmosphere of this night.

Up front, tattooed, shirtless kids with buzzcuts or shaved heads glistening under the lights and a few roosterheads dive mercilessly into the crowd from the stage.

"This is going to be fucking outrageous, Robbs," Gem screams, pulling us further into the insanity. Bodies crash everywhere in heaps and one of the glistening skins goes airborne, landing in front of Sammi and Lena, who prop him up, only to have Lena grab him by the belt loops and send him crashing to the floor again while letting out an ear crushing, manic tribal scream. Gem flashes the biggest grin and mischievously pushes and punches some buzzcuts out of our way. "Robbs, let's get into the mix! Misfits, are you ready to fuck this shit up?"

Otto and I let out a blood curdling war cry and Lena slides on her finger spikes as Sammi gives her a look of pure bewilderment. "Holy shit, Lena, what the hell are they for?"

"I told you, Sammi baby, if things get wild, I'll have you protected!" Gem spins around to hold me but gets caught up in a pretty intense slamfest before plunging headfirst with Tim and Skate into the epicenter of all hell breaking loose. Eventually crashing into Gem, she laughs when we're tossed hard into two skins and a few punks who topple madly onto to the floor. Not, even giving it a second thought, we hastily push them back into the whirlwind pit before another shirtless ball of sweat goes airborne past Otto, Gem and me. "YEEEAAAAHHH! This is fucking insanity, Otto!"

"I know! Are you not just fuckin' loving this?! EEEYYOOOOOOOO!" He grabs onto my jacket, spinning me around with sickening velocity. "OH SHIT, LOOK OUT!" A crowd surfing punk with an intense, acid color Mohawk almost lands on top of us but I get my hands up, as do Gem and Otto, sending him airborne once again. Otto and I do an old time pogo, eventually launching ourselves into the frenzied masses and away from a grasping Gem who eventually slams and barges her way to her tribe of screaming, cheering girls.

Otto and I get surfed over the slammers, moshers and pitched hard right past the Misfit girls who laugh their asses off at the spectacle of our crash and burn landing onto CBGB's floor. Two young skins yank us up roughly and one grabs me before reentering the war zone. "Yuh' spikes uh' sick as fuck, man!"

"Thanks kid! This is so fuckin' brilliant!"

"You ain't seen shit brutha', until the Cro-Mags go on! THE SHIT'S HITTIN' THE FAN 'DEN! Have fun punk asses," he roars, pushing us hard into the mob where the frantic pace of psychosis continues.

We look back quickly to see Flor and Steph draining some longnecks at the bar, but Dusty and Oren have 'taken the piss' on everyone, tossing, moshing and slamming their way besides us. Gem, Yuka and Lena are across the floor from us slamming furiously and holy shit...even Sammi is rolling some poor, chaos punk and his girl onto the floor.

Cause for Alarm is putting on a killer set. It's definitely gotten the crowd ready for the pure, sick madness that is the Cro-Mags. The band whips the audience into a pure fury, so the four of us lock arms around each other's shoulders. Yuka, Gem and Lena raise their arms up and let out a thunderous, "YO!" We replicate their horrific sound, running full steam ahead into the crowd which topples like rows of bowling pins. Roosters and skins continue to fly past our heads as our fellow moshers spew beer all over us in appreciation of our Trenton, Wall of Death, which has officially debuted on CBGB's floor. After aiding the stomped, toppled warriors to their feet, we cheer wildly when

Cause ends their set. We're bathed in sweat and our girls are just sexily shimmering.

A handful of punks and their girls come over to embrace us when a fresh-faced punk with a tall, purple Mohawk blows hard through the throngs and puts me in a bear hug. "You sick, Philly fucks! It's about time yuh' asses came back to CB's!"

"Alex, my Brooklyn brother, how is my Flatbush doing?"

"It's still turning into a puh' shithole, my brutha' Rob. You shoulda' called that you wuh' comin' t'day man…been missin' ya', hell, we all have!"

"Kid, I didn't even know I was coming here until about two hours ago."

Alex flicks at one of the flags in my spikes before giving me a big push. "That's my boy, Rob, the wind always at his back, nevuh' a care in the world but loyal as shit to his punk family! Hey, are you Philly folks ready ta' hit the alley and guzzle some pisswaduh?"

"Damn right, we're ready, Alex," Steph replies. "Listen, Flor and I got bottles stuffed in our pockets for the kids. Get us past Karen, 'cause she was on the warpath at the door."

The Misfits and our New York friends rush the door en masse, squirreling past an admonishing Karen and blast into the depths of the alley. Someone has already set a massive bonfire in two large steel drums, and the flames tickle the night sky.

Some ample sized sewer rats, with the oils of their hair shimmering from the yellowish glow of the dim street lights, scamper through the alley and slither away hissing and squealing after Lena adeptly tomahawks two of them with broken pieces of bricks and a beer bottle. "UGH! I FUCKIN' HATE RATS," she bellows and we laugh at the screeching rats' expense. Oren hands me a cold Bud before I blaze a Red for him. "Time to get cozy with the sexy, rat killer," he laughs, giving me a wink and then smoothly edging over to Lena and Sammi.

I find Flor, bring him into the center of our circle and hoist the almost spent Bud skyward. "AHEM! If I may have all of your attention, because a toast is in order here! To Florian McDonnell whose quick thinking turned a cancelled show on

Hallows Eve into a truly awesome, surely to be unforgettable evening. TO FLORIAN!"

"TO FLORIAN...PISS OFF...SOD OFF!

Dusty whips his empty bottle against the brick wall, grabbing Flor around the neck, as shards of glass explode throughout the filth filled alley. "Oi, and we mean that with nothin' but love, mate!"

"An' I tank' ya' wit' heartfelt gratitude," Flor replies in his best Irishman's brogue.

"FLORIAN, OI, OI, OI!"

The gang launch bottles in all directions and taking Gem by the hand, I dance with her around the ever-growing blaze. Her wild eyes sparkle in the firelight and we're soon joined by the whole tribe and a few more punks. The fire whips wildly and our animal yelps and frenzied screams fill the air. I admire the shadows swaying insanely on the wall behind us while the scene takes on a surrealistic feel, like we're in an urban, post-apocalyptic 'Lord of the Flies'.

Twirling Gem away from the flames, I press her body gently against the graffiti strewn, back wall of the club. The crisp, night air hits our hot, sweaty bodies, releasing torrents of steam from our pores. "God, you are gorgeous, I love you so much, Swan."

"Kiss me, Robbs, please, don't make this night end." Glistening lips find their way to my neck, her warm tongue twirls across it, before quickly finding my ear, which she nibbles softly. I repeat all of her moves...she exhales strongly...my hands, under her shirt and up to her bra. Gem's mouth finally meets mine and our tongues softly entwine; the loud voices around us, soon nothing more than a murmur...the dank, stench-filled alley of broken glass, broken pallets and broken dreams is now our punk palace.

Moving my hands to the small of her back, beads of sweat trickle through my fingers. Her heart beat quickens, I pop the clasp and hear her moan slightly, only opening my eyes slightly. Staring back at me so seductively, she delivers a quick peck on my cheek. "Mmmmm...as much as I would love to pursue this game of cat and mouse, we have an audience," which I realize has been cheering us on and I begin to chuckle. "I see what you mean, babe. Well, there's always tomorrow at your place."

"Now, that's my baby boy, talking about a much more intimate setting for me to do everything I want to do to you," and attempting to quell the excitement of such a statement fails miserably, when I stare into her fiery, wild eyes. "Everything, Gem?"

Her wet, glossy lips explore my neck again before turning loose a downright evil giggle. "Mmmmmmm...oh yes, everything, babe and I'm not going to lie, damn, you felt so good against me."

Taking a drag from my cig, I begin to smirk. "You know that you're not making this any easier..."

Snarfing my cig, Gem takes a long drag, ejecting yet another wicked giggle. "It's not my job to make it easy, babe."

••• 13 •••

This Epic Night

OUR LARGE CONTINGENT winds its way through the alley and back onto the Bowery. The Brody's are out in force and for some reason seem to be having an animated conversation with a burly, bearded man. Upon closer scrutiny, we realize it's Hilly and much as we'd like to tell him what an ass-kicking time the nights already been in his club, it's probably not the best moment to strike up a conversation. After producing our stamps to a very stoic Karen, we hurriedly re-enter the insanity of CBGB's.

The Cro-Mags take the stage, and their bass player, Harley Flanagan, revs up the atmosphere with some purely demonic licks. Within minutes, the Cro Mags are a whirling dervish of rage, so we're once again embroiled in the mad skirmishes of the pit. Bodies are furiously hurled in every direction, but the atmosphere is all aggressive energy, raising hell but not fighting.

Oren presses me into the heavens like a set of dumbbells, happily flipping me into the dense fray, so I'm airborne and immediately handed a beer by a screaming Steph. "YOU'RE KILLIN' IT, BABE!" Guzzling the suds with massive speed, I deftly hand the bottle to a roosterhead before Karen Kristal sees who I am and tosses me out of CB's. I'm not petrified of the Brody's outside, but Karen scares the living shit out of me.

Surfing over Gem who playfully pinches my ass, the goosing is repeated by a howling gang of Misfit and Alex's girls leaving me with a nonstop, cat ate the canary grin.

The Mags set moves along ferociously and all of the guys battling in the pit are faring well before Oren and Dust decide to hoist Otto and Flor to join me in the feverish riding of the wave. I get surfed right past Gem's outstretched arms and tossed into Alex's tribe. Oren and Dust get Tim, Skate and Flor airborne and once the four of us hit terra firma, we start elevating Alex and our New York family before I get hoisted again, making it onto the stage with Tim, Skate and Flor! Raining buckets of sweat, the jacket and shirt are tossed to the Mags crew with the other Misfits following suit as we start viciously windmilling around the stage.

The Mags singer, John 'Bloodclot', gives the three boys a hearty push into the crowd, which roars their manic approval. Our young charges surf famously through the madness and since I'm the only one up on stage with the band, I plan on a quick getaway before their crew tosses me harshly onto my neck. Backpedaling a few steps, I spot the tribe front and center, take a running leap in their direction but not before I try and master an acrobatic air twist. Admittedly, it's an equally euphoric and frightful feeling to be high in the air defying gravity, all the while hoping someone will catch you before splattering your nose onto the floor below and the boys valiantly hold on but going ass-over-head may be in my future.

Luckily, I flip over, land on my feet, but the momentum propels me into a wall of bodies, knocking beer, wild boys and badass skin girls to the deck. In the ensuing bedlam, the Mags crew begs our group of girls to attack the stage since this will be the bands last song. Lena still has a hold of Sammi around the waist, lifting her into the stage crews' arms. Lena hops up, imploring the other girls to join her and pretty soon, a seriously sexy, hardcore bump and grind is performed by eight sweaty, seductive punk vixens, including Gem, who pulls Yuka close and moves in perfect, erotic unison. Steph sandwiches Gem even harder into Yuka and with their legs entwined and hands freely pawing breasts and bottoms respectively, the crowd and band feed off their sensual energy.

Lena grinds Sammi even harder and our innocent one must be feeling her oats when out of nowhere, a dead-on lip-lock's applied to Lena for all to witness and thoroughly enjoy! Skate's retrieved me another beer from Oren but I lose its contents all over our tribe as we're left with our jaws hitting the ground at the seductive spectacle.

"HOLY FUCKING SHIT, ROB! OUR SAMMI IS ALL OVER LENA! WHAT IN THE HELL?! WHAT AN INCREDIBLE, FUCKIN' NIGHT!" Otto is beside himself laughing, the place goes nuts when we start our war cries and oi chants and once Gem realizes what's going on, her facial expression is priceless. Nudging Yuka and Steph, Gem and the girls stare in amazement as Sammi continues kissing Lena, whose hands run wildly over Sammi's hellacious body, and even the three New York girls who were bumping and grinding start boisterously cheering them on with their sexy howls of debauchery.

Oren, stands in stunned silence before I happily wrap my arm around his thick neck and pat his 'frohawk'. "I love you, Brother O but you ain't gotta' icebergs chance in hell of getting with either girl after that." The big man grins, shakes his head, laughs heartily, releasing a boisterous, 'PISS OFF, ROBB!" while squeezing my skull between his bear paws. "Gotta' admit bro, those two are hot as a firecracker together."

The song ends and the girls are helped from the stage to the sounds of raucous insanity, beer spewing and war cries. The band is totally spent but we give them a hell-raising shout for putting on a powerful, ass kicking show and wearing us out as well.

The tribes loudly spill onto to the street and everybody's still abuzz about the stage diving, crowd surfing, the bands psychotic sets and of course, the girls sexy stage act with Lena and Sammi being the center of attention on the Bowery's sidewalk. They hold hands, beaming endlessly before I walk over, planting a sweat filled kiss on their cheeks. "Samms, I don't even know where to start but...wow! You sure had yourself a helluva' debut into the depths of Bohemian life, babe! You've secured a place in our punk annals."

Laughing sweetly, they both roughhouse me, which invites both New York and Philly tribes to join the mix, having quite a playful go of it. The Brody's eyeball us but realizing it's all in good fun, they allow the energetic rumpus to continue. Florian comes over with all the gear the stage crew held for us and as I try to get my shirt back on, Gem delivers a pathetically, pouting face. "I was really hoping you'd stay bare chested, 'cause you're looking sexy as hell, baby boy."

A trio of punk girls passing by, decked out in shredded, worn through clothing and colored feathers twisted into their matted hair concur. "Your rebel, rebel...HOT TRAMP, is spot on..you got the whole package going, kid," one replies. "And the hair and the flags are fucking righteous!" replies another before they loudly walk off, singing some bawdy Slits lyrics and eventually disappear into the smoky haze of the Bowery's emptying, hollowed streets.

"Hey, New York punks, come ovuh' heuh' an' pay respects to my brutha'...the angel on my shoulda', Rob and his crazy as fuck Philly family who stole the show tonight," Alex yells out to anyone within earshot, so pretty soon, we're surrounded by CBGB faithful. A few punks ask us about the Philly scene, as well as Trenton's City Gardens, so Gem and I happily oblige, giving them tons of info about the venues and exchange phone numbers on small scraps of ripped up fliers to keep in touch.

After the crowds thin out, I pull the tribes in close for a quick chat. "Listen, I don't know about you guys, but I'm in no mood to head home tonight. I want to stay in Manhattan."

Otto blazes a Lucky, taking a hearty drag. "What's your thought, brother? I'm game for anything."

"Let's hop on the Lafayette line and take it to Bowling Green," I reply. Alex takes a swig from his bottle of Bud and grins. "Are you thinkin' Battery Park, Rob?"

"I sure as hell am, Alex. Look guys, I know the city at night can be fucknut crazy, but we'll be down by the Towers and we'll have safety in numbers. If you guys think I'm nuts, then I'll back off, but I know my Misfits will be up for an adventure. We'll take turns sleeping and being lookouts. How cool will it be to wake up to the Towers and the whole city behind us, while the sun comes out over the Statue of Liberty in the Hudson?"

Gem's eyes sparkle wildly. "I know I'll do it…soooo…what about my Misfit and New York girls?"

"I know we're there with you," Lena chirps, snuggling warmly into Sammi's chest. "Hell, Dusty and I will keep watch to start the night," Oren pipes up before a really cute, leather clad girl from Alex's crew walks over to the big fellow and smiles. "I'll stay up with you too, baby," batting her bright blue eyes at Oren, who now realizes that his night may be salvaged after all.

Our ragged but enthusiastic tribes give a final salute to some stragglers hanging under CBGB's awning and the victorious march to Lafayette Station begins. The armies of homeless increase by the minute, so we deftly maneuver around numerous, sleeping bodies on the filthy, dimly lit stairwell. One day, I hope our generation will fight harder than the callous Boomers and their parents, to try to put an end to these hardships. We have to do better or anarchy will truly arise in between America's shores.

Gem views the depravity and despair; her eyes rapidly losing their sparkle and I know where her thoughts lie. "She'll be all right, Gem. We'll look for Claire when we go back to Trenton, just like you promised. Hell, maybe we'll even take her some-place to eat. That little one could probably use a good meal." Wiping a tear from her cheek, she looks into my eyes for what seems like an eternity. "This is why I adore you, Robbs, because under that entire devil-may-care attitude or hard as nails exterior you try to portray, there really lies a heart of pure gold."

Waiting for the train, I hold her closely, her heart performing slow drum beats on my chest. "It's the same reason that I cherish you, Gem, because you'd try to save the whole world from itself, if you could."

Within minutes, a line of graffiti strewn cars squeals to an abrupt stop. The interior's even worse than that of our earlier ride and also reeks atrociously of vomit and piss. In a relatively short amount of time, we pull into Bowling Green Station, gladly retreating from the putrid stench. We adroitly maneuver through more bodies, blankets and belongings, finally reaching street level. Alex, Gem and I are in high spirits, stampeding across the streets and into Battery Park like wild bulls, with the rest of our tribes engaging in their equally, animated pursuit.

Even at this time of day, it never ceases to amaze me how many 'night creatures' truly dwell in cities. Whizzing past numerous homeless encampments, Brody's, junkies, drunks and handfuls of curious onlookers, Alex and Florian secure some concrete benches, giving us an outstanding view of Lady Liberty and a clear shot of the sparkling, massive monoliths, the Twin Towers of the World Trade Center looming skyward behind us. No matter whether this is your first time or hundredth, it's impossible not to be in awe of New York at night.

Dusty, Steph, Oren and his new gal', Allie keep a watchful eye on the tribe settling in for the night and Gem falls into my arms, allowing the heat of her body to warm my soul.

"Damn, Robbs, you're soaked to the bone from all that jumping around in CB's! You're going to get sick as a dog out here." I pull her even closer as the steam still rises from us. "I've got you with me, babe…that's all the warmth I need. I'll be up soon helping to keep watch anyway."

"I'll be up with you. I'm being very possessive tonight. I don't want you away from me for a minute."

"Lovin' the sound of that, Gem." Absorbing the grandness of the phenomenal skyline, it's easy to get swept up in the glitz and glamour of capitalism, ignoring the ills we've all witnessed tonight. For all the hell that can accompany being in New York, there is a romantic side to it as well and the Bohemian set of our crew gets it. Accompanied on our bench by Sammi and Lena, who nuzzles into my shoulder, whispering to Sammi about how she doesn't want this night to end, Yuka eventually squeezes in next to Gem, lovingly embracing her sister while Otto lies across their laps as the girls take turns poking at his mohawk.

Skate and Tim are looking shaky, so Alex takes them over to some dealers he knows, seeing if they can score speed for their morning rush. They still have the money Dusty fronted them and when the deal is done, Alex quickly hustles them across the street and into the bowels of Bowling Green's station.

The New York girls converge around Florian and even though it's not the true companionship he's seeking, he remains the consummate gentleman, watching over them, allowing them to rest, while a couple of the New York boys keep a keen watch over us with Oren, Dusty, Steph and Allie.

I'm trying hard to stay awake in case anyone needs me because when you get used to being the 'Guardian Angel' of the tribe; it's hard not to be on point. I say something to the girls but they're out cold, except for Lena who kisses Sammi's neck lightly. Noticing that I'm far from the point of sleep, she leans over Samms, kissing me softly. "Thanks for an incredible end to the night, cutie, this was a great idea…love you."

"Love you too, Lena." Cuddling into Samms one last time, she's asleep within seconds. The lights of the city blink, twirl and dance before my eyes but I fend off exhaustion, until I see a very animated Alex, Skate and Tim return and chat with Dusty. Relaxed, I allow the night to wash over me, hurriedly falling into a peaceful slumber.

● ● ●

Feeling a hard tug at my jacket, the fists are ready to fly, until my eyes fall upon Oren, Dusty, Steph and the New York crew smiling at me. "Ahhh, we figured you'd be ready to come out swinging, killer," Dusty laughs heartily. "So, you ready to let some tired warriors crash for a bit?"

"Yeah, sure…did everything go alright?"

"Well, outside of Skate, Tim and Alex takin' the piss and talkin' like they were shot outta' a cannon, yeah, everything went alright. They've been walking around the park nonstop, so thank

God there are too many different walks of life for the Brody's to mind or they'd probably be in some shit right now."

The flame of my Zippo hits a Red as I smirk at the thought of them zipping through the park like the human equivalent of a record on 78 speed. "Don't worry boys, I'll keep an eye on them, so get some rest. Hey, I'm taking it a wake-up call's in order when sunrise hits Lady Liberty?"

"You better believe it brother!" Dust shouts. "Damn straight, kid, we wouldn't miss it for the world," Oren adds before they all collapse on the benches and I'm able to fully appreciate the beautiful sight of our rag tag tribe of punk warriors.

We truly are Bohemians, friends...no...family, from all walks of life with a common purpose in music, in lifestyle, in our activism. We are rich and working-class kids bucking the system, the street urchins fighting for our last scrap of bread, our last inch of real estate, standing alone or bloodily brawling as a group down to the last person and I'm incredibly proud to be a part of this band of brothers and sisters.

Standing alone at the railing, I keep a keen eye on our spazzed out, young bucks, Tim, Skate and Alex, who've apparently made some friends. Tim's procured a wicked longboard and is chased by a cluster of rambunctious young skater punks who seem totally jazzed by his board prowess.

Skate commandeers what looks like a shark body G&S plank with neon green wheels. The boys tear through Battery Park, turning some sick Nosegrinds and Ollie's, igniting the crowd into howls of appreciation.

Becoming increasingly distracted by the breathtaking view of the downtown skyline, I think about if I'd taken the path of business school, inevitably setting myself on the familial, prescribed course of being a Wall Street master, amassing riches beyond my wildest dreams.

It was definitely upsetting certain people that I was leaning towards being a mill rat, a fighter for the worker; the proletariat. I was glad to hear Gem would truly support whatever decision I made because she understands that I had more in common with the working class, union life of my Grandfather, a leatherworker by trade who could make shoes, belts and everything in between. I want to be that guy stoking the furnace, pouring the steel that builds America.

Although the allure of the city's glitz and glam, the lure of easy money and unbridled wealth and power can be a tempting aphrodisiac, the boardrooms of The Street were crushing the people that I wanted to be a part of, churning up and spitting out their corpses at an alarming rate. Maybe that was part of the magnetism for me, to be on the right side of the good fight, to take down these wolves in suits at their own game.

Regaling in the luminous beauty of Lady Liberty, I imagine my Grandfather returning alone from Italy against his father's wishes. Although he was born here, his father kept residence in Italy and when his stone-mason jobs in Pittsburgh were completed, always returned to his small villa outside of Naples.

A few years younger than me, Giuseppe came here to work hard, forging claim to a new life worth fighting for. It's the same way I feel now, the fighting spirit to never yield, to disallow the halls of government or the boardrooms of corporate America from trampling our freedoms and hard-fought gains like some totalitarian nightmare come true.

The imagery of him wisps away like morning mist across the Hudson and I'm suddenly entranced by a vision of beauty approaching me. Securing my Zip, she lights a Newp, producing a pack of gum from her jacket. "A stick of mint for your thoughts, baby boy."

"Thanks, Swan...sorry that I didn't wake you but you were sleeping so peacefully with the tribe."

She taps her boot on the railing, chuckling lightly. "I was watching you the whole time, Robbs. You may have been keeping an eye over the tribe like you always do, but you were doing some deep thinking out here...about all of this, huh?" she asks, pointing towards the luminous beauty of the city. "Thinking about all the possibilities, the people who you're disappointing, thinking about that mill, fighting for the working man...I may have only known you for a while, Robbs, but I know where your heart lays." She takes another drag, smiling at me peacefully.

"You know what you want, so do it, damn it…start your adventure after this semester because I'll always support you." She places her hand over mine and closes it tightly. "I know that I was hard on you about the whole mess with Kellin.."

"Gem…it's over with, you don't…"

The beauty of her face radiates in the moonlight and her eyes sparkle like emeralds. "Please, let me finish, hon', because I am glad you took care of him that night. Yes, I was petrified of you getting hurt and I knew you could fight…but I could still lose you in an instant to someone hurting you…someone stealing you from me. I can't bear the thought of that, but I'm also madly, deeply in love with the loyalty and respect you show me. I'm so used to be some fellow's trophy…or with Kellin, even worse but I never worry about that with you, because you love me for me."

"I do love you for you, Gem. I love that you understand the artistic side of me, the poet, the activist writer, the musician. I'm in awe of your spirit and that you understand the fighting spirit I have in me for so many issues." I put my hands under her chin, kissing her softly and as my hands move under her jacket and shirt, I start to caress her back before laughing lightly.

"What was that laugh about, babe?" Gem asks shyly.

"I just can't believe how much I love you, girl…can't believe we found each other…can't believe that I could ever feel this way about someone."

Running silky smooth hands across my face she sighs. "I love those eyes of yours…how they shine when you're talking to me, like golden sparkles mixed in with beautiful brown. I could stare into them all day. Please kiss me again, Robbs…"

Becoming one with her, it's a feeling I have no intention of letting disappear, not now, not ever. "Please don't stop, Rob… the sun will be up soon. Kiss me again, make it last forever." Pressing my lips softly to hers, our mouths open, our love for each other revealed to the city that never sleeps, until the incredible beauty of the morning sky is there to greet us.

Leaning across the railing, Gem can't stop smiling, viewing the darkness of night evaporating, only to be replaced by vivid streaks of blues, oranges and pinks. "My God, this is unbelievable.

Thank you for doing this tonight, babe…no one will forget this anytime soon."

"I'll never forget this night, Gemma. Piss off if Flor didn't save it for us."

"He sure did, and you polished it off with perfection. Mmmmm…just wait until your thank you present tonight…"

"Now that's what I'm talking about, my girl, you are just killer. Well, you ready to roust this glorious mess to see this sight?"

"Yeah, let's get em' up!"

After hurriedly waking the combined tribes from dreams of glory, Dusty corrals Tim, Skate and Alex from their new skater friends and before long everybody's eagerly leaning on the railings, observing the colossal ball of fire rising behind Lady Liberty, setting ablaze not only her patina but swathing the windows of every skyscraper on the West Side in a mesmerizing palette of orange and yellows.

Dusty lights a cig and gives Steph a hug. "Robbs, this was fuckin' brill'! You and Flor should be damned proud of yourselves, bro. You boys made this night…this epic night."

"That's right, cutie, you put the icing on the cake with this," Lena chirps. Standing in awed silence with our arms locked in unity, taking in this incredible spectacle for all its worth, we acknowledge that very soon Battery Park will be overtaken with the rat race crowd, the earth shakers and money makers, but for right now, our inglorious warriors, battered and bruised from a raucous night of revelry, holds triumphant sway over this island.

We'll have to leave soon but until then, Gem and I proudly marvel at the spectacle that is our ragtag tribe of Misfits who are focused on the remarkable fall sky and bask in its intense sunlight.

"Golden and glorious, Swan? `A la vie de Boheme?"

"`A la vie de Boheme, Robbs, we'll always be golden and glorious."

···14···

The Way Home

IT'S FRIDAY, SEVEN A.M. and the island of Manhattan rapidly springs to life. Everyone seems to be rejuvenated, so it's suggested hitting the Empire Diner for some breakfast would be a befitting end to a remarkable trip.

Taking the subway on a workday, we're definitely out of place in appearance compared to last night and some of the 'suits' and 'dresses' glower condescendingly, having muted conversations amongst themselves. Gem and I overhear a middle-aged man in an expensive, tailored suit and overcoat express haughtily to the nattily dressed woman on his left, "This is our future? God help this country, they all look like animals and criminals. They need to take a bath, get a delousing, an education and some jobs."

The tribe stirs to his goading, but I ward them off, holding up my finger in a demonstrative, 'don't give them what they want' fashion. Gem and I both know how many punks are perceived by the general public, unfortunately some of our brethren fall into the trap with violent behavior and even though the animal instincts say for me to kick his teeth in for being such a pompous dickbag, my egalitarian senses take sensible control of the situation.

Playfully nudging Gem's ribs, I give her a wink. "Are you ready to give this sellout, Trump shithead a taste of his medicine the right way," I whisper.

"I certainly am, Robbs, let's do this." She pecks my cheek, arising to peaceably confront the gentleman in question before the nattily dressed woman tugs at his cuff linked sleeve, rolling her eyes in our direction and he stares at us with pure disdain. "Is there something you two vagrants want," I chuckle, which irritates him even more. "I don't see what's so funny with my question, street kid, now get lost before I call the transit cops."

"Excuse me sir, but you are being quite rude in your statements. All of us work in one fashion or another, we have our own money, some of us go to college and some are kids of the street figuring out ways to live every day without being larcenous or becoming petty thieves."

"I'm supposed to believe that a bunch of dirty drifters like you are better than just being common criminals? Please, move on..."

Gem smiles sweetly and speaks strongly for all to hear and it seems we have a rapt audience around us. "Sir, we'll only be on for a few more minutes so you can certainly believe what you want about us, but don't judge a book by its cover, for then I could look at you and say that you're a sellout to the generation you came from, a generation, mind you, which said to question everything.

"It seems as if you've lain down at the altar of greed and contempt. All we're doing is the same thing your generation did. Punks are questioning through their music and activism why so many in this country would turn their back on the common man and the frailest in our society," a statement which makes the pompous suit stare at his companion and snort. "The common man and the frailest in our society, come on you two. It's all code words for bums who can't hold their own in the new economy. You have a lot to learn, young lady."

His repugnance is astonishing but we remain undeterred, so it's my turn to turn the screws on this corporate hack for a bit…

"So, only the strong should survive, sir? That is a very short-sighted view, allowing a chosen few to reap all the rewards and spoils of a large society. That isn't even true capitalism, which in its original form, gave the average person enough money to continue having purchasing power, which keeps the proletariat working, content and able to provide for their family.

"What your generation professes is managerial capitalism which is Wall Street dictating what a company does, such as shutting down factories, leaving hundreds of thousands unemployed, losing everything they own and fighting over the meager scraps that are left. That is no longer capitalism, sir. That is a recipe for becoming what is known as being 'Third World'. Your generation which fought to stop such behavior is nothing more than feudal lords and tsars, which will eventually lead to a much-needed social revolution of the masses, overthrowing the powerful in their ivory towers and castles.

"Is that really what you want, sir? You're saying that most people in this subway car should be shivering under blankets in a subway station like many good people already are."

He goes to speak, but Gem cuts him off. "Sorry to interrupt you, sir, but you're the one who needs to learn something here. You're bringing the proletariat to their knees and worse, and for what, for avarice and shortsighted planning that will eventually hurt everyone and our planet? You're worried about my looks, my hair, my clothes…you need to worry about your vision for the world. It's a very despotic view."

The train screeches loudly when it approaches the station, I attempt to shake the man's hand, which he refuses to accept. "I hope we gave you some food for thought, sir and that for your children's sake, if you have any, that you'd please change your mind. You're heading the world into a very dark and dangerous future.

"For now though, we Bohemian, socialist peasants are going to enjoy breakfast at the Empire on our own dime. I bid you and your lady, adieu."

Gem takes a bow and blows them a kiss. "Change the world for the better, not for worse... please wake up, before it is too late."

A portion of the riders who'd been enthusiastically observing the animated discourse, actually applaud loudly and a well-dressed, older lady approaches us, going so far as to hug Gem and pats my spikes. "Thank goodness for you kids...you made my day. He was being so rude to you. I'm proud of the way you handled his condescending remarks." Turning to face the perturbed man, an admonishing finger is shaken in his direction. "I was ready to tell you to shut the hell up and leave these children alone!"

Laughing boisterously at her remarks, we depart the car to more cheers from the energized passengers, as our 'Master of the Universe' nemesis shuffles uncomfortably in his seat, averting everyone's glances.

The verbal confrontation has us psyched and hustling along, so within minutes, the door of the Empire is within reach. The diner's a total throwback to the pictures I'd seen in books of how the Metropolis looked like in its heyday, with gleaming chrome and stainless-steel jutting in every direction, as if a subway car had pushed up from below street level, landing unobtrusively onto the sidewalk. The inside has much of the same feel so it's nice being here after dealing with the Wall Street types, even though the working masses on the train made our day.

The Empire is a safe haven for the Bohemian proletariat of artists, musicians, writers, poets, gay activists, anarchists and dreamers, like our Misfits. A perky, middle-aged, dark haired waitress greets us happily, ushering us quickly to several rows of booths in the rear.

The conversation at the tables grows lively, vigorous and revolves mostly around the events of last night and who plans to cover the food bill, so once the monetary discussion gets settled, everyone's chatting so rambunctiously and simultaneously, even our sweet, motherly but exasperated waitress has to playfully 'take the piss' on us. 'Kids...kids! Christ almighty...one at a time...one at a time, please!"

Our usually sunshine Sammi reclines quietly besides us, grabs one of my Reds from the table and smiles awkwardly. "Gem, can you and Robbs join me outside for a smoke?"

"Sure we can, honey, is everything okay?" Sammi nods her head, grabs Lena's hand and pecks her cheek. "I'll be right back, Icy."

Lena stares lovingly at Sammi with her intense blue eyes. "I'll be right here, baby." Outside, we stumble into the blinding sunlight showering the city and Sammi taps her boot methodically on the pavement, incessantly smoking her Red, provoking a nudge from Gem to take the lead on the exchange. "Samms, you brought us out here to talk and I'm sure we know what it's about. You know us too well to hold back, so just go with your heart, girl."

Taking a deep breath, Sammi looks at Gem and nervously sighs. "Rob is right, Samms. Say what you're feeling, babe." Sammi burns through her Red, asks me for another one, takes a drag and exhales heavily.

"Look, Gem you know how I'm always flirting with Rob? I mean, I love Rob as a friend...but I don't think I like any boys like THAT anymore...probably haven't for some time. God knows, Rob...I enjoy being around you but you've noticed, you're the only guy I really hang with.

"What I'm trying to say is, for the past year or so I've really been feeling a lot stronger about being around girls. I mean, I pretty much slipped last week and you caught on, even though you kept it tongue and cheek, which I appreciated. I mean, am I being crazy here? I feel like I've fallen hard for Lena!"

Kissing Sammi's forehead, I happily drape my arm over her shoulder. "Samms, we know exactly what you mean. We're all good friends...hell, we're family so you don't have to explain. You've fallen for someone who makes you happy. Isn't that what really matters?"

Gem embraces her affectionately. "Oh my God, Samms... you're not crazy...you're in love. Listen, I've felt close only once to the way that you do about girls, I think it was more out of circumstance and concern…long story for another time…but I do know what love looks like.

"The way you and Lena stared at each other the other night at the apartment was intense…like how Robbs and I are with each other. That's not lust…it's not a passing fad…it's love."

"Does Lena know how you feel about her? I understand that you were kissing and all, but does she truly know the strong feelings you have?"

"She does, Robbs. I've been telling her constantly how I feel when we've been together and she feels the same way. Look, I know this isn't going to be easy and a lot of folks won't understand or like me because I'm in love with a girl, hell, I don't even have a clue as to how to approach this with my parents but I want Lena to be with me, so I guess I'll..we'll figure it out, somehow," she replies with superfluous, Samantha Baird optimism.

"Thanks for listening to me guys. You're like my best friends… hell…family and I'm so glad that I can tell you anything."

Gem tries to intone but we're interrupted by the door of the diner swinging open and the sound of heels approaching. "Hey, are you two gonna' take up all my girls' time," Lena inquires flirtatiously.

"Not at all, doll. Robbs and I are happy for both of you. We'll always be around to talk, if you need us. We know this is a big deal, and we also know how a lot of people will react to your relationship. All I'm saying is, if you need support, you have us and the rest of the tribe to lend you an ear."

Lena kisses both of us, thrusts her cig into the air and we happily follow suit. "Punks yesterday, punks today, punks for life!" she exclaims. We couldn't agree more…

"Punks for life!"

● ● ●

After a terrific breakfast and some hysterically enthusiastic banter, the Misfits sadly have to leave New York City. Alex's crew tags along on the subway ride to Penn Station and eventually we squeeze and squirm our way into the departing area for Jersey Transit.

Alex drapes his arms around Otto and me. "You boys be good, now. Take good care of yuh' girls. They are truly, as you say Rob…Punk Princesses." He gives me a hearty bear hug before we depart. "You are forevuh' my hero, brutha'. Love ya'!"

"Love you too, my Brooklyn bro' but you don't need to call me a hero, Alex," I reply with a hint of embarrassment. "You would've done the same for me last year."

Alex shakes his head and smiles. "Nah, sorry bro'…what you did was above and beyond…everybody still says we wouldn't be here…if not for you…"

Hastening to change the subject, I interject. "Listen, thanks again for being a surprise part of this night, brother, cuz' you and your tribe certainly helped to make this one memorable trip." The announcers' voice crackles through the speaker, announcing our train to Trenton's arrived, so, bummed as we are to depart, the journey home begins when the doors close behind us.

Upon taking our seats, Florian, Skate and Tim are already conspiring to hit Philly tonight and run the streets with the skater crowd. Dusty, Oren and Steph settle in for a quick nap, Lena and Sammi whisper sweetly to one another, until, like early this morning, they happily fall asleep in each other's arms.

Otto and Yuka are wide awake, as are Gem and I, so the conversation moves straight into the incredible night we'd just experienced, future plans and the like. Yuka professes her dream of becoming a designer, striking out boldly into the dog-eat-dog life of New York's fashion world. Otto really wants to take a shot at culinary school, hopefully becoming a chef in some posh Manhattan restaurant. Both swear they'll be CBGB regulars when they move to the city and that Gem and I can visit any time we want to.

I really don't know which way my path will take me, but I tell them how I hope to remain a writer, singer or lyricist of some sort, even if I had to supplement my income with a job like the mill for the time being. Gem definitely wants to do some kind of writing, keep playing in a band, especially if it's with me, she jokes and maybe teach underprivileged children in an inner city setting. Much like me, her future's a whirlwind of questions and opportunities. She loved her first true taste of New York and laughs that maybe we'll be Yuka and Otto's neighbors in some dive neighborhood on the outskirts of the Bowery.

During a lull in the conversation, Gem inquires why Alex calls me a hero, but I just told her to please understand there would be a better time and place to tell her the whole story behind that comment. Tired and somewhat unfocused to absorb what may be a long story, Gem smiles, replying maybe it would be better saved for a more private setting.

Gem thoroughly enjoyed our thoughts of the future...our hopes and dreams, but I notice her antsy behavior followed by a look of concern in her soulful eyes. The closer we're getting to Trenton, the more she thinks about little Claire. Yuka picks up on Gem's suddenly sullen demeanor and quickly holds her hands. "When we get to the station, we'll look for her, baby. You have my word."

"Me too, Gem," Otto adds.

"See that, Swan? We'll all look for that little one when we arrive in town." She leans into me and sighs. "Thank you so much, guys. I don't know what it is about her, but I just want to make her safe. Maybe it was her eyes, the despair...the soulfulness of her smile when she took our hands and thanked us for just caring. She was me, peering out from behind that raggedy blanket, looking so helpless and frightened.

"God, I am only a few years into getting myself back together but I wish I could just take her in and raise her myself." She begins to chuckle and lights a cigarette. "Christ, you must be thinking that I'm freaking cracked..."

"Gemma, you are the furthest thing from cracked...you've a heart of gold, hon. The little girl that most people would ignore, you embraced with warmth and love. If that is cracked, then cracked is an incredible thing to be."

"Awww...thanks, Robbs, you always know what to say to make me smile," she laughs heartily until the intercom suddenly hisses, "Trenton Station is our next stop, please make sure that you have all your belongings, and thank you for riding New Jersey Transit," so I attempt to get everyone's attention. "Yo, listen up Misfits, Gem and I are gonna' hang out with little Claire and see how she's making out today, so you're more than welcome to tag along, unless you have to get bookin'."

The tribe considers it to be a brill' idea, so when the train finally creeps to a stop, the rush onto the platform and up the stairs leading into the station commences. Moving hurriedly through the concourse to the place where Claire and her belongings were last evening, unfortunately, she's nowhere to be seen. Gem's noticeably nervous over this development but tries to be positive. "Well, maybe the Brody's rousted everybody out of here this morning," she conjectures in an overly hopeful tone.

Otto and I spot a transit cop standing next to the restroom doors and inquire if anyone befitting little Claire's vivid description has been witnessed here, sadly, he only recalls observing a few older homeless vacate the station earlier. When we're about to give up on our search, Gem and the girls scamper in our direction after she's discovered that another young street girl came around this morning and helped Claire get her things together upon their departure over an hour ago. "Maybe she went to get something to eat with the money you gave her, Robbs."

"It sounds like a good idea on her part, so hopefully that's what she did, Gem."

"I bet she did just that, sweetie," Lena chirps in. "I bet she's a tough cookie, just like us, Gem. She'll be alright." Gem smiles and pecks Lena's cheek. "Thanks Icy, you're probably right, well, let's get everybody home." After trudging across the potholed road, Dusty and I ignite our dew laden, maddening heaps of metal which are a chugging, calamitous, clanging mess from sitting in the frosty, overnight temps, but their warm-up time gives us a few minutes to say our goodbyes.

Everybody gives Florian another "PISS OFF, SOD OFF" cheer, thanking him profusely for transforming a total bomb of a night into the implausible, all-out fuckin' blitz that was CBGB's. I get thanked again for the magical overnight in Battery Park, culminating with the joyous pig-out at the Empire. To a person, they say it will never be forgotten. Flor and I lock arms, delivering a massively theatrical stage bow, for which we receive shouts of "bravo" and "oi" respectively.

Dusty's crew tumbles wearily into the belching Grenada, and we're already talking of meeting up tonight or definitely tomorrow, before he lays on his nasal, groaning horn and screeches out of the parking lot in a plume of pungent smoke and brake dust.

I ask Flor if we're dropping him somewhere but he wants to take advantage of the crisp, morning air and readies for his walk home. Meanwhile, I pull some change from Otis' ashtray, find a pay phone on the corner and give a painfully quick call to my house. Pronouncing that I'll probably not be home until sometime Sunday afternoon doesn't go over too well but I manage to assuage the aggravation level by adding that I'll gladly attend to any and all chores needing to be covered during the week, making me feel like a boot-licking pogue at the mo'.

After a hurried hang-up, Gem asks if everything's cool at home and I reply it's as good as it will ever be. She kisses my forehead, giving me a knowing wink before sliding into Otis. Lena and Sammi make themselves very comfortable next to Otto and Yuka, who grabs a hold of Sammi's hand. "I want to tell you how proud I am of both you girls. It's pretty ballsy to do what happened in that club and I applaud my honeys for it. Also, if any gal or guy gives you two any shit about your relationship, let me know. I'll be glad to tell em' to piss off!"

"That goes for me too, girls," Otto adds. "Nobody's gonna' talk down to you. Same thing I always remind Flor about too. We'll crack any fucker messin' with you all cuz' we're a punk family, damn it!"

Otis painfully putters through the lot and onto the streets of Trenton, so it's high time to get our ragtag tribe back to school and collect Sammi's car. Rolling across the "Trenton Makes" Bridge into Pennsylvania, the sun splashes rays of light everywhere, seabirds dance across the slightly rippling river below us and even though there's a chill in the air we keep Otis' windows wide open.

Gem happens across my box of cassettes and slides one into the player. "In honor of something that we hope never happens," she plays the Randoms classic, 'Let's Get Rid of New York', only to be followed by Fear's, 'New York's Alright if You Like Saxophones', and Exploited's, 'Dead Cities'.

"Great mix, Swan...keep em' coming!"

"You've got it, baby boy," she chirps, and as the Sex Pistols, 'Holidays in the Sun' kicks in hard with Steve Jones' guitar blaring, we're off to the races with Otis plowing ahead towards campus.

"A cheap holiday in other people's misery

I don't wanna' holiday in the sun
I wanna' go to new Belsen
I wanna' see some history
'Cause now I got a reasonable economy..."

The Misfits kick it up a notch with the chorus, before long, Otis' interior resonances resemble a deafening night at City Gardens, CBGB's or anywhere else our rebellious wanderlust take us...

"Now I got a reason, now I got a reason
Now I got a reason and I'm still waiting
Now I got a reason
Now I got a reason to be waiting
The Berlin Wall..."

The back seat becomes a violent mix of air guitars and drums, causing fits of laughter from Gem and me.

The big boat of a Chrysler soon slows to a crawl right next to Sammi's Torino and we thank her for finally hanging with us, before she peels out of the lot in a flash to destinations unknown with a radiant Lena sitting within inches of her on the cars bench seat.

Continuing our journey, we bounce enthusiastically into the city of Brotherly Love. "Wow! What they did last night was pretty intense. Do you think Samms is going to tell her parents, Gem?"

"I think she will, when she has time to take it all in herself, Rob."

She takes another drag of her cig and winks at me. "What a night, babe! I loved the shirtless look on stage too," she purrs. "Very sexy, indeed!"

"Thanks, Gem! I really wanted to do a bicep pose up there but figured Harley or Bloodclot would kick me in the nads and toss me off stage."

"Dude, that woulda' been funny as fuck," Otto snickers. "I have to agree with Otto, Robbs. That would have been hysterical, well minus the nad kick," Yuka replies with a giggle.

"No worry there, sis. Robbs lost his nads when he started rooting for the Rangers as a twit-shit kid," Gem dryly replies before they all explode into fits of laughter when I roll my eyes to the cars roof liner. "Yeah, yeah, yeah…laugh away with your Halloween colored, Philly goons. They're on a good win streak, but when the playoffs arrive, my guys will do you in." Gem clutches one of my Liberty spikes and flicks the Union Jack flag at the tip. "Robbs, you're usually an intelligent sort, but when it comes to following hockey, you're a big-time dipshit."

Yuka and Otto spew smoke out of their nostrils and fall about the back seat. "Piss off…all three of you! The Broad Street Bullshits are toast in the first round…guaranfuckinteed!"

"Oooooooo! Robbs is getting mad, Misfits!" and Gem looks so dead, fucking sexy making her point but I will not give in. "Hey guuuyyyys, should we remind him about the Rangers?" Oh shit, here it comes, the chant of futility, making any Rangers fans' skin crawl. "1940! 1940! 1940! 1940!" And there it is, the last year my team has won a Stanley Cup, laid bare, for all to see, a proverbial shot straight to the jewels from my own, supposed friends and my girl, to boot.

Tossing my cigarette out as we pull onto Fourth, I find a spot a few houses down from Gem's flat. "Ugh! Let's bounce, people. Oh, and piss off about your hockey team already."

Still snickering at me, I allow them to pile out of Otis, while I lean against the hood, giving them their spazzed out, pathetic moment in the sun. Gem approaches, grabs my chin and starts to coo. "Oooooo…my poor baby boy. I am soooo sorry you feel this way about my team, because I happen to have two tickets to see them and the…ummm…1940…Rangers play on December 5th, but if you feel so strongly about being seen with me, I could go elsewhere to see what guy's interested…"

My jaw drops at the thought of our insane, intense, pugilistic rivalry being played out in the Spectrum for thousands to see. I glance at Yuka and Otto, who are grinning profusely. "You two piss n' shits knew about this all along, eh?" Allowing some time to shower my Princess with a long, sweet kiss, I'm absolutely floored by the gesture. "Gem this is brilliant! Thanks!"

"Aww…you're welcome! Were you really surprised?"

"Oh, I sure was Gem, but not as surprised as you're going to be. Otto, would you be a good man, go into Otis' glove compartment and please grab the envelope under the owners' manual?" He hurriedly complies, handing the envelope to Gem, who's looking quite amused at the moment. "I was going to save this as an early Christmas present but go ahead, open it now, Swan."

The curiosity just kills Yuka and Otto, who crowd up behind Gem, as she pulls out two tickets and screeches with pure delight. "Oh, no effing way, this is just bizarre you two," Yuka gasps and Otto shakes his head in disbelief, because Gem is now the proud holder of two tickets to see the Rangers and Flyers play at Madison Square Garden on December 6th!

Gem jumps around excitedly. "How in the hell did you get these tickets? Oh my God, Robbs, this is going to be so fuckin' cool!" Pogoing around excitedly, Gem kisses me over and over, so when I finally get a chance to breathe, I tell her that Alex's dad, a season ticketholder, couldn't go to the game, so he let me have them. "This is going to be crazy fun!"

"Crazy fun, Gem? Holy crap, you two are going to brawl for two solid nights!" Yuka turns to Otto who's cracking up at the thought. "Yup, they're gonna' kill one another, Yuka."

Gem smirks and sticks out her tongue. "Piss off, you two! I don't care what they say Robbs, it'll be a blast." She pulls me close, biting my ear. "Sooo...you ready to get your thank you for a wonderful night and these tickets?" Smiling so seductively, I'm truly defenseless to her charms and she knows it, as does Yuka, who tugs at Otto's arm.

"Otto, let's get walking, babe. It's a beautiful day, so let's enjoy it before we crash at your place." Otto agrees this would be a good idea and tries to say something about the tribe meeting up tonight, but Yuka cuts him off, tilting her head in our direction as Gem continues her purring and nibbling. "Ohhhh...yeah... maybe we'll just give you a call tomorrow. We'll...ummm... hang out then..."

Yuka rolls her eyes to the sky. "It's why I love him so much, guys. My Otto's whirring, little peanut may take a while to catch on but he's a sweetheart! Well, whatever you two end up... ahem...doing, have fun, lovebirds!" Our two partners in crime thank us again for the great day, before departing down Fourth Street, disappearing into the emergent gathering of bodies.

Sitting on the stoop, we enjoy the growing warmth of the afternoon sun and Gem begins the slow purr. "Mmmm...I just love you, Rob Cavelli. Listen, why don't we go upstairs, grab a quick shower and head out for the afternoon? It's a gorgeous day, babe. I'm not ready to spend it inside yet. Besides, I want to be somewhere with just you."

I take another drag of our shared cig and smile. "It sounds like a perfect idea, Gem, especially the shower part..."

"Robbs..."

"You know you love this, Gemma Stinson."

She snuggles me tightly, breathing warmly along my neck. "Yeah, you're right, I do. So, how about we take my car? You can drive, if you'd like."

Breaking into a grin, I flick the spent butt from her stoop. "Are we thinking the same thing, Gem?"

"I think we are, love. New Hope it is then, Robbs?"
"New Hope it is, Gem!"

••• 15 •••

New Hope

BEADS OF WATER trickle down the bathroom mirror, spilling over its frame onto the sink below. "Damn, it looks like a London fog in here, babe." I move in again to cover Gem's glittering body with mine, pressing her against the bath tile and the chill from it makes her shudder. Running my tongue down her body, I catch droplets from her skin, tasting like the lavender soap she'd just rinsed off. "Mmmmm...you are getting way too comfortable up against me, love. At this rate, we'll never get out of the house today."

"You didn't seem to care about that minutes ago, Gem." I put my hands on her hips, press my weight against her as she becomes breathless. Holding her gaze on me, the eyes sparkle and there's not an inch between us when I give her neck a quick nibble, causing her to squeak. Snickering at the sound, I grab a towel to dry her off. "It kills me that I can make the rough and tumble, Punk Princess squeak like a bath toy."

Yanking the towel from my grasp, Gem snaps it off my thigh, before I can snag the end. "Keep being a wise ass and you'll only hear the sound of a pin dropping evvvvvery time."

"Ouch, that hurt worse than the towel snapping me."

Rifling the towel off my head, she haughtily steps from the tub. "Now you're catching on, baby boy!" she joyfully chirps, walking away slowly, making sure I catch every inch of her sexy hips swaying to the music playing in the other room.

"Damn, that's not even fair." Blowing me a kiss from the living room, she wraps the towel around her. "It's not supposed to be fair, babe."

After slipping on her bra and panties, she grabs a snug fitting black turtleneck and pulls a very short, red and black tartan skirt from her dresser. "Hmmm…what do you think of this and my boots?"

I stop dressing to take in the beauty that is Gem, shaking my head in utter amazement. "Your thigh high stilettos, I'm presuming?"

"Well of course…would I ever wear anything else with this skirt?"

"I think you just like being taller than me."

"Again…of course," she replies with a sexy, feline snarl before pushing me against the living room wall. "I find it to be quite intimidating." With our gear in order, we make sure the place is straightened up for when Misty arrives home and Gem tosses me the Bullet's keys.

"Am I winding her out today, babe?"

With a mischievous enough grin to make a leprechaun blush, she tosses her hair back, allowing the jet black and orange strands to cascade freely well past her shoulders, with the balance of it tumbling across the radiance of her light olive skin. "That's what she's made for Rob, so put her through the paces."

The afternoon sunlight through the windows catches her face, illuminating her exotic beauty and I can't take my eyes from the girl. She looks away awkwardly. "What…what is it, Rob, why are you looking at me like that?"

"My God, you're just so beautiful standing there, Gem. Why are you embarrassed when I say that?"

"Because if any guy said it to me before, it felt like they were only doing it to get one thing but not you, though. You value what I say, you admire my accomplishments. I'm not just a shiny ornament or a trinket to show off to your friends. I'm just Gem, the punk street kid and when you say I'm beautiful, I feel like a girl hearing it for the first time. I blush and look away because you mean it...because it really means something and I love you for giving me that feeling.

"You are so different than any guy I've ever been with. I could have told you today, or any other day for that matter that I just wanted to hang out...that I didn't want to do anything else and you know what I mean by that. You wouldn't have ever been upset with me."

"Why would I be upset with you? It's a decision for both of us to make." Putting her head on my shoulder, she plucks at my damp, but still spiky hair. "Hang on one second, cuz' there's something I want to take with us." Gem disappears into her room, returning happily with her guitar case. "I'm in the mood to play today, Rob."

"It sounds like an effing' brill' idea to me."

"Good, then let's get that Bullet bookin'."

Sporting a pair of black sunglasses which frame her face and hair dramatically, I open the car door and Gem smirks when a few high school girls in their hiked up uniform skirts smile, gawk and giggle when walking by. "Your hair is totally wicked," says one, as the others still giggle nervously.

"Thanks, not everyone thinks so."

"Is that your girlfriend in the car?"

"Yes, she is."

"Well, we think you're really cute, but we all think she's gorgeous. She looks like a model."

"I totally agree with you about that, girls. She's a beauty!" I exclaim before hopping into the car with a big grin that has Gem immediately amused. "Do we have a fan club of Catholic high school girls, darling?"

I crank the starter while Gem's baby roars to life. "So to speak dear, but apparently the big object of their affection is you, since they think you're gorgeous and look like a model," which makes her beam with pride. "They really said I look like a model?"

"Yup..."

"Oh my God, quick...speed up and catch them." Rolling down her window, she whistles loudly, startling the girls to say the least. "Thank you, girls, you are awesome!" She blows them a kiss before I rev up the Camaro, thundering away in a cloud of tire smoke.

"Did that make your day, Gem?"

"It made me feel good, but you...you've made my day, Robbs." I give her a quick kiss and within minutes we're heading out of the city towards greener pastures and placid settings...

● ● ●

The orange and yellow splashes of sunlight peek through the canopy of trees overhead as we navigate our way around the curves and straightaways of River Road.

Gem has control of the stereo and just about falls out of her seat when City Gardens own, Randy Now, hosting 'The Other Side' on WTSR from Trenton State College cues up the turntable with some new vinyl, allowing Gem to happily blast The Cult's latest song, 'She Sells Sanctuary' at max volume and after flicking her spent Newp out the window, she lends her powerful voice to compliment Ian Astbury's impressive ranges...

"And the sparkle in your eyes
Keeps me alive, keeps me alive
The world
And the world turns around
The world and the world, yeah
The world drags me down..."

Enraptured by her voice, ensnared by her intensity, the hand's removed from the shifter and soon across her long, lovely legs before the sultriness lures me to join her. "C'mon baby, you know the words, and you have the pipes. Sing it with me..."

"I'm sure in her you'll find
The sanctuary
I'm sure in her you'll find
The sanctuary
And the world
The world turns around
And the world and the world
And the world drags me down..."

"Damn Robbs, you sound so good with me. We're gonna' have some fun on the Landing today." Randy continues the tunes rolling with Flipper's, 'Sex Bomb', so I slowly parade Gem's Camaro onto New Hope's Main Street, where some bikers and punks don't hesitate giving an approving head nod to her silver shrine of Detroit muscle. I locate a spot in front of John and Peter's, the best joint in town to catch new bands, including punk acts. It's still quite early for the shows and after the battering and bruising of body, eardrums and wallet from CBGB's, we'll enjoy the respite for now.

Even though we're starting to fume out on funds, Gem and I bounce over to Random Records, seeing if we can bargain over any new or used punk albums or cassettes they may have obtained recently. Upon scouring through the racks of vinyl, Gem hears a familiar, squeakiness from the streets. "Oh my God, Robbs, come with me, baby boy...cuz' if it's who I think it is, you most certainly have to meet someone." Through Random's gritty windows I see Gem jump for joy, warmly embracing a short girl and a tall, lanky boy who are wearing some beat but very cool gear and respectively sporting a lime green and a purple mohawk.

"Rob Cavelli, I'd like you to meet Clarissa and Monk, two of the many corner kids with me when I was living on the street." I exchange a long embrace with Clarissa and receive a surprisingly strong handshake from Monk. "Always a pleasure to meet any of Gem's friends," I reply while blazing a Red, offering one to

177

Monk who happily accepts after inquiring about sparing one for Clarissa as well.

"I can't believe you're in New Hope, Gem. Do you live up here now?"

"No, I'm still in Philly on Fourth Street, 'Rissa, but Rob lives close by, so we love travelling here when we can. It's a welcome break from the insane hustle and bustle of city life. How about you guys? Are you living here, of all places? I figured you'd just disappeared into the abyss of the city forever."

"Nah, we're squatting over in Lambertville in a beat-up Victorian with about ten other punk kids. The Brody's try to roust us every so often but other than that and keeping the wild dog packs out of our grub when we chill under the bridge, it's a pretty peaceful existence," Monk exhorts before hacking on a long drag taken from his almost spent cig. "I gotta' give these damn things up one day...they'll fuckin' kill you." Informing Monk and Clarissa that we're heading to Ferry's Landing to chill and let loose some tunes on this awesome afternoon if they'd like to join us, they agree it's a kicking idea, matching us stride for stride down the Landing's path.

Gem grabs a spot on the bench, opens her case, grabs her guitar, before crossing her long, sexy legs, resting the weathered, wooden beauty across them while doing a quick tuning. "Hmmm...what to play...what to play?" Breaking into a slight smile, she starts with the opening bars from The Cult song we'd just heard on the ride up. I sit in utter amazement listening to the sheer perfection of Gem's playing, her ability to memorize a tune in minutes and replicate it within moments. "Do you remember the words, Robbs? C'mon, get ready to sing with me."

We belt out the lyrics to an awestruck Monk and Clarissa, who bob their heads to the rhythm. "Damn girl, how the hell do you even know this song? It's only been out since like yesterday," Monk yells over our playing. "That's our Gem, 'Riss, still amazing us with what she knows!" When Gem runs her gleaming talons across the strings for the last time, Monk, Clarissa and a few teenagers who scrambled down the alley when they'd heard the music cheer us on enthusiastically.

Monk pulls us aside, asking if we know a decent amount of songs to play, to which we reply "yes." He asks Gem if she feels like playing standing up and she replies, "what are you up to, Monk? You have that street corner glint in your eyes."

Snagging Gem's case, Monk clomps his raggedy, lace less, Doc Mart's towards Main Street, making a hurried stop into Farley's, the corner bookstore and within seconds exists the premises with a mile wide grin before opening the case, placing it next to Gem's feet.

"Rob and Gem, the bookstore is cool with this, so here's the golden opportunity for you to fill your car, have some spending cash and maybe get yourselves noticed on the streets of this town by some club owners. Rob and Gem, this afternoon, you are New Hope buskers."

"Are you cool with this, Robbs?" Gem squeaks happily before tuning up her acoustic.

"I think it's a bitching idea, Gem, so let's do it. We've done it in Philly, so why not here?" Amped up to deliver a knockout opener, Gem damn near tears the strings off during 'She Sells Sanctuary' again, and a small group of New Wave and punk kids mill around us, as do some adults who were in Farley's and the surrounding stores. Siouxsie's version of 'Dear Prudence', The Clash's 'London Calling', the U.K. Subs 'Warhead', are amongst the hastily put together list performed, and a number of people give a listen, throwing coins and dollar bills in Gem's case over the next few hours. We get a good round of applause after doing Killing Joke's, 'Eighties' and we tear through our original, 'Filthy City of Rats' bringing hoots, howls and laughter from the punk kids, so Gem decides to slow the pace down a bit.

"This next song's a favorite of ours and it's taken on a new meaning after befriending a young homeless girl recently. For those of you in the crowd that can donate goods or money to local shelters, please do so because living on the streets is something no one should have to do. I should know, I was one of those kids you saw shivering in the cold or sleeping on the sidewalk.

"If any of you know this song and love it as much as we do, feel free to sing along. This is for Claire," and when Gem plays the beginning chords of The Replacements, 'Unsatisfied', a handful of young punks smile knowingly. We take turns singing, eventually imploring the kids who know the words to come up front and join us before Gem finishes to some very well-received applause. "This was awesome, love," she chirps excitedly, throwing her arms around me, her gleaming, emerald eyes begging for some form of passionate reply, so I have no choice but to kiss her pursed, wet lips. "I love you so much, Robbs. New Hope always ends up being magical for us, doesn't it?"

"It sure does, Gem. What another unforgettable experience and thanks for letting me sing with you. I can really make this a habit…you and me performing together." Jubilantly entering Farley's, we thank them profusely for allowing us performance time alongside their business. Gem and I each try to purchase a magazine as a small token of our gratitude but the manager refuses to accept our money, instead pulling out a ten spot in appreciation of the outside entertainment and imploring us to set up shop by their doors when we hit town again.

Monk and Clarissa snag the guitar case and head to the Landing to count our spoils. "With the managers ten, you guys made over thirty dollars. Wow, an unbelievable bagging of coinage, folks." Gem and I huddle together, deciding to give them half of the take, since it was Monk's brill' idea anyway. Initially, they refuse but Gem's adamant. "So, when's the last time you two had a full cabinet of food?" she asks, to which they both shrug their shoulders. "Yeah, neither one of you will answer me, so take the money and get some food before you get sick." Clarissa thanks Gem, hugging us forever before Monk looks dejectedly at the large, ornate, iron clock standing regally in the center of town. "Guys, thanks for the entertainment…you really made our day and we hate leaving but we have to watch some of our friends' kids so they can work tonight." Walking across the bridge, they eventually wave goodbye, mixing in with the early, Friday evening diners of Lambertville's swank, new eateries.

Gem and I sojourn at the halfway point of the span, with our feet straddling the painted Jersey and Pennsylvania border designations underneath them and we share a smoke. The late afternoon sun beats warmly against our backs, the gentle autumn winds wisp around our faces Gem remarks on how the peaceful, shimmering tides on the river below remind her of our one trip to Seaside Park this past summer.

"I loved being down at the shore with you...our bodies so close and glistening in the sun." Reminiscing even more about the day, Gem giggles continually about how I tried to teach her to surf as she tumbled repeatedly into the waves. "I was dead tired...getting so frustrated...but there you were, being ever patient, just showing me what to do. I was so excited when I finally stayed up and rode a wave!

"I was in awe watching you surf, Robbs...how free and at one with the waves you looked. I hope one day I'm good enough so that we can both enjoy that feeling together.

"And then lying on the beach with you at sunset...getting under our blanket when it was chilly and so dark. Making love to you with the waves crashing in the distance was incredibly intense and then when we looked into each other's eyes, the way you just held me so strongly in your arms until I fell asleep. It's a night that I remember non-stop, Robbs."

"It was a memorable night for me too, Gem. It was when I realized how much I was really falling in love with you. I couldn't stop telling you either...ha, ha...you were probably tired of hearing me say that to you."

She stares intensely, unashamedly whispering her reply. "I'll never tire of hearing that." Kissing me tenderly, the walk back culminates with some well-deserved rest by the Delaware's serene waters, just holding one another tightly. There's so much connecting us now, our love of the punk scene, our great friends, our writing, the music, our feelings of what's politically just, and most importantly the strength of our feelings for each other.

The wind slips and whistles in between the bridges support beams, making Gem snuggle me even closer. "It'll be getting dark soon, Swan, are you ready to head back to Philly?" Pushing the lustrous, windswept hair away from her face, she contemplatively sighs. "I'm so ready, baby boy, even though New Hope was a great way to top off an already incredible couple of days."

Viewing the breathtaking sight of the river again, I smile at the beauty surrounding us. "You know, there's going to come a time when I have to figure out what I want out of life and settle down. I think settling down here would be a very easy and peaceful choice for me."

Holding her hand lightly, slowly meandering through the dinner crowds scurrying about the Borough, we reach the Bullet. Gem awaits the opening of the passenger door but not before I press my body against hers, holding her arms back against the roof of the car, never averting my eyes from hers, as she nervously laughs. "What's that look for, Rob?"

"I was just imagining the thought of me settling down here and you being around to see that happen...maybe even settle down with you."

"I would like that very much, love. You know, I say this whenever we come here and maybe the thought of us settling down makes this have a lot more sense to it...so, here it goes... I'll love you forever, Rob."

"Forever sounds glorious, Gem."

"Golden and glorious...Rob."

Slicing the SS through the rolling curves of River Road, the music of Social Distortion, The Minutemen and Husker Du blasts in the background while Gem and I share more smokes, stories, laughs and dreams. The sun descends quickly, dancing through the orange, yellow and red canopy overhead until our adopted town is all but a darkening memory of faintly flickering lights in the rearview mirror.

··· 16 ···

Where Is She?

NIGHT'S FALLEN OVER Yardley Borough and although the meandering journey along River Road comes to an enjoyable completion, Gem plays The Clash's, 'Straight to Hell' at a low volume, leaning across the shifter to embrace me. Making solid eye contact, her sunny demeanor rapidly transforms to concern. Across the river, the lights of Jersey's capitol city glimmer in the distance. I rub my hand across her legs and slowly bring it up to caress her cheek. Rolling past the Calhoun Street Bridge, I give her a kiss, quickly understanding the soulfulness that is Gem. "At the next light, we'll be able to turn onto the Trenton Makes Bridge so we'll bolt to the train station from there."

Casually touching my cheek, her smile radiates through the darkness of the car. "I just adore the way you can read my thoughts, Robbs. It gives you an even more endearing quality." The hard-shell exterior of Gemma Stinson still can't hide the fact that inside comprises the soul of an amazingly caring and compassionate young lady. She hasn't stopped thinking about that soulful eyed, little, raggedy waif since last night. "Hang on tight, Gem, we'll check up on little Claire." She thanks me for doing this, but she really doesn't have to because it's always been our code, a punks' code, our socialist roots, if you'd like, to look out for those who need a hand.

Hastily spotting the parking field, Gem grabs my hand as we hustle our way across the street, deftly dodging the evening rush hour traffic, blaring horns and rude catcalls. The clicking of her heels can be heard across the tile floors of the cavernous train station and the yuppie set is definitely getting an eyeful with us tonight but to hell with their stares, our only objective is finding Claire.

Gem and I approach the spot where Claire previously resided, but agonizingly realize she's still not amongst the throngs of homeless entering the station for nighttime refuge. Dejectedly, we're ready to give up but Gem appears to have found out some information and from the sullen look of dismay, I presume it can't be good. Tapping her boot heel rapidly, she relays the message from the haggard, older woman who is now picking through a trash can by her belongings.

Claire departed with another young girl like we'd heard but there was no way she was going for something to eat. The girl she'd bounced with was a known prostitute who enticed young girls off the street with the promise of a warm place to crash in return for 'testing' the latest strain of heroin being pushed by her dealer-pimp. Gem tells me where the house is located and I can't even attempt to hide my growing concern for our newly found, young friend.

"Rob, how bad could this be?"

"You did say Perry Street, right?" Her impatience and unease with the situation is growing worse. "Yes, I did say Perry Street, so how bad is this going to be for Claire, Robbs?"

I kick at the tile with my combat boots and grab a Red from my jacket. "This could be some deep shit, Gem, possibly like K & A." I exhale, allowing the smoke to billow around us; a thick fog enveloping our gloomy situation. "A girl was recently killed there, Gem. She was young, got lured into a building and that's where she was found a few days later."

Gem grabs my Red, pacing frantically, her eyes revealing the personal pain of years gone by. This is striking too close to home for her and anxiety grows with every ticking second of the large, digital clock she can no longer ignore…its red glow spattering about the floor like the agonizing droplets of blood spilled throughout her harrowing, formative years.

"Rob, we can't leave her out there. We have to try and find her!"

"I knew that's what you'd say, Gem. This is going to be pure hell we're walking into…" Crushing the half spent Red under my boot, I shake my head, take a breath, give her a wink and dart through the station into the crisp, Fall air. "Let's get going girl because nightfall isn't going to make this any easier of a task."

We sprint through the calamitous nighttime traffic back into the lot. "Do you have anything in your trunk we can use in case the shit hits the fan down there?"

"I have a tire iron and one of Ronnie's old baseball bats is in there."

"Ok, that's a start. Listen, I know we can both tear up some folks if need be, but that may not be enough. What time is it, babe?"

"Almost seven, Robbs…what are you thinking?"

"Jump in, Gem, I've got an idea."

● ● ●

The desolate, dimly lit streets of Trenton, sinister on this night more than ever, sucks the life out of anything left in its presence, save for the silver steed rocketing through the decay, despair and hopelessness. Punching the accelerator almost to the rumbling floorboards, this Motor City nightmare snorts, scoffing as if to inquire, "that's all your bitch ass has for me," so I thrash on it, throwing her through the battle scarred avenues of the metropolis like one of the Four Horseman of the Apocalypse on their final ride towards hell. Through the foreboding landscape, a glimmer of light appears on the horizon.

Racing manically towards the unknown in hope of salvation for one innocent, I spin the 'Bullet' harshly through the gravel after seeing a few cars and some roosters milling about in the smoke and filth of Hades playground..City Gardens...we are home. A familiar face runs over to greet us when the dust settles and the steed rests, occasionally snarling and braying, readying itself, begging for more action.

"Damn, I didn't expect to see you lovebirds hard charging it this soon after last night."

"Flor, we got a big fuckin' problem! Who else is here that we know?"

"Trent and some of the local boys are here already and getting restless." Perring in the car, he's totally aware of Gem's helpless expression. "What the hell is going on guys?"

"Flor, do me a favor, get the boys over here, we may need some bodies. You remember the young girl we befriended last night?"

"Yeah, Claire...sure I remember. We couldn't find her this morning, why, what's up?"

"Grab the guys and I'll fill you in."

Flor hastily corrals Trent and five other rough and tumble punks we know from the shows. I fill them in about Claire, as does Gem, who is very concerned about what may be happening to her right now.

"Look, I know most of you don't know her and I understand if you don't want to look for her, but those of us that have been kids of the streets...or have known kids of the streets, let's try and save one tonight. She may have put herself in a very bad situation.

"She's young, she's alone...I know how that feels and so do some of you. If you don't mind putting yourself in harms' way just this once, we could save a young girl from some really heavy shit tonight. It's the right thing to do, guys. It's part of the reason we're punks...it's part of our fuckin' code."

"Gem, we got your back, doll. Anything you and Rob need tonight, it's yours. Yo' Rob, you ready to show me a repeat of that Fairmount beatdown if need be, son?" Trent smirks, stopping only to run, his battered knuckles across his tapered, brown mohawk.

"I will if I have to, buddy. Claire's on Perry Street, and since Gem, Flor and I know what she looks like, we'll jailbreak her outta' that shithole. You gotta' be our eyes and ears outside if shit gets weird. You all still in?"

"Fuck yeah, we're in, son. Boys, get the car and let's follow Rob."

"Thanks for this, bro! You know this could get real fucked up, real fast, right Trent?" I ask before the black, rusted Cutlass full of punks screeches to a stop. "Sounds like my goddamn kinda' night, son," he grins, chomping at the bit to brawl and spill blood.

Running like bats out of hell, we get to the car and Gem damn near stumbles on her heels but Flor grips her hard. "Thanks, sweetie," she says breathlessly.

"Anytime, Gem," Flor replies with some very nervous energy. I pull anything out of her trunk that we may need to start swinging if we catch some resistance on the streets. "Get these bats and crowbar under our seats, Gem!"

Gem grabs the pillows and blankets out too, handing them to Flor. "We may have to wrap her up and keep her warm if she's got smack in her system."

"Gotcha', Gem." Flor is really psyched up to look for our little waif. "C'mon! Let's haul ass, Rob!" Smoking the SS down Calhoun, the Cutlass within inches of our taillights, the silver streak thunders onto U.S. 1 and I let the girl have a full head of steam on the highway, slide furiously within seconds through the Perry Street exit, past the offices of the Trenton Times and bring her to a snarling crawl, as does the Cutlass.

No need to go fast through this part of town since it will only draw the Brody's unwanted attention which is the last thing we need right now. The streets attain an eerie silence only witnessed in a truly blighted and decimated area. Poverty and misery rule many of the Wards of Trenton and Perry Street is no exception.

Gem's head is on a swivel, surveying the landscape like a top notch military scout in case the shit hits the fan out here because as much as she's the girl I love, who'll lend a hand to anyone, she's also a street kid who can punch, kick and literally claw her way out of back alley brawls that should've put her in a hospital or morgue; instead she's pulverized girls and guys into submission so brutally, one self-proclaimed badass greaser even soiled himself and bawled like an infant upon Gem pounding him and slashing a chunk from under his Adam's apple because he stole her money and slapped her hard across the face.

"Robbs, there it is. The old lady said it had a red door and the buildings around it were burnt out. Jesus Christ, this is as rancid as anything I slept in the K & A or past Seventh and South…oh, Claire. Rob, they'll mutilate that little girl in a place like this.."

We park further down the street, trying to not draw too much attention to ourselves. Trent and his boys get out of the Cutlass and we go over our plan. "Gem, Flor and I will hit the house, see if we can make a score, then I'm going to try an' get us in. I'll tell him that Gem heard her girlfriend is here and she can't shoot up without being 'serviced' by her."

Trent grins at that. "Son, that's fuckin' brill! Those cocks will totally get off on the lesbo shit. They'll let you right in."

"That's what I'm hoping for and as soon as we find her, we'll pay for the shit, dump it in that alley and get bookin' with her back to the car. Claire may not be in any condition to walk so get ready to help us out."

"Anything you need son, you got it. Go get your girl…and Miss Gem?"

"Yeah, Trent?"

"You stay right by Rob and Flor, girl. I know yer' tough as nails, but we need you stayin' safe. Ya' got me?"

"I got you, Trent…Robbs and Flor have my back…see you soon."

Approaching the burnt-out house with the cool, calculated demeanor of panthers stalking their prey, the area around the shooting gallery is surveyed repeatedly. In the alleys, piles of rotted garbage, piss and shit mix together to permeate the air with a noxious odor. Several shadows lurk ominously between the two structures and from the sound of things, they've already drifted into the euphoric highs or death throes of the poison obtained from the house with the blood colored door.

Sensing the tensing of my muscles because I thoroughly detest what these dealers do to an area, Gem holds me close. She must know I'm thinking of Kellin, peddling his shit to a young, desperate Gem just to fuel his sick desires with her. "Keep calm, babe. We're here to get her out; nothing more, nothing less."

"I'll be good, Gem…no hair trigger reactions from me, babe. You ready to do this, Flor?"

"Never readier, guys, let's get her the hell out of here." We walk past a few strung out junkies and up the steps of the house. I stare at Gem, giving her a wink to let her know I'm calm, my breathing is low, slow and ready for anything.

"Gem, you know I'm going to have to talk trash about you to these creeps, so…"

"Unfortunately, I've heard it all before, Robbs. Say what you need to say," she replies nonchalantly.

Rapping on the solid, wooden door loudly, the recessed slot opens quickly as a set of cold, darting eyes meet mine. "Nice hair, porcupine. The fuckchoo want?"

"I hear you got some prime smack here, brother." I pull a twenty out, swaying it back and forth across the slot. "I got some friends who want to party tonight."

"Gimme'it through the slot, bro and we'll getchoo hooked up."

"Tell you what, son, another ten to let us in so my bitch back here can look for her girlfriend. They only shoot up together after little bitch pleasures her and you know what that means for me, kid."

The cold eyes lighten up and I hear him deviously chuckle. Cracking it open slightly, he waves us in. "Yeah, I know 'zactly what you mean, man. Your bitch here hot as shit man, you must be a crazy fuck cracker takin' her into a neighborhood like this.

"Gimme' the money up front and take a look. Everybody in that room right there…no fuckin' 'round now. We got a business goin' here…ya' got me?"

"Loud and clear, brother...loud and clear." Cautiously, the gatekeeper leaves us to scatter throughout the dilapidated living room searching amongst the bodies lying everywhere. The foul den of misery reeks of numerous bodily fluids and it's enough to make me wretch, yet I have to keep my wits about me and focus on saving Claire from this madness. We move around for a minute or so, kicking through spent hypos and crack vials but I can tell the gatekeeper is growing impatient. "Yo' bitch find her girl yet, bro?"

Stopping by a small, lumpy blanket, Gem kneels down, stroking at the hair of the girl under it, embracing her strongly. Holy shit, we found Claire. Flor and I stand nervously over them and I tap Gem's shoulder as she gently extracts the poison bliss filled rig from our girls' razor thin arm. "We'd better get the shit from this asshole and get going," I whisper. "Gem, babe...are you listening to me?" I ask her again, however she keeps stroking at Claire's hair and whispering in her ear.

"Rob, she's not moving, she doesn't hear me." Kissing her forehead, Gem pulls away from Claire fast. "Rob, she's burning up. We've got to get her out of here." Shaking furiously, she balls up her fist, hitting the floor hard next to Claire. "What the fuck did these animals give her?" The anguish, the rage from a painful past has finally boiled over, so I motion for Flor to get Gem moving but she grabs at Claire, crying out to her, "baby wake up, please baby wake up."

Scooping Claire from the ground is ridiculously effortless...Jesus fuckin' Christ, she's so emaciated. Pressing her body against my chest, I can barely feel her heart beating. "Let's haul ass, guys...we're gonna' lose her."

The gatekeeper spots us moving with Claire in my arms and begins snickering. "Hey, I thought yo' girls would give us a show tonight. Well, maybe you bring her hot, tall ass to have some fun with a girl who can hang next time," he says pointing to Gem.

"Look, just keep the cash, we gotta get her outta here, she's really sick." I want to cave this fucker's skull in but my main focus is getting Gem, Flor and the very ill Claire out of this shithole.

"Thanks for the dough, bro…and don't think you mutha's gonna' blame us for yo' bitch lookin' like that. She came here that way."

Flor grabs the door open and almost has Gem out, until she hears the gatekeeper's snide remark. "You're full of shit, asshole! She was alert and smiling last night."

Placing the volcanically feverish Claire into Florian's arms, ushering him down the steps with Gem's car keys now in his hand, we give one another the knowing look we'd feared would occur. "Get the boys ready, this could get ugly," I murmur.

The gatekeeper and a scantily dressed street whore start towards Gem until I cut off their progress. "Yo, you better curb yo' bitch's temper, cuz' I been patient til' now."

"Back off from her and we'll be cool, kid. Everyone gets what they want here and we'll leave."

The gatekeeper grins and spits on the floor in front of Gem. "Damn right ya'll leavin', now get yo' raggedy asses outta' here."

The street whore isn't about to stop running her mouth and flails her hands wildly in Gem's face. "You heard my man, get the fuck outta' here wit' your raggedy lil' bitch. She all crying like a bitch for her mom and some Gem pussy. Guess that's you, tramp. Heh, well, you a little too late for yo' bitch."

A blur of orange and black streaks past me and the crack whore gets strangled, punched and tossed down the front steps in a matter of seconds. Gem repeatedly stabs her heel into the screaming girls' ribs while darting headlights swirl around the empty buildings before the Camaro and Cutlass come screeching up to the curb.

Jumping from the stoop, I swing Gem away from the girl who is damn near unconscious from the repeated blows and kicks but not before Gem's dagger like nails rip into the girl's face, leaving a vicious, bloody gash under her left eye. I push her towards the SS with the gatekeeper in hot pursuit and Flor swings open the passenger door, pulling Gem in and sliding me the bat from across the front seat.

Two more people have joined the gatekeeper, but Trent and his friends' gang tackle the goons, delivering them a quick stomping.

Furiously breaking loose from Trent's grip, the gatekeeper relentlessly storms in our direction, reaching into his pocket, but not willing to discover what he has in store for us, he has the unfortunate displeasure of meeting a swift shot to the ribs from a Louisville Slugger. Writhing on the ground, bellowing screams of utter pain, I give the prick a solid crack to the face with my fist before reaching into his pocket and tossing his concealed piece into the car. Adding insult to his various injuries, I grab our money back. "That's what you get when you poison young girls' who are just looking for a place to get out of the cold, you fuckin' asshole!"

Trent has the Cutlass pouring smoke and ready to bolt and Flor implores me to hop in Gem's ride. "Come on, Rob...more are coming," he roars, pointing out three more goons running from the alley. Flor mashes the pedal, swings a hard U-turn on Perry Street and with the Cutlass glued to our bumper, we turn wildly onto U.S. 1, only slowing down when out of harm's way. Pulling onto the shoulder, I sprint towards Trent and toss the gatekeepers' piece over the barrier, listening for the eventual splashdown into the depths of the Delaware. "Son, that was fucking insane! Gem and you thumped the piss out of those assholes!"

"Thanks for getting the other goons, guys, we really needed the help."

"Ah, no problem, son, it was all in a night's work. How's her young friend doing?"

"Not so good, T, we have to take her to Saint Francis. She's in bad shape."

"Well, let's haul ass, son, we'll see this through with you."

Sprinting through the crisp, evening air, I find Florian in the back seat helping Gem bundle Claire in a mountain of blankets before cautiously placing a pillow under her head. "That's it, angel, please wake up, little one," Florian begs of her.

Claire stirs just enough, her eyes opening slightly to see who's caressing her. "Gem...Gem...you found...me...don't leave...I'm sorry...just wanted...a place to...sleep," she painfully smiles, fading in and out of consciousness.

Gem kisses Claire's forehead, sheltering her fledgling like a mother bird. "Shhh, baby, I'm not going anywhere, I'll take care of you. You're safe now, the bad people are all gone.."

"So sorry...Gem...help me..."

"Hang on, guys, I'll get her to Saint Francis." Looking in the rearview, Gem goes ashen in appearance. "Robbs, hurry! I don't think she's breathing anymore. Oh my God, I can't feel her heart beating. Oh, my God! Please breathe, little angel! Breathe!" And as tears from the years of pain inflicted on her by life on the streets stream down her face, splashing onto Claire's very frail body, Florian implores Gem for some room to administer CPR on our little friend. I catch Gem's eyes, begging her to stay focused. "We've got this, babe, Claire's not dying tonight!"

The SS leaves smoke pouring out its rear and the Cutlass rushes to catch us through the city, which becomes a blur when we hit Route 29 and after a furious run-down West State Street and a frame bending turn into Hamilton, I slide furiously into the lot by the Emergency Room, and help Flor gently extract Claire. Once our delicate, little angel is in my arms, Flor, Gem and Trent's crew make a mad dash to get into the E.R.

"HELP US! NURSE, SOMEBODY HELP US," Gem cries desperately. Two E.R. nurses' race towards us immediately with a gurney, doing their best to asses a desperate situation. "Try and calm down dear...tell me exactly what happened to this little girl."

Breathing heavily, explaining that we found Claire in an alley on Perry Street with a needle in her arm, it's a brilliant lie on Gem's part, negating a chance of us being placed in that drug house or the beating we put on the gatekeeper and his goons, because the Brody's would certainly put us through the wringer and none of us need to get hauled in for assaults on lowlife crap, so corroboration of Gem's story is readily expounded.

Gem cries again, putting her head on the nurses' shoulder. "Please, please help her. God knows what was in that needle besides heroin."

"We'll do our best, hon. Let us do our job now," she replies warmly, consoling Gem as more medical staff appears rapidly around the gurney and it's only then we begin to tell the excruciating toll unforgiving streets have placed on this fragile, little bird of a girl. Fresh needle marks show this isn't her first trip down the lane, with a repeated amount of quick highs to forget the meanness of how she ended up in this catastrophic nightmare.

The baby faced E.R. doctor arrives, surmises her condition, hurriedly ushering Claire towards the doors of the O.R. with tribe in tow. "We're losing her, team!" he bellows and Gem continues holding Claire's hand as they pick up speed. "BREATHE BABY, PLEASE BREATHE!" The emergency staff calmly tells us we have to wait out here but Gem's still running alongside. "I want to go with her...please, let me go with her. She knows me...PLEASE!"

I finally catch Gem, holding her tightly. "You have to let them do their jobs, girl," I whisper softly. "We'll all wait here. We're not going anywhere, Gemma, except outside to get some fresh air and a smoke."

A few of Trent's tribe locate the cafeteria to snag some coffee. Gem's hands tremble poorly in a mixture of nerves and adrenaline from the night's insanity, with the incredible journey into New York, the beautiful enjoyment of New Hope seeming like some distant, dashed memory.

Time passes and we're running through cigarettes like water. A few hospital staff and Brody's question us about Claire and where we found her but there's only minimal information we can give them about a girl we'd befriended from the streets last night, so we corroborate the story of finding her in the alley by a drug house on Perry Street.

The Brody's realize the information they're receiving is fairly scant and depart, so Trent takes Flor to get more smokes at his house and upon their return, Flor informs me he's made calls to most of the Misfits and that whoever he could track down is on route to the hospital.

Within an hour or so, more cars pile into the lot until we're surrounded by Dusty, Steph, Oren, Skate and Tim. Yuka, Otto, Lena and Sammi show up about ten minutes later to occupy the majority of the E. R.'s lobby and a few of our tribe occasionally show up outside to worrisomely monitor Gem's and my condition.

Trent and his boys catch up the Misfits about what transpired and instantly, Sammi, Lena and Steph are draped over me on the curb. Yuka kneels down, exploding into my face out of sheer frustration. "Baby boy, what the hell were you two thinking? You didn't get close enough to getting sliced up in Fairmount, so now you storm a drug house?!" She grabs my shoulders, shaking me hard. "Goddammit Rob, you fucking can't save everyone, not even someone who deserves to be saved," but I only look at the girls before reaching to have another cig and Gem arises, protectively placing her arms around me. "Don't blame him, sis. I wanted to find, Claire. This little girl is so much like how I was when you saved me from the streets. I just wanted to try and save her too."

"Gem, Yuka is right. You can't put yourself in harms' way like that to save every little bird with broken wings," Lena adds contemplatively, but I take the time to stand, pulling another long drag, shaking my head derisively. "Listen, I love you guys, fuck it all, I'd battle anyone who'd hurt any of you. Yuka…Lena, I understand your concern and I love that you care about Gem and me so much…but you're wrong on this.

"I was too young to do anything about my pop being killed… God knows if I could have done a damn thing to save him anyway, but I'll tell you this much…if I can try and save even one person in my lifetime than it's truly been a life worth living."

Yuka wipes the tears streaming slowly down her cheeks and nods. "Damn you and your college debating, Robbs! I hate when you make a point that I can't argue with!" Her comment allows for a much-needed laugh. "You're still crazy as shit though, Robbs. Batshit crazy! You know this, right?"

"I know, Yuka…I know," I reply before leading our large circle of friends into the lobby to keep vigil for this wild-eyed little girl who within a few days' time has captured all of our hearts.

• • •

Another agonizing hour passes, however we've heard nothing new about Claire and restlessness turns into a non-stop inquiry of Claire's progress at the main desk.

Arising from the couch with Gem in tow, ready to pester the very sympathetic but groggy desk nurse again, the doors from the operating area swing open, revealing an exhausted, baby faced doctor and the nurse who'd consoled Gem earlier.

He commends our valiant efforts to save Claire from insurmountable odds and continues speaking of her feeble condition, something about a toxic mixture of heroin and traces of poisons in the cocktail with which she'd been injected and the endless times resuscitating her, only to fail once again from the weakness of her heart and a diminutive frame which had probably been ravaged for months by the poisons of the streets.

The nurse reaches out to touch Gem's trembling hand and we give each other a look of utter bewilderment when they explain no measure was spared to save her, until she finally expired a half hour ago. Expired…expired…EXPIRED…

The words strike painfully, like a lead pipe across the face and try as we may to comprehend these final words, it's all a blur, a cruel fucking blur, and before long the equally dejected doctor and nurse depart with their heads held low.

Gem releases her grip, backing away panicked. "No, she's not gone! We saved her from that damn place, Robbs! She's not supposed to DIE! She's supposed to be saved…she's supposed to get cleaned up from that garbage! She's supposed to live a happy life!"

It's hard to hold back the tears and I try to console the hard-scrabble, girl of the streets but Gem's relentless in her escape, eventually breaking free, darting for the hospitals' entry. "NO! She's supposed to be saved, Rob!"

The glass doors swing open with violent emphasis and she collapses to the wet blacktop. The previously star filled skies have been pushed away by harsh bursts of wind, while the rain comes in torrents, tears for a young angel taken away much too soon. "WHY, GOD? WHY, GODDAMN YOU?! WHY?! WHAT THE FUCK DID SHE DO TO YOU? What did she do to God, Rob? What did she...WHY?" I envelop her like a cloak, refusing to let go. Tears from pained, lonely green eyes cascade into the rainwater swirling around us before Gem's screams and cries of desperation echo through the mean, ice-cold, unyielding night air.

••• 17 •••

No Good Time to Say Goodbye

The constant drone of road noise and water lapping against the Bullet's undercarriage keeps me tortuously focused on what's becoming an infernal journey through the boorish hell of Interstate 95. Wiper blades shriek like agitated crows across the windshield as I go over what transpired a thousand times, with each frame of reference presenting differing conclusions, altered scenarios tragically being played out in true, Shakespearian style.

Nevertheless, the outcome is always the same, a pretty, little young angel named Claire has died. A Red's been dangling in perpetuity from my lips and after attaining a good, long drag, it sails aimlessly across the flooded highway...the highway seemingly stretching on fucking forever. Escaping the confines of this groaning, tin box is tantamount in my thought process but lamentably, I can only drift back to the evenings painfully, final events.

Upon returning with Gem to the Emergency Room's down-trodden backdrop, we repeatedly answer the Brody's insolent enquiries as to the whereabouts of the ramshackle, Perry Street house of horrors. Gem composed herself enough to query what will happen with Claire's body since she was a child of the street but the nurses seemed to have no discernable answer. Exiting the hospital soaked, shivering, bewildered and bedraggled, I thank all the boys for their help tonight before Gem embraced them one-by-one, with an especially big hug for Florian.

"You were so brave tonight, Flor. You tried your best to keep her alive in that car and that angel knows what you did for her." Clearing his throat, Flor emitted a frog-throated thank you, before departing in hollow, dejected silence.

Mashing the pedal to alleviate some pent-up aggression from the night's tragic outcome, the passenger seat remains painfully vacant, evoking an even lonelier experience for this solemn driver.

In the rearview mirror, she rests on Yuka's shoulder, who gently strokes Gem's soaked, matted hair, kissing her forehead, while Lena wraps her arms around Gem's waist. "We're all here, Swan and will stay with you all night, if you want us to."

Sammi and Steph have also joined us for the ride back to our Philly digs and straddle each other across the floor mats in the rear of the car, using a blanket from the trunk to keep Gem warm. Sammi repeatedly takes hold of Gem's hands, eventually placing her head on Gem's knees. "Lena's right, honey, we'll stay all night and keep you and Rob company. We can't leave you alone after what's happened."

"Thank you for being here. You're probably so tired from last night and today. You didn't have to do this," Gem replies soulfully.

Steph finger combs Gem's hair away from her face. "Listen up, girl, we wouldn't be anywhere else. When Flor called, Oren and Dust sprinted down to South and Third, snagged Tim and Skate and by the time they returned, Yuka called to say the whole tribe was Trenton bound."

Steph stares into Gem's eyes, softly voicing her undying allegiance to the Misfits, Punk Princess. "We're not just your friends when it's time to have fun. We're not punks just for hitting the shows, or sharing fanzines, smokes, beers or a laugh. This tribe of Misfits is way more than that. I've never been around a bunch of more fun, crazy, caring and loving people.

"We'd fight tooth and nail...would spill blood for one another. There aren't many people in life willing to do that for you. There's a reason, my young beauty, why we stood shoulder to shoulder, arm in arm, looking at that sunrise over the Statue of Liberty this morning...all of us smiling, seizing the moment for everything it was worth. It's because we're not just a tribe, not just friends' girl, we're family...hell, and better family to one another than most of our blood relations has ever been to us."

"Thanks, Steph, it means a lot coming from you because I've always looked up to you and Dusty as the elders of our tribe. You lead, we follow."

Steph smiles lovingly at her street sister. "Baby girl, you couldn't be more wrong. It's you who leads this group and when you brought Rob into the fold, it solidified everything. YOU TWO make us what we are. You are not just punks for the music, you are activists for many causes...poverty, homelessness, the working class and so much else.

"You enlighten and enliven us. When either of you speak, everyone listens...fuck, even the people you protest against and piss off pay rapt attention to your words. You and Robbs truly are the Punk Princess and Prince of South Street."

The drenching downpour dissipates to a trickle against our fortress of steel, chrome and rubber, before an outwardly shaken Gem trembles slightly when speaking of Claire. "You know, Steph, for the brief time she was awake, she kept repeating how she was sorry, that she just wanted a place to stay warm tonight. Why did they have to do this to her? She was just a baby, just like I was, a baby of the streets. She needed someone to keep her safe and look out for her."

"It may have only been for a little while but she did have a savior. She had Flor, Rob and you. No one could have done a better job of protecting her, my sister. At least she passed on knowing that she was in your arms when she left us tonight."

"Thanks, Steph…you've all…been…too good to me." Gem's tears fall like rain, the girls valiantly attempt to comfort their stricken, street girl and as another glowing Red dangles precipitously from my lips, the wet blackness of the road enshrouds us once more with anguish.

• • •

Gingerly navigating through the revelry of another untamed, South Street, Friday night, I luckily discover some parking within a stone's throw of the apartment. Alighting from Gem's saturated, silver chariot, awaiting the tribes' arrival, the girls continue consoling Gem before she cries aloud, with painful, green eyes begging me to assist in her comforting. "It's all right, girl, let's get you upstairs and warmed up."

Sobbing heavily, she buries her head into my shoulder. "Thank you for everything you did for that little girl tonight… you were insanely brave. I don't know…what I'd do without you…by my side."

"Thanks, Gem but don't sell yourself short. You were willing to put yourself into danger for Claire even more than I did. You're tough as nails and have the heart of a lioness." Wrapping her arms around my neck, I seize the opportunity to gently lift her into my arms. "Hold onto me and rest, I've got you."

Dusty quickly unlocks the front door and the commotion we've caused in the hallway stirred Fred and Beth from a peaceful respite because they're both out of their apartment in a flash and inquiring about Gem. A handful of the Misfits remain downstairs to recount the night's harrowing events, while Dust opens the apartment, sending Steph, Big O, Yuka and Otto scurrying in all directions to assist.

Soon, more footsteps approach. Beth and the girls help Gem into her bedroom, out of her wet clothes and into some warm sweats. Keenly observing my grimy, downtrodden appearance, Otto suggests a shower may do me some good.

Conceding that Gem is well tended to, I kiss her lips softly, retreat to the bathroom, crack open the creaky window whose layers of white paint, from years gone by, bead up from the condensation and after the steam loosens my spikes, I untangle the flags from my tips, returning my long locks to society's bogus norms.

Upon toweling off some sore muscles, I slide into Gem's room, spotting a worn-out Rangers sweatshirt, a baggy pair of sweatpants and a wool, longshoreman's hat Otto's piled on her bed for me.

Beth and the girls continue conversing with Gem, before she spies me venturing from her bedroom and smiles peacefully. "Come here, Robbs. I need your arms around me."

Kissing me warmly, I fall under the spell of those soulful, mesmerizing eyes. "Thanks again for everything you did tonight, Robbs. You put yourself at risk to keep that little girl safe. You were so brave."

"It wasn't bravery, Gem, it was just the right thing to do." Kissing her forehead, I force a smile but we're both too pained at the loss of such a young life for it to last. Beth takes hold of Fred's hand and nods towards the door. "We're going to let you get some sleep, Gem. If you, Rob or any of you children need anything tonight, don't hesitate to come down and call on either one of us."

"Thanks so much for being such good family to Gem and I," I respond before saying good night and returning to Gem's side. Our tough, girl of the streets has put up a brave front, but the evenings exhausting, emotionally draining events eventually reveal their circuitous toll. "I think I'm ready to go to bed, tribe."

"It sounds like a good idea, babe." Lowering her voice to a whisper, she asks if I'd be upset if the tribe stayed with us tonight. "I don't want to kick everyone out after what our incredible friends did to support me."

"I think the company of true family would be a fuckin' brilliant idea." Gem tiredly smiles, revealing a peaceful beauty in the midst of such tragedy. "I really would like you to stay. You are my family and I love you all."

"C'mon tribe," I boisterously add. "We can make room in here, you guys can move the sofa bed in too or you could even crash upstairs in the attic."

"Oi! We wouldn't be anywhere else BUT here, girl," Dusty bellows. "C'mon boys, let's pick this up and get it into the bedroom." Skate, Tim and Oren hastily lift the sofa, while the girls help Gem into bed. Snuggling into her long, warming body, she releases a long, contemplative sigh. "I love feeling your arms around me and the warmth of your breath against my neck, Robbs. It makes me feel safe."

"You are safe, Gemma. No one can hurt you here, Swan… not the drugs, the evils of the pushers or even the sinister likes of Kellin can harm you. You're surrounded by your tribe."

Lifting her head slightly, she absorbs the glorious sight of our Misfits. "If you need anything Gem, you just let me or Skate know," Tim whispers from beyond the massive, wooden spindle stretching across the foot of the bed. Dusty and Steph give her a 'thumbs up' from the sofa bed, as does Oren. "We're here for you too, Punk Princess," he retorts in that deep, baritone voice.

"Thanks Oren, you guys are all too good to me."

Otto and Yuka fall in at the end of the mattress. "Wouldn't be anywhere else, sis," whispers Yuka. "We love you so much."

Lena and Sammi join us, nestling into Gem, showing love for their girl. "You know we'd do anything for you, sweetie," Lena declares warmly, stroking her fingers through Gem's long, flowing hair. "Lena's right, Gem, we'll always be here for you, beautiful girl," Sammi states emphatically.

Gem's exhausted but manages to give us her signature, radiant smile. Placing her head onto the soft, lavender hued pillowcase, she turns to kiss me. "I love you so much, Rob," she lightly whimpers before being showered with kisses. "I love you too, Gemma Stinson."

Otto switches off the bedroom light, with Skate taking care of the night table lamp. The rains finally ceased, allowing for a surge in action further up Fourth. These are the nights in which the Misfits own the street, but our place was here, consoling

Gem, with the punk code as it should be; taking care of our own in a time of need.

The whimpers of a beautiful but tortured soul become mournful cries as the sounds of Friday night Philly become muffled, background noise when Gem repeats her heartbreaking refrain. "Good night, little Claire…you're safe now. Ronnie will watch out for you in heaven, Claire…good night, little angel… you're safe now…"

• • •

The sun cracks through the long, flowing, translucent curtains, leaving the room with an ethereal feel. Everyone's still crashed out so I toss on my gear, slinking quietly out of the room to make some coffee. Gem's still in the warm embraces of Lena and Sammi but I sneak around to give her a light peck on the cheek.

With the coffee finally percolated, I pour a cup of black gold before treading lightly downstairs to my place of refuge, the stoop. I've enjoyed this vantage point of city life since childhood in Brooklyn, missing it immensely after being hijacked to Pennsylvania's cow towns, so to have it back again is a welcome pleasure, especially when I share time here with Gem or the tribe.

Endlessly replaying the previous evening's chaos, admittedly, I did not sleep very well, even after Gem fell off an hour or so later. Thankfully, the coffee warms and wakes me instantly on this beautiful but chilly morning, even though I pull my wool hat down to cover my ears before allowing the inhalation of some very welcomed nicotine to the bloodstream.

I'm thankful for the Misfits support in these past hours but I'm hoping to get some down time with Gem. Let's see how the day goes before we even fathom about what to do tonight. It's almost surreal to think that a little angel was robbed from us just hours ago and yet here I sit, wondering why the world has to be so damn brutal to the innocents, so cruel to the ones who fucking need our help the most.

For the moment, absorbing the odd solitude of early morning Philadelphia is a peaceful, welcome distraction. The old, brick colonial rows take on a measure of exquisite charm in the morning light peeking through the grand trees lining the block, while the pleasant, constant singing of burnt orange bellied Robins and jet black starlings give my soul some well needed harmony.

Eventually, the door squeaks open and turning to observe a familiar, smiling face in my presence, she's already changed into grafittied jeans, open laced black work boots and Yuka's leather jacket. Her hair's damp from taking a quick shower and the dye has washed out, revealing the full beauty of her deep, auburn color cascading slightly past the center of her back as she pushes a few strands away from her face. Taking her place on the stoop, she wraps her arms around me. "Did you get any sleep at all, Robbs?"

"A little bit, but I saw you were sleeping peacefully with Samms and Lena, so I didn't even want to disturb you. Are you doing any better?"

Her eyes twinkle in the daylight. "I think I'm coming to grips with it, hon'. I've seen so much death in my life already that you're almost desensitized to it at times." She swipes at a tear, regaining her composure rather hastily. "I'll admit to you, this little Claire really gotten to me."

"I know she did, Gem. Listen, if you just want to stay in tonight, ya' gotta' let me know. I'm taking the lead from you today."

She snags the Zippo from my pocket and blazes a Newp. "I appreciate that but I think I need to hang on the street tonight. I say we get some alone time in the afternoon, then we'll hit South Street. I have to go to the diner and SKULLZ to check my work schedule anyway. Maybe we can stay local and see some of our friends' bands tonight in the underground clubs. It would be a welcomed segue and I can honestly use the music to clear my head. I'm certain that you can too."

"Let's see how you really feel by then, hon' but it does sound like a good idea at the mo'." Feeling her body shiver, I place the mug in her hands after I pause for a sip. "Have some, Gem, it's still very warm."

"Thanks doll, it will hit the spot." She tugs at my hat and smirks. "You look real kickin' like that. You should wear it if we go out tonight."

"I think it will be on all day cuz' it's feelin' quite chilly out."

Gem stares longingly before doling out another embrace. "I'll keep you warm, Robbs. Listen, would you like to take a walk with me this morning? I have some blueberry muffins upstairs and we could fill up a thermos with some tea...maybe jazz it up with some good Irish whiskey to drown our sorrows?"

"Sure thing, Gem, I'm game for anything right now and the tea and whiskey would kick the morning in something fierce after all that's happened. Let's alert the tribe that we're jetting, just so they don't panic. You know, I think they still worry about Kellin doling out his paybacks."

"Smart thinking, so let's get booking." Gem readies our provisions, unloading the backpack's contents on the kitchen counter and replaces them with food, a thermos full of enjoyment and some smokes. Gem articulates frequently that she likes using my pack because of all the political and punk bands pins I've adorned it with, calling it "the billboard of our movement."

I slink quietly into the bedroom, tugging lightly on Otto's shoulder. "Oi Robbs, is everything cool, brother? How's Gem?"

"So far, so good, man. She wants to go for a walk with me, so I didn't want to cause any worry when you guys woke up and didn't see us."

"No probs, we'll lock the casa, so take your time, man...just be careful...you know, I still don't trust Kellin," he replies groggily while patting my wool capped head for good measure.

"Thanks, Otto...don't worry about that prick, buddy. Been carrying a little insurance in my pack lately...a mini bat hollowed out with some lead cylinders in it.

"More than likely, you won't see us back soon. Gem's talking about maybe going to the do the underground tonight, since it's a little more of the political punks, serious music lovers and not as much the posers."

"Yeah, we could use a night like that, man. Tell Gem if she's really up for it to call later and we'll kick it to the underground."

"Good deal, bro…hey, tell the guys to grab some grub and thanks again for everything last night."

"Anything for my man and his Princess, you guys are the glue to the Misfits, brother. Enjoy your walk." Snaking past all of our awesome, slumbering tribe, I throw Gem a sly wink. "I told Otto we won't be back any time soon and that they should all grab breakfast here. He said the underground sounds like a kickin' idea, so just give him a call when you want to head out."

"Good," she replies as I get a quick peck on the cheek. "We need a night of bare bones punk. No glam at the old factories, I'm keeping my hair down and rocking into a trance like state tonight, baby," eliciting a nervous glance from me but she assuages my fears about that statement. "No worries, love. Trance like from the music, nothing else. I'll stay the straight and narrow, 'cept maybe for some of that tea and whiskey."

"I'm glad to hear that, babe. You have a lot of people in your corner, hoping it always stays that way." Grabbing the backpack and her hand, we bound aimlessly downstairs. I'm truly exhausted but catching her radiant smile in the suns glorious rays while she tosses her long, lustrous hair to and fro allows torrents of energy to resuscitate me. Gem just has that effect on you.

"I really love you for doing this with me, Robbs. You have to be so tired and yet you give me all of your body and soul."

Briefly taking on an air of supreme seriousness, she speaks. "I want to take you on a little journey of my life because you should understand everything about me that I can possibly relay to you. I feel you're owed that much because I've never trusted any guy like I do you."

"Lead on, Gem. Whatever you feel you can tell me about your life, I'm all ears. I love you, girl."

"Love you even more, Robbs. I know you'll never judge me and I know you'll never break my heart."

We cross Fourth, stopping at the massive, wooden doors of Old St. Mary's Church. "The story of my journey will be in bits and pieces, Robbs. Some things happened earlier than others, some later, but I'll try not to get too wrapped up in confusing details.

Taking in the expansive cathedral, Gem sighs, smiles and sighs again. "Now granted, you don't know me for being a religious person, but this church means a lot to me."

"I noticed you always stop and blow a kiss to the statue of Mary, so what started that tradition, if you don't mind me asking?"

"You can ask whatever you want, Robbs, since the journey today is as much yours as it is mine. I blow a kiss to that statue on high because this church was once a place of refuge for me, when I was just thirteen and on the streets for the first time. I had a little school pack with some clothes and a warm blanket in it as my only belongings. I travelled downtown using the subway, eventually meandering onto this peaceful swath of land because my mother had just put a beating on me after she found my father doing some pretty horrible things to me. She always blamed me for seducing him."

Gem lights a Newp and takes a hard drag. Holding her hand and sensing the compassion in my eyes, she continues. "She was such a sick, human being to even think her little girl was capable of doing such a disgusting thing but that was my mom for you. She was a stone-cold junkie and I followed right in her footsteps.

"Strung out on dope, tired and scared, I jumped this fence and hid on the church grounds. It was nighttime and only then, under the bright moonlight, did I realize I was in a graveyard. I wasn't scared though...I found it strangely serene and the beautiful smell of lavender planted to and fro really comforted me, so I took out my blanket and propped my pack against a headstone to use as a pillow."

Sharing a drag with her, we walk through the cemetery grounds as I try to imagine the bizarre peacefulness she must have felt that first night. "So, that's where the love of your lavender scent came from...always wondered about that. So, who eventually discovered your secret hiding place?"

"After a few days, one of the priests discovered me asleep and asked why I was here, so I unraveled my story. Father Kevin was a young, understanding man, who prayed for me while I wept. When I calmed down, he told me the cemetery was no place for a young girl to spend her nights but I adamantly responded that I'd never go to a shelter and unquestionably would not return home, so Father Kevin reached a compromise with me that morning. Anytime I was around the church in the evening, I was to ring the bell at the rectory and ask for him.

"He opened the church for me at night, allowing refuge inside its peaceful walls and ornate statuary. At least you will be warm, dry and safe in here, Gemma, he said to me. His only stipulations were that I respect the sanctity of the church and that I make my best attempt to get off whatever drugs I was using at the time."

"Did you stay here long?"

"I was in and out of here quite a bit over the course of a few months but eventually I thanked Father Kevin for being so nice to me and left. Unfortunately, the lure of what was happening a few blocks away began taking hold of me."

Departing the solitude of Old Saint Mary's, within a few more blocks, South Street emerges in all of its decadent glory. Work crews piled up trash from last night's party crowds while some unfamiliar, jackbooted Brody's angrily roust a handful of groggy, tattered homeless kids from their perches around the storefronts.

"Why do they have to be so cruel to us, Robbs? None of us wanted to be homeless."

"They'll never know what it's like, until one day, it may be them getting pushed from a doorway, Gem.

"Yo' Beat, give 'em a break, they're not hurting anyone. What the hell's wrong with you?" I angrily inquire from across the street but it earns Gem and I only a menacing stare and a 'move along' swing of his truncheon.

"It's just the way they treated me when I was going from alley to alley on this street. They'd slam their nightsticks on the dumpsters or trash cans. I used to scream and start running, while some of them would be laughing at me.

"I was only thirteen, alone and just wanted somebody to love me. Some of them were so nasty to us..the things they called us were deplorable. The diner Brody's were the only ones that were ever kind to us." She smirks, trying bravely to appear upbeat but her eyes can't hide the pain from those years, the prolonged agony of never knowing what she did so badly at home to be abused and misused like she was. "So sad..."

The Newp's cherry tip connects violently with the curb, before the green eyes menacingly meet the beat Brody's dead stare, prompting her to spit into the street. "C'mon, babe, fuck him, there's more to see but not before I find out my work schedule from the Diner."

We cross over Second Street and into the South Street Diner where Gem's greeted with a huge grin from Amy, the head waitress. "HEY! There's my tall beauty. How were your shows this week, Gem?" she asks, snapping her gum with machine gun precision and twirling her shoulder length blonde hair. Amy is a little shorter than Gem, slim in build and probably close to her mid- forties. She has two daughters around Gem's age and Amy rivals them all with her energetic pace.

"Hiya, Amy. Rob's and my show went well and Motorhead got cancelled, but we ended up in New York City at CBGB's, stayed all night with our Misfits, watched the sun come up over the Statue of Liberty and then went to the Empire to grab some breakfast. It was a lotta' fun, Momma," she replies happily to the woman who, in many ways displays the only sweet, mothering ways Gem's ever known.

"Oooh...New York City with your honey, how romantic! I used to sneak into the city on the train with my boyfriend and catch all sorts of rock acts there in the Fifties.

"So, Rob, were you good to my sweet girl here? Kept her out of harms' way, I hope." Gem's eyes widen but I give her a peck on the cheek. "Absolutely, it was nothing but a fun-filled time for our Punk Princess, Momma."

"Good to hear, honey. Well, are we going somewhere special today, lovebirds?"

"I'm taking Robbs around Philly today and giving him a little tour of my life, so to speak. I figured it was time he knew a lot more about me." A customer momentarily distracts Amy's attention but she puts up her finger quickly. "Hang on a sec', Marty...be right with you." Pulling us close to her, she smirks mischievously. "So, my tall beauty's in love, is she?" The question makes Gem's light olive skin attain a rosy hue.

"OH MY GOD, YOU ARE," Amy screeches before taking hold of Gem's hand. "Oh, it's about time! You don't know how much I wished for this. I keep telling her that you're the one. Don't I tell you that, Gemma?"

"Yes, Momma...you made that emphatically clear to EVERYONE in the diner after the first night Rob came to visit," Gem replies with the shyness of a young girl experiencing true love for the first time.

"Well, you just made my day, kids. I can't wait to tell my daughters the news. They're going to scream!"

"Ya' know what would make my day, Amy," a voice barks from the counter, but Amy's finger shoots up like a rocket, pointing ominously towards the older gentleman from whence the barking emanated. "Unless you want to take a bath in your coffee, Marty, you'll zip it, doll. My girl is in love!" Marty rolls his eyes and grunts, "yeah...aren't we all," before disgustedly spinning his stool towards the counter.

"Gem, let me write down your times for the week so you kids can be on your way." Amy grabs her pad, hastily jotting down everything Gem needs to know. "Here you go, honey." She begins doing a little dance and smiles brightly. "Oh, you kids are awesome, I just love you both. Now, shoo...get a move on! The day is long and beautiful, so get your journey started."

Gem embraces Amy, giggling like a girl on her first date. "Thanks, Momma. You don't know how happy you just made my day."

"Glad to hear it, doll." Lifting a glass dome from the platter on the counter, she grabs a few Danish's, tossing them in a paper bag and then to me. "Some goodies for the trip...now get going."

Gem's beaming and her energy level perks up a few notches after seeing Amy, so she begins skipping down the street ahead of me. I know there are still thoughts of Claire whirring through her head but she's a tough girl, working through it in her own unique way and I'm beginning to comprehend how much her street existence has framed this ability to bounce back from adversity or tragedy without pause for too much thought.

Catching up to her, she pulls me close and whispers in my ear. "Thanks for not letting Amy know what happened in Trenton last night. She would have been very distraught if she'd known about us being in danger and especially about a young girl dying like that. She worries about me very much. I wish she'd been my real Momma."

"She's a sweet lady, Gem, so there's no way I was bringing up that mess to her. There's a time and a place for everything so I'm sure you'll tell her when the time is right and I'll come with you when you do so. She can yell at me instead of you," I reply with a chuckle. With her head firmly resting on my shoulder, Gem laughs as well. "You're too sweet but be careful what you wish for. Amy may hurl an ashtray in your direction if she knew her Gemma was ever in danger."

Tousling handfuls of Gem's hair, I eventually find her neck, massaging it, much to the delight of the now purring Princess. "Mmmm, that feels so good. Keep it up, Robbs. We have some distance to cover before reaching our next destination."

The morning sun shines ever more brightly and the makings of quite the radical day lie ahead. Hiking further away from the more well-known parts of South Street, it's virtually impossible to ignore the change in scenery since the neighborhood attains a more solemn, gritty feel, reminiscent to the Bowery around CBGB's. Although many would shy away from traversing through this part of town, Gem has an invulnerable comfort level here because for a while, this was home.

"Over there, in that broken down, garbage strewn, graffiti riddled house, was the refuge for the Wild Girls. That's what the Brody's used to call us because of the way we dressed and acted, so it kinda' stuck with us." Confidently approaching the shabby row, we kick some debris around before pushing at the broken front door, which is tagged with gang names, and a giant, unwelcoming, 'FUCK OFF PIGS' design is sprayed dead center on the rows brick facade.

Taking the lead, I head a few feet into the dank, shabby space, which at one time was probably a family or living room but go no further. Rats and mice scatter about when a small hunk of wood is tossed near their vicinity and the smells of fresh piss, mold and burning embers pervade in the ramshackle, junkyard of a house.

Where once probably stood a television cabinet, sofa and a side table with a lamp, a metal trash can, pieces of plaster, wood and various odds and ends probably pilfered from other parts of the house now displayed themselves somberly, unproudly in their stead. Local punk band names haphazardly adorn the walls and concert fliers are strewn to and fro. Quietly coursing through this squatter's hellhole, I touch the can, "still has warmth to it. Someone jetted recently."

"Was smart of you not to venture too far in, Robbs. Wow, the place has gotten even worse in the years since I was here." We both light up a smoke just to kill the overwhelming 'stank' of the house before Gem looks towards the stairs and smirks a bit. "I used to sleep up there with the Wild Girls. This is where Lena and I met. It's hard to believe that we've survived long enough to still be friends." She takes a quick spin around the room, motioning towards the splintered front door. "C'mon, let's head out before we roust up the night dwellers, if there's any left."

Wandering further into the netherworlds of South Street, I move closer to Gem. It's nice having this time alone, getting a better sense of the bond we've made since meeting in school. There are some days where I feel as if I've known her forever and most days, I wish that I had. Truth is though, much as we've talked or hung out, I'm still only scratching the surface of Gemma Anastasia Stinson's life and although infrequently it's a rough life to fathom, I'm thankful she's entrusted me entrance into her world.

"How old were most of the Wild Girls, Gem? Were they all like you or Lena, from broken homes?" Gem sucks out the last bit of life from her Newp, snapping the butt from between her talons. "Most were my age, a few of them were in their late teens, and Sissy was twenty. Believe it or not, some of them had more precarious home situations than me." She takes a long breath before replying again. "Sissy was the one who brought me to that house. She was a wild haired, little snip of a gal and the first chick I ever saw with a Mohawk. She found me huddled up in an alley between Second and South with some real rough and tumble girls.

"Sissy grabbed me before the Brody's smashed the dumpsters and cans around. 'C'mon Stretch, let's get you the fuck outta' here before the Pigs or Truancy Nazi's finally get tired of seeing your pretty ass and arrest you.' She loved calling me Stretch, hell even at thirteen, I towered above most of the Wild Girls and upon arriving at the squat, Lena was there and took an immediate liking to me.

"That's when she and the other girls started calling me Swan. Lena said it was because of how beautiful and graceful looking they thought I was." Gem's blushes and scoffs at the thought. "Ahhh...they were so silly about that. They were very protective of me, especially Lena. First thing she did was clean my hair."

"Ha, ha...Robbs, you should've seen the work that went into bathing yourself since the place had no running water, no gas, no heat...but the neighbor had a hose bib outside, so we'd fill pots of water from it and leave them all over the kitchen. There was an old hibachi we found in the backyard and once we 'procured' our charcoal, lighter fluid and lighters...viola...heated water for baths.

"To this day, Lena just loves to look pretty. She was our expert cat burglar in the local markets for any kinds of soap, shampoo, hair coloring, deodorant, toothpaste, toothbrushes, mouthwash...you name it, Lena would get it. Hey, even we street girls didn't want to smell or have mule breath," she remarks with a giggle. "Sissy took to calling Lena, Icy, partly because of her beautiful, ice blue eyes and also because of her icy demeanor when it came to stealing or fighting.

"Sissy was also Lena's first crush on a girl and the feeling was mutual. Quite a few of the girls in the house had a thing for each other because, hey, when you're pressed together for body warmth, things tend to happen, the boys weren't always around for companionship and a lot of us realized that the boys were not always as good to us as the girls were.

"In some cases, our broken homes opened us up to revolutionary sexual thoughts going against society's norms once we were on our own and we were fine with that. The girls loved each other not for shock value to the outside world and their hang-up's but because they were really in love.

"Some of the street punks took to derisively calling us the Wild Dyke's but they only emboldened the girls' stance towards openly loving who they really wanted to really be with."

"You said Lena enjoyed being with you from time to time, was that when it happened?" Gem notices my wariness about asking and lets out a hysterical, squeaking laugh. "Why, Robert Cavelli, are you getting all shy and sheepish over the thought of a girl being with me or even making love to me? How cute are you?"

She laughs again, wrapping her arms around me. "Lena, this cutie punk named Birdie, Ski from the Knockabouts and this rarified beauty named Stace all tried at one point or another. Now, body warmth was another thing altogether.

"I didn't mind snuggling for that reason and sometimes Lena, Birdy and Stace would kiss my lips, my neck, nibble my ears or nuzzle really close to me, sometimes they'd even press themselves against me or touch me tenderly but that was as far as it got. I know Stace really wanted it to go further but I just wasn't into being with a girl that sexually at the time.

"Ski was always kissing and touching me, begging me to give up on hurtful guys and run away with her, to be her lover but I wasn't ready for any of that. The thought of giving myself to another girl in that manner was still so foreign to me.

"Now, I'll be honest with you, there was one girl more recently that I got a little heavy with, when I was really doped up and we made love sometimes out of feelings for each other, sometimes I think out of pure loneliness, but in the end, it didn't work out. I cared for her, but when we departed each other's company, I swore off any mental or physical relationships of any kind. I had to get my life straight and live for me...to learn to love me first.

"Listen Robbs, the story behind this girl is long and sometimes, very painful and I'll have to save it for another day. I'll tell you a lot about my life today but her part's still hard to discuss because it involves a guy I don't want to bring up again," Gem says in a soulful whisper.

"Kellin...fuckin' Kellin...". Gem picks up on my frustration, holds me close and soothes my anger with her softened, sultry voice.

"Please understand, there's a time when you'll know everything, just bear with me, ok?"

"Gemma, I know you went through so much in your young life compared to me and I can't even imagine what you encountered out here, so of course I'll be patient. You've entrusted me with so much already and I love you for putting that kind of faith in me.

"And as far as the Wild Girls go, who am I to question their love for you? They gave you love when nobody else was willing to, so who am I to judge. You loved each other and that's all that matters."

Placing her head gently on my shoulder, we slow our pace, strolling by fellow Philadelphians pounding the pavement towards their own life's journeys on this sunny, Saturday morning. "Thanks for understanding Robbs. God, I wish I'd known you growing up. Maybe we could've been little ones in love, you know, destined to be together forever. We could've run away together when the shit got heavy for us at home...been true Bohemians...true punks. It's not like any of the norms ever understood us, so we wouldn't have been missed for too long."

"We could still run away now, you know, Gem," I say quietly, holding her hand tightly but she strokes my face gently with her blood talons. "Tempting as that sounds, you've helped me understand, more than you know, that running away is not an option. I need to face down everything and you're even helping me do that today. For that reason alone, I love you, Robbs. Now, let's continue the journey!" she exclaims radiantly.

Moving along these gritty, grimy blocks of row houses with a purposeful spring in our steps, we approach Broad Street's Theater and Music District and Gem's eyes sparkle with delight as warm, yellowish sunlight dances between the edifices of the art world. "I've always treasured these theaters and do you see the building resembling a temple from ancient Greece? That's the University of the Arts. I would've loved attending classes there, becoming even more immersed in musical studies.

"Up further by the Union League is the Academy of Music. They call it 'The Grand Old Lady of Locust Street'. I still enjoy walking past the beautiful, red brick topped structure and even tried sneaking in a few times but with no luck. I really hope to see the Orchestra play there some day."

Descending into the Lombard-South Broad Street Station, preparing to take the Orange, or Broad Street Line as it's widely known, Gem hands me a few tokens as the arduous wait to head uptown begins. I hold her very close to me, since the clientele is not much better than anything witnessed in New York City the other night. The poverty, homelessness and joblessness are hitting our City of Brotherly Love rather harshly and the scope of its toll's becoming too precarious to absorb.

With numerous bodies sleeping under mounds of filthy blankets while shopping carts store their worldly possessions, we can only shake our heads as the rats' screech and race wildly through these underground catacombs between shards of broken glass, reams of discolored newspapers and piles of God knows what. As our song states, "Don't matter if it's subway tunnels or halls of power under Billy Penn's hat, one thing you know quick, it's a filthy city of rats..."

Kicking away at the filthy debris in our path, Gem blazes another Newp for us to share. "You know how I've had an affinity for any music. I wasn't always into punk, until I hit the streets. Sissy, Lena and Birdie introduced me to it. Birdie loved music with a passion, just like I do. I listened to a lot of different music because of my Uncle Ronnie. He turned me on to the 60's sounds, Motown and even classical and jazz. He was the only person in my family that dared to be different and become learned."

The somber subway stop quickly illuminates when the SEPTA Broad Street Line squeals harshly into the station. Gem and I are but just a handful of folks riding at this early hour, so we take up residence on a broken, torn bench seat with most of its stuffing missing. Reclining, resting my wool capped head against the funky, discolored detritus peeking from under the graffitied windows, Gem comfortably lies across me, recounting more stories about the Wild Girls.

"Birdie knew how much I liked music, so she and Icy get this crazy ass idea to snag a boombox right out of an electronics store on Walnut Street in Center City. Lena still laughs hysterically about how they even had the 'tits' to bogart a boatload of batteries too.

"Now, Birdie and I loved New Wave music for dancing. Birdie was short, cute with a shoulder length, white rat, spiky do and Rob, could she move her voluptuous body and she made everybody know how proud she was of her curves! She loved being provocative, grabbing you by the hips and just moving dead sexy up against whichever girl happened to be there...and a lot of times, it would be yours truly," she slyly giggles. "The two of us would get the party started, dancing to songs like Gary Numan's 'Are Friends Electric?' or the Furs 'Love My Way'. Pretty soon, all the girls would be on their feet and dancing like crazy.

"When Sissy and Lena got me into playing and listening to punk, everything went completely wild and when Kelly, Joanne and Annabelle, who became our beloved, now famous Knockabouts entered the squat for a while, playing their raucous brand of music on their guitars, my guitar or any crude instrument they could invent or find, we'd be windmilling, pogoing, slam dancing...hell, that place was our personal mosh pit at times. The upstairs would shake from us when punk music was on and we'd be falling all over one another, screeching, laughing like crazy, and just trying for even a minute to forget how rough life could really be."

After softly kissing her wet lips, a final drag of her Newp is elicited before being extinguished onto the subway cars pitted, filthy floor. "You said the Wild Girls had a number of problems and demons to face down, so, were there a lot of drugs in the house? How'd everybody make their money?"

"Some of us had odd jobs, others were professional criminals. We always had each-others backs' when it came to the Brody's, though. Nobody in our group was a rat or tried to dime the other ones out. Drugs in the house...oh goodness yes, there was quite a bit of pills, meth...and of course, my infrequent escape drug, heroin.

"Occasionally, it got out of hand and I know this was no excuse but there were times when you felt a need for the escape that only a needle full of bliss can give you, especially when the girls returned to this shabby existence because they'd go right back to the same, horrific abuse at home, thinking it would get better only to find out it had gotten worse. The only problem is, you find out quickly that the bliss is a fucking lie and it's better to deal with your demons head on."

The earlier twinkle in her eye dims, her mood retains a certain solemnity and I smartly allow the sounds of the subway car to wash over us for a few minutes before broaching any more questions. "I guess one of those girls returning from time to time, was you?"

"Until Yuka got me into the sanity of her home environment and cleaned up from the drugs, which was pure hell to endure, I was back there quite a bit, Robbs. It may have been a dumpy squat and some days the situations were dicey, but it was still home. Some of my beautiful Wild Girls have sadly passed on. Sissy died from smoking crack last year. They found her frozen body in an abandoned row and my poor, little Birdie was shot and killed by her abusive step-father in 83'.

"Beautiful Stace was another one, an absolutely entrancing nineteen-year-old. Oh, Robbs, to me, she was gorgeous and at times, I can admit to having sort of a crush on her. She had such captivating features, courtesy of a Dominican father and a French mother and the most alluring, hazel eyes. She was about 5'7" and always wore stiletto boots, ripped clothing, short tartan skirts, leather jackets with biker chains through the belt loops and she had this radiant, chestnut hair when it wasn't spiked or dyed. Needless to say, I emulated a lot of her styles.

"Stace and Lena were the ones who suggested the sharpening of my rock hard nails for protection from my family or anyone else for that matter and I don't think they ever fathomed that I'd transform them into the dagger point weaponry you see today but they've been useful."

"What happened to Stace, Gem? If it's too painful to mention, you don't have to tell me."

"Poor Stace had her throat slit by a jealous lover named Trix. Trix was pissed because she thought Stace had become smitten with a girl who worked at a local flower shop, but we found out the only reason Stace was spending time around that girl was because she wanted to get Trix a beautiful arrangement of white and red roses to celebrate a year of them being together." Sniffling slightly, she turns away, the hardened Wild Girl averting the stares of the few riders on the subway.

"Gem, I'm so sorry. So many young girls are on the streets, going through this every day. I wish they were all still here, babe, I would love to have met them." Circling her finger around my lips, the eyes sparkle, the morning radiance returns to her face.

"They would have adored you, Robbs, just like Lena does and Birdie and Sissy would have danced with you incessantly. I think Stace would've initially been jealous, but once that simmered down, she'd have admired your intelligence, wit, especially your passion to fight for what's right and when she saw how much you truly loved me, it would have made her happy for me."

"I'm glad to hear that. I'm certain I'd have adored her too." Moving in closer to her beautiful, pursed lips, I kiss Gem for what seems like an eternity in this cold, heartless world.

Smiling sweetly, she eventually pulls away to eye me up. "Don't ever break my heart, Robbs."

"No way that I will do that, Gem…no way."

••• 18 •••

The Underworld

"NEXT STOP...ALLEGHENY...ALLEGHENY...NEXT STOP!... THE garbled, scratchy early morning voice of the engineer bellows through the gnarled, subway car speaker. Gem springs up from her comfortable quiescence, nudging me along. "C'mon cutie, our journey continues." Wrapping my arms comfortably around her svelte waist, I sandwich her between the pitted, rusty subway car stanchion and my body's full weight. "Mmmmmm, now this is why I still like to nuzzle," Gem purrs.

The incessant brake squealing makes it hard to even think and after a few quick lurches and jerks, our car comes to an uneasy rest at the stations platform and the doors barely release, allowing for our escape before hurriedly alighting through the turnstiles. A maddening obstacle course ensues navigating these steps too, with an overabundance of exhausted souls using them as beds and a gauntlet of spent hypodermics to circumvent. "Watch out for those needles Robbs, they seem to be everywhere," Gem cautiously whispers.

An alarmingly young looking punk with golden warrior spikes lies in a comatose state at the top of the graffiti strewn vestibule. Newspapers, empty coffee cups and food wrappers amass around him but he's too gone to notice. The smell of spray paint lingers, there are traces of silver around his nostrils and from the looks of the two shiners under his eyes, someone decked him pretty hard before the huffing rendered him completely useless.

"Is he even making any sounds, Robbs?" Gem inquires before I meander close enough to hear his short, labored breaths. "He's alive babe, but hurtin' pretty badly." With Gem's assistance, I manage to lug him up the steps and into the crisp, autumn air. He's still pretty much shot in the ass but at least he's not lying in a puddle of piss anymore.

Our young junkie is a microcosm of the bigger picture plaguing the Kensington and Allegheny sections of North Philadelphia. Once a large, blue collar manufacturing region, the only industries growing amongst the dilapidated factories and tattered, brick rowhomes were drugs and prostitution, with a multitude of their clients finding their way to the never empty, Temple University Hospital.

Surveying this landscape was a harrowing experience, to say the least. On every corner, in every alley, down every sidewalk were depression, destruction of property, mind and soul caused lately by the crack cocaine epidemic and the fall foliage, blue skies and regal sunlight hovering above does nothing to liven up the sadness on display.

Even at this early hour of Saturday morning, the drug and skin trade was in full effect further away from Broad and West Allegheny. A number of the girls, dressed in nothing more than tight, short dresses and go-go dancer heels stumble their way over to Gem for the only warm, meaningful embrace they'll encounter today. She breaks off pieces of the diner muffins, which the girls inhale within seconds, even licking the sticky crumbs from their dirty fingers and nails and I hear Gem whisper these words over and over to them, "be safe...get out, before these pricks get you killed."

And before the dealers and pimps curse mercilessly at the girls to once again man their corners and peddle their prospective wares to the suburban masters of destiny, who travel far and away from their lush lawns, pedigreed wives or girlfriends residing in gated communities, to sample the pleasures of pure decadence behind the doors of filth ridden squats overrun by rats and littered with soiled cots stained by numerous bodily fluids, you can't help but notice the vacancy of feeling in the young girls cold, hard stares when they leave Gem's warm embrace. These are more of the forgotten ones, a dozen or more little Claire's, doomed to meeting a similar, precarious fate.

Gem knows the pimps are especially uncomfortable with her strong, unexpected presence here today and glare menacingly in her direction. Undeterred, she responds in kind, smirks and flips them a hearty fuck you for good measure before returning her attention to me. "Fuck those assholes. They'll never stop me from talking to the girls down here, unless they're prepared to kill me for doing so."

Extracting the thermos of 'special' tea from my backpack, I liberate more of the muffins from the comfort of their pouch, handing one to Gem as we lean on a freshly stripped, new red Cadillac Eldorado convertible that was torched and deserted in an overgrown, debris filled lot to die its lonely death amongst the ruins of capitalism gone awry. Gem shakes her head, tossing her hair from side to side, hoists the thermos cup and offers a toast. "Welcome to the American underworld, baby boy, in its entire rancid, horrific splendor. You're witnessing the fall of a modern day Roman Empire and punks like us have the soundtrack for its destruction."

Taking residence on the Cadillac's torn up, burnt frame, I struggle to make sense of the amassing, broad daylight chaos which reminds me of the stories written about the South Bronx when I was still in New York. "Gem, is this where your family lived before you moved up by the Yamaguchi's?"

"This is it, Robbs, the junkie proletariats' Rodeo Drive. Take a walk with me. It's a number of blocks to East Allegheny, the alphabet blocks and the El and yes, it's quite depressing but it'll give you a glimpse of how your girl grew up and where my evil father earned his street reputation."

A beater Toyota Celica full of little shit punks rolls by blaring The Clash's, 'Working for the Clampdown,' laying on the horn mercilessly to curry favor with Gem. North Philly is just another place where I hastily ascertain through our travels that the presence of Gemma Stinson still holds a mighty amount of sway.

Sharing another muffin, I ask Gem about how they finally got Lena away from the total street life existence. "Icy got really shook up when Trix murdered Stace. Hell, how many young girls do you know who've watched three of their girlfriends die within a year or so of one another?"

"Not too many, Swan."

"Mister Yamaguchi...bless him...found her a good paying job at the Budd Company manufacturing rail cars and in return, she promised him that she'd at least finish high school to earn her diploma. Listen Robbs, Icy still has a lot of her street ways, as do I.

"I've tried to lower mine a notch but it's not always that easy because the lure of the street is very tempting...it can be very hard to turn away from.

"You witnessed how fast Lena can become a handful of trouble for someone by the way she acted in Fairmount. She would've torn those skinheads to shreds if they'd laid a hand on you and even Yuka got a taste of what street life was like by hanging around with us in high school. Her fists are quick, Robbs. I've seen her deck a few people really hard.

"Even you have a street brawler mentality, mixed in with some pretty lightning quick fist work. It's just wicked to watch you have a go at people, but admittedly I'm much happier when we don't have to fight anyone."

"No argument there, Gem. Peaceful is much better but it's nice to know we won't take any wankers shit either."

Travelling further through the chaotic dangers of her old stomping grounds, there's an odd sense of security being around Gem, a strange acquiescence taking place in the bowels of

Allegheny, so wherever Gem seems to travel this morning, there's almost deference to royalty approaching which visually unnerves her. "They know who I am, Robbs. No harm will probably ever come to me up here because of who my asshole father was. Even in fuckin' death, he holds a level of fear over people.

"People in the K & A knew the brutal enforcer of the street... the stone cold killer who could charm you with his handsome smile, right before he beat you within an inch of your life with his iron fists, just because you owed money to the Italian or Irish mobsters who retained his services but only after his life was taken did they learn about what an animal he was in his own home.

"Even my mother was feared by most when she was younger and not all strung out. If my father ever did get himself caught up in shit from time to time, she'd think nothing of sliding a barrel of blue steel to your temple or lodged in between your teeth. It really was a demented way to live and makes you wonder why in the hell they'd ever bring a child into this kind of world."

Another group of black, middle age roughs, with their flat rimmed ball caps turned askew, step aside when Gem and I approach, bowing their heads either out of a shallow respect or the trepidation apparently still existing when a Stinson travels through these broken streets filled with one residence more neglected than the other. She smiles ever so slightly but grunts mildly in disgust. "God, it's so fucking humiliating...the influence that bastard still commands down here."

Remaining silent, I can't imagine the burden it must be for Gemma returning to these badlands of hell and hardship. Whereas she is revered, loved, respected and feared only by those who are up to no good in the punk enclave of South Street and its environs, you can bear witness to the pain it causes when the denizens of her birthplace still react in this manner. "Let's backtrack and pick up the pace, Robbs," she snarls as a SEPTA train roars above us. Some street urchins defiantly blaze 'rock' on stoops and car hoods while others add their tags to the volumes already existing on the steel girders of the colossal, Frankford Elevated or 'El' as it's famously known here.

Retracing our steps through the human and bricks and mortar rubble that have become North Philadelphia, we eventually pass the entrance for the Broad Street Line. "We'll be back soon enough to take the subway, Robbs, but there's one more place I need to see before I depart this sorrowful landscape. Hang tight, we're almost where I want to take you," she sighs heavily, lamentably.

Turning onto North Fifteenth Street, Gem slows to a crawl, eventually pointing across the street to a derelict row house, veiled by overgrown shrubs, thick, weed trees and lathered with crude graffiti. The faded words "DEMON" and "RAPIST" are splattered across the splintered, wooden front door in red paint. Gem asks for another Red and takes a long, portentous drag, sighing heavily. "There it is, Robbs...3250, North 15th...where my life of hell with Allan and Gabriella Stinson ended."

"Gem, you really don't have to do..." but I'm admonished with a mild rebuke. "Yes, I do have to face my demons, Robbs. That's why I needed you here by my side...the only person who can help me do this."

Calmly, I take hold of her hand, lifting it towards my lips. "I'm here for you, no matter what, Gem."

"This is where Allan Stinson, a machinist by trade, coming from the hard-working stock of German, Dutch, Scotch, Irish and the Cherokee tribe brought his bride, Gabriella, a tall, slender, lovely woman of Italian, French, Icelandic and Russian lineage to live and die and on the in between years, they copulated on a booze fueled evening, bringing an unwanted little girl into their alcoholic, junkie world.

"I can't find it in my heart to forgive what they did to me since they seldom tried to love me, even when times weren't so bad for them. My father was too worried about being the enforcer who'd crush skulls in for non-payments on 'debts'. They were too worried about partying their asses off and leaving their daughter to fend for herself. They laughed when I was beaten, they laughed when I was a young girl and they spiked my orange juice with vodka to get me drunk...the list of their evil goes on and on, Robbs."

A stiff breeze suddenly whisks through the street, sending debris whirling into the air like dry, fallen, autumn leaves. Gem swings her hair to and fro, tenaciously approaching the house through increasingly ferocious, heavy winds, before suddenly stopping.

Violently balling up her fists, she takes no notice that one of her switchblade sharp nails digs into her palm, sending slow drips of blood to the cracked, filthy pavement. The winds die for a moment but return harsher than before, the superlative beauty of the sun increasingly disappears, replaced by menacing, gray clouds which makes the fetid landscape ever more ominous.

Gem's eyes darken in a way that I've never seen before, as if summoning up forces from above to do her bidding against this place of evil. "Hold my hand, Robbs...no matter what I say, don't stop holding my hand."

"I'm not going anywhere, so say what you have to, Gem," who glares at the domicile of heartbreak while the wind whips her flame like auburn hair in all directions. A wicked smile creases her face and a low growl's summoned from the depths of her soul. "You know that I'm back again, after all this time, don't you, Al and Gaby? Did you think you could keep me away forever? Did you think people wouldn't know what you two assholes did to me?

"I see your shithole of depravity got tagged for the whole neighborhood to see. Icy and Stace said they were gonna' do it and I'm glad they did. They should have included MURDERERS, because you broke Uncle Ronnie's spirit, hastening his pain-ful death and God knows how many people you sent to their untimely deaths by your other monstrous actions."

The winds drive against us maliciously but Gem remains undeterred, emitting inundations of venom against the howling gusts. "You two pieces of shit can pummel me with winds, rain and hellfire to drown out my voice but I WILL say my piece! I HATE YOU FOR WHAT YOU DID TO ME...FOR WHAT YOU LET BE DONE TO ME BY OTHERS...

ALL I WANTED WAS LOVE...ALL THAT ANY LITTLE
GIRL WANTS FROM HER MOM AND DAD!

She whimpers soulfully, gathering her thoughts until the
ferocity of Gem returns in spades. "YOU both hurt me beyond
belief but now I'll be strong in your presence, because this house
of hell represents the two of you! DEAD and BURIED...it's
where you belong so you can't hurt anyone else!

"I just want you to know that I've found LOVE and HE'S
WITH ME RIGHT NOW...he's brought a smile to my face
....and a song to my heart...AND BECAUSE OF HIM...
YOU WILL NEVER HURT ME AGAIN!

"NEVER! NEVER! Never...never..." Lightening her grip,
low sobs have joined Gem's fury. Gathering a loose brick from
the sidewalk, it's heaved maddeningly through the only full pane
remaining on the derelict structure. "FUCK YOU...GABY
AND AL! NOW, YOU'RE TRULY DEAD TO ME!" she
bellows while shards of glass fall, exploding onto the street below.
Winds whip feverishly around us as Gem pulls me closer, emotionally battered and fatigued she regains enough strength to
whisper placidly, "I...love you so much, Robbs. Kiss me...just
kiss me...I am madly in love with you...kiss me and tell me it'll
all be all right..."

Our lips meet, leaving my mind racing with thoughts of us
doing this over a lifetime. I've never felt like this about anyone
and it gives me peace, something I want to share so badly with
her.

Gem's body goes limp in my arms from the sheer exhaustion
of two days filled with triumphs and tragedies and as if on cue
from a Hollywood movie, the winds suddenly taper, delivering
the sun's warmth and blue skies happily to the sorrowful, barren
landscape of Fifteenth and Allegheny.

The eyes of pure green return and she emits a long sigh. "You
must think that I'm crazy, Robbs. Christ, I even cut my palm
open from being so infuriated."

Kissing her wound before compressing the razor thin cut
with my hand, I manage a calming smile. "You're not crazy,
Gem, you're just a hurt little girl, who wanted to make peace

with yourself today and I was glad to be here for you. Shit, for a while there, I thought we were gonna' have a fuckin' exorcism on this block. You proclaimed the truth with pure conviction!"

"Well, I don't know if our college shrink would agree but that felt very fuckin' therapeutic!

"Seriously though…all that wind…I believe that was them. I know you think I'm probably wiggin' out but I haven't been here since I left for the last time. Believe what you want sweetie, but that wind kicked up out of nowhere for a reason. Spirits, baby…spirits.."

"Yo, it could be fuckin' gremlins for all I know but it bordered on lunacy. I was waiting for the house to land on the wicked witch, for fucks sake."

She giggles slightly, tweaking my earlobe for good measure. "You're crazy, Robbs, but I love the way you make me laugh. It's been a mix of incredible and rough the past two days, still you make me smile and I adore you immensely for that, now, let's get the hell outta' here cuz' we're being watched."

Sure enough, a few older folks perched atop their stoops stare and gossip amongst themselves. "Yep, they know who I am. They're probably going, 'there's that crazy ass bitch of Al and Gaby's. Well, let them get a taste of this, Robbs. This will be one time that the fear of my parents in their memories will play to my advantage." Taking another long breath, she emotes in ways only a purely tortured soul can conjure.

"Good morning, neighbors who did nothing while a little girl was drugged, raped and beaten in this house! You spread rumors and innuendos before turning shamefully away when I walked down this street because you were scared shitless of my father, my mother and what they could do to you, so like cowards, you permitted a little girl to lose her innocence and almost her life at the hands of pure evil.

"When I left you didn't care, when I came back you cared even less! So now I leave, hopefully for good and have no reservations telling you all to go fuck off!"

After thrusting her chin proudly skyward, I let out a hearty laugh, embracing her strongly in the face of her neighbors' stunned silence and timidity. "Now, let's get going, Robbs. Fuck this place, I feel rejuvenated and cleansed."

Returning to the downhearted streets of Allegheny, an older, wild eyed, raggedy, hulking character covered in blankets impedes our progress to the subway, muttering some inconsequential nonsense before repetitively bellowing an odd sound... BEEEE BOOOO! Preparing to throttle this character if need be and possibly get me ass kicked by this mountain of a man in the process, I adeptly produce the mini bat from my sack until Gem's smile disarms my hostile demeanor.

"Oh, don't worry about Be-Boo here, Robbs, so you can put the mahoska away," she replies in a warm, motherly tone before bequeathing this John the Baptist of the Badlands with a muffin. "He's harmless to those who respect him and always has an ear to the street so I know what's going on back on my home turf, isn't that right, Be-Boo?"

"Thas' so right, Miss Gemma," he sputters through a myriad of blackened, crooked teeth. "I'm the eyes or ears o' dis' here land." Giving me a good once over, he raises a finger into the air. "Aha! Beeeee Booooooo! This must be the stomper of the Kellin Titus. This must be the righter of wrongs...Beeeee Booooooo!

"Be ever so careful, my friend...for in 'tween all these der'licts lie wolves in sheep's clothing waiting for the protector of Gemma Stinson to falter but Be-boo hear this youngin' is quite the enforcer too, Miss Gemma.

"Well maybe he keep the one who is still quite safe 'round these parts even more protected. Maybe he be revered an' feared here in the Badlands madness too just like the Gemma is. Maybe he can protect some other young ones who still be needin' protection. You know one...Miss Gemma...she may have 'scaped away but I heard she back...if she is, she may need big help... BEEEE-BOOOOO!"

Patting Be-Boo's soot covered, Eagles ball cap, Gem hands him another muffin before advancing through the ramshackle avenue. "Yes, Be-Boo, you make sure everyone knows that Robbs will do just that. Now we must go, so be careful," she adds while happily stuffing a five spot in his jacket. "Ahh...Miss Gemma and Robbs, beater of the evil Kellin…Be-Boo always car'ful!" he exclaims, his words echoing loudly over the harrowed landscape as we dart through the insane, never ending procession of 'burb zombies.

Proceeding at a jackrabbit's pace we float down dark, piss riddled steps, through the clanging, rusty turnstiles, returning to the wild but more homespun feel of South Street, via the Broad Street Line.

● ● ●

Blue skies and sun continue to grace our walk back from the subway station and upon stopping again by the former residence of the Wild Girls, Gem smiles warmly. "For what it's worth, there were some good memories in that house."

"Gem, if you don't mind me asking, who was Bee-Boo speaking about before we hopped onto the subway?"

"Robbs, that would be a part of the story from my harrowing past. Please, again, let me have some time and you'll know everything…I promise."

Lighting up two more Reds for us, I relay a warm, understanding smile. "Take all the time you need, Swan."

It's still early in the day, but the neighborhood spills over with amassing crowds pushing us down the street like rustlers during cattle drives and before we know it, we're in front of SKULLZ. "Hold on a sec, Robbs…I need to get my schedule." She skips in to give her anime look-alike, raven haired friend Sydney a big hug. Syd works the makeup counter and I can already see her persuading Gem's purchase of the latest lip gloss or fuck it all knows what.

Returning happily to the mayhem of our punk environs, she leaps into my arms and pecks my cheek. "I really do adore you. Oh, Syd's going to meet us in the Libs', since she knows where our boys, Crack are playing tonight. Dilby broke the lock and has already taken residence in one of the factories out past Callowhill."

"Very cool, I can't wait, babe." Rejoining our journey towards the refuge of Fourth Street, Gem glances curiously at Old Saint Mary's. "How cool and strange is life that my travels would come full circle, to be here with Misty just hundreds of feet from where my journey began?"

"Gem, it's strange but very beautiful and thank you for letting me be a part of your journey today. Don't ever be afraid to keep telling me about your life, because I'll always listen to your story."

Checking out the slight wound on her palm, it's already begun forming a scab. Gem smiles and rubs noses with me. "I'm fine, my protector. It only stings a little. I'll clean it up when we get inside." She decides to knock on Fred and Beth's door remaining only long enough to thank them for their caring help last night and after retreating upstairs, we're greeted with a note taped to the door.

Gem and Rob,

Glad you guys took your walk on this beautiful, sunny day, especially after the horrible ordeal of little Claire's passing. Sweetie, we're all still heartbroken but know you did everything you could to save that beautiful girl. You don't ever have to thank us for being there for you guys, WE ARE FAMILY. Get some rest.

We'll call tonight and yes, the underground sounds bitchin' if yer' up for it!!!!!! Can't wait to show off my gorgeous Sammi to all of the Punk Tribes!!! I am smitten!!!!

LOVE YOU, PUNK PRINCE AND PRINCESS!!!!
XOXOXOXOXO

Lena and YOUR Misfits

Everyone else signed the note, which Gem absolutely loved. "I have to tape this to my mirror," she responds angelically. Upon entering the seclusion of the aromatic apartment, we discover that Otto left us fresh coffee, whipped up some scrambled eggs, smattered with onions and peppers, and a plate of bacon and biscuits. Another note adorns the two wrapped plates.

To my bud and his girl,

Sprinkle a little water on the eggs, bacon and biscuits so they won't dry out in the oven!!
Enjoy!!!

Otto

"Wow Robbs, we really do have an awesome punk family, don't we?"

"Yo, the best punk family ever, Princess…we're truly blessed." Upon devouring Otto's scrumptious breakfast and hastily cleaning up our mess so Misty arrives to a spotless house if she actually shows up tonight, Gem throws open the living room windows and lights up some cigarettes before turning on her boombox which contains the new Replacements cassette.

Snagging her guitar from the bedroom, Gem bursts out, "hey hon, fast forward it to 'Bastards of Young,' I love that song." After gladly obliging, we take residence by the window to people watch. Gem starts picking away, continuing to amaze me with how rapidly she absorbs chords after briefly listening to the music.

"I'm rewinding, so it's your turn to amaze me, Robbs. You may have been watching me intently, but I know you were deciphering those lyrics. Come on, baby, belt them out for me." Westerberg and I wail out another anthem so befitting of the Misfits lives that Gem drops her guitar to hold me close when the last verse is sung…

"Unwillingness to claim us, ya' got no war to name us…

The ones who love us best are the ones we'll lay to rest
And visit their graves on holidays at best
The ones who love us least are the ones we'll die to please

If it's any consolation, I don't begin to understand them...

We are the sons of no one, bastards of young
We are the sons of no one, bastards of young
Not the daughters and the sons..."

"This is us in a nutshell, babe and you nailed it with that voice of yours. Dilby's going to be batshit cracked up when he finally gets to hear you sing somewhere besides a street corner. Hopefully, it'll be sooner than later." Staring into one another's eyes for an eternity, speaking volumes of thoughts without ever making a sound, I lift Gem from the floor, carrying her into the bedroom...our bedroom. In another day, I'll have to leave her again but at this moment, we're inseparable and it's all I allow myself to think about.

Laying her gently on the mattress, we're soon intertwined. "I love when we can do nothing but this. I'd die to stay in your arms forever, Gem." Her thick eyelashes flutter as she never loses sight of my gaze. "This past year with you has been amazing. I wish we'd met so much sooner..."

Placing her finger over my lips, she flashes her incredible, sunny smile. "You came into my life for a reason, Robbs. It was perfect timing as far as I'm concerned. I wouldn't have written it into my life's story any other way. Now, lie here in my arms and fall asleep with me. Let's dream the afternoon away."

Closing my eyes, I feel her wrap around me like a protective cocoon. Finding the nape of her neck, I breathe in her wonderful, lavender scent and she sighs lightly as I exhale. "I just love the feeling of your warmth on my neck, baby boy, it's the feel of pure love..." Her grip tightens and as she takes in the powerful lyrics of New Order's 'Leave Me Alone' playing on WXPN's afternoon show, the Princess is soon asleep.

Falling into darkness, I find my own peace. I know I've finally found the true love escaping me, until now. Love is Gemma...

••• 19 •••

The Underground

CATCHING THE FINAL glimpses of sun escaping the day, my head slowly lifts from the pillow. With the sounds of early Saturday evening fanfare in Philly enveloping our room, Gem's continues sleeping soundly, so I try my best not to disturb her while heading to the living room phone where I call Otto, who per his usual frequency picks it up after the first ring. "The Misfits hangout, Otto speaking…to whom may I direct your call?" Chuckling into the receiver lightly, I don't even get a chance to reply. "YO, my brother, so did you and the Princess have a restful day?"

"Ha, ha, you always have a knack for knowing who calls don't you?"

"Let's just call it Otto's sixth sense, brother Robbs," he replies in his gruff but elated demeanor.

"To answer your question, we had an eventful day and yes, we did make some of it very restful. By the way, thanks for the eats, man, they sure hit the spot."

"No probs, Robbs. Cooking is my gig, bro. Listen, speaking of gigs, Crack is doing their show tonight at the shuttered factories by the old, AJAX Foundry. Dilby told us exactly where they'll be, and get this, he wants you and Gem to jam with them, so tell the Princess to get Robins Egg warmed up and ya' both better have your pipes in order!"

Could this be THE CHANCE...our dream? "Man, that is way cool! I can't wait to tell Gem."

From the shadows of the bedroom appears a vision of beauty slinking towards me on her tiptoes. Flicking strands of hair away from her face, she nuzzles onto my shoulder and yawns mildly. "Mmmm...you can't wait to tell Gem what, love?"

I tell Otto to hang on for a sec, fill Gem in on the nights' events but before I can even finish, she jumps and squeaks for joy, like we've won the lottery. "Otto, prepare for the insanity which is about to erupt here," I laugh hysterically.

"Oh my God, I can't believe this! Robbs, you and me on stage together with our friends! No fucking way! This is brilliant! This is just what we needed! Oh shit...fuck it all...what are we going to sing? We have to discuss this! Oh, my GOD! WOOO HOOOO!"

"I surmise you've heard the commotion you just caused here."

"Ha, ha, ha! Yeah, we hear everything!" Otto explodes over whistles and the clapping of hands. "Lena wants to know if Gem is darting all over the apartment," so I turn to witness Gem's full force of activity. The boombox blares from the bedroom, the lights shine brightly throughout the household and Gem zips back and forth, gathering her clothes while tossing fresh ones out of my backpack.

Retrieving her Gretsch by the neck, the old tube amp is juiced up for its initial warm-up "POP!" The playing commences with some chords, then a few more, a pause, some murmuring, cussing and a book launched into the netherworlds of her closet for good measure, followed by a look in my direction, a squeak and presto, another cover is coming our way. Gemma Stinson's officially in full, 'golden and glorious' mode.

Trying to regain my composure but failing miserably, I let out another hearty laugh. "Yeah, you guys have to witness this for yourselves because it's pure 'chaos punk' in here right now. It was sorely needed after the past few days she's had."

It sounds like a party at Otto's place, but I'm able to hear him say they'll be over soon. "Awesome! We'll be waiting for ya', Otto!

Switching into a somewhat clean, Black Flag tee, a new set of ripped Levi's and combat boots, I tie bandannas' over my boot tops, put my longshoreman's hat back on and head into the frenzied sounds of the bedroom. The underground events are typically bare boned, so I'll save the multi-colored do's for the roosters having ample time to display their plumage tonight. I'd rather stay in a Ramone's mode.

Gem seems to have the same idea as well; a tight-fitting Replacements tee, a new pair of tight, shredded black leggings and her combat boots. She also does the bandana look over the top of her boots, one is colored black, "for my Wild Girls…Sissy, Birdie and Stace," a bright green one, "just like the color of little Claire's jacket," as she puts her fingers to her lips, kneeling to touch each one. "They'll be there in spirit for you and me."

"You're an incredibly, thoughtful girl, Gemma. I know it may not be the right time to say this but your parents were fools for missing out on the inner beauty that's you."

Kissing my cheek, she tugs at my hat and smiles. "Thank you, love. I think my Prince owes me a kiss, don't you?"

"I think I can do that, but just a kiss. No messing around before a performance, young lady because it gets the body all out of whack, ya' know."

"Get over here, you goof!" she laughs as our emotions spill over and we're all alone in this crazy, cruel, beautiful world again. The blaring music becomes nothing more than a murmur and we are one…or are we?

So embroiled in our little slice of nirvana, we neglect the sounds of a creaking door, the mild laughing or the clearing of throats emanating from the living room and only then do I notice Lena and Sammi standing beside us in Gem's room.

Startled, Gem jumps and almost falls over her own boots. "Holy crap, you two Betty's scared the hell out of me!"

"GET A ROOM, YOU TWO LOVEBIRDS!"

While the rest of the gang gets a good laugh at our expense, I twirl both girls around, ushering them beyond the door and give Sammi a light boot kick to the butt. "We do have a room...now if you'll excuse us," I reply, with a wink for good measure.

With the tribe's mouths left agape when the door closes, I'm left free to chase my girl again. The game of cat and mouse continues...Gem screeches loudly as I playfully give her a nudge towards the bed. "ROBBS! Oh my God, you're crazy! Everyone will hear us! ROBBS! Ha, ha, ha...RRROBBS!"

• • •

Darkness sets in dramatically on our street and the Misfits are ready to roll. The obligatory, 'yes, I'm still alive, mom' phone call has been dealt with, although honestly, it's quite a pain in the ass at my age to do so, but if it keeps her at bay until she rails on tomorrow night about what a problem child I've become and how she should have kept beating me into submission, so be it. Gem's left a note for Misty, directing her to our whereabouts since we may be performing at some point.

Yuka's borrowed her pop's work battle wagon, a 72' Pontiac Bonneville and I place Gem's Gretsch gently into the trunk, wedging some old towels around it, so the case doesn't slide. The crew piles in the green bomber but I wait for Yuka to get behind the wheel. Perched on the carrier sized hood, I place a hand to my forehead, searching high and low and get ready to 'take the piss' on our girl. "I know she's here somewhere...I just know it." Otto lets out a roar, as Gem snorts, "you're so fuckin' wrong, Robbs."

Yuka peers through the wheel, sees what I'm up to and grins before a well-placed middle finger is hoisted upon the dashboard. "Can you see this, dickhead?" The cars' inhabitants crack up, as do Dusty and his wild bunch who flip me the bird before falling in the Grenada. Sprinting hellaciously towards the open drivers' door, I hop in, tumbling onto Yuka's lap to deliver a big, wet kiss on her lips, nibble her ear and grin. "I love you sooooo much, my little Yuka Yamaguchi!"

Smirking, trying hard not to lose her composure, she nibbles my ear and launches me from the Bonneville onto the blacktop. "Love you too, Asshead...now sod off, wipe the gravel off your crapper and get in the back with your girl."

"But of course, Madame Yuka!" Immediately receiving rabbit punches in the arm from Lena, Sammi and Gem, I prepare for the boxing match soon to come. "You're such an airheaded, dipshitted doofus sometimes," Gem scolds me playfully.

"Correction, my girl...I am THE airheaded, dipshitted doofus and very proud of it."

"Oi, here's to being an airheaded, dipshitted doofus," Otto blurts out from the front seat, eliciting a quick, violent slap to the neck from our driver. "Keep egging him on, Otto...you'll soon be a hood ornament."

"That's alright, brother Otts, I've got your back," I reply boisterously, understanding too late how vastly outnumbered I'm in this back seat.

"Who, pray tell has your back, Robbs?"

I size up my pretty but very rough and tumble competition and sigh, "point well taken, Gem." I slap Otto mournfully on the shoulder. "Once again brother, the Punk Pirate Princess and her legions are victorious..."

Otto exhales a plume of smoke, hanging his head for the moment. "Bro', we're always screwed when it comes to this tribe of Wild Girls."

Yuka peels away from the curb and smugly smirks into her rearview mirror. "You boys are finally learning a valuable lesson and it's that you can't beat the Misfit girls."

"Yeah, but the Misfit girls can sure beat up the boys!" Gem blurts out before the pouncing commences. Realizing there's no escape, I claw for the back window as the melee continues, trying in vain to get Dusty's attention, only to receive Steph flipping me the bird, laughing her ass off and Dusty flicking the bucking Grenada's high beams before mouthing, "Yer' fuckin' screwed," through his hazy windshield.

Yuka and Dusty wail on their horns when they pass Otis, an automotive version of 'Taps' played in requiem for my sputtering, belching, doddering, not to be trusted in lieu of an escape from the Brody's, fucking car. The girls resume their brutal rough-housing, dragging me under, so Otis is delivered my one finger salute for his ineptness, while my mind says what I can't right now...'I coulda' been driving, Otis...avoiding these girls thinking that they can always win...then again, getting pounced on by three gorgeous punk girls before a show is kind of an enviable position for an eighteen-year-old guy to be in.'

"Thank you, Otis!" I blurt out with a grin, voluntarily succumbing to whatever it is the girls have in store for me on the ride to the underground.

● ● ●

The cars snake in slow procession to a designated area where the rule of thumb is, everyone parks approximately two to three blocks away from the actual event, so if the Brody's come around, we have ample time to alight from the premises. Most times, if the cops do 'raid' an underground event, it's because whoever owns the structure happens to stop by, checking on their useless pile of shit real estate, and then raises hell to the local authorities that we're breaking and entering the premises.

This entails the Brody's making their presence known, smashing their truncheons against cans, dumpsters, metal doors or what have you and unless you're a daft fuck, putting up a fight, Brody's very rarely arrest you since there are too many of us, too few of them, and probably too much paperwork to deal with for processing us. In other words, "here's your free pass punk kids, so on to the next factory or warehouse, and we'll see you in a week."

Word around South Street is that apparently Dilby takes care of the local Brody's handsomely which certainly must alleviate a multitude of hassles. I guess when you're a Beat Brody making dick for pay from the filthy city of rats, any extra cash is a welcome extravagance to have fall into your lap.

Yuka and Dusty creep into spots around the corner from the looming monoliths of America's now failed industrial centers which are bathed eerily in only moonlight and the faint glow of incandescence from the few operable streetlights.

With the fun of our roughhousing behind us, Gem snags her guitar from the trunk, mulling over what we should play if Dilby stays true to his word. At the age of twenty-eight, Edward 'Dilby' Dillard is an elder statesman of the Philly punk scene who's played in numerous bands, hosted hundreds of underground concerts around Philly, Chester, Camden and the local suburban counties and his events have had the pleasure of being visited by some well-known acts including members of Black Flag and Fugazi, or even the likes of Patti Smith, Springsteen or Gem's fav and my boyhood crush, former punk Runaway, Joan Jett.

Crack is Dilby's latest brainchild and they're becoming a well-known, highly respected band on the local punk circuit, so even being considered to jam with them is quite an honor for Gem and I. We may be buds with these guys but our best, strongest performance better be on display tonight. The underground may be a lot of friends getting together to listen to the best local punk and rock has to offer, but the audiences take their music seriously.

A young punk with a messy purple mohwak repeatedly whistles the Pistols, 'Anarchy in the U.K.' pointing us towards our destination located just beyond the hulking, Schmidt's Brewery which gloriously tinges the surrounding air with the aroma of beer.

If you've ever been to an underground gig, it's masterfully organized by Dilby, right down to sentinels being posted every few blocks serving as traffic and money handlers. Dusty and Oren usher the tribe through a peeled back, chain link fence, leading to the fire exit of a massive factory site, which probably dates back to the late 1800's.

The door creaks loudly, paint and rust flake from the hinges and upon closing behind us with a thunderous thud, we're able to view the makeshift stage for tonight's festivities and Dilby's

242

boys have done their usual magic locating some type of rudimentary power for the amps, stage lighting and the soundboards which are set on an iron platform in the rear expanses of the space. Perusing the dingy, grimy setting, you can't help but take notice of broken machinery, hoisting chains and parts for pianos scattered about the landscape. What sheer perfection for a hard driving night of partying and music! It's pure effing' crust! Bohemian punk at its crudest!

Dusty puts his arm around my shoulder, taking a drag from his cig. "Dil' tells me they manufactured pianos here years ago and even unearthed one in a maintenance shed that's still in fab' working condition. It's by the side of the stage."

"Dust, this is just way too cool!"

The boys of Crack prep for their soundcheck while we Misfits enter the industrial arena like Centurions ready to pillage the joint, so Gem and I give their lead singer, Tommy 'Acer' McShane, a big "Yo, oi, oi," when we spot him and he tosses his shoulder length brown hair away from his slender, Irish facial features. "Ahhhh...yeesssss, there's my two superstar punks! Are you ready to kick ass with us tonight, Gemma and Rob?"

"We're ready to tear this place up, Acer," Gem replies gleefully.

"YO', now THAT'S the kinda' spirit I like to hear, girl. How about your boy here, is he ready to show this crowd what kinda' pipes he's got?!"

"He will not disappoint them, or you, Acer!"

"Fuckin' brill, I'm just juiced by the level of fucking confidence, Gemma Stinson!"

For as talented as Crack is, there are no prima donna's or pretentiousness amongst the bands' members. They perform diligent, solid work on their covers and crank out numerous, lightning quick, balls to the wall originals. Their bassist, Randy and their drummer, Stacks are flat out intense, their lead guitarist, Viktor, leaves all of us, especially Gem, awestruck, while Dilby is just masterful on rhythm guitar. If this band doesn't become famous in the annals of punk history, the music world has been done a major disservice.

Dilby ambles over, bellowing, "ay', my sideline act has arrived! The boys are looking forward to giving you some ample jam time with them and very excited to hear you two amplified and not just busking on a corner or in a coffee house getting' your boots shit on by rats." He lights up a Red while running his free hand through his jet black, spiked hair. "Gem, Viktor left you a spare axe up on stage to do a soundcheck with the band."

Gem shyly smiles before wagging a talon into the chilled air of the factory. "Thanks for the offer Viktor but I brought Robins Egg with me tonight," eliciting sighs from both men when it's pulled from the case. "Damn! Much like you girl, she's a thing of beauty."

Gem impishly winks at Dilby and struts away, swinging those hips of hers with an air of playful confidence before hopping upon the stage to confer with the boys, who usher over a slick saxophonist named Zip to join the conversation. Everyone beams brightly while Gem lets them in on what she's got up her sleeve to impress Dilby, the Misfits and a growing number of show-goers milling about.

Taking hold of the robin's egg colored Gretsch, which gleams in the spotlight, Gem plugs in and steps to the mic. "Hello, everyone! I just want to thank the boys of Crack for letting me do this soundcheck with them, so Acer, why don't you take a break with our Misfits and I'll take care of the singing for now."

"Sounds great, Gemma girl, sing away…I can always use a suds break!"

Viktor approaches the other mic, relishing his role to play rhythm for this sassy, punk newbie. "Gemma, I know you play a wicked axe, so don't be afraid to lay into it with those claws of yours."

Gem takes a deep breath, smiling to all of her adoring Misfits, before blowing me a kiss. "Thanks, Viktor. I'll do my best not to disappoint you all, sooooooo are you ready to ROCK THIS CHECK, CRACK?"

Prepping for the onslaught, I see Gem's hands flash across the Gretsch, allowing the wicked sounds to force the early arriving punks to cut conversations short and scatter for the stage with mouths wide open upon realizing this gorgeous, statuesque beauty with the auburn hair and black leather is no goddamned joke as the opening riffs of GBH's 'Race Against Time' explode through the amps and our fellow street busker and soundman for the evening, Eddie 'Nails' Evans is already having a time keeping up with her guitar savagery .

The thundering, ass kicking licks of pure speed place Gem on display for a growing number of friends and strangers to behold and her crushing chords and strong voice have people forgetting that she's only nineteen years old.

Dilby breaks into a shit eating grin, shaking me around like a bear pawing over a prospective meal. "Goddamn it, kid! What the hell have you two been up to?"

"Honestly, Dil, Gem and I have been so busy with school or work that we've only been busking here and there and playing small shops when we get the chance."

Emphatically throwing his hands towards the monstrous factory's ceilings, he bellows, "here and there, the kid tells me. HERE AND THERE!" He points to the stage, absorbing Gem's persona, but Swan is nowhere near ready to stop this ass kicking assault, with the boys following her chaotically into the madness, so just when we assume she'll give her hand a rest, our girl slows down just a tad, seguing perfectly into Romeo Void's, 'Never Say Never'.

Dilby and Acer are righteously floored by Gem's extreme confidence, voice and the adept handling of her vintage Gretsch, as are the crowds which flow like the rapids into the now buzzing underground. Zip lets loose on his saxophone and Gem harnesses his energy into her playing. "HERE AND THERE!" Dilby bellows again while I let out a massive wolf whistle for my girl, who's ripping through Deborah Iyall's terse vocal stylings...

"The slump by the courthouse
With windburn skin
That man could give a fuck
About the grin on your face
As you walk by, randy as a goat

He's sleepin' on papers
When he'd be warm in your coat.."

Gem winds down her stage act to some thunderous and warranted applause. "Oh my God…thank you so much! Thank you, Crack! So Dil', do we have time for one more song, babe?"

"It's your stage, Punk Princess," he laughs while Gem blushes over his awareness of her new nickname. "Really, guys? You just couldn't wait to let Dilby know that, huh?" Gem smirks, pointing my way like she's picking me from a 'Rogues Gallery' lineup. "Oh Robert, my handsome Prince, when you're done cackling with those wiseass Heckle and Jeckle kids, Tim and Skate, would you care to join me for this last song?"

Well, I can't just leave my girl stranded up there, so with some goading and ribbing from the tribe, I hop on stage. Gem steps to the mic, beaming once more. "If you're having fun already, buckle up for the ride street punks, 'cuz you ain't seen nothin' yet!"

"You ready for this, Robbs?" she playfully pries. "This is fuckin' bril', girl, so hell yeah, let's give em' some righteousness," and as if shot out of a cannon by my prompting, her talons flash across the axe, ablaze in Phoenix-like glory from the crude, bright stage lights before X's 'Los Angeles' pounds across the massive factory floor at an unbridled pace.

The crowds of punks amass and the underground resembles a hot, hazy, Philly summer evening from all of the cigarettes and weed being blazed simultaneously and the whirlwind of maddening activity in the pit and its surroundings gives the wasteland aspects of the venue a portentously enjoyable feel.

Dilby and Acer flip a thumbs-up while I grab the mic, trying to do justice for John Doe's epic tale of how L.A. life could eventually make you viciously hate everything or everyone and Gem couldn't be a more exceptional backup vocalist, channeling Exene Cervenka's inner demons.

And just when you thought Gem would tire at playing so furiously, there's not a chance, because the dying sounds of her guitar immediately flow into The Exploited's, 'Dead Cities', permitting the rooster set to unleash a serious war whoop when

Wattie's frenetic, growling Scottish vocals come shining through in my hastened adaptation.

I'm truly feeling euphoric about the results and the Misfits appear rather gobsmacked about the performance, but Gem has always acknowledged that my persona transforms outrageously when I plant my boots firmly onto a street corner to busk or a small venues stage.

Drained from the adrenaline rush but equally riding a massive high, Gem and I depart to an insane level of applause but not before Dilby retrieves his rhythm guitar and acknowledges our raw energy. "Hey, underground punks, would you like to hear from them again later tonight?"

"YEEESSSS," is the deafening response, as we return to the blitzkrieg energy of the tribe and some new admirers.

Gem jumps into my awaiting arms, screaming with delight, "what an incredible night, Robbs! I am so happy...so in love with you! Maybe this is THE CHANCE!"

"Gemma, I love you too. Enjoy this chance, Swan, 'cuz it's only gonna' get better, I just know it!"

···20···

"She's Tearin' It Up!"

THE EVENING MOVES along without a hitch and the Brody's have left us to our own devices for the moment. The Misfits and other tribes have pogoed, slammed, ska punked, windmilled, and moshed ourselves into near blissful exhaustion. Oren was thrown into service as a bouncer by Crack and his muscular forearms shake from continuously launching punks into the pit while simultaneously keeping them away from the stage.

Crack careens through a wicked set of covers and originals, rocking the well over three hundred punks, wavers and wannabe's into a pure state of frenetic energy. During a well-deserved intermission, Dilby makes haste through his adoring throngs of fans towards our crew. It's pure magic watching him perform because his animal magnetism and raw energy are a sight to behold. A crew member tosses Dil' a towel to dab at the volumes of sweat gushing from his pores.

"Dil, that was a knockout set…boy, you are a tough act to follow, bro'."

"Glad to hear you say that, because you and your girl will be giving me and Acer a break for a while. The stage and the boys are yours again in twenty minutes so get with em' and figure out what you plan on playing."

Gem jumps into my arms, bellowing, "Fuckin' bloody hell! I'm going to faint! This is unbelievable! Thank you so much, Dil, you won't regret this!" We excitedly haul ass to where the band's slamming some gulps of whiskey straight from the bottle and with my nerves tingling, I don't hesitate to partake in a swig when its contents are passed my way.

Hastily conferring with Stacks, Viktor and Randy, they're quite jazzed upon hearing our thoughts for covers and some other surprises but in what seems like just minutes elapsing, Acer returns to the microphone, continuing the evening's festivities.

"I'd like to give big thanks to all the fuckin' tribes who made it out here tonight. We've got a surprise in store for those of you who'd not arrived early enough to witness some ass kicking, raw talent.

"For this set, we have Crack teaming up with eighteen-year-old Rob Cavelli taking over on lead vocals and get ready to be blown away visually and audibly by our nineteen-year-old, axe smasher, Gemma Stinson…so let's give our street buskers a big welcome to our underground!"

Hearty cheers of 'fuck off' and 'oi' resonate throughout the dingy factory until an eerie silence finally ensconces us. Gem plugs her 50's rockabilly Egg into an amp, readying herself for our debut. Grabbing the microphone, I welcome the crowd to the show and Gem happily finishes her setup. The Misfit girls scream out, "Kick their ass, Gemma and Robbs."

"You can do this, Swan," Sammi blurts from the pit as Lena playfully kisses her neck and when 'Nails' gives us a big thumbs-up from a lighted platform in the rear of the factory, we're ready to go until suddenly, a cocky, crass young rooster down in front, mischievously takes the piss at Gem. "Hey, tall and gorgeous… are you done holding the guitar for your boyfriend? So…are you a punk girl or a poser?" he chides, eliciting a smattering of chuckles from the group of pubescent bucks around him.

Gem holds steady, placing fingers to her lips, bending over to 'kiss' each bandana, readies herself again, directs her shit eating grin towards the snarky snot and snarls, "I'm a PUNK, you fuckin' little BITCH, so don't fuckin' forget it," and with a ferocity second to none, she plows into the opening riff of X's, 'Johnny Hit and Run Pauline,' which immediately instigates a moshing frenzy below us.

Gem and I stay irreverent through the vocals and as the audience continues to absorb our manic energy, we're exhausting each other in the intensity department and it's only the FIRST FUCKING song! In other words, we love this bitchin' night already.

Swan's kicking Egg compliments my vocals perfectly and we can't stop grinning.

> *"L.A. bus doors open*
> *Kicking both doors open*
> *When it rested on 6th Street*
> *That's when he drug a girl inside*
> *He was spreading her legs*
> *And didn't understand dying*
> *She was still awake..."*

The song ends with a mashing stroke across smoking hot strings and Gem stares into the totally electric, screaming crowd, flashing her infectious, radiant smile. Pointing out the now mesmerized rooster heckler and his crew to the legions of howling tribes, she purrs into the microphone, "Was that punk enough for you, little boys?"

The crowd goes wild, while Dilby, Acer and the Misfits can't stop roaring their approval at Gem's moxie. "WOOOOOO HOOOOO! You did it, Swan!" Lena screams from the madness of the pit while holding onto an equally excited Sammi and our little, Yuka wipes tears of pride from her cheek. "You killed it, sis!"

The tribe gives me some bitchin', piss off, sod off chants but this is Gem's chance to shine so I happily enjoy the ride. "You folks ain't seen shit yet. You ready Gem?"

"Hell yeah, baby!"

"We ready back there, Crack?"

"OI, OI, OI!" comes the boys' reply with ear splitting thunder.

"Hey, underground punks, welcome on the mic, Gemma Stinson!!! One, two, three…GO!"

Gem runs to my side, sharing the mic on X's remake of Jerry Lee Lewis', 'Breathless'. Her guitar playing and vocals just scorch the old factory setting and a hundred years of metal dust is probably ready to loosen from the goliath ceilings of this rusty relic at any moment, raining down like snow on the masses of rowdies and anarchist punks tearing up the mosh pit.

In the eerie glow emitted from the few overhead, turn of the century relics the crew were able to power and the ample stage lighting, the scene takes on a wild, orgy like appearance, with outlines of bodies twisting, slamming and jumping to and fro.

Skate, Tim, Otto and Dusty can't contain themselves any longer after storming the stage and launch themselves into the crowd along with three young mohawk girls who happily join Steph, Lena and Sammi, pitching themselves into the frenzied masses while the crowd begs loudly for more music.

Not in any mood to disappoint, I jump right into Killing Joke's, 'The Wait'. 'Jaz' Coleman's lyrics come growling out low, allowing Gem time to build up the momentum with her finger picking, black talons making the gleaming Egg's strings beg for mercy.

I'm absorbing every minute of this night…a night we would never fathomed even a few months ago, especially after never looking at ourselves as anything more than two crazy punk kids playing music by the artists we appreciated for shits and giggles, painstakingly trying to create our own sound, busking, or just for the love of doing it in small settings like the coffee shop in Queen Village. Now, here we are, onstage with one of the hottest Underground Philly acts, playing our asses off in front of a truly energized, music loving throng of punks.

We give the crowd a chance to catch their breath...nah... fuck that...we ain't giving them shit of a chance to breathe tonight. Grabbing the mic, I keep them lively, if not off balance with our choice of music. Smiling...hell, beaming from ear to ear, I give Gem a nod. "You ready to give this crowd some rockabilly punk, Gemma?"

"Damn straight, I'm ready to rock these 'Roosters' to the rafters!" She swings back, eagerly viewing the Crack boys' expressions of pure enjoyment.

"This is a song for ALL my boys out there. You'll relate to these lyrics whether you're one or not. Randy!"

"Yeah, Rob?!"

"You ready to give me some earth-shaking bass to set this girl up?"

"Fuck yeah!"

"Viktor...Stacks?!"

"Yeah, Rob?"

"You ready to give me some hot licks back there?"

Viktor finger picks with amazing speed in approval while our young Stacks lays some hot, hard stick work across his drumheads'. "Awwwwrriiiight! Let's do this..." Randy thunders out of the box with his wicked bass line and the crowd goes apeshit when they realize it's the 'Runaway Boys' by the Stray Cats.

Brian Setzer's blues driven voice flows coolly from my throat while the band slays the audience...

"Get kicked out for coming home at dawn,
Mom and Dad cursed the day you were born,
Throw your clothes into a duffle bag
shoutin' as ya' slam the door home is a drag

Who can I turn to and where can I stay?
I heard a place is open all night and all day
There's a place you can go where the cops don't know
You can act real wild they don't treat you like a child

Runaway boys..."

Gem roars through the song with Setzer-like chops...fuck it all, man...she's having a goddamned blast! Sammi and Lena can't take it anymore, so Oren lifts them up and they ultimately shake and shimmy their way around Gem, who's crushing the guitar solo, tossing her hair like long, auburn whips, stomping her boot to the beat of Randy's wicked bass and the ripping slaps of Stacks' skins. Our sultry, sexy Misfit duo set their sights on me and shaking their hips fiercely, elicits wolf whistles from guys and gals alike.

Two of the young mowhawk girls find their way back up, deciding to give me a peck on the cheek. Gem cracks up when she spots the goings on but Lena and Sammi are having none of this tomfoolery, so they politely dance the girls to the end of the stage and into the waiting arms of Oren and Dusty. "Piss off, pretty girls! My babe Gem has this guy all to herself," Lena shouts above the ear-bleeding loudness.

Lena's send-off of the Wendy-O Betty's gives me a chance to enjoy the madness arising in front of the stage and what a mix it is tonight; roosters, Wavers, I even spot some rude boys and girls here and of course, the Misfits are right in the middle of the fray, with Dusty and Otto tossing bodies into the factory's dark, shadowy environs. Much to our surprise, they are soon joined by Flor, Trent and the City Gardens boys from the other night on Perry Street. It's turning into quite a family night for Gem and I and upon looking further into the audience I spot sexy Syd with quite a few of the SKULLZ vixens in tow, drinking like fish and howling loudly.

I find myself wishing Sissy, Birdie and Stace could see their beautiful Swan in all of her glory on this magical night. I wish little Claire would have viewed her big sister savior relishing this moment for all its worth. Somehow, I believe they're here in spirit.

Using this as the perfect chance to introduce the tribes to some of our sound, I wave out to the masses. "Alright! Well before we get in to some more tunes that you know and love,

Gem and I, with the help of the boys from Crack have one to introduce.

"It's a nice play on words but it sums up our feeling on the human and pest version described here. Hey Lena...this is for you...rat killer! Underground, welcome to the 'Filthy City of Rats.'

Well, here it goes, the days of busking and doing some quick practices with Stacks and the boys is coming to fruition. It's all or nothing and Gem is out of the box like a machine gunner and from the raw, ass kicking reaction on the floor, it's working like magic.

Keeping a keen eye on the anarchy unfolding, I'm keeping the counts rolling through my brain. This is going to be rapid fire singing and I don't dare fuck it up...the band sounds so tight and Gem's already slaying it, so...two, three, four...

"Scurry from the alleys
Tumble down squat stairs
Nibble your feet while sleeping
Tangle in your hair

Sniveling, slickened snarling mess
If you wanna' live without 'em
Move to the 'burbs, I guess

Cuz you'll never escape them
Venturing out after dark
They'll close your nightclubs
Overrun your parks
Don't matter if it's subway tunnels
Or the halls of power under Billy Penn's hat
One thing you learn quick
It's a filthy city of rats..."

The tribes are going nuts with the level of energy exploding from the stage and the Misfits and apparently a few others who've seen Gem and I busking on the streets are ready to blurt out the chorus along with us. "IF YOU KNOW IT, FUCKING SING IT! COME ON UNDERGROUND...HERE WE GO!

"Filthy city of rats, filthy city of rats
If they got any bigger, they'd fuckin' eat the cats
Filthy city of rats, filthy city of rats
If they got any bigger, they'd fuckin' eat the cats!"

The roof has officially been blown off the underground and the pit has swelled in size...the punks have gone apeshit with Gem and Crack's enormous wall of sound and hopefully with my lyrics. With no time to waste, Gem runs next to me, hammering away at Robins Egg like there was no tomorrow and for us, we have to play this night just that way...there is no tomorrow, The Chance starts now.

Building up a good head of steam, another bottle of Schmidt's is guzzled and sprayed all over the pit and my bandmates for good measure. With a heavenly mix of beer and sweat stinging the eyes, I attack the mic like a wolf devouring its prey.

"Dirty politicians, dirty cops
Try and MOVE them out
Or it's a bomb they'll drop

'Cuz the jobs are all gone
And they don't fuckin' care
'Cuz the rats love to feast
On your despair

Hell if I know how to duck 'em
So I'll get a steak at Pat's
Hope the fuckers don't eat it
Filthy city of rats..."

The adrenaline explodes through my veins, Gem's head is banging a mile a minute, sending wet whips of flaming hell in every direction and joining me at the mic, the words roll out from us like dagger throws into an unsuspecting victim's chest. "FUCKIN' SING IT WITH US UNDERGROUND!"

"FILTHY CITY OF RATS, FILTHY CITY OF RATS, IF THEY GET ANY BIGGER THEY'LL FUCKIN' EAT THE CATS...FILTHY CITY OF RATS, FILTHY CITY OF RATS IF THEY GET ANY BIGGER THEY'LL FUCKIN' EAT THE CATS!"

It's relative pandemonium in the factory right now. Gem's grin is fucking glorious, Stacks launches his drumsticks into the crowd and the boys from Crack are amped when they hear the underground punks begin chanting "FILTHY CITY...FILTHY CITY!" as if their lives depended on it!

Trying not to let our steam run out, I usher Gem up front again, thank everybody for the absolutely gobsmacked reaction to our song and introduce Zip to the crowd so Crack can make quick, blistering, genius work of Romeo Void's, 'Never Say Never' again.

Gem has the underground eating from the palm of her hand after the 'Filthy City' performance; however she graciously turns the microphone over to me. "Rob, are you ready to give this crowd some 'Godfather's of Punk' for the next few songs?"

"I would love to oblige, Gem! Are you and the boys ready to have some fun?"

"Ready when you are, baby," she bellows after removing her leather jacket, revealing the very snug fitting tee. Blushing in acknowledgement of the wolf whistles, she still hits the count in jackrabbit speed, blazing perilously into a righteous cover of The Ramone's, 'Rockaway Beach', which allows Dusty and Steph some stage time, screaming "OI" at the top of their lungs before disappearing into the spazzed, moshing masses below.

From up here, the old factory setting is taking on the look of a club more by the minute, aided by the returning smells of cigarettes and weed. Trent tosses me a bottle of Schmidt's, which I happily guzzle away in a matter of seconds before showering the underground faithful with the rest.

Bathed in sweat, I grab the mic, giving Gem a big smile. This is the way we always pictured The Chance to be...the music, the white hot lights and us giving nothing but love and energy back to our punk fam. "This next song is for all of you Roosters who got screwed out of seeing Motorhead at City Gardens the other night! Apparently, the band didn't care for their surroundings and gave us all a big sod off at the last minute."

The crowd boos derisively but I quell their hostility with a smirk. "Now, hold on a sec, my punk brethren, because in retrospect, I know our Misfits would like to thank them for the cancellation anyway, since we went to CBGB's instead and had one hell of a fuckin' night! Didn't we, Gem?"

"We sure as hell did, baby!"

"So even though we still love you, Lemmy and Motorhead, you really were a bunch of tossers in Trenton!" The crowd cheers wildly but are quickly drowned out by Gem and the boys churning out a purely vicious rendition of 'Ace of Spades' so, once more, my girl and I are off to the races on who will be more intense here...her axe smashing, or my impression of Lemmy's grizzled vocals. From the looks on everyone's face and the anarchy taking place in the pit, it must be a dead heat, but just to raise up the ante, Gem lets loose an incredibly nimble, athletic leg kick while still handling all the quickness of her playing with some ferocious dexterity. Jaws are dropping left and right over her kick but the Misfits can only howl and whistle at their girl...they've witnessed this mastery before.

Gem's hair whips in every direction, sweat pours like a waterfall down her body and even though the abandoned factory is cool and damp, I'm drenched from the spotlights heat and the giant metal cans around the stage, ablaze with pallets; hell, I could probably ring my wool cap into a large bucket as steam wildly escapes my pores, but I'm having too much fun to care... this is the fucking night we've waited for.

With the crowd screaming uncontrollably, Swan and I still have an ace up our sleeve. She waves Acer over to the stage and as he takes position behind the piano, Dilby has his boys aim one of the spots directly on Gem. Soon, everyone attains a hushed silence, viewing this Punk Princess in all her glory, bathed in ethereal light as she tosses those lustrous, deep auburn strands over her shoulders. Grabbing the mic, Gem smiles broadly, looking like a vision of beauty in this enormous, dark, hallowed space.

"Rob and I want to thank Crack, Dilby and Acer for a truly bitchin' night. We're so grateful for having such good friends to make this happen." Gem swings Robins Egg behind her like a gunslinger of the Old West would do with their most trusted rifle. The old girl got strummed, thrashed and pummeled but came back for more every time. "We're going to slow it down a bit before we leave you. This is a favorite of mine…a song for ALL young lovers here tonight."

The piano warbles out a familiar strain as Gem cradles the mic; softly singing the lines Springsteen and Patti wrote with sheer, emotional perfection…

> *"Take me now, baby, here as I am*
> *Pull me close, try and understand*
> *Desire is hunger is the fire I breathe*
> *Love is a banquet on which we feed…"*

With one good smack of Stacks' skins, Gem, Crack and Acer are bathed in light. I take my place by the mic Gem vacated earlier, giving her the backup vocals, which really aren't needed. This thrilling night is hers and I'm just feeling the high of being part of the whole deal!

Gem handles the powerful lyrics with sheer brilliance before ushering me to her side for the chorus. Looking into those blazing green eyes, hearing that strong, spirited voice, I'm more mesmerized than the audience at Swan's prowess…

> *"Because the night belongs to lovers*
> *Because the night belongs to lust*
> *Because the night belongs to lovers*
> *Because the night belongs to us…"*

Peering through the smoke and haze enveloping the punks of the underground, I see smiling faces…the bodies entwined in a lovers embrace…lighters being held aloft by the purists who realize they witnessed something pretty special tonight because Gem's had a totally unrehearsed, smashing debut.

Acer brings our set to an end with a roll of his knuckles across the piano keys and is immediately drowned out by whistles, applause and cheers which go up from every corner of this former leviathan from the city's industrial past. Dilby leaps eagerly onto the stage to give us both a big shout of approval, and his new phenom, a long, warm embrace. "Are they not something, 'Underground' punks?" he asks, imploring the crowd to beg for more and they do not disappoint our mentor, boisterously screaming for an encore. Gem whispers something in Dil's ear, causing him to grin broadly. "I like your thinking, Gem! Confer with your boy here and get him on board!"

"Dare I ask what it is you're both up to?"

Gem nuzzles into my frame, bringing her lips to my ear. "I have a special request to ask of you. I want you to sing the last two songs." She tells me what's in store for the playlist, smiling broadly. "Tell me that's not, as you say, effing brill!"

Feeling my heart sink slightly, I try to dissuade her from doing this. "Gem, you just gave the most incredible performance. 'Because the Night' was a perfect way to end this evening for you. You should think of something to do, instead of me."

Shaking her head, she can only grab my chin and smile. "Baby boy, you still don't get it, do you? YOU are the reason I'm doing these things. You've helped me become confident enough to do this…to be up here, in my world, happy and free, for the first time in my life. Please, do this for me."

How can I even begin to say no? She grabs the band, tells them what we'll be playing and they look psyched about the idea. Gem swings her hips over to the microphone, holding up her hands to quiet the murmuring crowd. "Did you all like what you heard tonight, my punks?"

"YEEESSSSSSSSS!" comes the deafening reply. "Well, sit tight. We have one that's pure punk gold, followed by a very special song. It's not punk but some of you who know it, will just love this. Please welcome back to the lead mic, my truly kick ass guy, Rob Cavelli."

I absorb the applause and trying my best to be workmanlike with my stage demeanor, give Gem a quick nod before lowering my head, grabbing the mic, wrapping my fingers tightly around the stand, not making a move, not making a sound. Gem nervously approaches her mic, staring at me blankly. "Are you ready to do this, Rob?"

I lift my head slightly, still saying nothing.

"What the hell is up with you, Robbs? Let's do this!"

Grabbing the mic harder, I turn to her wild eyed, with a level of rage building in me. "You wanna' know what the hell is up with me," I snap. A buzz runs through the crowd, the band starts to shuffle around, even the Misfits appear nervous.

"You're damn right, I wanna' know what's up! What's your fucking damage? You're acting nuts right now and it's pissing me off!" Stomping her foot demonstratively, I rip the mic from the stand, furiously approaching my green-eyed nemesis. The night has taken a turn for the worse...

"I told you we should've ended on your song...now you're pissed off?"

"Yeah, I'm pissed off!"

...or has it? "HEY GEM!"

"WHAT ROBBS?" Gem screams...her eyes blazing furiously.

"You're pissed?! SO FUCKING WHAT!"

Gem pulls away, ripping her fingers wildly across Robins Egg's strings. Stacks pounds on his drum set, Randy thunders in on the bass, while Viktor churns in some hammering riffs on the rhythm. The stage is ablaze with white hot spotlights, raging thunder from the amps and Gem's talons scraping wildly down her strings before continuing her pulverizing, axe playing with the biggest smile on her face. I think the Anti-Nowhere League boys would be quite proud of our 'pissed off' showmanship.

Once the crowd sees Dilby and Acer grinning wildly, the jig is up. The openness of the pit rapidly encloses under the massive crush of bodies being hurled to and fro, so it's easy for me to snarl and snap through Animal's foul, condescending, and putrid lyrics of debauchery on the League's, 'So What'…

"Well I've been to Hastings and I've been to Brighton
I've been to Eastbourne too
So what, so what
And I've been here, I've been there
I've been every fucking where
So what, so what
So what, so what you boring little cunt

Well who cares, who cares what you do
Yeah, who cares, who cares about you,
You, you, you, you…"

Oren and Dusty have gladly given up trying to hold the crowd back, so the stage becomes a launching pad for everyone having the sack to sail aimlessly through the air, hoping someone will be on the receiving end to catch them.

Gem takes a wide stance like X's, Billy Zoom, churning her black, switchblade tips madly across Robins Egg's strings; head-banging so wildly that her auburn mane's swirling in every direction again. "Holy fuckin' shit!" I hear Dusty bellow. "Lookit' Gem…she's tearin' it up!"

The Trenton and Philly Misfits invade the stage, even big Oren gets in on the action, diving off the stage full force, until everyone catching him buckles or sways under the strongman's weight. Trent, Flor, Skate and Tim scream out my name and tumble riotously into the pits' insanity…holy shit! I can't even see where the hell they've been surfed to.

The glory and the fury of the past few days has draped over me like a cloak of pure venom and with a death grip still on the mic, I kneel down, teetering on the precipice of the stage, grabbing the hands of our Misfit girls who are either singing or screaming wildly and almost get pulled into the boisterous pit. Catching myself, Dusty helps right me to finish the song while

I keep one foot perched on a floor amp and upon spotting Trent and the boys bellowing like only Pan's Lost Boys would...just tempting me to go airborne, I run to Gem who's exhausted and bathed in sweat.

"You were just insane tonight, girl! I love you so much!

Giving me a sweet kiss, she pulls me close. "I love you too, Rob." The boys keep imploring the jump, so what's a friend to do? Gem's bellows out, "YO!", while waving a hand in their direction.

"Gotta' fly now, babe!" So with a running start, I soar through the air peacefully, into the waiting arms of my punk family, while getting surfed through the turbulent waves of 'Underground' faithful.

• • •

After a few minutes of wild cheering begins to dissipate, Gem playfully grabs the toppled stand and replaces the microphone while giggling audibly.

Her radiant smile and wild energy have the crowd hanging on every word. She begins to 'shyly' shuffle around behind the mic, tapping her boot on the stage again. "Umm...if it's ok with my beautiful punk family, we really need our singer back to close out this set."

From the rear of the factory, I get some roosters to surf me back stage-side and next to my girl. Acer takes his place by the piano as Dilby grabs two, tall workbench stools which were probably rescued from the scrap piles littering the maintenance shed next door. "Enjoy this, kid, you've earned it," he adds, while patting my back.

"Thanks, Dil...this is a dream come true," I excitedly reply.

"Zip, I hear you know how to play this next one so would you please do the honor of joining us?" Our young saxophonist hurriedly enters the scene, while I ask Gem to sit beside me. "Robbs, this is your moment to shine, let me see it from the ground." This is Gem at her best, pure selflessness.

"No way am I going to let that happen, Gemma. I'm here because of your faith in me. See how that street goes both ways, darlin'? I want to sing for them, but I also want to look into your eyes when I do this song."

Smiling lovingly, she immediately acquiesces. "Then there's nowhere else that I'd rather be."

Acer gives me a thumbs-up, so it's time for me to get the undergrounds attention. "Wow! Thanks again to all of you for making us feel so welcome. I'd like to dedicate this next song to all of us. It was written and performed by Bruce Springsteen. He may not be a punk rocker but he certainly understands the life of a punk. He gets what it's like to be the misfit, the Bohemian, the vagabond, so with that being said, I give you 'Meeting Across the River'."

A Red is procured from my pack and blazed immediately to get the mood and the voice just right; rough edged, not soft. Acer taps the keys lightly setting the frame for this great song. Zip intones with some sweet licks on his sax, trying his damned best to replicate the trumpet blasts from the original and acing it. The crowd is hushed, Gem reels me in with those eyes…the stage is ours…

"Hey Eddie, can you lend me a few bucks
Tonight can you get us a ride
Gotta make it through the tunnel
Got a meeting with a man on the other side
Hey Eddie, this guy, he's the real thing
So if you want to come along
You gotta' promise you won't say anything
'Cause this guy don't dance
The word's been passed, this is our last chance…"

Whether it's the first time they've heard it or not, the crowd gets it, because it's their life story. It's the story of us…the dreamers, the schemers…running full steam ahead, running on empty…golden and glorious…our generation of punks. It was the saga of anyone whose street life came down to a live or die existence.

It was the 'Wild Girls' freezing through a harsh Philadelphia winter in an abandoned, ramshackle squat on South Street, trying in vain to escape the pain and suffering inflicted through their horribly tragic home lives. It's the story of little Claire, tired, hungry and alone, losing her young life to the harsh, remorseless streets of Trenton.

It's also Gem's story, the one of an unloved, sexually abused girl whose parents lives revolved around dashed dreams, broken promises, booze fueled nights and drug filled days. The story of the girl who's hopefully expelled their demonic hold over her with the strength of her voice…with the fury of a rock crashing through their house of hell this morning.

I put my focus solely on her as Zip's lonely saxophone entices a single tear down her cheek. With our gazes permanently locked, I exhale another drag of a Red, finishing this epic tale of hopefulness and equally downtrodden heartbreak…

"Cherry says she's gonna' walk
'Cause she found out I took her radio and hocked it
But Eddie, man, she don't understand
That two grand's practically sitting here in my pocket

Tonight's gonna' be everything that I said
And when I walk through that door
I'm just gonna' throw that money on the bed
She'll see this time I wasn't just talking
Then I'm gonna' go out walking

Hey Eddie, can you catch us a ride…"

The Red's extinguished into the dirty, beer soaked stage floor…plumes of smoke escape from me and I bow my head, listening to Zip's gleaming sax capture the song and the grimy factory's feel with his pure, gritty performance. The piano's final note and Zip's sax float through the massive space, taking us all for a high only found in music...

The light slims to a single beam on just Gem and I, sitting there in silence, staring, understanding everything we need to know about each other. Rushing from her stool to hold me in a never-ending embrace, the stage is ours, the night is ours and the lights dim, enveloping us and a cheering audience of glorious punks into the welcome darkness...

• • •

You would've thought this to be the perfect way to end the evening, but Dilby is having none of it, having been told by Stacks that there's still one song left to play. Appearing puzzled, Gem shrugs her shoulders but I'm as perplexed in my reaction.

"Fuck no...they don't get to leave that easily, underground punks. I hear we have another original to do, so Gem, get your ass back up here." The jaw drops, the eyes grow wide and the boys of Crack nod and smile. Turning to me, she looks ready to cry. "Rob, I wanted this to be a surprise but I wasn't expecting any of this tonight."

"Gem, it's ok! Just let me bounce to the soundboard with Nails before you start playing. I want to get the whole feel, the pure sound of this song." Bringing her close to me, my eyes close, our lips meet and the heat of the moment takes charge. The underground will have to wait for a just another minute to hear their newly adopted star work her magic.

The wild sparkle of her eyes greets my return to the reality surrounding us and we both smile knowingly. "Kick their ass, Swan...leave nothing on that stage!"

"You know it, baby boy. Thank you for this."

"No, thank you, Gem...if not for you, I'd be sitting in a Podunk, cow town watching my life pass me by."

"And if I didn't ever have you to help me find my voice... these words..."

"You'd still be right here, Gem. It's your time to shine...go get 'em. They'll be floored by this."

Strutting away confidently, the boys pull her up to take her place out front; the Punk Princess of South Street's rightful throne. Laughing, shaking her head as if not to believe this magical night, she composes herself to speak seriously. "Thanks for this chance to perform a song that's very personal for me and has become even more personal after the events of this week when we lost a beautiful, young punk angel of the streets to its evils.

"Some of us, myself included, know what it's like to be abused, misused and treated like we're garbage. For all the girls...even some of the guys...and for little Claire..this is for you.

"Thanks Rob, for the lyrics completing my journey to this song of personal heartache and hope. Underground...this is 'Never Looking Back Again.'"

Prepping myself near Nails for a heart-wrenching ballad, Gem walks over to the amps, raises all the volume levels and gives a wink to the soundboard platform. "Sorry boys, but you're in for some ear-splitting sound," and right out of the box Gem is shaking the factory to its core.

With a strike across the strings and the facial expression of a woman possessed, her words, her voice are strong and serious. The moshing has come to a crashing halt and everyone's attention affixed on the auburn-haired hellcat in the white hot spotlight. Gem's prowess mesmerizes the underground and even the Misfits, Acer and Dilby are transfixed to what's transpiring right before their eyes; Gemma 'Swan' Stinson's star has shot into the stratosphere.

The beauty and pain of the lyrics are not lost on the audience and many mouths are left agape and others absorb the lyrical and musical prowess through their body movements. No stage diving, no moshing or slamming, this is pure, punk rock at its best and has everyone's attention.

The sparkling, green-eyed beauty finally hits the last, gut punch, "Never fuckin' looking back again," stretching the last word onward, going higher and higher, holding it for what seems like a glorious eternity...into the heavens until as hard as she and the band are winding out the song, it doesn't matter; her range has hit a peak which literally loosens a blizzard of metal dust onto everyone from the rafters of this dirty, old factory, leaving the crowd of hardened punks in jaw dropped awe. 'THE NIGHT IT SNOWED IN THE FUCKIN' UNDERGROUND!" I bellow.

Nails lets out a "HELL FUCKING YEAH, ROBBS..AND I NEVER EVEN RAISED HER VOLUME! BROTHER... IT WAS ALL HER...FUCKIN' ALL HER," shaking his head in utter disbelief as he keeps Gem's last blast of vocal magnificence shaking throughout the factory while Crack plows on into the raging hellfire being sent from the blazing guitar strings of Gem's, Robins Egg. Choked up, mentally drained from her raging, musical animosity and the last verse which left me on the verge of tearing up, I smile broadly at the undergrounds new star.

And when the last chord is struck, save for the echoes of the amplifiers left to resonate throughout the factory, she looks at me and only me; the audience going wild, Nails, Dilby, Acer and the Misfits roaring their loving approval...it's all drowned out by our never ending stares acknowledging what's occurred tonight.

THE CHANCE has been met head-on and Gemma Stinson kicked its ass sideways.

● ● ●

The rest of the evening is a blur. Our old friends, new friends met, Dilby, Acer, the band, even people asking us for autographs and when is our next gig...it careens right past us like a rushing freight train and after receiving no static from the Brody's, our exit from the underground goes off without a hitch and we bid farewell to countless well-wishers before collapsing into Yuka's Bonneville. Drenched from head to toe, Gem and I sit back, letting the conversations wash over us.

Dil already expressed readying ourselves for some big news very soon, but I've a sneaking suspicion his sights are set on Gem and why not? She's the perfect complement of talent, beauty, with an enigmatic stage presence and a take no prisoners attitude. Like she said earlier, this is her world, happy and free.

Yuka creeps onto Fourth Street, double parking so Otto can haul ass to the trunk and carefully extract Robins Egg from its depths. "You're one hell of a rocker, Gem. I'm in awe of you, Punk Princess and your voice...I never even knew you could achieve what happened on that last song. You had all the girls in tears and those lyrics choked me up, girl."

Hugging him tightly, Gem kisses Otto's forehead. "You're too sweet, Otto but I'm still just Gemma Stinson, the girl from the street. I'm still just Swan."

"That's right, you are just Gemma Stinson," Yuka intones from the Bonneville. "That means you're an incredible girl, who's faced incredible adversity, pain and sorrow. You're just Gemma Stinson, who gives so much of yourself to everyone else, doing it all with grace, power and a beautiful smile. YOU are a brilliant goddess...never forget that!"

"Thanks, sis...thanks to all of you for another unforgettable night. I couldn't have done this without my tribe."

"Wouldn't have been anywhere else, honey," Yuka chirps. "Oh, by the way, baby boy..."

"Yes, my little Yuka Yamaguchi?" I ask with a chuckle.

"You just like, kicked some major ass tonight! The Misfits are very impressed with their Punk Prince, his songwriting and his singing!"

"HELL YEAH!" exclaim Lena, Sammi and Otto. "FILTHY CITY OF RATS, FILTHY CITY OF RATS...Oi, Oi, Oi!"

Yuka yells for us to get some sleep and with SoCal's ass kickers, Social Distortion's, 'Mommy's Little Monster' ear-piercing the night air from within the car, the green bomber peels down Fourth, quickly turning onto Pine.

Clomping slowly up the stairs, expecting to see Misty eagerly waiting up to find out how our evening went, we find a note instead.

To my beautiful Gem and her incredible Rob,

Went to SKULLZ to find out from Sydney what my kids were up to, so my date was nice enough to accompany me to your event, where we witnessed, from the rear of a rundown factory, the fun insanity which is your nights. The first band was loud, fun and wild, but the young girl and gentleman who accompanied them for the next set were just incredible!

Sorry we couldn't stay for the whole thing, but after your set and encore, we older folks had to get our hearing back and escape to the calm respite of a local eatery. I will say this much though, I was duly impressed and extremely proud to watch you perform!

Both of you were amazing and Gem, what a voice on that last song! I could only cry out of sheer pride. Will be home in the morning and I can't wait to hear about everything.

Love you both,
Misty

Proceeding to the bedroom, Gem gently leans Robins Egg next to the dresser. "You kicked ass tonight, my blue girl. Thank you," Gem pronounces sweetly to her partner in crime. From the opened window, excitable sounds of the night creatures have not fully dissipated from the streets of Philly, but we're too exhausted to join them. Collapsing onto her bed, we can only stare at the ceiling, laughing like a couple of little kids. "Robbs, did tonight really happen? Please tell me this was not a dream."

"Ha, ha! It definitely happened, Gem. Your dream…THE CHANCE became a reality. You were incredible, girl, just pure effin' brilliant!" I reply excitedly.

"I'm so glad you shared the experience with me, babe, because you just knocked me out with your sound and presence up there. You were rock solid," she declares before kissing my cheek.

"I hate to tell you this, but I was scared shitless until I saw people smiling and the floor erupted into pure chaos, Gem… then it calmed me down. After that, it was nothing but fun!"

"Oh my God, me too!" she giggles. "I was ready to bag barf when Dilby told me to rehearse! I had to catch my breath just to play 'Race Against Time'."

"You were something to behold, girl…underground famous tonight, Gem! And that mezzo range at the end would've made any opera singer green with envy."

Wrapping her arms and legs around me, she whispers into my ear. "I couldn't have done it without you. You bring an energy from me that I never knew existed," and after she yawns a few times, I have to politely disagree with her statement.

"You had this talent before I met you, Gem so take the credit that you deserve. I appreciate that you want to say I helped your confidence but you took the bull by the horns, just like when we busk. It was all you out there."

Feeling her warm breath lay heavily across my neck, Gem has fallen into a deep sleep from all of the excitement and pure exhaustion of the evening.

I'll never know if she'd disagree with my comments but one thing's for sure, Gemma Anastasia Stinson, has been introduced to the music world, and there's no turning back now…

••• 21 •••

The Bet

THE WEEKS HAVE been flying by for me. Gem and I have been busy with school, work, practicing our asses off; many times with Crack and enjoying our time together with the Misfits at City Gardens, where we've seen Suicidal Tendencies and the Dead Kennedy's on successive weekends. Suffice it to say, the shows were great, with all of us, Gem and the girls included, getting pummeled into youthful oblivion. Jello Biafra ran through a hell of a playlist with the Kennedy's while 'Cyco Miko', Mike Muir of Suicidal had us screaming for more. His performances are pure, psychotic, raw energy.

The whole city of Trenton had to be shaking loose from its foundations because from inside the bowels of the Gardens, the noise level was utterly volcanic. How Randy Now was able to keep the club in one piece on either day was beyond me. The insanity of the punk scene was something to behold anyway in the Gardens, but these two shows really put it out there for me. Gem and I left the cavernous, graffitied bunker of punk just awestruck.

Gem and Yuka also got their first taste of freight train hopping with Otto and me before the Suicidal show. Sneaking our way onto Staley Syrup's plant grounds in Morrisville, the flatcar was 'hopped' with lightning quick precision and we all cursed, screamed and laughed our asses off viewing their guards stumbling, bumbling, failed pursuit.

Gem initially held onto me for dear life, but soon enough, the fearless redhead had only a fingertip grip and a hysterical surfer pose on display while crossing the Delaware River on the high, concrete rail bridge schussing us into Trenton. "Don't let go of me, Robbs!" she shrieked with pure delight. What a sight four multicolored, spiked haired, mohawked punk kids must have been to onlookers from Route 29, as we passed overhead, surfing the flatcar and emitting a torrent of war cries.

A week later, it was Gem's chance to introduce me to something I was too young to experience before leaving the Big Apple, although I'm sure the way it happened wasn't intended. Returning to Erie and the pure hell of K&A, Gem had to deliver something "to an old friend," as she put it. "Just another part of my past I need to check on, Robbs. I promise, you'll know all about it soon enough."

Not wanting to pry into who she was visiting, I awaited her return from the beaten row of apartments by blazing a Red on the cracked, weathered stoop, but not before drawing some unwarranted attention from six shaved heads down the block.

Sensing that this wasn't a welcoming party, I kept a keen eye on their movements and when Gem spotted them, clenched her fists and growled menacingly, my suspicions were confirmed… Kellin's boys were about.

"Fuck it all, it's Gordy and the goons from Fairmount! Haul ass to the El, Robbs, c'mon!" Blazing down the Avenue with jackrabbit speed, the pursuit began as the hooligan six unleashed howls and tribal screams. "Yer' fuckin' dead, Gem's bitch boy!"

Flying past the tattered, patchwork apartments and shops, Gem and I flipped over trash cans, abandoned shopping carts or anything we could get our hands on to impede Kellin's assholes from gaining ground but damn, they were still quick as lightning.

Reaching the El, the clamorous clanging up the metal steps resembled a symphony's cymbal section gone awry. "Hurry Robbs, the El is coming," Gem yelped in between breaths and as I reached the platform, I knew Kellin's goons weren't far behind. Running even harder, I glanced up long enough to hit the brakes and change direction, when, with wild hair whipping in every direction, Gem sprinted madly towards the steps with a metal trash can in tow.

Between the El screeching into the station, the can exploding into five of the skins who went toppling down the steps like bowling pins and Gem screaming, "die, you pussies," at the top of her lungs, I had just enough sense left to coldcock the one Gem called Gordy, catching him behind the ear while he leapt the can. Much as I wanted to relish in his shocked expression when he bounced down the steps and over the can, the other skins were relentlessly mounting a comeback.

Pulling on me hard while I unearthed the mini-bat from my pack, Gem scampered through the trains' open door, sprinting past stunned riders until we were outside the car and climbing the next ones ladder. "Gem, what the fuck? We're gonna' subway surf this bitch?"

"Do you wanna' explain to the train conductor or the SEPTA Brody's what just happened," she queries before unleashing one of her devilish laughs. "Well, when you put it that way Swan." Yanking me up, we kneel on the cars roof. "Shhh...lay flat, Robbs. They're not onto us yet."

"Who, the Brody's or Kellin's jerkoffs," I snigger.

"Neither, now shut the fuck up you goofball," she hisses. Holding me close, she kisses me quickly as the train jolts and for the first time, I'm the one wondering if we're going to make it. "Yes, we're moving!"

Sitting up, I follow her lead and shimmy to the end of the car long to laugh out loud and flip the bird to the helpless, platform stranded skins.

"This ain't done Gem! You an' yer' boy are dead...FUCKIN' DEAD!"

"FUCK OFF AND DIE, GORDY!" Gem howls. "PISS OFF, KELLIN'S LITTLE BITCHES," I add, and while Erie Station and our skin stomping becomes a mere memory, we get to our knees, extend the arms and grip at each other's finger tips. "Let the surfing begin, Gem!" Zipping past the avenues and endless apartment buildings, we try our best to stay up on the sleek, steel roof but quickly lay flat when we approach another station.

"One more stop, and we're in the heart of the K&A, Robbs. Then it's down the ladder, onto the station's steps, a possible, narrow escape from the SEPTA Brody's, then haul ass for a few blocks on Allegheny's 'Junkie Row' to catch the bus and hop off and snag the Broad Street Line by Temple University's hospital.

"Sounds like a walk in the park," she giggles as the train picks up speed. "WOO...WOOO! Ha, ha...God, this was a blast!"

"WOOOO...WOOOO! EYOOOO! It's never a dull moment with us, Swan!" I reply happily, sitting on the roof with my arms wrapped around the leather clad, Punk Princess.

● ● ●

The underground events have been pure enjoyment for us. Gem and I have performed frequently with Crack and some-times on our own, with Gem's guitar work and my singing getting some very positive feedback. Admittedly we're both starting to wonder where this may take us down the road, leading to some pretty interesting, vigorous late-night talks at the South Street Diner with the Misfits.

Sammi and Lena have already taken to loudly announcing us as "world famous punk rockers" every time we enter the diner or our other favorite haunt, the Famous 4th Street Deli (where Gem is absolutely adored by the owners, who've known her since her street days), causing Gem to blush in utter embarrassment, while I just laugh my ass off.

And if that weren't enough, a new Fanzine, called the Punk Perception, wrote a blazing article about Gem and I playing with Crack, our small venue shows and completed the excitement for us by adding a killer picture of Gem shredding her axe, with me singing by her side. "The Night It Snowed in The Underground," was how it was surprisingly titled; thanks, I'm one hundred percent positive because of Nails, the soundboard man being interviewed. Jeff Janklow, the 'Zine contributor, says he wants to do one with Gem and I in the near future. The CHANCE!

● ● ●

On a more somber note, Gem and I took a trip back to Saint Francis Hospital in Trenton to see if we could find out any more information about Claire. Luckily, we ran into one of the E.R. nurses who remembered us from that sorrowful night. The story she told us was even more heartbreaking than we could have anticipated. Apparently, little Claire was abducted from the streets of her hometown in Lorain, Ohio and had been missing for over a year. Trenton Police surmised she'd probably escaped from her kidnapper somewhere in Jersey and they were still trying to find out what the connection was to her ending up here, if there was any at all.

Gem cried helplessly at the thought of Claire's young life becoming so traumatic and fatal. "Her poor parents, I can't even imagine what they're going through right now. I wish there was a way I could write to them and offer my sympathies."

Betty, the nurse who was so kind to Gem, offered some advice after handing her a tissue. "Sweetie, go to the police, they may be able to give you some information. Her name was Claire Woods and I'll get you directions to the station. The Desk Sergeant's name is Tim McNulty. Tell him Betty from Saint Francis sent you there. We're good friends and I can guarantee, he'll be very helpful to you."

Without delay, we met with Sergeant McNulty, who was indeed, quite obliging. The jovial, barrel chested Sergeant offered us the address of the Woods family after Gem informed him of her intentions to write a note of sympathy and include a few minutes of our encounter with Claire at the train station.

"That's a very thoughtful gesture, young lady. I'm sure her parents would like to hear from you. You two seem wise beyond your years to do something like that for this grieving family that you've never met." He also thanked us again for our brave efforts to save Claire's life. "The officers who questioned you that night told us the whole story.

"You know, they arrested the piece of garbage that ran the drug house. Apparently, a story started filtering through the neighborhood about a bunch of crazy ass white punk kids and a tall girl with switchblade nails kicking the crap out of the whole drug house to get that girl to safety. Hmmm...don't know anyone who fits that description, do we kids?"

Staring down at the floor of the station house, Gem awkwardly shoves her hands deep into the pockets of her leather jacket, leaving Sergeant McNulty to chuckle, shake his head and return to his paperwork. "That's what I thought too, because nobody fitting such a crazy description would even exist in that part of Trenton," he adds with a smirk.

"Very gutsy what those kids did, wouldn't you say? My advice to them would be not to make a habit of doing things like that, though. Sometimes, you're only lucky enough to escape a bad situation once. Wouldn't you agree kids," he inquires before we sheepishly nod in affirmation. "I thought you would," he replied with a wink. "Now, you two have a great and ummm... safe Thanksgiving."

Returning to Misty's flat, Gem penned out one of the most heartfelt letters of condolence I'd ever beheld with a conclusion bringing tears to even the most hardcore punks we know.

"By the time we left the train station after meeting her acquaintance, your little girl had captured our whole tribes' curiosity with her beautiful smile and childish innocence. We talked about her endlessly on the ride into the city and being a child of the streets myself at her age, I anxiously awaited our return so we could reunite.

I hoped to convince her to seek help and maybe even come live with me so she'd be safe until we figured out what her next steps would be. I cry myself to sleep a lot of nights wishing that

I'd just taken her with us that evening. If I had, she'd still be alive. I only knew her for a few moments of my life and I miss her so.

Please know this much, when we heard she was in harm's way, our tribe of friends and my boyfriend Rob fought valiantly to get her out of that horrible house and our one friend tried endlessly to bring life back into her heart and lungs. She was purely angelic and will be loved and missed by all of us." No one could have written it any better or warmly than Gem.

● ● ●

Thanksgiving Day was spent in New York. Even though I enjoy visiting with family, I was really missing Gem something awful, especially when the political talk erupted over the dinner table and everyone was purely aghast when views were spilled from the "Commie kid, who didn't know a damn thing about real life," or so I was told.

Gem ended up going to the Yamaguchi's for the day but we did spend a few minutes on the phone, although not as long as we'd liked, since these long distance calls can just kill your bill; so much to my surprise when I returned to Yardley in the evening, I received an awesome call from New Jersey.

Needless to say and much to the chagrin of Mama Cavelli, I bolted out the door, sling shot Otis across the Calhoun Street Bridge and into City Gardens parking lot where a black jacketed, auburn haired temptress sat atop a Silver Bullet awaiting my arrival.

"Gobble, gobble, baby boy…what took you so long?"

Kissing her endlessly, I had to laugh aloud when we came up for air. "Gobble, gobble?"

"Piss on this holiday, Robbs and screw the pillager pilgrims. I want to dance and stomp the floors like my native ancestors tonight! So, you ready to join the tribe inside on what's known around here as Dysfunctional Family Dance Night?"

"Hell yeah, Swan. Lead the way and let's dance with OUR fucked up family like there's no tomorrow…"

• • •

With the short, holiday break behind and our ears still buzzing from a gobsmacked weekend of dance and live music, we met at the Student Union the other day where Gem was beaming with pride. Not only had the Socialist Office been a bigger success in creating a stir around campus than we could have ever imagined, it also paid off with some issues of neglect and injustices being addressed.

For one, the 'Berlin Wall' between the Gulag and the norms lunchroom was protested, rallied and voted against, thanks in large part to Gem's demanding of a debate with Abby Rothschild, who was largely left in tatters after Gem's excoriating, passion-ate speech which called out the campus and certain students on trying to drive "a never-ending wedge between the classes and the masses through racial, religious, physical and emotional sep-aration." A week later, we were told the 'Berlin Wall' will be torn down before next semester begins. Now, if only the real Berlin Wall could be demolished due to passionate debate and not bloodshed. Maybe there's hope after all.

Another source of pride came in the form of an envelope run my way by a sparkling, happy, auburn haired beauty. The winter courses and maddening pace of maxing out her credits paid off in the attainment of an Associate Degree when this Fall Semester culminates. Handing over the envelope with Villanova University imprinted on the top left corner she exclaimed excit-edly, "open it Robbs, open it!" and there, before my eyes, were the next few years of my girls' life set in stone upon being accepted to 'Nova on a full, academic scholarship, starting in the Spring Semester of 1986. I could have never been prouder of her accomplishment and embraced her warmly. "This is going to be the start of something brilliant for you, girl."

"My God, Robbs, I'm so nervous! Nobody has ever made it this far scholastically in my family. What if I can't do this?" I could only smile, emitting a light chuckle at her statement. "Gemma Anastasia Stinson, if there's one thing I've figured out about you, is that when you put your mind to something, you always manage to achieve greatness."

Throwing her arms around me, she kissed my neck, letting her tongue roll up to my earlobe. "Mmmm...you always know how to say just the right thing to make me happy," she purred.

Making Gem happy was becoming quite an easy and enjoyable undertaking as of late. Why wouldn't it be, I'm madly in love with this girl. I'd already informed her of my intentions to put school on hold for the time being, even though my grades remained pretty solid this semester.

Although initially nervous with my perseverance, I allayed Gem's fears slightly, informing her that I've already secured a job in the up and coming semiconductor market and I'd be leading their Production Planning department with a starting salary of almost $30,000 per year; not a sum to sneeze at in this day and age.

The choice of working for U.S. Steel was put on hold for now, due to some pretty fierce unrest between the Steelworkers union and their sleazy, corporate overlords before their upcoming contract talks. Once the dust settles, I'll probably apply, start earning some even bigger dollars and ultimately venture out on my own. Gem becomes uneasy with the idea of me in that hellish environment, but I think she's accepting the benefits of toiling there for at least a few years.

Anna Cavelli, on the other hand was extremely pissed off about the decision to give up. "Oh, I see it being another James situation for me all over again, leaping from one rainbow and dream of yours to another. Damn it, why can't you just be like your cousins and Perry? They finished college and are successful. Don't you ever want to be successful, Robert?"

Personally, I don't know why she was still complaining about James especially since he was accepted into Columbia University on a partial scholarship, essentially taking the entrance exam for the hell of it but that was my brother for you, carefree and aloof. Personally, I loved the whole idea of him going to a school which was the hotbed of activity for protests during the Sixties because it fit him to a tee.

Monetary success and another son to brag about was of much more concern to Mother Cavelli than the happiness of actually doing something you may enjoy. I wanted to keep writing, explore where an exciting musical future with an insanely Betty redhead may take me...who knows? At least I knew one thing; if or when I returned to college, it would be for what I wanted to accomplish, not to achieve someone else's dream and it would be attained with a well-padded bank account to boot.

My mother honestly seemed more concerned with turning me into a Reagan disciple, a religious zealot, or both. Recently, she invited me to some Charismatic Catholic deal going on at her parish, so for shits and giggles I tagged along. It was fucking bizarre, to say the least, with all of these people swaying about and speaking in tongues. I'm glad that I drove there myself, because after about fifteen minutes of that insanity, I escaped to Otis, lit a cigarette and hauled ass.

Now, she's starting to watch these two, odd bird evangelists on TV...Pat Robertson and some other gay hating shitbag named Jimmy Swaggart. My lifestyle may be Socialist, Solidarnosc radical, but the scene she's into is for the fucking birds. I could quite possibly be living with the mother from the movie 'Carrie'.

Informing Gem of the bizarre goings on at casa Cavelli, all she could do was giggle incessantly. "My dear love," she purred in that sultry voice of hers, "you'd better keep a Cross Dagger under your pillow. She may try to take your soul away one night." I'm glad someone finds it amusing but living here is honestly giving me the creeps anymore.

Whilst finishing off my time in college, I worked maddening amounts of hours at both jobs and hid the burgeoning cash pile in a stash box in my closet.

There was a method to the madness of burning the candle at both ends, but I only let the Philly Misfits, Alex, and Florian, who was a great pal to have accompany my anxious self on a very secret journey and the reaction from everyone about what the journey exactly entailed culminated into a wicked eruption of sheer pandemonium and I almost couldn't hear myself think!

• • •

The hell with December Seventh, I have to get past my own 'Pearl Harbor' tonight...December Fifth, a day which will truly live in hockey infamy. Robert Cavelli, adorned in his Ranges jersey, will have to face down the legions of Flyers goons and his rabid girlfriend at the Spectrum, or as I lovingly refer to it when the Flyers are playing there...the Rectum.

Gem is a nonstop chatterbox on the short ride up to the game and although we could have taken the Broad Street Line, she figured a brawl would ensue at every stop with me sporting the Rangers colors tonight, along with my, 'Piss off, asshole Flyers fans' attitude making matters worse. "Outside of the fact that is a Rangers jersey you're wearing, you do look extremely cute!" she blurts out while The Clash, 'Know Your Rights' warbles from the Bullet's stereo.

I thank her for the back handed compliment while I take in her fabulous look of thigh high boots, torn jeans, and a (yuck) Peter Zezel, Flyers jersey. A few days ago, Gem took the time to sew two, small black numbers (31) onto the jerseys' shoulder in honor of the Flyers young, star goalie, Pelle Lindbergh, who died tragically in a car accident just a few weeks earlier. "It's going to be so sad to not see him in net, Robbs," she says quietly as she runs her hands across the numbers, pushing her hair away from them as if out of respect.

She has taken to wearing her hair down a lot lately, especially when it's just the two of us heading out. "I really liked when those girls said I looked like a model," she says with a hint of youthful embarrassment.

"One of these days, Gemma, you're going to realize just how beautiful you really are."

She smiles broadly, giving me a mischievous push as we enter the Spectrum parking lot. "Thanks for the compliment, hon. You really know how to make me smile. Now, are we ready to get to some much more serious business?"

"And what would this serious business be?"

"Why, THE BET, of course, Robbs."

"I almost shudder to think what our bet will be, knowing your competitive nature."

I immediately get swatted across the arm, making our way through the throngs of boisterous Flyer faithful to our seats. "Wait a second, my competitive nature? Let's talk about whose competitive here, 'Mister I Break Hockey Sticks Over Goal Posts' when I lose! Like, there's no buggin' there, right?" She gives a quick wink, happily swatting me again before settling into our seats.

"Really, Gem? Who broke a TV antenna over her team losing to mine in a freaking exhibition game and you're going to call me competitive, but you're not buggin' right?" giving her a push back and receiving a smattering of boos and catcalls from around us when people spot my Greschner jersey. "Hmmm... alright, you've got me there. You're such a dork when you're right," she replies with a succession of quick rabbit punches to my arm. I can tell already, there will probably be more violence occurring between these two seats than what may actually take place on the ice.

Wrapping my arm around her neck and giving her a nudge, I am ready to hear the terms of the bet. "Focus, Gem...focus...I know you Philly people have comprehension issues, sooooo... let's discuss the bet." I expect more rabbit punches and Gem does not hesitate to disappoint.

"Oh, how freaking funny we are tonight! Alright, hotshot... here's the deal. You win, I have to wear the...barf bag...Rangers jersey outta' here tonight. I win, you have to wear this beautiful Flyers jersey outta' here but only after you quite vocally profess your love for my team."

Damn, she's cornered me! This girl is ruthless, callous, merciless...I'm fucking loving it! "Okay, hotstuff! This bet goes for tomorrow as well except when you put on my Greschner jersey and you WILL be wearing it at the end of both games, you must announce your total love for the city of New York to everyone around you, while admitting that Peter Zezel is nothing more than a pretty boy hack!"

"Grrrr...that's not even fair! I don't have you saying anything about Greschner!"

"What's the matter, Gem, no faith in your team, little girl?" It was a low blow by all accounts but the green eyes seethe with pure contempt. "Oooo! You get me so mad sometimes, Robbs! You're on, baby boy! You and your 'Smurf' Rangers are going down Cavelli!"

I chuckle with pure delight as she maybe, not so good-naturedly, wallops my arm this time. "We'll see about that, Stinson...we'll see..."

● ● ●

"The Flyers are the greatest hockey team in the world!" I almost taste the fucking acid puke building in my throat, knowing these words have just emitted through my pie hole and deafening applause goes up in the seats around us as I continue to feel thoroughly nauseas.

"Oh Robbs, you look so adorable in orange and black!" she replies sweetly while more whistles, catcalls and laughter erupt around me. Strike that, now I can get thoroughly nauseas. To say the least, I'm not caring for the Rangers very much at the moment. Outside of a fight filled game, my Broadway Blueshirts were manhandled and mauled 4-0 in front of the mostly obnoxious Flyer faithful at the 'Rectum'.

Adding insult to injury, Gem got to screech, chirp and squeak about her pretty boy Peter assisting on the Flyers last goal of the game. The only solace I have is that she did do a pretty sexy bump and grind, so it elicited the only reason to smile before she shed the Zezel jersey, handing it over to me immediately. I must truly love her because there is no other damn reason in the world I'd endure this kind of mistreatment.

So now, here I am walking through the bowels of this horrible arena in the freaking Halloween colors of a team whom I despise even more than Wall Street yuppies. Gleefully, she takes my hand to retrieve her car, happily tossing my Ranger colors into a ball on the back seat of the Bullet while I try to slump below the passenger side window. "Oh no, no, sweetie, you have to sit up straight so everyone can proudly see you wearing YOUR colors for the night."

She giggles incessantly and I know I've probably shot her at least a hundred death stares but eventually she wins me over with a long, sexy kiss and soon we're already talking trash about tomorrow's matchup. "Just remember, Gemma Stinson, we still have a bet riding on that game too."

"Mmmmm...you're gonna' look so adorable parading around Manhattan in your orange and black attire then as well." The giggling becomes even louder as the agonizing ride to Fourth Street continues.

● ● ●

Finding a spot about a block away from her place, I retrieve my beloved Greschner jersey, finally to be rid of this black and orange buffoonery but she lights up a Newp, puts hands to her hips and laughs haughtily. "Hold on there, Robbs, since we must have some official documentation of this great event."

Taking a drag from my Red, slumping even more in defeat... how much more abuse can one guy take? "What, now you want a photo of this mess you have me in?"

"Oh, no, no, no...more like taking a walk with me to the Diner before you leave."

"Woooo now, you want me to parade down South Street looking like some Halloween, smacked asshole in this thing? Oh babe, even you wouldn't be this cruel."

Flashing that 'melt you' smile, pursing her lips, I'm a goner. "Oh, wouldn't I be, babe?" The sultry voice too? Damn, I'm done...

Arm in arm we go, laughing, joking, talking some massive shit about tomorrow's game, until Skate and Tim spot us slipping onto South Street. Mouths gaping, snorts and chuckles abound, followed by a long, "Whaaaaat? Damn, Rob! Gem got you burned real good!"

"Piss off, you two and not another word or what I did to Kellin will look like a toddler spanking compared to what I'll do to your asses." I smile but the death stare is noticed by both of my young compatriots. "Ummmm…yeah…ummmm…yeah.. no, not a word, Robbs…not a word."

"Thanks boys, I knew we'd reach a quick understanding here," I jokingly snarl, tossing a couple of Reds their way before we go. A few more 'roosters' that we know can only gawk at the sight of me in enemy colors but start laughing when Gem mouths behind me, "he lost the bet."

The diner is looking more like a fortress of solitude by the minute, until I open the door and my head drops in pure disgust when every Misfit has assembled to hoot, holler and basically take the piss on me. "Check out ol' Robbs sportin' the Zezel," Dusty blurts out hysterically.

"Awww…sweetie you look so cute in Petey's uniform," Lena giggles incessantly while Sammi gets a quick photo of me flip-ping them all the bird and when Steph, Otto, Yuka and Gem, along with Amy behind the counter, lead the whole diner into a boisterous, "1940" chant, I can only slump onto the counter, helplessly burying my head into my hands.

Gem raises a hot cup of coffee, the Misfits hoist their smokes. "To my Robbs, the lowly Rangers fan on this glorious night of Flyers victory, for being such an all-around good sport!"

"To Robbs! PISS OFF, SOD OFF! OI, OI, OI!" The diner patrons join the Misfits in their raucous applause which breaks me up, until I take a bow and stand on the counter to say my piece. "All I can say is wait until tomorrow, Flyers fans," but I'm promptly drowned out by hearty Philly boos, catcalls, derisive whistles and hilarity before Gem comes over to give me a con-soling kiss. "There, there, baby boy. I figure you'll be saying the same thing when the year 2000 rolls around."

Everyone gets another good snicker, so I have no recourse but to rest my head on Gem's shoulder. After getting a quick bite to eat, I dejectedly point towards the clock in the corner. "Gem, it's been a fun night but I'd better get bookin' because we have a busy day tomorrow in the Big Apple."

"Oh my God, you're so right and you still have to warm up Otis." Gem thanks everyone for waiting and becomes mobbed with hugs, grins and wishes of "good luck tomorrow" from the Misfits and Amy, leaving Gem with quite the quizzical expression once we abscond from the diner. "Ummm...why was everyone wishing us good luck tomorrow?"

"Oh, you know, because of the game. I guess they just hope my team plays better."

Gem smiles wryly, batting her thick eyelashes while she pulls me close to her. "What are you up to, babe? I'm getting suspicious."

"Nothing, Gem, they just want us to have a good time in the city and at the game. Seriously, that's all..."

"Uh huh...ok...I'll believe you...for now," she responds gleefully, lighting up a Newp when we reach Otis and I get the warming up process started. A belch, a blow of smoke, the old boy is running, for at least fifteen minutes. Gem tosses over the key for the flat so I can grab my backpack and sits patiently on the hood until I return. "You know, it's times like these when I'm really happy Otis takes such a long time to move along." With eyes twinkling brightly in the streetlights glare, she draws me in closer and after wrapping her legs comfortably around this delighted punks' waist, our lips meet passionately.

"Even though I enjoy debating with you, Gemma, I thoroughly agree with you on this point."

She breathes warmly near my ear and giggles. "Mmmmm.. that's because my Robbs is smart and knows he's got something good right here," she coos before tossing back her hair. Pulling off the Zezel jersey, to hurriedly replace it with mine, Gem sulks as she hops off Otis' hood. "You look so damned cute in mine! I should make you wear it home tonight and hold yours hostage until we go into New York tomorrow but I'll be agreeable."

Holding her gaze for only so long...I wish so much to stay here, but it's time to go. My heart skips excitedly while I give her a quick kiss before jumping into Otis. I let the window down as she leans in to say goodbye. "Is everything ok with you? You seem really hyper right now."

"I'm good, babe…just real excited about our trip to the city tomorrow. You and me alone in the Big Apple, I'm really psyched, that's all."

"Ok, as long as that's it. I'm really excited too." Skipping away from the car, spinning around before heading upstairs, she blows me a kiss from the stoop. "I'll be by your house at five, Robbs but until then, I'll love you forever in my dreams…"

"I'll be waiting for you, Gem. Enjoy that dream."

"I plan to, Robbs…I plan to." Before pulling away from the curb, I already see her solitary figure in the window, waving goodbye, making this day another fond memory in the many occurring between us.

Slicing through the streets of Philly, I get Otis fueled and flying onto Interstate 95, navigating us towards Yardley. In a few hours, Gem and I will be in New York and my heart races furiously thinking about the day ahead and about how my young life will quite possibly be changed forever.

Thank You

Many thanks to Lori Kay, the Wordsmiths, Ink staff and Debbie O'Byrne at JETLAUNCH for their professionalism, help, patience and perseverance in making 'PUNKS' become a reality.

Thanks to all of the talented bands who entrusted me with providing the majority of their lyrical workings and lead vocals. What incredible, 'gobsmacked' times we shared, and what friendships we've forged. Whether it was a street corner, a backyard, basement, abandoned factory, or a smoke-filled venue; every day, to borrow a line from one of our songs, was, "a new experience to write home about.".

To Randy 'Now' Ellis, at City Gardens and countless other band promoters in the Trenton and Philadelphia areas who gave any young kids like us a place to play, go watch other bands perform, or had the club DJ's spin records for us so we could dance the nights away, thanks. You truly don't know the impact you had on our teenage lives or moving forward into young adulthood.

To 'Nayls'. You've been a source of inspiration for me and I appreciate all of your help and guidance when I began thinking of turning 'PUNKS' into more than just random thoughts on paper. Good luck with your new ventures. We finally grabbed for the brass ring and are holding on tight.

To friends, too numerous to name, thanks for the constant cheerleading and well-wishes. Know that you'll be thanked in person when we meet throughout our travels. A big thank you to a wonderful writer, Shelby Kent-Stewart and talented photographer/artist, Sharon Roark. Your constant never give up attitudes, were a big boost at times. .

And the biggest, most important thanks of all; to my wife and best friend, Jenn. You came into my life at a turbulent, chaotic period and your loving heart gave me peace for the first time in years. You've had my back for over two decades, whether it's been through some tough illnesses early on in our relationship, being the biggest supporter of my aspirations, being front stage at some of our loud shows and practices, even though some nights I knew you'd rather be dancing than having your eardrums endlessly pounded by our music, to being on your own with the kiddos many a night and for years on end while I've toiled for days, nights, weekends and even holidays at the mill, your faith in, and love for me has never wavered.

I knew from that first time we hung out on South Street and Penn's Landing, talked for hours about everything and anything, laughed ourselves silly until near the morning light and couldn't take my eyes from yours or your beautiful smile, that you were the one for me.

You always say that you're my biggest fan, but without a doubt, I am yours. This is for you and the five wonderful, feisty and fun children you've blessed me with. Punks for life!!!

About the Author

Whether busking on street corners in Philadelphia, New Hope, PA or Lambertville, NJ, singing in venues the size of a postage stamp, large as a theater or as dank and devious as the underground settings could be, writing lyrics, poetry, fiery political or social articles, hitting the streets or the airwaves to fight for the poor and homeless (especially teens), workers' rights and many other causes close to his heart, or finding the time to sit down and write a series such as 'PUNKS', the sounds of anarchy also known as punk rock have been Rich Cucarese's lifelong soundtrack and fueled his ambition to continually fight for what is right and just.

With a background as patchwork as his musical influences, Rich spent a few years in college (Pennsylvania State University, Ogontz/Abington Campus 1985-86), toiled in the massive mills of United States Steel Corporation's, Fairless Works not too far from Trenton or Philadelphia, and when the majority of the plant was shuttered, he went through a series of changes leading him back into music, activism and a never-ending stream of writing.

Eventually returning to what had become a much smaller steel plant after the Free Trade shakeouts, Rich became more involved in the Steelworkers Union (USW) as Local 4889's

Rapid Response Coordinator; writing many timely, socially active pieces including 'The Battle for Prosperity Over Poverty', which was awarded Best News Story of the Year by the United Steelworkers Press Association.

He's been interviewed by CNBC, MSNBC, BBC America and VICE News, as well as various print sources about everything from Free Trade and its social impact on communities, to protests he was involved in such as Occupy Wall Street. As always, he will credit much of his social and political enlightenment to his punk tribe and the anarchistic upheaval of the norms that many punk rock groups espoused, whether they were on this side of the Atlantic or across the pond. .

Rich resides in Bucks County, Pennsylvania with his four fiery but equally kind-hearted daughters, his funny, gregarious son and a wife who has actively supported his writings, his music; even though their musical tastes are worlds apart, and still manages to forgive his teenage stupidities like jumping headfirst and happily into mosh pits at an advanced age.